Nothing Is As It Appears

by Guerdon Monroe

DORRANCE
PUBLISHING CO
EST. 1920
PITTSBURGH, PENNSYLVANIA 15238

Dorrance Publishing Co
585 Alpha Drive
Suite 103
Pittsburgh, PA 15238
Visit our website at *www.dorrancebookstore.com*

ISBN: 978-1-4809-9915-2
eISBN: 978-1-4809-9910-7

Prologue

Entering her cramped den, Katelyn reached under the dark green shade protecting her desk lamp bulb and pulled down on the chain. Straightening up, she scanned her tiny tongue-and-groove knotty pine hideout in the dim serpentine light. Her husband took special care to fit the boards tightly and trimmed the edges with precise cuts. She loved her small but cozy "woman cave." The wood came from bark beetle-killed ponderosa pine. The lumber salvaged from the dead trees displayed streaks of pale to darkish blue intrusions along the smooth wood. She learned the "Blue Stain" occurred due to a fungus that entered the trees on the bodies of the attacking bark beetles. The stain caused no structural weakness but lowers the grade, i.e., value of the lumber. Initially, she thought her husband chose to build her den on the cheap. He just said, "Trust me, you'll enjoy the contrast." He knew his wife well and, of course, he was right…again. With a clear finish, the bluish stain randomly infused across the boards gave her hideaway individuality and character, much more so than just plain knotty pine.

While sitting down behind her desk, Katelyn turned her gaze out through the large, north-facing, wood-framed window to the garden, orchard, pond and forest beyond. The dichotomy of life in Northern California versus her first thirty-five-plus years on the East Coast could not be more stark than black and white. While scanning everything and nothing, she heard a faint knock at the door.

"Enter at your own risk," she offered.

Young Justin poked his head through the door slowly, as if looking for booby-traps. Wearing his ubiquitous University of California baseball cap, Justin smiled at his mother. While stepping into her lair, he said, "Hey, Mom."

As he walked up to her desk, Katelyn replied, "Hay is for horses, young man."

With exaggerated effort, Justin tried again. "Helloooo, Mother."

"Hi, son, what can I do for you?"

"I was just wondering.... you know—"

Rocking back in her chair, Katelyn interrupted, "I'm not a mind reader; spit it out, Justin."

"It's just that when you start writing, you disappear in here for hours, days. Why do you want to do this book anyway?"

"You saying you'll miss me?"

"Na... yeah...well, a little. You just get so abscessed."

"Obsessed," Katelyn corrected her youngest.

"Pops says abscessed and you don't correct him. He only uses it when you get locked on to something and won't let go."

"He's using a play on words, and your father's one to talk about obsessions." Focusing on Justin, she realized how much he looked like his father. Katelyn thought about her son's question, then said, "It's a good story, mostly based on the truth, at least as much as we'll ever know. It's about your dad and his childhood friends. Like your dad most turned out well, some turned out... okay, and one fellow turned into a very dark, spiteful and malicious monster. I think it has all the earmarks of a great read."

"Like what?"

"It's a classic story of good versus evil, with betrayal, murder, revenge and redemption all wrapped up with plenty of cliffhangers. And, of course, I've included a healthy dose of love and passion."

"Ah, Mom, are you going to write about Dad and you and...."

Katelyn just smiled.

"Ah, gross, Mom, really? I won't be able to go out in public or see my friends without the fear of...more comments. They already think you're one of those old free-spirit hippies."

"Believe it or not, I'm too young to be a hippy, at least the original San Francisco, Haight/Ashbury types." After registering all that her son said, Katelyn added, "What did you mean by your friends making more comments?"

Realizing he'd slipped up, while turning away, Justin said, "Mom, I really have to pee; see you." Justin bolted for the door. He didn't make it.

"Justin Abraham, you turn around and march your little fanny right back here."

Dropping his head and letting go of the doorknob, Justin turned around and trudged back as if wading through molasses.

With her son's fear of getting too close, or even looking at his mother, Katelyn leaned forward and grabbed both of his wrists. She tugged on his arms and he reluctantly walked up to her knees, eye to eye. "Have you been talking to your friends…about your father and me?"

After a long pause and a quick glance at his mother to gauge how mad she looked, Justin said, "Welllll…."

"Well is a deep subject and does not pertain to my question."

"Deep well, ha, that's a good one, Mom," Justin offered, hoping to defuse a little of his mom's focus.

"Nice try. Stop deflecting; now answer me."

Justin took a couple more darting looks at Katelyn, then exhaled, "Okay." After a pause to build up a little courage, he continued. "I might have told them about the, um…laundry room."

Oh, shit, Katelyn's brain screamed. Her eyes grew large just for a split second, and Justin registered the brief panic. Not really sure if she wanted to hear what her son knew, a far less confident Katelyn said, "Go on."

"Well, you know when you ask Dad to help you, you say something like, 'Can you give me a hand, Hon,' or, 'Hon, can you help me?'"

"Yes, and your father usually ignores me, at least the first time."

"Or Pops says, 'I don't do skirt work.'"

"Yes, your father's a real comedian." Katelyn prompted, "Okay, so?"

"Well, sometimes, you say it different, you change your…um…."

"Inflection?" Knowing where this was going and resigned to her fate, Katelyn couldn't help being curious about how badly she had misjudged their youngest.

"Yeah, inflection, and it's always when you're doing laundry. It's like you're not asking, you're telling. Like, 'Hon, your presence is required in the laundry room,' or 'It's time you helped with the laundry.' And Pops just drops whatever he's doing, jumps up and marches right in there."

Katelyn, as nonchalant as she could muster, said, "So?"

"And he closes the door; you never close the laundry room door when you're doing laundry alone."

Katelyn put her hands up to stop her son. "Okay, okay—"

"And why do you two have toothbrushes and toothpaste in the cupboard above the washbasin?"

Katelyn thought, *For coffee breath, you little spy.* Pointing both her index fingers straight up, she said sternly, "Alright, got it, that's enou—"

"And sometimes just the dryer starts but you haven't washed any clothes yet and—"

Leaning forward, Katelyn demanded, "I said stop, you observant little shit."

Super-fast Justin spewed, "And sometimes when you two come out—"

Katelyn grabbed the back of Justin's head with one hand and his mouth with the other to shut him up. Their eyes met, and Katelyn felt her son start to grin against her hand. They both started laughing. Katelyn had to let go of Justin, she laughed so hard. When she calmed down, she opened her arms and Justin ran into them. She hugged her little man and said, "Damn you, Justin, what am I going to do with you?"

"Don't squeeze too hard, Mom; I really do have to pee."

Holding him at arm's length, Katelyn slowly shook her head and said, "My, it seems we should have had a little talk long before this. I'll leave the details up to your father. But for now, understand this: I'm crazy about your dad and it's not just sex; its love. One compliments the other, but there is a huge difference. You'll learn this for yourself someday. Safe to say, though, what your father and I have and what we do stays right here. Your twelve- and thirteen-year-old friends are not to be privy to any private, personal family matters, from this day forward, understand?"

Pursing his lips together, Justin quietly muttered, "Yes, Mom. Sorry, Mom."

Justin surprised Katelyn by not asking to be excused; plus, he still looked a little perplexed. She questioned, "Obviously we're not done yet?"

Justin asked, "Well, if you write this book, isn't everyone going to know about you and Pops and…you know?"

"Don't put your dad on a pedestal; he's no puritan. Besides, he's packed full of quirks, faults and idiosyncrasies a hell of a lot worse than mine. Remember, I've put up with him a lot longer than you; I know. Plus, he's a hopeless romantic, though he won't admit it. But, your father has taught me so much; I've changed more than you can imagine. You should have seen this…old hippy, before I met your dad."

"What's Pops say about you writing about his past?"

"You know your father, he's very private, almost introversive about his personal life. He wants me to use fictitious names and I don't. But when all is said and done, he'll leave it up to me. Your father lets me be me."

With a smirk Justin said, "Shit Howdy, Mom."

Slapping the bill of Justin's baseball cap down over his face, Katelyn scolded, "Do not use that word."

"Sorry, but you say that to Pops sometimes and it makes him laugh." After a pause, Justin saw his mom wasn't going to respond, so he added, "Is that going to be in the book? Will I finally find out what that means?"

Smiling back at her son, Katelyn said, "Shit Howdy, son."

Justin's eyes grew as he started to protest. "But you just—"

"Now you scram," Katelyn scolded. "I need to collect my thoughts. Why don't you go out and play with your friends, you know, while you still can?"

Justin gave his mother that same slow grin his dad often gave her. He stopped at the door of her den, turned around and said, "Too funny, Mom, too funny." Then he was gone.

Staring at the closed door, Katelyn smiled. *Love you, you sharp little whelp.* Finally, she spun around to her desk, leaned forward, put her elbows down and dropped her chin into her hands. Katelyn thought, *No more laundry day sex, damn. Well, at least not when the kids are around.* She closed her eyes and allowed her memory to summon her last, assisted, laundry day.

———————————

Katelyn liked sex in the mornings, especially if she'd wanted but didn't get a good "roll in the hay" the night before. Sometimes she just needed morning sex because someone kept beating her to the finish line too many times in a row. Dutiful husband Whit seemed to work a little harder to please Katelyn in the mornings. And he always knew exactly why Katelyn summoned him to the laundry room.

It was Saturday morning, and Whit had just returned home from picking up motion cameras he'd set up in the woods. To detect predator activity prior to a logging project, timber companies often hired Whit to set up carnivore camera stations. Basically, Whit attached a motion camera to a tree pointing at another tree where he stapled a wire basket full of chicken necks. The information derived from the critters that showed up added to the overall pre-project environmental research. Fourteen-year-old William and young Justin enjoyed helping their dad view the pictures triggered by any movement in front of the camera. Both were scanning every speck of each new frame hoping to be the first to detect anything different. Hundreds of pictures needed painstaking review. The boys, so far, verified a bobcat, a spotted skunk, two raccoons, a pine marten and just a speck of an animal's tail behind a tree, possibly a gray fox.

From the back of their long rectangular cabin they heard, "Benjamin Whittingham, I require your assistance in the laundry room."

Whit looked first at William, then at Justin and groaned, "It's the devil's work, boys. Stay free as long as you can."

As their dad stood up, the two boys looked at each other and rolled their eyes. They silently watched their dad scurry down the hall.

Justin asked, "Are we going to end up like that?"

William replied, "I don't quite understand how it happens, but I don't see any way out. That's just what married people do, I guess."

Justin turned back to the computer and said, "We're doomed. Well, let's see how many frames we can get through before Pops returns from…laundry duty."

As Whit walked into the laundry room, he noticed bluegrass music playing on the disc player. Closing the door, he looked at his wife sitting on top of the running washing machine in her three-quarter-length bathrobe. She was naked otherwise. The front of her bathrobe parted, just short of revealing her nipples, but did show off her flat stomach. Paradise remained hidden at the juncture of her slightly parted long legs.

The washing machine wiggled her butt slightly; the movement jiggled her breasts. Whit said, "Warming things up a little there, babe?"

Whit watched his wife point to her lips and say, "Brush your teeth, mountain man, or you won't get to kiss these." Then pointing to her chest, she added, "Or these."

He tilted his head and smirked as if to say, "Not even a little kiss?" Whit walked up to Katelyn. She shook her head while putting one hand over her breasts and pointing to the sink with the other.

Whit returned a half-salute and spun around to the basin. He grabbed his toothbrush and noticed some thoughtful person had already added toothpaste. While brushing away, he looked up at his wife in the mirror. Katelyn pretended to play a banjo to the music. She looked up while rocking her head, picking away with her fingertips right in front of her nipples. Whit laughed and sprayed toothpaste on the mirror. Still smiling and losing most of the rest of the toothpaste, he bent over the washbasin to spit. As soon as he did, Katelyn stuck her big toe up his butt. He reared up straight but did not turn around. He grabbed the basin with both hands and just shook his head. Finally, he said, "Gosh, honey, your nose feels as cold as ice."

She poked him in the butt again and when he turned around she asked, "Am I really going to get it, mountain man?"

"That's a big Shit Howdy. You'll be lucky to walk when I'm through with you."

"Promises, promises."

Whit walked up to Katelyn and parted her bathrobe. Then he grabbed the material near her knees and slid her butt to the edge of the rumbling machine. As they kissed, she started unbuckling his belt and pants. While still kissing he brought his hands up the side of her thighs, around her ass, and up her ribcage. He stopped at the outsides of her breasts and, using his thumbs, rotated little circles around her areolas. She responded quickly with hard erect nipples. As they continued to kiss, her exhales became stronger and louder, as did his. They parted lips and, with their foreheads still touching, Whit whispered, "Washer or dryer?"

Katelyn slid her lips to Whit's left ear, bit the lobe and whispered, "I'm fine right here."

She had his pants down and just slid out what she wanted from his boxers. With Whit's boots on he stood the perfect height for washing machine sex. Barefoot, Whit had to tip up on the balls of his feet. One time his calf cramped, temporarily interfering with an otherwise glorious laundry day.

Katelyn rocked back slightly and lifted her legs; she was ready. This was Katelyn's time, and Whit wanted it to be. He noticed the CD playing "*Wagon Wheel*" by the Old Crow Medicine Show. He toyed with entering her but didn't. Twice she reached down to insert him. Both times he pushed her hand away and kept kissing her deeply and rubbing her nipples. Finally, the verse he waited for started. He entered her slowly and rhythmically.

"*Rock me, Mama, like a wagon wheel,*

Rock me, Mama, any way you feel,

Heyyyyy, Mama, rock me."

Katelyn pulled her mouth away from Whit and tipped her head back while holding on to Whit's neck with both hands. She panted and moaned at the same time.

"*Rock me, Mama, like the wind and the rain,*

Rock me, Mama, like a southbound train,

Ahhhhh...."

Katelyn squeezed hard, then finally let go; her contractions were violent and her whole body shuddered. She was wet and breathing in gasps. She rode out a few more series of contractions, then relaxed.

As her breathing calmed down, she opened her eyes thinking she'd see Whit's smiling face. Instead she found herself staring out through the large, north-facing, wood-framed window at the garden, orchard, pond and woods beyond.

What the hell? Katelyn stopped gently rocking. She also realized she had one hand flat on her desk and the other one down the front of her pants. She opened her eyes even wider. *Shit!*

I'm in my woman cave! Oh my God! I just gave myself a monstrous orgasm while daydreaming. Not making a sound, she listened to make sure no one had heard her. She thought, *Didn't see that coming, damn...I'm good. Just thinking about making love with my man, I get off. Am I the perfect mate for a horny guy like Benjamin Whittingham or what?* Katelyn smiled, then thought, *What the hell am I doing? I was supposed to start the book. Well, that's not going to happen. I need to change and not get caught.* Getting up and walking to the door, she listened for any sound. Looking down she thought, *Jesus, Kate, nice wet spot.* Katelyn cracked the door and looked both ways as best she could. Seeing and hearing nothing, she scurried off to the larger of the two bedrooms.

Leaning back from her typing position in her tiny Enfield, Connecticut, condo, mystery author Sam Lund, aka Katelyn Summers, stopped for two reasons. One, she felt fairly satisfied with her prologue. Katelyn's agent used Sam Lund as the author of Katelyn's first two books. He told Katelyn that way too many men just won't pick up a murder/mystery or thriller written by a woman. Eventually, if her books took off, they'd switch to Samantha Lund, to shock her male readers and tweak the literary world. They'd also add a vague but intriguing biography. All good press, as Sam Lund strictly demanded anonymity, which was true with the real author as well. Katlyn's only stipulations to her agent—a nom de plume—and no one could ever know Katelyn's true identity. Those points were especially important now, as the storylines for her third book were true and involved Whit and Katelyn. The blowback could be substantial because the murders, destroyed lives, and tragedies were real.

The second reason Katelyn stopped typing—she was crying, crying hard. She blurted, "Goddamnit." *It would have been like that, Whit and me, I know it. If only Whit hadn't….*

Shaking her head, she said again, "Goddamnit." *The cabin in the woods, their two boys, her perfect little den, and Whit by her side every night. It should have been…my life, not just a bunch of bullshit on paper, a façade, a mirage, just a beautiful damn dream of what should have been.*

Rocking back farther in her chair, Katelyn wiped her eyes and scolded herself. *Jesus, Kate, get ahold of yourself. He's gone…. You'll never get through this book if you don't stop crying and start controlling your emotions.* Tilting her head back, she used the heel of her thumbs to wipe the tears from the corner of her tightly shut eyes. Katelyn crossed her fingers on top of her head. *Okay, okay, damn you, you can do this. You want to, you need to, get it all out.* She'd already decided to use real names, places, businesses, everything because she could recall events easier and write the story faster. Katelyn would add fictitious names, locations and anything else potentially libelous later during editing.

With pursed lips, she leaned forward while hitting her head with the palm of her right hand. *It's all in here, all of it; the good, the bad, the passion, the pure evil and the tragic end that left me without the love of my life.* She dabbed at her eyes with bent index fingers. *If I can get through the first chapter, it has to come easier and easier, I know it will.* Katelyn heard her own voice cry out, "So start writing then, damn you."

Katelyn closed her eyes and took a deep breath. *I'll start by what I know best…what else, how Whit and I met.* Katelyn opened her eyes, scooted forward and began.

Chapter One
Somewhere in Virginia

Holy crap, Benjamin Whittingham thought, *what in hell made me think I could do this?* Leaning against the wide windowsill, at the base of huge drapes, Whit peered through the small opening where the thick fabric met. His sad blue eyes scanned the expanse of the large, well-manicured backyard. With his back to the other guests, Whit took a sip of his watery drink and marveled at the well-lit, putting-green smooth lawn that covered the rolling hills. Just enough magnificent old hickory, maple and oaks blocked his view of any building or other man-made object. It gave the impression that the woods extended on into infinity, though Whit knew homes and buildings resided out there close by. After all, this is Virginia, home to millions of bureaucrats, lawyers, lobbyists, pollsters, government contractors, and all the other lampreys firmly attached to their life support system…the federal trough. Whit thought he'd tell the next person who asked what he did in the beltway, *"I'm the under-secretary, to the assistant, to the secretary, to the deputy director of the Department of Redundancy Department."*

So, this is how the Kennedys live. Yes, the Kennedys. Whit didn't even really know if this walled mansion, fortress, compound, whatever the hell you call it, actually resided in Virginia. If not, it was close. *Maybe I'm in Maryland. Hell, as out of place as I feel, maybe Mars. If I could click my heels three times right now and end up at Auntie Em's farm, or anywhere in Kansas for that matter, I'd do it.* Bored to tears, Whit absentmindedly closed his eyes and rocked forward in his borrowed shoes, *There's no place like home, there's no place like home, there's no place like home.* Whit opened one eye, looked out through the crack in the drapes and thought, *Nope, didn't work. Okay, dumbass, stop acting like an idiot. But I am an idiot...an idiot who wants to get the hell away from here.* But home meant a place far west of Kansas. Whit had dropped everything and left northern California because of a call for help from an old high school buddy. Whit had no clue that rubbing elbows with the who's who of the "progressive" elites in Washington, D.C., would be part of the deal.

So here stands Mr. Duck-out-of-water, the wallflower, the bump on a log, dressed in an ill-fitting borrowed suit about an inch or so too short in the sleeves and legs. What the hell did I do in some former life to deserve this? Do any of these liberal beltway elites recognize or have a clue that a right wing, gun-toting, tree-cutting hunter stood among them in this gigantic room? It's more likely they all suspected...or clearly could tell...an outcast, an intruder, a "stick out like a sore thumb" imposter lurked in their midst.

With the polite smiles and the appropriate distances maintained, the latter seemed accurate. Whit made it easy for them and he knew it. Never one for small talk, the pleasantries or putting on airs, he projected the desperate energy of a trapped animal, wary and unapproachable. As easy as they could read him, he could do the same with them. Their vibes said, "What's he doing here; he's not one of us." *Well, dittos back at you, you stuffed shirts. But that isn't fair; I'm the one who doesn't belong here.* Ostensibly Whit arrived as a guest to a Kennedy gathering that included the birthday of a granddaughter of Robert Kennedy. At least Whit sipped some pretty smooth bourbon from a substantial crystal highball glass. Too bad they inadvertently served it with a ton of ice and, since he was nursing the drink, the flavor waned as the ice melted. Whit wondered if this amber liquid came from Uncle Teddy's stash. He moved to the corner of the window, leaned his left shoulder against the wall and thought back to the errant decision that ended with him standing in this very spot.

"Janet, I am not going to a Kennedy kid's birthday party, especially alone. I'll just wait here for Mike and you to come back."

"That won't work; the party and where Mike and I have to go are over an hour from here, but only ten minutes apart. We'll pop in the Kennedys' with you; greet the hosts, then sneak out. Mike and I will meet Mike's prospective new bosses and be right back. We won't leave you for long, I promise. And the birthday girl is not a kid; she's a high school senior, in Paul's class."

Whit replied, "Well, don't I feel better. Make your youngest go then, to represent the family, or don't you have any control over Paul?"

"If we had any control over our youngest, we wouldn't have called you. Why that boy, all our boys, bonded with you...I'll never know. You're such a...pill. But, Paul can't go; he can't stand her. Plus, that's not the point. It's the logistics. Besides, we already broke protocol by asking to bring an uninvited out-of-town guest."

"I'd feel terrible if I made you break protocol; I'll just stay here."

"Whit, in this part of America, the Kennedys still pull a lot of weight. You get an invitation from the Kennedys, you go. Look, Whit, I feel bad enough that you came all the way out here to help us and we're double booked on your first evening. Mike's retired military buddies are going to introduce him to some important contractors and try to get him a job at the Naval Yard. We can't stay here and put our boys through college on my pay and a retired Lt. Colonel's salary."

Knowing the answer but vying for time to conjure up a good excuse, Whit said, "And how again did Mike get so chummy with the Kennedys?"

Mike answered, "Right before Desert Storm, the higher-ups reassigned my general to the Pentagon. When he left Saudi Arabia, I returned as part of his luggage. I eventually received an assignment as one of the liaisons between the Army, at the Pentagon, and the Senate. Uncle Teddy took a liking to this Catholic, Chinese-American, Lt. Colonel. I tipped back a few with him on three or four occasions. The rest is history, but you already know all this. I know you, Whit; you're just stalling."

"But, I won't know anybody; it will be way too awkward, for everybody. I'll say something politically incorrect or, for God's sake, stick my middle finger out instead of my little pinky when I sip my tea. I'll embarrass your good name and you'll forever be banished from Kennedy functions."

Janet cut in. "No, you won't, and you won't be alone. I've asked Brenda to be your date and take care of you at the Kennedys."

"Brenda? Your nurse friend, Brenda? She'll ditch me for the first guy who winks at her."

"No, she promised to be good. Besides, if you'd paid her any attention, she wouldn't be on the hunt."

"Oh, come on, Janet, we've already been through this before. She's just not my—"

"I know, I know, too needy, too liberal, too chunky, talks too much. Blah, blah, blah. Did I ever tell you men are pigs? Did I ever tell you you are a pig?"

Whit looked up like he was thinking then said, "Not this visit...until now."

"Believe me, I'd rather stay; the Kennedys throw great parties. But, it's important for these contractors to see the dutiful wife beside her stable, hard-working husband. Image is everything around here. And when we get back to the party, I'll still have time to introduce you to some lovely ladies."

"I don't want to meet lovely ladies from this town. They're all GUs."

Looking at her husband, who just shrugged, Janet turned back to Whit. "I'm almost too afraid to ask; what the hell is a GU?"

"'GU' is short for a 'Geographic Undesirable.'" Pointing to the west, Whit continued. "Don't forget, I live three thousand miles that way and distance makes the heart grow fonder...for someone else. Why start something with absolutely no future?"

Exasperated, Janet looked at her husband and said, "Mike, what are we going to do with him?" Turning to Whit she vented, "Whit, the perfect woman doesn't exist, the perfect situation never happens, and the perfect timing never occurs."

"It did for Mike and you."

"He's got you there, hon," Mike piped in.

"That's different," Janet retorted. "Mike wasn't...isn't...difficult." Turning to Mike, Janet stabbed a finger his way and said, "And quiet, you; back up your wife when she's trying to make a point."

Whit chided, "Yes, dutiful husband, be a team player while your buddy gets RFed."

Shaking her head, completely frustrated, Janet lowered her voice and said, "Look, Whit, just forget my point; please do this for me, please. Mike has a great opportunity for a good job, close to home, with more time off to be with the boys and me. We really need this."

After a short pause Whit rocked his head back and said, as if talking to the ceiling, "Okay, Janet, okay, I'll do it."

Before Janet could hug Whit, Mike offered, "Hon, he was going to do it all along. He just wanted you to squirm a little first."

Janet looked into Whit's blue eyes and wasn't sure if her husband was right, but she launched toward Whit anyway. Whit curled his arms up defensively as Janet slugged him. She finally hugged him, and said, "You are such an ass, Benjamin Whittingham…but, a lovable ass. I'm starting to understand why the boys look up to you."

Well, that was that. A shave, shower, a neighbor's slightly too short, but nicely cut gray wool suit, another neighbor's black oxfords, and they were off. At the Kennedys, after some air kisses, perfunctory greetings, painful small talk, and a quick walk through, Mike and Janet ducked out. It took Brenda less than fifteen minutes to forget her promise to Janet. She slipped away with a Kennedy lookalike. The guy had the accent down, the Bobby Kennedy hairdo and even mimicked the buck tooth smile pretty well. Hell, maybe he was a Kennedy. Brenda looked over her shoulder at Whit as she disappeared into the crowd. She gave him a sad, cow-eyed look that was supposed to convey "Sorry." Whit glared back at her with his most sincere "Screw you" sneer. Looking around the crowd, now completely alone, Whit realized time suddenly slowed to a crawl. Every second took three to pass. *Man, I knew this would happen. I feel like a mouse sensing a rattlesnake nearby but not knowing which direction to scurry.*

Half daydreaming and back to peering through the drapes into the backyard, Whit didn't notice the tall, slender woman walking up to the only guy in the room who looked totally lost and out of place. She asked the back of the tall, fit, frumpily dressed, dark-haired man, "So what are you doing here?"

Almost jumping, Whit involuntarily raised his head while turning around, "I don't really know," he confessed.

Whit lowered his head slightly to focus on the attractive woman with a piercing stare. Though her complexion said fair-skinned, her straight hair shined midnight black. In fact, except for her deep red lipstick, everything was black. Her sleeveless black dress clung to her figure like cellophane, revealing well-defined features.

She shot back, "What does that mean? Were you kidnapped, brought here by aliens, lose a bet?"

Whit chucked slightly and said, "Nothing so dramatic, but I am here against my better judgment."

"And what does that mean? Don't you like the Kennedys? Are you a Republican?"

"No, I mean yes, that is I—" Whit had to stop to collect his thoughts. She just stood there, sipping her wine, staring. She had him out of step and fumbling. He could tell she enjoyed his torment. "I was going to say it wasn't my idea to come here."

"Whose idea was it?"

"My buddy's wife."

"You let another man's woman tell you what to do? Don't you have one of your own to do that?"

"Yes, wait, no." Whit put up his hand. "Just hold on a second." That did it. Now Whit stared back. He became instantly annoyed at this smartass yanking his chain. Just as she started to say, "Cat got your tongue?" Whit cut in, "Okay, Miss 20 Questions, let's slow down a bit. I'll answer your questions, one at a time. But first let's exchange introductions, so we know, to whom we are speaking."

"Hmmm, proper English. That tells me you at least had some formal education."

"Or, how about a father who was a stickler for proper English and would rap you on the temple with his knuckles if you spoke poorly, used slang, or forgot your manners."

"So, you're saying you were an abused child?"

"No, not at all. My folks were fine, just strict."

"Well, sounds like abuse to me. But, Mr. Ideal Childhood, we have hit on our first coincidence. My dad's an English teacher and refused to accept poor speaking from his children. His efforts helped me become a journalist—well, a reporter." Putting her wine glass in her left hand, she extended her right and said, "Katelyn Summers, from *Progressive Politics*."

Receiving her firm handshake, Whit thought, *Oh, great, not just a liberal, a super liberal. Just pile it on.* Now instead of just trying to hide in plain sight like a brown moth on dark bark, Whit felt exposed and naked, like his little moth wings had just turned pure white. *She's going to make a scene if she discovers anything more about me.* Glancing quickly around the room he thought, *Where the hell are Mike and Janet?*

"Are you looking for someone to rescue you, or did you lose your date?"

"No, I mean yes, sort of. Actually, I'm just checking out the guests, you know."

Whit could tell she didn't buy that one bit. *Okay, Whittingham, focus and engage this assertive, beltway savvy troublemaker. Handle this or she's going to expose you. She just happens to be gorgeous and works for a liberal rag; correction, the most liberal rag in the beltway. If she finds out I'm a conservative, I'll be wearing her drink.*

Katelyn broke in. "I thought we were making introductions?"

Covering poorly after a long pause, Whit blurted out, "Oh, uh, I'm Ben, a, ah friend of the Kennedys?" *Jesus, Whittingham, nice effort. It even came out as a question.*

Staring hard, she nodded slightly with a smirk of satisfaction, like she'd ferreted out an imposter, a shyster, a bullshit artist. Then Whit noticed an expression that he took for real disappointment. Finally, she spoke with a flat tone that meant *we're done here, liar.* "Well then, uh, Ben, a, ah friend of the Kennedys, I'm sure you won't mind if I check."

Katelyn spun around and walked away. If Whit had not registered that trace of almost sadness on her face, he would have just blown off the whole encounter. *Screw you, witch.* But there was something there, like he'd let her down. He quickly said to her back, trying to only speak loud enough for her ears, "I cut down trees for a living."

His words stopped her cold. She stood facing away from Whit for a good five seconds, debating whether to just keep walking. Finally, she pivoted on her heels.

Trying to recover, Whit offered, "Well, that's not all I do, I also—"

Walking back, she cut in with, "Well, uh, Ben, what else do you do, club baby seals?"

"We don't have baby seals in the Sierra. But I do pull the wings off little birds. There, make you feel better?" Whit held up his free hand to stop her from responding and continued. "Look, my name is Ben Whittingham and I do work in Northern California. I help private landowners manage their timberlands. I figured as soon as you knew what I did for a living, you'd fling your drink in my face and walk away. I know I came off a little shady, but your guilty-until-proven-innocent approach didn't help. Plus, can't you tell I am a little out of my element here? I know you know I was BS-ing you, but hey, I was just trying to save some other guy's suit from a wine bath."

Katelyn held up her glass and shot back, "I was damn close to flicking this very nice merlot right in your face. I hate men who lie to me."

Wow, did we hit a tender nerve or what? Whit asked, "Look, I'm sorry; can we start over?"

After a pause, Katelyn smiled and said, "I don't often hear apologies from men in this town. Okay, let's try again. So, what are you doing here?"

With a smirk, Whit said, "You're quick, Ms. Katelyn Summers. Not that far back. Okay, how about I explain why…or how…I ended up here."

Turning off her charging-bull manner, Katelyn said pleasantly, "I'm all ears."

"An old buddy called me with a problem."

"The same guy whose wife made you attend this party?"

"Correct."

"Okay, what kind of a problem?"

"Kid problems; he and his wife have three teenage boys and, well, they're starting to get in trouble."

"What's that have to do with you? Are they cutting down trees and pulling wings off of little birds?"

"Tell you what…let's try to have a conversation without the little digs and jabs."

Backing off another notch Katelyn said, "Sure, okay, I'll try to be good."

After shaking his head and downing the rest of his water with a splash of bourbon, Whit decided to continue. "I seem to be able to connect with kids, most kids. My buddy and his wife are worried about the direction their kids are heading. Even from the West Coast I've always been close to my buddy's three, and care about them. Their youngest seems to be slipping the most. He feels like the low man on the totem pole and fights boundaries, structure, limits. I was there once. So, I came to Virginia to help, if I could." Pointing down, Whit added, "How I ended here is another long story."

"I'm starting to get the picture, Mr. Benjamin Whittingham."

"Whit. My friends call me Whit."

"Are we friends already?"

"Well, no, not exactly, but you did come over and talk to me."

"You looked so out of place and forlorn standing there. It looked like you wanted to open that window and escape into the woods. Most people beg to get here; you were fighting the urge to flee. You piqued my reporter's curiosity."

"Believe me, I feel it. I even clicked my heels three times trying to get to Kansas."

Laughing, Katelyn said, "I saw you; I thought you had something in your shoe." After another little pause, Katelyn asked, "Well, uh, Ben, ah, a friend of the Kennedys, do you want to get out of here and go someplace where you can relax or at least feel a little more comfortable?"

"Pardon me?"

"You heard me, mountain man. I won't make the offer twice."

Looking over Katelyn's head, Whit saw an alien world he never should have tried to navigate. He found himself smiling broadly and saying to himself, *What the hell am I doing? Out of the frying pan and into the fire?* But, to Katelyn, he just replied, "Absolutely."

Chapter Two
The Watering Hole

As old Gold Rush bars go, Pete's Place fit right in, exhibiting the classic mid-1800s façade. Sandwiched in between two other similar structures with common walls, the front contained a tall, wide window set inside geometrically perfect rustic red and orange bricks. The ancient thick glass displayed old technology including wavy impurities and tiny bubbles frozen in place. Massive, thick riveted iron shutters guarded each end. The wood-framed glass door on the far right also included a thick riveted iron door, open during business hours. Eighty feet long but only twenty feet wide, the long hardwood bar and eighteen barstools ran down the left side and used up more than half of the room's width. Small little two-seat tables barely fit along the right wall. Where the bar and barstools ended, a couple of four-seat tables just fit. Down a short, narrow hall, two restrooms used up the far back. The men's room retained a functioning oak overhead tank, pull-chain toilet. Between the end of the bar and the larger tables, an open entryway passed through into the adjacent building. The area contained a space big enough for a small group to meet, a storage room, and a back door accessing the bar's parking lot.

Two of Benjamin Whittingham's childhood buddies and lifelong friends sat on their usual barstools, at their favorite watering hole. Greyson Milner and Ned Penrose met at Pete's Place in the tiny Northern California mining town of Cedar Creek almost every Tuesday evening. If Whit didn't need to work late and found himself close to town, he'd also drop by to meet, throw back a few and shoot the bull. This evening, Grey, as most called him, dismissively explained to Ned why he'd just dumped his latest squeeze.

"That's it?" Ned Penrose blurted out, spilling some of his drink. He put his glass back on the bar, licked his fingers and turned to face his buddy. "You're dumping Janie because she has...troll legs? That's bullshit, Milner. Tell me you're not that shallow; there has to be something more."

"No, that's it, troll legs," Grey replied.

"This is a new low, even for you." Ned paused, waiting for a response but none came. Finally he said, "No, I take it back, Milner; this only ties your lowest low. Who was the gal you dumped because her vagina was too big? What was her name?"

"Brooke."

"Yeah, Brooke, another nice gal dumped by Mr. Sensitive."

Ned thought about Brooke. *Sorry I didn't remember your name, Brooke, but you really didn't last that long with Grey. But I do remember you. You were great, even to me. I would have treated you a whole lot better than—*

"She is a very nice girl." Grey's response cut short Ned's reminiscing. "She just has a huge who who."

"Well, Stud, maybe you just didn't measure up," Ned shot back.

Milner ignored Ned's slight, or at least Ned thought he had. Then Grey asked out of the blue, "What was the name of that pendulous dude in the porno movie we watched at Mike's bachelor party?"

"Long Dong Silver."

"Yeah, Long Dong Silver. He couldn't fill good old Brooke's void either. But you know, thinking about your memory, it says something about a guy who can't remember the name of a hottie like Brooke but can easily recall the name of a dangling porno star. You have something to tell me old buddy? Need to get a dark secret off your chest or...out of the closet?"

Wide eyed, Ned stammered, "What? Me? Guys? No, no way." Then he noticed Grey's got-you smile. "Ah, fuck you, Milner. You always do that. Stop the bait and switch. We're not changing the subject. Right when I try to make a point about your 'no woman is perfect enough for you' phobia, you sidetrack me. Well, not this time. You'd have dumped Brooke even if she didn't have a big muffin. She stood taller than you, another fatal flaw. Once you scored, that ended your interest. And now, Janie; man, you're nuts."

Grey turned his head Ned's way, tilting it slightly and said, "Why can't you just let my little encounters, trysts, affairs...whatever you want to call them, go? I do."

Ned shot back, "No. That's the problem, you moron. Women are a lot more than just a body. Have you ever thought about that?" Emboldened and on the offensive now, Ned continued. "You'll never find the perfect girl because you'll never be satisfied until you find the perfect body. But, in your warped, narcissistic, self-absorbed little mind, that woman does not exist. Haven't you ever heard of the old saying, 'If you can't put up with the mind, you can't put up with the body'? You can't separate the two. If you ever really do fall in love, you'll find out, you'll see."

"Oh, thank you, Mr. Love Expert. And how many times have you been married?"

Ned turned his head away and said nothing.

Grey dug in, "That would be two, right? Well, if you don't count the annulment after, what, six days of bliss? Too bad, too; I liked Sherry. I just didn't like her first husband; you know, the guy she was still married to."

After a short pause without a word uttered from Ned, Milner continued. "Let's move to relationships, shall we? Let me see...oh, yeah. There was Tina, who professed to you her undying love. You bought her that car and she dumped you for a dishwasher at Paradise Lake Lodge. And we can't forget sweet Bridgett, who moved to the Bay Area after you put her through nursing school." With that annoying Milner smirk, Grey finished with, "I could go on, but, I think I've made my point."

Ned just stewed. *Yeah, Milner, you made your point. Easy for a good-looking guy to be...how should I put this...less desperate, trusting, gullible. In the world of looks, I don't measure up to a guy like Milner. Hell, in the bar scene, I don't measure up to most guys, period. A little too tall and gangly, a big nose and a huge Adam's apple; I would kick ass in an Abraham Lincoln or Ichabod Crane lookalike contest. In fact, my dear old buds nicknamed me Abe about twenty-five years ago and it stuck. I know there's more to me than just what people see on the outside, but sometimes it doesn't feel like it. If you can't get past a hello, how will women—who go for a guy like Milner—ever give me a chance?*

Since Ned refused to respond, Grey knew he had gone too far. Milner toned it down by saying, "Look, sorry for the jabs, old buddy. You just make it too easy." Still after no response from Ned, he added, "Okay, what I'm trying to say is, that was mean and uncalled for and I'm sorry. But you have to admit, with your track record, it's kind of funny you giving me advice on women. All good humor has to have an element of truth, right? And back to Janie, I am telling you the truth. It's her legs, or more accurately, her lack of legs. I mean, she's cute and fun and all, and damn nice tits, but she's all torso. When she's naked and walking away from me, like heading to the bathroom and I'm checking out her backside, everything's fine until I look below her ass. She goes from butt to feet. No legs; there's just a little space above her ankles keeping her tight little hiney from touching the floor."

Ned finally couldn't remain silent anymore and blurted out, "Jesus, Milner; you absolutely amaze me. Do you ever think about their feelings? How can you dump them and just never call? Don't you think they deserve a smidgen of respect?"

Milner gave Ned a look like he was listening to a telemarketer…blah, blah, blah, blah, blah. "Shit, Abe; you treat them like goddesses and they treat you like crap. You're too nice; I'm just making up for you. I bring balance back to the universe."

"It's still mean; you never used to be like this."

"Ah, hell, Abe, they're all players; especially the ones that come into a bar alone. They're testing the water. You either go for the hotties or go home with…how do I say this, delicately?"

Ned finished for Grey. "Easy marks? A woman a little overweight, maybe a tad homely or lonely, perhaps the poor thing is a little too desper—"

"Okay, okay, you've made your point. So, I became a little more…aggressive, assertive, and I upgraded to women we all used to shy away from. Hotties are players too; you just have to be willing to get shut down and move on to the next one."

They both just sat there saying nothing. Grey knew Ned had a point… sort of. Ned knew Grey had a point…sort of. But all the banter was about to end. Ned's indignation always lost steam when Stacey, their bartender, planted herself right across from Ned and started washing glasses. Grey knew Ned's smitten feelings for Stacey, and her presence always distracted his thought process. Sadly, Ned's affection for Miss Stacey fell into the category of unrequited love. She only seemed to be attracted to guys with big biceps, tattoos, confidence and, Grey and Ned assumed, access to recreational drugs, none of which could be found in Ned's quiver.

Grey leaned over to his buddy and nudged him on the shoulder. "Hey, big fella, something bugging you? You seem particularly edgy tonight; more combative than usual." Trying to lighten Ned up a little he added, "If you were one of the Seven Dwarfs, you'd be Grumpy."

Ned turned to Grey and said, "If you were one of the Seven Dwarfs, you'd be Sleazy."

Shaking his head Grey said, "There's no Seven Dwarf named Sleazy."

Ned shot back, "No, and there shouldn't be one here either."

Grey jerked his head. "Whoa, good one Abe; nice shot." Grey reached around, stabbed himself in the side and moaned. "Right between the ribs."

They both became quiet again. Stacey came by to see if they were ready for their second round. "Kind of noisy at times down here tonight. You girls cat fighting again?"

Grey said, "Oh, Abe here's got his panties in a bunch."

Defensively, Ned said to Grey, "I do not." Turning to Stacey, he repeated, "I do not."

Stacey looked at Grey then pointed at Ned, "So, did he just confirm he's wearing panties?"

Grey jumped in. "I'm thinking, yes."

"I am not...you two...why do you two always...ahh," Ned threw his hands up in frustration.

Stacey leaned over the bar and smacked Ned on the shoulder. "Hey, buck up, Princess; we're just teasing."

Ned just nodded his head but didn't say anything, so Stacey asked, "How about another round Ned...on the house?"

It was impossible for Ned to stay mad at Stacey. He smiled at her, shook his head and said, "Okay, sure, thanks."

Grey tapped his chest and asked, "Hey, what about me?"

Stacey winked at Ned and said to Grey, "No friggin' way...Sleazy."

Ned mocked at his buddy. "Ha, serves you right." In a whisper, Ned added, "Any doubt that Stacey can eavesdrop on our conversations from just about anywhere behind the bar?"

Grey, glad the conversation had moved away from his relationship with women, asked, "When is Whit coming home from visiting Mikie?"

Ned replied, "I think the end of this week. I'll bet he'll be backlogged with work and we won't see him for another week or so after that, though."

"Whit sure puts in the hours; but at least we'll get an update on Mikie, Janet and the boys."

Ned replied, "Whit loves his work and at least gets paid well to do it. Better than me. After bills and taxes, I've been working for less than minimum wage lately."

Grey knew Ned's stationery store hadn't been doing too well. *Maybe that's why Honest Abe's in such a dour mood?*

Chapter Three
Layers of Evil

The smallish, serious-looking man exited the SUV—a rental procured from Enterprise at the San Diego International Airport. Stephen Sliger's huge bodyguard and driver, Moose, closed the back door and followed his boss to the elevator in the basement parking area. They rode up to the top of the four-floor building. The doors parted, but before Moose could check the hall, Sliger marched out holding his small briefcase tight to his side. Moose made a face but said nothing, other than to himself: *Impossible to do my job.*

Moose hurried forward and did bypass his boss enough to quickly open and enter the psychiatrist's outer door. The receptionist, Donna Atkins, squealed and half leaped out of her chair. Knowing that Sliger and his bodyguard were coming didn't help; she retained a full-fledged, scared-to-death-fear of both men.

Still holding her chest, Donna chirped, "Please." Clearing her throat, she tried again in a little more controlled voice. "Please go right in, Mr. Sliger; the doctor is expecting you."

She noticed both were smirking, enjoying her apprehension and dread. Sliger actually never stopped walking as he moved past Moose and through the door to the doctor's office. The six-foot-six, 360-pound bodyguard closed the outer door. He grabbed a chair and moved it to where he wanted, then sat down. Donna knew better than to offer the giant a cup of coffee. She tried on the two previous sessions and Moose returned the gesture with a menacing stare and audible exhale.

Sliger entered the doctor's office and, without greeting, started in on the doctor. "Doctor Zulov, save your breath and my time. Lay off the distant past.

We are not going back to my years in high school. You're just like the other shrinks I've seen. It's nothing, of no consequence...irrelevant. I've climbed so far above and beyond those assholes I knew then, who cares? How could giving them a second of my time or even acknowledging their existence matter to someone like me? They're insects. I just don't see how those miserable little pricks could affect me now or be the root of my problems. I refuse to think about them."

"Mr. Sliger, Stephen...."

"If you are going to address me casually, its Steven or Steve. I hate Stephen."

Another well-orchestrated lie Sliger used to put people off guard and set them back. It fit his decades-old identity and the way he treated...outsiders. His name wasn't Stephen or Sliger, but only the "Inner Circle" knew his real identity, and even they only knew bits of his former life. To the world, he was Stephen Sliger, owner and CEO of Serpentine Solutions, Inc., a small but successful computer programming company that diversified into environmental research, habitat improvement and hazardous site reclamation. The rapid decline of a larger competitor turned SS Inc. into the West Coast's go-to player in the very profitable world of large government-funded environmental grants.

"Steve," the therapist paused for effect then continued, "listen to your anger, listen to your denials. We have been going around in circles for two sessions. You seem to truly want to find out why, even with all your success, why, you are so...out of sorts. But you steadfastly resist any attempt to delve into what could be the primary cause or causes. As I understand it, I am your third therapist since your latest divorce. You want answers, you want help. I can tell you're searching and sincerely want resolution. You shut out the other psychiatrists and you are doing the same to me. I can't help you if you won't let me."

"Isn't that why I'm here? Isn't that why I'm paying you the big bucks? Aren't you the top quack?"

Ignoring the insult, Zulov continued. "Yes, okay, yes, I hear you. Paying double my fee is very generous, but that's not the point. If we can't get beyond the walls you've erected to block out your past, you can double my fee again and it won't help. Release what's locked up inside you, and together we will find answers, resolution, relief." *There it is Sliger, my best pitch. We go forward or end it now.*

Steve Sliger glared briefly at his newest therapist, then turned his head and scanned across Dr. Zulov's plush fourth-floor corner office. Finally, he sat down and turned his gaze to the open window. He watched the tops of the ever-present palm trees. The fronds swayed gently in the morning breeze that blew in from the Pacific. Sliger breathed in the cool salty air in what guaranteed to be another perfect day in San Diego. He sighed a little and thought, *I'm tired of trying to ignore this… whatever it is gnawing at my brain. I hate this overriding feeling of bitterness, resentment and sorrow, all at the same time. Those are the emotions lesser people exhibit after I've destroyed them. What do I have to feel bitter about? I control whatever I want. Why do I feel resentment? I make sure no one bests me. And why in the hell do I feel sorrow? I'm not weak. Besides, what do I have to feel sorry about? I have money, power, success; what else is there?*

After sitting back in his chair, Sliger closed his eyes and tried to be honest with himself. *Then why don't I feel…better? I used to feel satisfied; no, much more than that…on top, powerful, in control of my surroundings. Why has that been replaced by…all this crap?*

Opening his eyes and briefly glancing at Dr. Zulov, Steven Sliger's self-analyzing continued. *Maybe I can open up to this guy, a little. If I can let my guard down just enough to find out what's eating at me then I can crush it and get on with my life. To do this, I'll have to break the golden rule to my success: complete secrecy and total control of information. Okay, Zulov, we'll try it your way; but only after I complete a background check on your sorry ass. Everyone has dirt, secrets, an Achilles heel. Everyone hides something, something useful. Once I know your past and own your future, then we'll talk about my dear high school friends. Then, finally I'll fix this shitty limbo. Well, Dr. Zulov, you better believe in doctor/client confidentiality because, if you don't, you'll find out how deadly serious I can be when people dare cross me.*

Dr. Zulov observed his newest client, staring blankly out of the west facing window. Zulov believed Sliger to be his richest client. That was saying something when you considered all the movie star's spoiled, drugged-out children and the dumped dumpy first wives of zillionaires that Dr. Zulov saw on a regular basis. Yes, the good life…profiting off of the messed-up lives of the LA basin's wealthy.

Of course, it didn't start out that way, not even close. After picking up his sociology/psychology double major from the University of Chicago, he added a master's in behavioral science. When his favorite professor offered him a research job with time to pursue his Ph.D., he jumped at the chance. Unfortunately, it turned into a work-your-ass-off, no-credit-for-anything, penniless, party-less, sexless three years. The same day he received his doctorate, he quit his now much hated professor. Unfortunately, the brand-new doctor of psychiatry could only find a government job, running a county clinic. A bad move, stuck with three more years of unfulfilled, unrewarding financial goose eggs.

Finally, at thirty-two, he borrowed a substantial stipend from his elderly parents and put out his own shingle using his real name, Dr. Wayne Butterfield. Everything looked rosy and felt right. Unfortunately, it didn't take long to learn the rich and just about everyone else didn't feel comfortable spilling their guts out to a shrink named Butterfield. After three more pathetic years of barely breaking even, he found himself at wit's end.

Frustrated and angry, he started seeing a therapist himself. Toward the end of what would ultimately be his last session, his therapist, half in jest and half in disgust, suggested, "If money and self-gratification drive you more than helping people, just change your name to Weinstein and move to LA. Set up shop near the rich and famously screwed up."

That's when the lightbulb in Butterfield's head flickered to life. He felt the Jewish angle would be a little too much to pull off, but everything else fell into place. Other than his age, he faked everything. His fabricated past sounded perfect; his degrees appeared authentic. Wayne Butterfield became Dr. Ivan Zulov from an obscure school, a satellite affiliated with the University of Moscow.

Once again, he hit his parents up for another, never-to-be-repaid loan and put his plan into motion. After putting 20 percent down on a high-end office space in downtown San Diego, he bought furniture and used the last of his poor unsuspecting parents' money to blitz the San Diego and LA area with a monstrous add campaign. His business took off and he never looked back.

The well-to-do, with Bloody Mary in hand, loved to brag to their peers, during brunch, about their worldly and brilliant Russian therapist. *Zulov is the best; you just must see him yourself. I credit the genius of Mikhail Gorbachev and his glasnost and perestroika for the opportunity to finally have access to a real psychiatrist, blah, blah, blah.*

Dr. Zulov did have all the answers…at $400 an hour. Even his lack of accent he attributed to a strict Russian father and nurturing but stern East German mother who forced him to learn perfect English. No one checked; not even the licensing board questioned his masterful but very phony credentials. With money and notoriety came women, lots of women, mostly needy and gullible clients. Unethical to take advantage of these vulnerable women, damn straight, but hadn't he paid his dues? And the most amazing part, most of the time, the women eventually moved on to someone else and apologized to him for breaking off the affair...incredible! Of course, banging clients definitely fit into the category of unprofessional doctor/patient...privileges; but hell, this is Southern California, right?

Seeing Sliger's menacing glare transfixed on something out of the open window brought the good doctor back to the present. He said to himself, *Be careful with this one. He's packed with delusions of grandeur, narcissism and manic self-preservation. And he seems to have the money and power to bend the rules to fit his needs. That huge goon of Sliger's, who sits in the waiting room scaring the hell out of my receptionist and other clients puts an exclamation point on my concern. I don't want to wake up with a horse head in my bed...or worse. I have a good gig here and don't want to blow it.*

Dr. Zulov continued to watch his client stare out the window. Doctor Zulov observed a short, maybe 5' 4", fortyish-aged man with straight flat gray hair. His light complexion, skinny pointed nose, and thin frame gave him the appearance of a wiry, hungry coyote...lean and sinuous. He exuded the classic Napoleon complex. That was Zulov's impression when Sliger marched aggressively into his office for the first time wearing loose fitting casual clothes and very expensive leather oxfords...with two-and-a-half-inch heels. The first two sessions confirmed his original impression. This guy possessed a ruthless streak like megalomaniac rulers. Maybe the Napoleon comparison was too light. Dr. Zulov absentmindedly sketched out a swastika on his notepad.

The doctor figured he had two options; milk this nutcase for a bundle while stringing him along or dig out the core of Sliger's anger and then give him the name of a good doctor specializing in Sliger's specific psychosis. Self-preservation won out and Zulov decided to get this dangerous man the hell out of his office.

In talking to Sliger, he could tell the guy kept layers and layers of deception perfectly choreographed. He never forgot what he said or in what context. Most people can't remember the truth, let alone the lies, but Sliger could.

He figured Sliger retained an IQ of 160-plus, and Zulov didn't want this clever and scary loose cannon mad at him. Just then Sliger opened his eyes wide and turned his gaze from the window back to Doctor Zulov. Those cold, dead eyes frightened Zulov; they were remorseless killer's eyes. The top of Zulov's thighs started to tingle and he quickly looked down at his notes and blocked in the swastika.

Trying to gain composure, Zulov chose a different tactic. "Why don't we just try talking in general about one old classmate and see how that goes?"

After a pained look and a long and awkward pause, Sliger opened a door sealed shut long ago, and simply said, "Won't work."

Zulov thought, *Maybe this is my ticket out and I can end this right now. I'll send this loon off to some other poor unsuspecting doctor.* "Okay, well, that kind of puts us in what we call in the profession, an impasse. I really don't see how I can proceed any further with—"

"I agree, Doctor, you don't see," Sliger interrupted sternly.

Dr. Zulov froze but tried to look neutral. Sliger's comment came out as a pure threat. Zulov was now very scared; he couldn't have spoken even if he knew what to say.

Finally, Sliger broke the silence. "They were a gang, a clique, a club. You can't just talk about one of them without including them all." Just bringing up that little tidbit of information about his past turned Sliger's stomach. He felt them winning again; laughing, mocking, and he sensed the same humiliation and helpless frustration he had suppressed for so long. It raised more bile in his stomach, all the way up to the back of his throat.

Zulov realized the huge leap forward that just occurred. Though he felt elated, as he always did when he reached a breakthrough moment with a client, he also felt a chill run down his legs and the hairs on his thighs stand on end for the second time in two minutes. He instantly felt both excited anticipation and frozen-in-place fear. To continue, Zulov knew he'd be poking into a very disturbed man's very disturbed past. *Who pokes a viper with their bare foot?*

Zulov's mind flashed to an all too familiar scenario from old horror movies. The beautiful, but tormented, woman awakens abruptly, as wind and rain pound outside the elegant guest bedroom of a large 16th-century estate. Inexplicably, she's drawn to the one room forbidden to her by the baron of the manor. She lights a candle and slides out of bed. In only a revealing lace negligée, she walks barefoot down a dark narrow hallway, as menacing shadows dance around her in the flickering light. *Zulov could even feel the cold air seeping out from under the door at the end of the hall.* She can't stop herself; compelled forward she reaches the last door. Slowly she leans down for the crystal door knob just as a cold musty breeze extinguishes the candle. *In Zulov's mind, it's his hand. Dare he twist the knob and confront the horror that lurks inside?*

Chapter Four
No Touching, No Talking

Katelyn and Whit left the Kennedy party long before Mike and Janet returned to pick him up. Chaperone Brenda was nowhere to be found; probably in a dark den or library 'bobbin the nobbin' of her newest and soon-to-be ex-boyfriend. Katelyn's apartment resided less than twenty minutes away—-well, during non-commute traffic. She lived just outside of Alexandria.

On the drive, Katelyn asked Whit if he wanted to smoke a joint. He wrinkled his nose and shook his head. She lit up and said, "You might want to roll down your window."

Whit said, "If I roll down my window the smoke will be sucked out my way. Why don't you crack yours?"

After she did, Katelyn said, "Oh, how about that, you're right. I bet you know a lot of stuff like that, don't you?"

"I could teach you tons of stuff like that back home. Not so much here."

After a long pause, Katelyn said, "You're quite the oddity, Benjamin Whittingham."

"Well, you are quite the odd one yourself. Tell me—changing the subject—why would a reporter for Progressive Politics pick up a sad sack like me at a Kennedy party?"

Putting her joint down she explained that it was his absolutely pathetic look of lost bewilderment that made her seek him out. The reporter in her smelled a rat. Though to herself, she had to admit it was more. She wanted a change…something, anything…new, different. She thought he looked attractive, in a rough sort of way. He definitely did not exhibit prissiness, vanity or arrogance. She was tired of the plastic, cookie-cutter same-old, blah, blah,

blah, self-important, ladder climber, egotistical users she seemed to attract. This man was different, seriously different, and showing up poorly dressed to a Kennedy party took balls…or meant he was crazy. It was early on, but so far, she was not disappointed.

After another awkward pause, bam, direct as hell, Katelyn Summers hit Benjamin Whittingham with the big questions. "Do you have AIDS, genital herpes, hepatitis, or something else I need to know about?"

Whit put his thumb under his borrowed belt and pulled the slacks forward. After peeking around, he replied, "Nope."

"Good, me neither. Are you fertile?"

"As far as I know."

"Me too, but I'm on the pill."

Whit thought, *Bingo bango, pass go, collect two hundred dollars. This emancipated woman would fit right in on the Berkeley campus.*

Katelyn glanced at Whit deep in thought and asked, "What are you thinking in there?"

"Oh, just a move in the game Monopoly."

"Monopoly?" *Monopoly?* "Am I boring you?"

Whit looked directly at Katelyn's beautiful profile and assured her, "Most certainly not."

Giving her head a little shake while rolling her eyes, Katelyn turned left into the right side of a wide, short driveway. The Tudor-style structure, a combination of brick and wood siding, displayed the standard colonial appearance. The lawn and shrubbery showed superior care as did the outside of the house. Whit noticed the window shutters were fake, just for show. But then so were the shutters on just about every other home.

Katelyn cut into his assessment by saying, "It's a duplex; I rent the right side. Progressive Politics owns both sides. They provide fairly reasonable housing for many of their employees."

Getting out of the passenger side Whit said, "Very progressive."

Katelyn waited until Whit opened her door. *A small but important test for the country bumpkin; he passed.* Holding his left hand in her right, Katelyn's high-heels clicked softly as she led him down the well-lit walk. They stepped up a short flight of stairs. At the top she let go of Whit's hand and walked across the short landing to her front door. Unlocking the door, she pushed it open and put her purse and keys on the small table just inside. Turning back to Whit, who was standing on the last step to the landing, she smiled and closed the distance between them. With Whit on the last step they looked at each other nearly eye to eye. She reached up and held his face in her hands, leaned forward and kissed Whit for the second time. This time she inserted her tongue and Whit felt a surge of excitement and a flush of blood flow. *He could taste and smell the pot and a lingering sweetness from the red wine.* Stepping back, she grabbed his hand and walked him into her place.

Whit could sum up Katelyn's condo in two words: white/black. Walls, carpet, living room furniture, cabinets were white like fresh snow. Well, bone or ivory or one of a thousand shades of white...the difference, only women can distinguish. The countertop, window shades, table and chairs, and stair railing reflected back shiny and blacker than black. Whit thought, *Definitely, no pets.*

Still without a word spoken she kicked off her shoes. He did the same. Katelyn walked Whit down the hall and right past the kitchen and living room. She was all business now and didn't even ask Whit if he wanted a drink. They walked to the white carpeted stairs and he followed her up to her bedroom. She sat him down on the edge of her high queen-sized bed covered with a large, thick, cream-colored quilt. After turning on the black lamps on both sides of her bed, Katelyn pointed toward the bathroom and said, "Do you need to...?" Since Whit had used a tennis-court sized bathroom at the Kennedy fortress prior to leaving, Whit said he was fine. Katelyn turned and walked into the bathroom. Before she closed the door, Katelyn poked her head back into the bedroom, looked at Whit and said, "Go ahead and take off your clothes but stay on the end of the bed, leave the lights on, and no talking when I come out."

Whit nodded and made a zipper motion across his lips as she closed the door. *Well, Janet Ho,* he thought, *did you know about this? Did you set this up? Is she really a reporter or a high-class hooker you hired to get poor old perpetual bachelor Whit laid. If it was the latter, Janet, you have my type of woman down pat.* Katelyn, if that's her real name, fit Whit's kind of perfect. Maybe 5'9", she possessed wide, light-brown eyes on a face with strong features. Her nose might be a little too long for a movie star, but not to Whit. He never cared for mousy, soft featured women; they seemed pouty looking and weak in some way. Her hair was a little longer than shoulder length, parted in the middle and shaped around her angular face. The one feature, her hair color, dyed way too dark, didn't quite seem to fit. Katelyn was definitely slender but shapely, with square shoulders like a distance runner.

Doing as he was told, Whit stood and stripped down quickly, half folding and half dumping his borrowed suit in a pile on the carpet, at the corner of the bed. He sat right back down on the bed where Katelyn originally put him. He noticed or sensed he was aroused even though Little Benny didn't show it.

He could hear Katelyn making noises from the bathroom doing whatever women do. As he looked around, nothing seemed out of place other than his bare-assed naked body, three thousand miles from home, sitting in a beautiful liberal reporter's bedroom. Getting picked up like this and actually making the conscious decision to go through with it was not what the very reserved Whit did. *So why now, why me? Why did I say yes? Was it because I was stuck at the Kennedys'? No. Was it because I'm so damn desperate? No; well, not completely.* It was Katelyn, something about her. Alluring, quick-witted, damn good looking, even her assertiveness attracted him. But he also knew she possessed something…something more. The attraction clobbered him instantaneously.

Then another overanalyzing thought hit him. *You better get focused on the task at hand here, Benny Boy, whatever that task turns out to be. Don't think too much, don't think at all. Turn your mind off and let go. Good, bad or indifferent, it's happening, so focus.* Just then the bathroom door opened, and Katelyn emerged wearing a bra and panties, both light pink, and tall stiletto high-heels, also pink. She had pulled her hair straight back into a tight little ponytail which accentuated her facial features. Whit's first thought was, *Uh-oh, the dominatrix type. No handcuffs for this guy, sweetheart! No whips, no chains, or Great Danes either.* But her movements were delicate and feminine, not stalking and physical. *Will you please calm the hell down for once in your life?* She sauntered right up in front of him, bent over at the waist, and kissed him on the lips. It was a long kiss, but not so hard that she pushed him backwards on the bed. He reached for her and she took his hands and put them down by his sides. In a throaty voice revealing her own growing arousal she whispered in his ear, "Don't touch. Your turn will come; be patient."

Violating the no-talking rule also only seemed to apply to Whit, but he wanted to see how this played out. Whit said only to himself, *Patience is not a guy thing, Miss Pretty-in-Pink, but you seem to know what you want. Let's do this your way.*

She straightened up while still looking down at him, reached behind her back and unfastened her bra. She brought her shoulders together slightly to allow the bra to slide off of her chest. Katelyn intently watched Whit's eyes travel to her breasts. *What's a guy to do?* They were like identical twins, grapefruit sized and firm with long erect nipples that actually pointed up. Whit had seen breasts like that in magazines but never in real life. *Arousal meter going up.*

Katelyn was breathing deeper now, obviously excited by Whit's response. She slowly turned around facing away from him, bent over straight legged once again, and started sliding off her panties. As she slid them down just below her ass, Whit could tell the pale pink material in the center was damp. As the panties passed her knees, she lifted her right leg, then her left leg. They dangled on the left heel briefly then fell to the floor. She stayed bent over and started using her thumbs and index fingers to massage and pull at her nipples.

With her legs spread widely apart, she gave Whit a bird's-eye view of her backside, not two feet away. *Patience; she does this to me and wants me to be patient...Christ Almighty.* She had absolutely no hair around her vagina, but Whit noticed soft short blonde hairs running up the crack of her ass. *Blond. Blond? Focus, damn you.*

Whit turned his attention back to her slightly parted and reddening vagina. He could smell the combined scent of her body and the fragrance of musty feminine sexual arousal. His own arousal meter headed for the red line. *Hell, don't focus too much; Little Benny's going to blow.*

Katelyn backed up slightly, squatted down and straddled Whit's right thigh. For balance, she used her left hand to firmly grip the top of his left thigh and placed the heel of her right hand on Whit's right knee. Katelyn shifted her position a little, then lifted slightly and started sliding on Whit's thigh. She was so wet she slid easily back and forth rubbing her now parted lips. Sometimes she bent way forward to include her clitoris in the movement. Whit put his arms back behind him on the bed to support their position. He could watch her head bobbing slightly as she began to moan and sometimes make short quick squeals. More frequently she'd bend way forward exposing her ass as she made long slides back and forth. Finally, she sat up straight and moved very little. Whit realized she was controlling her stimulation. He was fully extended now, totally wanting to be a part of this sexual encounter and wondering how much longer he or Little Benny could be…patient. It took all of his willpower to be this close, to have all his senses so stimulated, and not just grab her and take her.

She was getting close, he could tell. The motion had slowed to only slight movements. She was fighting between the urge to prolong the rise to ecstasy and the desire to let go. She gave in with violent shudders, muffled squeals and strong constrictions that Whit could feel on his thigh. The orgasms rose and fell many times with just the slightest movement on her part. Moist slipperiness covered Whit's leg. Whit thought he would lose it right then and there. *Damn, this is erotic as hell.*

Eventually, Katelyn's breathing settled down. Still facing away from Whit, she rose slightly and reached under herself with her left hand. Whit was thinking, *Now what? No more patience, no more damn patience!* She slipped her moistened hand out from between her legs and grabbed the base of Whit's hard-as-a-rock member. Making a circle with her thumb and index finger, she started stroking him with a grip like a tight vagina. She always stopped short of his head, which Whit took as maddeningly torturous. Then he realized she was doing to him what she'd done to herself; she was prolonging his climb. Katelyn listened to Whit's breathing as she worked him. She could tell he was getting close, so she quickly turned around, dropped to her knees and wrapped her mouth around his head. She cradled his tightly constricted balls in her right hand. He could take only two more strokes then exploded. Whit fell on his back as thrusting spasms shot multiple spurts. She swallowed the whole load. As she was milking him, Whit finally had to speak. "Sensitive…getting a little too sensitive."

She looked up at him with a devilish smile, pulled her mouth away and said, "Just trying to get every drop."

Whit remained on his back and Katlyn rested her head on his left knee. Katelyn looked up between Whit's legs as his flat, hairy chest rose and fell. Katelyn rubbed her hands up and down the top of Whit's left leg, leaving most of the slipperiness there. She slid up beside him, wiped her mouth back and forth on his left shoulder, leaned over his chest and kissed him. After their lips parted, she slid up past him pulling slightly on his arm, urging him to slide up to the pillows. They pulled the quilt and blanket back and slid between the cold silk sheets. She snuggled under his left arm and crossed her left leg and thigh over his waist. She purred, "That was really, really good."

"Shit Howdy," was all Whit said.

She laughed and said, "Shit Howdy? Where did that...? You are one un-usual guy, Mr. Whittingham."

"You are one unusual woman, Miss Summers. That was one erotic per-formance you walked us through. Did you come up with that little scenario all by yourself?"

"As it turns out, yes. I know what turns on a guy, and as you can tell, it works well for me too. Guys are so...visual and so impatient. I figured out a way we both get to the end zone. Agreed?"

"Shit Howdy."

They lay quietly in each other's arms for quite some time.

Finally, Katelyn said, "You kept your mouth shut and didn't touch me the whole time. That's the first time anyone ever...." She stopped herself realizing she started revealing past intimacies.

Whit broke the tension by asking in a surprised voice, "You mean, you're not a virgin?"

Laughing a little again, and thankful she didn't have to finish the thought but feeling okay to elaborate more, she said, "Virgin? Well, no, not really. But you know, I've been told if a woman doesn't use it in six months, the hymen grows back. So, tonight, yes...I'm a virgin."

"You have not had sex in six months?"

"Shit Howdy," she responded, making Whit laugh. "Long time and long story; let's just say I learned the hard way about love and one's reputation in the beltway. So, what about you? What makes you such a patient lover?"

"Oh, even though I've never been married, I learned to mind well at an early age, to be a good listener, pick up on a woman's moods and avoid poten-tial pitfalls like forgetting birthdays and Valentine's Day."

"Really?"

"Hell no, not even close."

Katelyn made a face, slapped him playfully on the shoulder and said, "You suckered me in."

Whit stuck his little finger in his cheek and pulled, "Hook, line and sinker."

"I thought you were going to be different."

"I'm no saint; I'm just a guy from a small town. It's just tonight; I'm so far out of my league here, like walking around in pitch black. I didn't know what the hell to do or what to expect. When you said sit on the edge of the bed, don't talk and then later don't touch, I thought well, if I do what she says, I can't screw up."

"Good answer, country bumpkin." Seeing Whit look somewhat in thought she said, "Now what? Are you judging me? What are you thinking?"

"Oh, ah...I...."

"Not that again. Come on, cough it up."

"Okay, okay. I just was thinking...well more accurately, I couldn't help noticing...you're a blonde."

"Oh, that; it's a beltway thing. Dark-haired women are thought of as more assertive, confident, in control. Plus, in this place, there is a perception of blondes as bimbos. I'm actually sandy blonde. Yeah, how do you know? I took care of that...down there."

"Well...almost; it was the soft little blonde hairs along your taint area."

"What the hell is a taint area and, more importantly, where is it?"

"You know the area in between your...parts: taint pussy and taint ass—"

"Oh, don't you dare finish." With wide eyes, Katelyn shot up on her right elbow. "Oh... my... God. I can't believe you just said that. I see you are going to take some getting used to, Benjamin Whittingham."

"I've heard that all my life."

After a while Katelyn ran her hand down under Whit's balls and rubbed lightly with her middle finger. "Taint?"

"Uh-huh. It's also called the tweener area, as in between your—"

"I got it, okay? Enough." Tugging lightly on his balls she said, "Back to the...situation at hand. What do we do now?"

With a wrinkled brow, as if in deep thought, Whit responded, "Well...for the next few minutes, I suggest we snuggle. Then, I'ma thinkin' we should give it another go."

"Whoa, stud, you ready?"

"I'd say we've nearly given the ole parts enough time to settle down and recharge."

She leaned close and asked, "Any rules?"

"Hmmmm...let's keep the lights on, but softer; no talking, and this time let's face each other. And touching is definitely top priority."

Katelyn moved her lips up to Whit's ear and said, "Good answer." She slid to his side while pulling on his shoulders for him to get on top. When he did, she saluted and said, "Aye-aye, Captain; welcome aboard."

Chapter Five
Return to the Past

"Good afternoon, Steven."

"Dr. Zulov, I presume?"

Hmm, why did he make my name a question? Such an odd fellow. "Please sit. I think we'll just dive right back in where we left off. We spoke in broad generalities last session and I'd like to try more detail…if that's okay with you."

"I'm here, aren't I?" Sliger snapped.

"Yes, yes, of course." Dr. Zulov thought, *Yes, twenty-five minutes late and in your normal surly mood.*

That worrisome dread also returned. Dr. Zulov suddenly wished he had never taken on this client or his damn money. He also wished he'd taken a little something to calm his nerves. At the same time Zulov couldn't deny or control his craving to find out what, in this crazy bastard's past, remained locked up inside his very sick and protective mind.

Barging into Zulov's thoughts, Sliger said, "Before we start, that is continue, I have something for you. Since our last session, I spoke with one of my attorneys. He's drawn up a little contract."

Taken aback, Dr. Zulov responded, "I see; do you really think—"

"Basically, it states you can never tape or record any of these sessions; you can only take written notes, and they go with me at the end of every session." With a forced smile, Sliger added, "That's basically it."

"Mr. Sliger, this is unprecedented. I understand your need for complete secrecy and I assu—"

"Sign it. Read it if you like but sign it." The fake smile was gone. "Let's avoid any future unpleasantries, shall we, Dr. Zulov? Or, should I say…Dr. Butterfield?"

As Dr. Zulov processed Sliger's last word his eyes flared, displaying shock. He couldn't stop his mouth from falling wide open.

As Zulov's lower lip started to quiver, Sliger continued. "You see, I, like you, have a past to protect. But, unlike you, I have the means to ensure mine stays buried. Let's not mince words, Zulov; cross me and your future will end in one of two ways. You'll either wake up financially ruined and professionally humiliated, or you'll wake up…dead."

Dr. Zulov's mouth kept moving up and down but nothing came forth. He wished he had never tempted fate, he wished the damn hair on his legs would stop standing on end and he wished his hands would stop shaking as he signed the unread document. Zulov's mind raced. *How much of my past does Sliger know? There must be something I can do. Shit, what's the difference; he already knows I'm a fraud. My bank account, my investments, my special little arrangements, my lifestyle…my life!*

After Dr. Zulov's pathetic scribble and Sliger returned the contract to his thin briefcase, nothing happened. Unlike most clients, Sliger felt completely at ease with long periods of silence. Most people just start talking to fill the vacuum, but not Sliger. He seemed content to just let Zulov absorb the crushing weight of his new completely servile, subservient and submissive position.

He can ruin me, ruin me, ruin me! Zulov realized his tenuous situation would only get worse if he didn't stop freaking out. He recognized his out-of-control nature mimicked some of his worst patients, but he could not stop himself. *This crazy monster owns me, but for Christ's sake, what should I do? What can I do?*

Finally, Zulov concluded he must continue the session, just go forward. *Get back to work; get him talking so I can think. If I help this loon it will be okay. Just focus on this session; it will be okay.*

Dr. Zulov pulled himself together enough to offer, "I understand, Mr. Sliger."

Settling back in his chair and looking straight ahead, Sliger jabbed, "You bet your ass you do…now."

Zulov needed a drink; at this point, he didn't care what Sliger thought. He reached for the bottom-left drawer of his desk and pulled out a pint of brandy. He drank greedily, right from the bottle. After a large inhale and slow exhale, he capped the bottle and put it back in the drawer.

In a tone far more confident than he felt, Dr. Zulov said, "At this point, I think, the best we can do now is to just proceed with the session." Clearing his throat and trying to sound calm, Zulov offered, "Even though your high school classmates were in some kind of a gang, to help me help you, I really hope you can allow me to know—"

"Stop patronizing me, you spineless worm. If you're going to ask me a question, ask it. Now that you understand you're as insignificant and as easy to flush down the toilet as soiled shit paper, my childhood is now open for discussion. Get on with it."

Zulov blurted out a little too fast, "I just need to know a little about each one of them…your old buddies."

While Sliger mulled over the request, Zulov thought, *I'm dead, I'm dead, I am so dead. I don't know if I can do this. Jesus, I'm scared shitless.* Coming from somewhere way down deep inside, with a little more fortitude Zulov stated, "I think it's crucially important. Could we start with one of them, any one of them?"

Just the thought of opening up, letting go and reveal bits of his long-suppressed past caused Sliger's beady eyes to suddenly dart around the room. He looked like he was trying to find someone hiding, lurking, sneaking up from behind. Slowly he settled down and sat back.

Zulov could almost hear Sliger say, *Okay, okay, calm down. Zulov knows now not to mess with me; I own his future, his life. He can't hurt me so I can open up.*

Sliger tilted his head back to the headrest and put his hands on top of his head. He slowly closed his eyes and didn't say a word for two minutes. Dr. Zulov thought Sliger may have fallen asleep. He was just about to say something when all of a sudden Sliger started talking. The words came out in an easy conversational manner. "There were seven of us, in the gang I mean." At nearly a whisper, Sliger added, "As it turned out, I was number seven."

Like shaking off a bad thought, Sliger continued. "There was Michael Ho, Catholic up the ass; we called him 'Mikie.' A great big giant oaf, like 300 pounds, a rancher's son named Alex Bean; we called him 'Tiny.' A brainiac named Tomas Horayosa; he and I traded top grades in every class. We called him 'Professor.' Then there was the core, or should I say, the inner circle; Benjamin Whittingham, Greyson Milner and Ned Penrose. Whittingham became 'Whit,' Greyson Milner, 'Grey,' and Ned Penrose, we nicknamed 'Ichabod'… you know…like Ichabod Crane. But as he grew older he started looking more and more like a young Abraham Lincoln, so we changed to 'Abe.'"

"And you?"

"Oh, yes, and me. They called me Trevor when we were kids. They changed it to Trevrep in high school. I didn't know why or who thought it up...until the end."

Knowing for certain now that Sliger changed his name, Zulov remained too scared to ask the psychopath his real name. Instead he repeated Sliger's last words. "Until the end?"

"Oh, we'll get there, Doc, we'll get there."

"Okay. Why did they give you the nickname of Trevor?"

"Easy enough...the British actor Trevor Howard; he almost always played the same part in movies. He became synonymous as the stoic, insensitive, black-and-white, no bullshit British officer in charge...giving life or death orders without emotion. The gang thought my...personality traits most resembled ole Trevor. That's because they were always soft, didn't want to hurt anyone's feelings, didn't want to win hard enough."

Nice editorializing, Sliger, Zulov thought but said instead, "Then why change it to Trevrep?"

Sliger stewed on that question. He became physically angry and his eyes danced around, unfocused again. Finally looking away, he said in an almost whisper, "Spell it backwards, Doctor."

Zulov wrote it out, p-e-r-v-e-r-t. *Pervert! Jesus, this is going from bad to worse. His childhood buddies turned on him. Why? Sliger must have twisted into something dark in his adolescence. I'm in serious trouble. Act like it's no big deal.* "That seems odd; why do you think they would do that to a friend?"

Sliger piped right up, like he had rehearsed the lines often enough to believe them. "As it turned out, they had issues with how I treated animals and...lesser people. They didn't get it. Even the good book says we have dominion over all other creatures. Well, tell me; what's the difference between animals and weak people... simpletons, buffoons, dimwits ripe for exploitation? I possess an innate ability to read people, know their failings, weaknesses, fears. I'd be an idiot not to take advantage, to exploit and dominate them. How else do you succeed? Guidelines, boundaries, rules of engagement, fair play, decency, honor, respect, are all limits for losers."

Zulov pretended to write furiously but his mind screamed, *I don't even know how to respond to this...this...complete lack of boundaries. This guy possesses absolutely no empathy.*

Zulov flashed on his personal exploitation of female patients. He quickly blocked any further thought, refusing to believe that what he did had any resemblance to Sliger or his view of life. *I need to move off this subject.* Zulov switched gears and asked, "Tell me about the core. What does that mean?"

"You know, the go-to guys, the top dogs, the leaders."

"How were they the leaders?" Looking at his notes, Zulov continued. "Who picked, uh, Whit, Grey and Abe?"

"That's a very good question, Zulov. One I've pondered for a long, long time."

Dr. Zulov realized a huge clue into Sliger's hatred of these guys started forming, so he remained silent and just waited. Eventually, Sliger continued. "Whittingham evolved into the ringleader, sure as hell. Not like an Alpha dog, more like just the organizer. He set up most of our outdoor stuff and we all participated."

"Outdoor stuff, like?"

"Oh, camping, fishing trips, hunting trips, backpacking, swimming at the river, all kinds of adventures like that. He even set up work projects like fence building or mending at the Bean's ranch. When we were little, he'd always check old man Arbogast's apple orchard in the fall. When the fruit started turning or falling off the trees, we'd all meet there for rotten apple wars. Damn, that was fun; but man, would we stink."

Again, Zulov marveled at the dichotomy. Sliger spent most of his adult life despising his old buddies. Yet, now he candidly talked about some of them with such reverence. What the hell happened?

"Those other two guys, Grey and Ned, how those two became part of the inner circle, I...." Sliger's elevated voice trailed off. "I was way smarter than those two. Hell, I proved to be smarter than all of them, even the Professor. I was just as cool, just as...." As before, Sliger's words trailed off. "All those years, thinking I was—"

Risking an outburst but not capable of stopping himself, Dr. Zulov prompted, "Thinking you were?"

"Thinking I was right there with Whittingham, in the center, the core, one of the other inner circle guys. All that time...my friends didn't give a rat's ass about me. Goddamn them all, leading me on, laughing at me behind my back. All those years thinking I was...I was one of them.... those fuckers."

Wow. How could he think he was so important, respected and liked? There must have been signals. Sliger acts like he has no clue. They must have been nice to him, felt sorry for him, or just put up with him. "But how do you know you weren't in the center, the inner—"

"Oh, I found out," Sliger cut in. "I outsmarted those bastards."

Dr. Zulov kept his head down again, pretending to write. He suddenly felt his chest go hollow as he said to himself, *Shit, Sliger will be taking my notes at the end of this session. I have to start putting something down, something he'll like.*

Sliger startled Dr. Zulov with a terse question. "Don't you want to know how I learned the truth?"

"Yes, yes, of course, this is all very enlightening, insightful, useful. Please continue."

Though Sliger found Zulov's response and tone again too patronizing, he was on a roll, and it felt good to finally get it all out. "Even though I always thought I was next to Whittingham, you know, as leader, I conducted a survey to confirm…what I thought I knew. This chubby girl named Peggy Foster was scared to death of me, so I used her. I talked her into doing a psychological profile questionnaire as her senior project. The seven of us in the gang were the subjects. Each guy had to rank the others in the gang on a list of subjects; funniest, sincerest, most loyal, most trusted, who they looked up to, stuff like that. Each question had seven names and seven boxes to fill, ranking each one of us. One represented the highest mark and seven being lowest. It was supposed to be anonymous, but I knew who authored each."

One of those patented long Sliger pauses ensued. After ninety seconds, Zulov decided to cut into Sliger's brooding and ask, "And?"

In a flat emotionless voice Sliger said, "As anticipated, the sun in the center of our little solar system belonged to Whittingham."

"And?"

Sliger spit out, "And I was fucking Pluto."

"Certainly not everyone listed you so—"

"Every fucking one of them! Oh, Whittingham, the consummate leader, put himself down as seven. Tiny and Ned put themselves down as seven too; the pussies, who couldn't hurt anyone's feelings. I was surprised Grey didn't also. But there my name sat at six. The rest of them stuck me at seven…dead last."

"How did that make you—"

"Don't give me that shit, Doctor. You know damn well how I felt; fucking humiliated, violated, lied to, used, mocked. My whole childhood turned out to be a lie."

"But you must have had some doubt, some clue, some insight that something wasn't right, or you wouldn't have asked Peggy to—"

"They hated me because I was smarter than them, all of them. They resented my intellect, I know that now."

Oh, brother; classic protective deflection. But I have to calm him down. He's interrupting and getting riled up. "Let's switch gears a bit and address each one of them, so I get an image or clearer picture of who they are. Just choose whoever you like."

Back to a near whisper, Sliger said, "Pretty Boy."

Sitting up straight and leaning forward, Dr. Zulov said, "Pardon me?"

"Greyson Milner, my personal nickname for him was Pretty Boy; I hate him the most."

That wasn't what Dr. Zulov had meant, but he knew to keep silent. He nodded to Sliger.

Sliger whispered again almost to himself, "Slacker, not tough enough to be a leader." Then he fell silent again.

All of a sudden it all started pouring out again. But it wasn't venomous; it was just matter of fact. Sliger leaned forward and said, "Pretty Boy had everything. He was the type of kid everyone wanted to be around, to be his friend. You ever know a kid who never got caught…never got in real trouble? Well, except for his mother; she busted his balls all the time. Barring her, that was the charmed life of Greyson Milner. When we were little, just before a teacher would turn Grey's way, he'd stop whatever he was doing, like he sensed it. I or someone else would always get caught talking, pulling some girls hair or throwing a spit wad, even though Milner started it. He didn't even go through that geeky teenage boy stage, at least not like the rest of us. He always looked and acted cool. In high school he was the teacher's pet type. Plus, lots of girls liked him, but he seemed just a little too self-conscious or unsure of himself to pursue or take advantage of them."

"Can you describe him for me, so I can get a mental picture?"

"Oh, sure; about 5'10", maybe 5'11", kind of dark blonde hair with lazy waves, greenish blue eyes, beach boy-looking features and pretty well built without trying. Grey could play any sport. He excelled at just about anything, though he just seemed to lack confidence, balls, the killer instinct."

"Well, what about his personality? How about scholastically?"

A little agitated, Sliger sniped, "It didn't matter, don't you get it? Teacher's pet, the chicks loved him, he received good grades without trying, he could treat the girls with indifference and they still ogled over him."

"He sounds a little spoiled."

"Not spoiled, just not confident enough to take advantage of his talents and abilities. Looking back, he was weak, but he kept it together enough to be cool and funny."

"Funny?"

"The guy had a quick wit and always pulled stunts." Sliger sat back and thought for a moment. "One time Grey started sneaking into our history class early to put a gift on Miss Palmer's desk. She was our first-period teacher, a big-titted thirtyish woman. She exuded the free spirit hippy attitude. The way she jiggled, you could tell she didn't wear any…support. She would open the surprise package at the start of class, look up and thank her secret admirer. Milner played it cool, acting like he had no clue. He really had her going. One week it was an apple, the next a rose. After about a month this bigger package sat on her desk. The whole class waited as she opened the gift. Somehow Grey got ahold of this lacy red bra. He cut the cups out and had sewn in their place, a pair of huge boot socks. Miss Palmer saw the neatly folded socks and lifted them up, one with each hand. She looked up to thank her secret admirer but became puzzled when the class erupted. She didn't notice the bra attached to the socks at the bottom. The look on her face when she realized what she held…man, it was perfect."

"Didn't Grey get in trouble?"

"Oh, at home his mother tore him a new asshole, but at school, not really; it was Milner. The vice principal and principal were men and they couldn't even keep a straight face while chewing him out. Because he owned up to it and apologized to Miss Palmer, nothing happened. Even she finally said it was inappropriate but kind of funny. The golden boy."

"What does this Greyson Milner do now?"

"He took over the family's farm and turned it into an organic busi—" Sliger blurted out, then stopped. Sliger realized he had just slipped up. If he didn't keep track of his ex-buddies from high school, how did he know what Milner did? He tried to recover with, "I assume he does anyway, how the hell should I know?"

Zulov thought, *Your first slip-up, Sliger; so you are fallible.*

"I think I have a good impression of Mr. Milner. Can we move on to some-one else? The choice is yours."

Sliger said nothing for a while; Dr. Zulov just about asked if Sliger needed a break, when Sliger said, "That would be Nature Boy."

Dr. Zulov pretended to be writing again and didn't respond. Finally, Sliger continued. "Benjamin Whittingham, everyone called him Whit, but sometimes, Nature Boy. I think he liked being in the woods more than being around people. He loved to fish, hunt, camp, hike, trap, ski, swim at the river, cut wood, and work on ranches or farms...anything that had anything to do with the outdoors. He fibbed about his age and started firefighting in the summer before we turned seventeen."

"That seems young. Didn't anyone notice?"

"Nah, he was a big kid, maybe 6'2" and 180 pounds back then. Matured early too; I think he was shaving before any of us. He used to set up all kinds of campouts and trips into the woods for the gang. Man, we used to have fun; they were—" All of a sudden Sliger again stopped in midsentence, then made a face like he'd swallowed vinegar.

Zulov anticipated, or at least strongly suspected, Sliger had a great childhood before something changed and it all came crashing down. Dr. Zulov didn't want this easy flow of information to stop but he remained perplexed. Since high school, Sliger spent every waking minute hating these guys, pretending they didn't exist or had ever really meant anything to him. Now he speaks of them in almost sincere admiration. What the hell happened? Did it change Sliger into today's rigid, vicious control freak or was he just a blossoming psychopath all along? How did Sliger fit in with the gang, or did he? What destroyed their friendships? The prospects fascinated Zulov, but his overriding concern for his own survival kept him restrained from digging too deeply. Give it time to surface on its own. He really didn't want the real Sliger to return. Zulov also realized Sliger's session time ended a long time ago. He already kept a free hour after Sliger's appointment, but that hour had also passed.

Zulov tried again. "What does this Benjamin Whittingham do?"

"How the hell should I know?"

"You've never heard anything about him since high school?" Dr. Zulov asked, already realizing Sliger had kept tabs on all of them.

"Well...maybe I heard Whit went to UC Berkeley. If he applied himself, he was smart enough. He just didn't care about money or power or anything important. He just liked being outdoors, trying to figure it out, how nature worked." After a pause, Sliger added bitterly, "The more I think about him, I take everything back; what a dumbshit."

"Well, Steven, it's almost 4:00 and—"

"Honest Abe would be next in line."

Obviously Zulov no longer possessed the ability to set the length of their sessions, and he had to pee so badly he thought he'd explode. He told his bladder to hold on. Finally, Zulov asked, "Abe?"

"That was his nickname. His folks named him Ned, Ned Penrose. We used to call him Ichabod, but eventually Abe stuck. He had dark curly hair, walked like a gangly dork and had kind of a big nose and huge Adam's apple. Ned really did look a lot like pictures of a young Lincoln."

"Did he take it well?"

"Oh, yeah, Ned's easygoing personality didn't take offense. He's what you'd call back then a nice guy. So were his folks; not a mean bone in their bodies." After a pause Sliger added, "Weak, really, easy to push around, if need be. That's what I can't figure out, how did he rate so high with the rest of the gang?"

That was a present-day Sliger comment slipping into the conversation. Trying to get back on track Zulov asked, "What did, ah, Abe's folks do for a living?"

"They had this mom-and-pop stationery store and print shop. Abe's great-grandfather started it sometime during the Gold Rush. It was a little skinny brick building packed with stuff. You needed pens, pencils, envelopes, folders or anything like that; they were the only game in town. They printed business cards, wedding notices and stuff like that, too."

Sliger stared off into oblivion. Suddenly, he snapped back and said, "Hey, I'm getting hungry."

Dr. Zulov nodded his head and struggled to his feet. *Thank God. Jesus, I'm afraid if I try to walk I'll wet my pants.* "Same time next week?"

"No way, Zulov. I want to get this out and done with. I'll come back after dinner."

Dr. Zulov thought but didn't say, *But it's going on five now.* Nodding his head again Zulov said, "It's best to have a little time between—"

Sliger interrupted, "I know about your date tonight with one of your patients, break it."

Shit! Somewhat recovering Zulov offered, "We are making such good progress. Okay, that sounds like a good idea." *Like I have any choice.* Afraid he'd wet his pants any second, Zulov had to ask, "When can I expect you back here?"

Sliger stood with his hand out for Zulov's notes and said, "After dinner, like I said."

Placing the doctor's notes in his briefcase, Sliger walked out of the office leaving the door wide open. Zulov heard Sliger yell, "Moose!" The monstrous goon in the reception room lumbered toward the outer door and yanked it open.

Obviously, Zulov's receptionist had already bolted for home. He shuffled in misery toward his bathroom as quickly as he dared.

Chapter Six
The Offer

Grey sat himself down in Pete's Place the next Tuesday after his buddy Ned, aka Abe, had displayed an uncharacteristic huffy attitude. Grey started on his second drink, wondering what could be holding up Ned. He scanned the bar and smiled at a pretty dark-haired woman sitting with what appeared to be her husband. At least the guy looked like his wife dressed him. The wife vaguely reminded Grey of Veronica Sanchez, his mysterious, bizarre, fascinating and once-in-a-blue-moon, hookup. The woman drifted in and out of his life...on her terms. The difference between Veronica Sanchez and all the other beautiful women Grey just gawked at but never pursued was that, in Veronica's case, he had marched right up to her and tried to buy her a drink. Jesus; to Grey, that encounter became a life changer. He hadn't seen Veronica in quite some time and actually felt like he sort of, kind of, maybe missed her...a little. *How can you miss a woman more like a ghost, a shadow, a wisp of smoke, than a real human?* Grey remembered back to when he first met Veronica. *What was it, three years? Jesus, almost four years ago.*

Veronica walked into Pete's Place all alone. Ned didn't even notice her, but what's new. Grey figured Ned had an excuse for being so oblivious. He happened to be going through his second divorce, right after putting wife number two through nursing school. She said thanks and ditched him for a job in the Bay Area. Ned found himself a tad in debt and adamantly proclaimed to swear off women forever, for like the fifth time.

Grey nudged Ned and tilted his head toward the hottie that just sat down. Ned followed Grey's gaze then quickly turned back to Grey and shook his head. Grey knew his buddy's facial expression said, *No way, man.*

Veronica sat by herself and ordered a shot of well tequila and a shot of Patron. She slammed the house swill then sipped the call drink. Wild and dangerous looking in her black biker clothes, Grey felt cautiously intrigued. Without her boots Grey guessed she stood maybe 5'6". She had short, tomboyish, straight black hair, parted on the left side. Some of her bangs dropped down and across her dark, thick eyebrows. When she ordered, Grey picked up a slight Spanish accent, but her strong nose and chin gave her more of an American Indian look than Mexican or Latino. She scanned the bar slowly, eventually stopping at Ned and Grey. Ned sunk his chin into his chest and looked away. Grey smiled and tipped her with his glass. She gave him a beautiful smile displaying straight, white teeth. She continued to slowly survey the occupants in the bar like she was putting faces to memory. As far as Grey and Ned knew, she never looked in their direction again. Over the course of two double orders she dispatched two separate guys who walked up to talk to her. Grey couldn't hear what she said but they didn't sit down or stay long. Grey couldn't erase the image of those brilliant white teeth surrounded by that beautiful smile. He continued to glance past Ned.

Nervously, Ned said, "Jesus, Milner, stop staring at the biker babe. She gives me the willies."

"Willies my ass, Abe; that woman scares the shit out of you."

"At least I have some sense of self-preservation."

"Hell, Ned, you're just a serial monogamist who's too quick to draw a line in the sand. She's probably a sweetheart once you get to know her."

"Oh, I seriously doubt that."

"Okay Ned; just crawl back into your safe self-preservation little hole and you'll never find out."

"Oh, so she doesn't intimidate you?"

Grey just shrugged.

"Can't you feel those negative vibes? Jesus, Milner, she'll chew you up and spit you out."

Grey just smiled at his buddy.

Ned had had enough. "Okay; well then, big man, just march right over there and be the third stud she shuts down. A fiver says you come back with your tail, and whatever's left of your fragile ego, between your legs."

Grey thought, *Now you've gone and done it. Why do I do that? That cavalier cool-guy shrug always seems to get me in trouble. Now I'm stuck. If I just sit here I'll be a pussy, like Ned. If I walk over there and she bites my head off, Ned will tell the gang and I'll be a laughingstock. Either way the gang will hear about it and get a good chuckle at my expense.*

Looking down the bar again, then at Ned, Grey said to himself, *Ah, hell, getting shut down in front of Ned won't be as bad as being called a pussy.* Without looking at Ned, Grey stood up.

As Grey walked behind Ned, he heard his friend hum the funeral march. Grey pinched Ned's boney ribs.

Moving up beside the dark beauty Grey asked, "Can I buy you another drink?"

She put down her glass and turned to Grey. He thought, *Oh, shit, here it comes.* She didn't say a word for quite some time.

Grey felt naked as she looked him up and down. Not knowing what to do, Grey almost repeated himself, but she finally said, "Sure, I'll have another, but it's two." Even before Grey could order, she followed with, "But if you're going to try to pick me up, be more assertive. Don't ask if you can buy me another drink; tell me. Try it again."

"Oh, uh…." *What the hell? What have I stepped into?* Again, before Grey could process a way out of his predicament, he heard himself say, "I'll buy you another two drinks."

She smiled and said, "There, much better." She tipped her head toward the empty barstool to her right. "Have a seat." Grey started to introduce himself, but she cut in, "One more thing; if I let you pick me up and I fuck your brains out, you better not give me a disease. Because stud, if you do, I'll kill you." She set her gaze on Ned, who once again quickly turned away. She followed with, "And that gangly stork down there, your drinking buddy, he'll never see you alive again or ever find your body."

All Grey could muster was, "Oh, okay."

———————————

That's how it all started. Greyson Milner the student became Greyson Milner the lady killer, thanks to the tutelage of Veronica Sanchez, the teacher. For three years plus, she'd drifted in and out of Grey's life; her terms and her schedule. Veronica would call about two days, sometimes two hours out, and tell him to clear his schedule for a day or two, sometimes just a night. He always complied. The anticipation of her visits released endorphin he didn't even know he had. That first night, after six drinks, she smoothly handled her Harley and followed Grey to his Victorian. As he looked back, those six drinks probably saved his life. Veronica left him raw and exhausted before she fell soundly asleep. Without the effect of those drinks, Grey felt fairly confident that she would have honed him down to a nub. Veronica was older, he knew, but nothing else. Another one of her rules that came out more like an order: her work and past were off limits. Through their shared experiences, she taught Grey how to please a woman physically; but more importantly Veronica taught Grey how to look, how to act, and how to approach women and make them feel comfortable, interested.

He thought back to the morning after they met.

Awkward for Grey, though she seemed unfazed, they sat naked at the corner of his kitchen table drinking coffee. When the small talk tapered off, she said, "Look, Grey, I don't want or desire a steady man or any kind of relationship. I needed last night to decompress, to relax," then almost unperceptively, she added, "to forget."

They both remained quiet, awkwardly just sipping coffee. Eventually, Veronica continued, "I'm looking for someone I can trust who's available when I am. As long as it lasts, that's it. You could be that guy."

Scooting forward to allow his tender parts to hang over the kitchen chair, he sighed in relief. Looking up he noticed Veronica smiling. She asked, "Sore?"

He smiled back and lied, "In a good sort of way." She seemed waiting for an answer, so he finally said, "I'm definitely interested, Veronica, but—"

"V."

"What?"

"No, not what, when you talk to a woman, don't say what. Women hate 'what.' Save that for your guy friends. Use 'excuse me' or 'pardon me.'"

Grey thought, *Jesus, is she assertive or what? Oops, glad I didn't say that out loud. She's so damn different.* Grey smiled and said, "Excuse me, Veronica?"

"Much better. But I said V. You can call me V."

"V, I like that. Okay, V, I'm interested but...what's in it for me?"

She cocked her head back with an inquisitive look, then spread her legs and pointed at her dark shaved hair trimmed like a Mohawk.

He quickly added, "Oh, I'm not talking about last night, holy crap that was incredible...and painful." His added comment made Veronica grin. He continued. "You know you're good, very good. I'm talking down the road; what's in it for me, if I'm supposed to be this always available guy?"

After taking a sip of coffee and thinking, Veronica said, "Okay, stud. You want to know how to be a lady's man, right? Pickup lines like 'Can I buy you another drink' won't cut it. I can give you some pointers. What you do when I'm not around, that's your business. I can teach you how to play the game... get good-looking women to spread their legs for you. And Milner, in that category, you need help. That's the 'what's in it for you' I'm offering."

"Yeah, but if I give you the clap or something you'll kill me."

"True enough. But Milner, life is full of risks; that is, if you're willing to live it. Are you?"

As Grey pondered the thought, Veronica added, "Look, I'll give you your first lesson, well, your second lesson on how to treat a woman right, right now."

"Shoot."

"Okay, Romeo, think about a hot little number coming over for dinner. What's the most important item in your house?"

Milner thought maybe a mirror on the ceiling of his bedroom; no. Then he guessed pictures of cute little animals, like puppies; no. Grey realized he was stumped. He figured he better say something, so he guessed, "A good stereo system, you know, mood music?"

"Nice try, amateur; way more basic."

"Shit, V, I give up."

"Two-ply toilet paper."

"What?" Milner's eyes popped wide open as he quickly corrected, "I mean, pardon me?"

"Think about it, Milner, think. A clean bathroom with two-ply TP sets the right image. Of course, that includes no hair, stains or dirty underwear in the corner, too. Women like to feel clean and comfortable before they get wild and dirty. Wiping their twats with that one-ply sandpaper in that kennel you call your bathroom won't cut it. Fortunately, I'm not like most women."

"Shit Howdy to that, V."

Veronica laughed, then turned serious. "I need this…time…to laugh, to get physical, to feel safe enough to sleep."

"Look, V, I know your past is off limits; but I'm not blind. You're in insane shape, like granite; and, those scars…."

Veronica turned her gaze away from Grey and stared out through the large kitchen window over the sink. Almost in a trance, she seemed lost in thought.

Grey wondered, *what's lurking out there, Veronica? Are you running or chasing?* He continued. "My buddy's dad was in Korea; he has scars, shrapnel tears, like yours. Your tattoos cover some of them, kind of. I'm no expert, but that jagged spider web on your ass looks like an exit wound."

Finally, her eyes returned to Grey's; they were wet. She said softly, "I've lost…."

She couldn't finish and dropped her head. With her arms tense and her hands clutched in fists on the table, she didn't look up for quite some time. Violently, she snapped her head up; her eyes blazed at Grey's. She yelled, "Look, asshole, I told you…." She stopped herself again and put her hands up in a stop motion then put them over her face. Slowly, she shook her head from side to side and exhaled hard. Grey heard her say softly, "Sorry." She stood up and walked toward Grey.

Grey slid back in his chair, drawing his dangling goods to a more protected position. But Veronica turned sideways and sat on his lap. She was still damp from their lovemaking.

She put her arms on his shoulders. He didn't know if she was going to kiss him or snap his neck. He tensed, not knowing what to expect, but she remained relaxed. He relaxed a little too and she said, "Look, Greyson Milner, I like you. I think our arrangement can work for both of us, but let's take it…one step at a time." Grey nodded slightly, so she continued. "I was in the military; I'll give you that. And I have demons…horrible demons…mine to sort out. And my work, what I do now, I'd classify as…intense. Can we leave it at that, for now?"

"Legal?"

"That depends on your definition of legal; but let's just say, for the right side." Before Grey could press further she added, "Grey, questions end now, or we end now."

Through the finality of her statement and sternness in her eyes, Grey also saw a measure of pleading. He smiled and said, "Let's try this...your way, V."

She smiled back and kissed him hard. He wrapped his arms around her then slid his left hand down to her rock-hard ass. He was surprised to feel his mangled parts responding to their intimacy. She felt him too, and while kissing him rose up and straddled his lap. She pulled her lips away long enough to whisper in his ear, "This is going to hurt."

Chapter Seven
Game Plan

Worried that if he left to eat he'd miss Sliger's return, the starving Dr. Zulov's fear overrode his hunger. After blissfully relieving himself of what felt like a quart and a half of fluid, he started searching for food. Coming up empty handed in his office, other than his pint of brandy and bottled water for the coffeemaker, he tried the waiting room. In his receptionist's desk, Zulov found a long-forgotten energy bar and some gum. The peanuts left a rancid aftertaste in his mouth, but he ate the bar anyway, crumbs and all.

Still hungry, Dr. Zulov sat at his desk pondering how Stephen Sliger had discovered his real name. Concerned...no...scared witless; his future lay in the hands of a very wealthy, very dangerous and very unforgiving man. Zulov leaned back and rested his head against the back of his polished leather chair and rocked gently. *Come on, think, damn it. You've done very well and made it this far on your wits; think. I'm the psychiatrist. I have the power. I need to use what I know. But, what do I know?* Dr. Zulov closed his eyes. Even before taking Hitler's twin on as a patient, Zulov knew a little about Steven Sliger and Serpentine Solutions. Sliger came off in the press as a mysterious saint; politicians praised his work, environmentalist hailed his progressive company, but there was dirt. Sliger mostly controlled his company's image well. But some of his competitors and ex-employees provided the tabloids with plenty of contradictory fodder. Serpentine Solution's number one competitor in California self-imploded due to a very public and very salacious sex scandal. The competitor blamed Sliger...in his suicide note. The negative press included the death of a disgruntled ex-employee in what the tabloids referred to as unusual circumstances. Rarely seen in public, the reclusive Sliger mostly used his very attractive and articulate press secretary and human resources officer for comment. She portrayed her employer as nothing more than a selfless champion for the environment surrounded by rainbows, unicorns and cute little puppy dogs. The dichotomy between the tabloid stories versus Serpentine Solution's outward image left no middle ground. Zulov definitely now knew the dark side.

Dr. Zulov needed a way out and fast, but what? *Come on, damn it. Think outside of the box; go unconventional. Come on.*

Suddenly, he opened his eyes and slowly rocked forward as he thought. *Hmm, unconventional, crazy stuff, that's it. I'll use Sliger's self-absorbed, narcissistic ego to my advantage.* Slowly a plan emerged. *I've got it. I can end this tonight, if I'm as good as I think I am. The perfect solution to direct his anger away from me.*

A slight smile and sense of relief crossed Dr. Zulov's face, then just as quickly it disappeared. *What if Sliger doesn't bite? What if he suspects I'm just blowing smoke up his ass?* Dr. Zulov involuntarily put his hands up defensively. *Stop, don't think like that. Be positive; use your professional skills, it will work... it has to. It fits Sliger's warped sense of reality and brand of justice.... that is, injustice. It's perfect. Sliger will leap at it. Give him a few weeks and he'll think it was his idea. I've got my life back. He'll do it, I know he will. Better his old classmates than me.*

Dr. Zulov realized he could have eaten dinner twice by the time Sliger and his bodyguard, Moose, returned. Zulov let Sliger and his goon in. Moose walked over to his usual seat in the reception room while Sliger marched into Zulov's office.

Sliger seemed in a particularly good mood. Dr. Zulov thought, *Perfect; it's now or never.* "Please have a seat, Steve; I'm so pleased with our progress."

"Yeah, well, I'm a solution-oriented kind of guy and I like answers. This session better be good."

The guy's walking right into my salvation. He's ready, I'm ready. Jesus...I hope this works.

Dr. Zulov took a deep breath then said, "Mr. Sliger, the revelations of our earlier session have opened up an opportunity to begin the healing process and could very well return you to the person you want to be." *Hitler, Mussolini, Stalin, Mao, take your pick.* "It's really quite simple, though unorthodox."

"I'm listening."

Here comes the bullshit. "Just recently some studies have revealed very positive results for certain successful and resourceful individuals with your specific, ah, symptoms. Not everyone fits into this unique category; however, you fit the profile perfectly."

"What do you mean, profile? You saying I'm unstable?"

No one spoke.

Finally, Sliger said, "Be very careful with your answer, Doctor."

"Oh, it's quite flattering, really. The profile pertains to achievers with high IQs and the ability to take charge of their problems, shall we say…forcefully, if necessary. The type, that by any means necessary, always wins."

Interested now, Sliger asked, "Unique individuals like me, and they get fixed, right? That's what you're telling me?"

"Absolutely."

"Well, let's hear it."

"Your symptoms are a classic case of what we now know, and call transferred burden. You are carrying the weight of other's failures due to a lost sense of loyalty. In your case, either through jealousy or envy, individuals from your past transferred their weakness, their guilt, their inadequacies to you. You cared for them, and they…," Zulov struggled for a good medical term but gave up and said, "crapped on you."

Sliger just sat there looking straight ahead, nodding slowly.

Eat it up, you son of a bitch, so I can get my life back. Jesus, what a crock; transferred burden…more like transferred bullshit. Well, let's see if he bites. He should, he's crazy enough. I just hope he doesn't look into this…new research…and just goes with it.

After forty seconds of silence, Zulov started to worry. Sliger stopped nodding and started to frown. *Ah, shit. He's not buying it. He's going to call for that giant creature to come in here and break my neck.* Another whole minute went by; Zulov's empty stomach churned bile and acid. He felt nauseous as sweat started saturating his armpits.

Finally, Sliger nodded again. "Yeah, yeah I see that. I repressed what they did to me and now I'm paying for their weakness. They are the ones that should feel like this, not me."

Drawing in a huge amount of air, Zulov exhaled and managed to say, "Exactly."

"Okay, so I get it, this…."

"Transferred burden."

"So, how do I fix it?"

"That's the point, most people can't. It's—"

"Bullshit," Sliger barked "I'm not most people."

"Yes, yes, that's right. Only the rare individual with the inner strength, resources, and drive to win have the ability to ever overcome transferred burden."

Sliger's mood, body language and demeanor suddenly turn dark. "Listen, Zulov, I've spent my life observing people, assessing them and exploiting their weaknesses. I can ferret out a liar in my sleep. That also includes someone trying to patronize me. You are doing both."

Scared to death and talking way too fast, Zulov blurted, "Okay, Mr. Sliger, okay; it's just my own theory. Please don't hurt me. I'm only trying to help you, really, I—"

"Then, spit it out! Your future depends on what you say next. I came here to resolve a problem. I don't give a damn about you or your future. I care about mine. You can have your milk-the-rich bullshit career back, but only if I get mine back. If I don't, you don't. Now, you said you had a way to fix my... dilemma. What is it?"

Grasping for the tiny lifeline Sliger offered, Zulov straightened up and spoke with as much confidence as he could muster. "What I told you is a solution. It's a way to get back at them and ultimately make them suffer. It's a solution that can work, but it will take a huge commitment. You have the resources and drive to do it."

Still angry, Sliger hissed, "Get to it."

"You do to them what they did to you. I told you it's unorthodox and will take money and time, but that's the cure. You take what's precious to them away. Give them a taste of the misery they have caused you. It will have to be anonymous to work. They're unaware of the pain they've caused you; make sure they're unaware that it's you causing their pain. Eye for an eye."

After what Zulov felt like an eternity, Sliger said, "Son of a bitch, Zulov; two minutes ago you were walking dead. But your proposal, it feels right. Those other two therapists kept alluding to my past as my problem and to confront my past. I never thought about taking it to my ex-buddies. It's brilliant; strike back, destroy their lives like they've tried to destroy mine."

Zulov knew he had just released unholy hell on innocent people, but did he really have a choice? Better them than he; just their bad luck. He glanced at what was a jovial Steven Sliger and saw that cold ugly look return to Sliger's face. Zulov's empty stomach erupted and those damn hairs on his legs twitched to life again. He froze, expecting Sliger to summon Moose for neck-snapping services.

"Dr. Zulov, do you remember the contract?"

Zulov's wide unblinking eyes just stared. His mouth, twisted in fear, uttered nothing.

Sliger turned and coldly stated, "For the record, I will no longer require your services."

Walking to the door, at the exact same moment Sliger yelled, "Moose!" Dr. Zulov lost all control and wet his pants.

Chapter Eight
Fish Cop

Gene Perkins, a thirteen-year veteran warden for the California Department of Fish and Game, pulled into the parking lot at his new assignment in the small northern Sierra mining town of Cedar Creek.

Gene had just transferred to the Sierra after seven years on the North Coast. While working there, Warden Perkins made quite a name for himself. His most notable bust took down an abalone poaching ring and the San Francisco restaurants buying the illegally acquired mollusks. A sudden spike in the availability of nice sized abalone steaks at a few finer Bay Area eateries and an anonymous phone call to the department's poacher hotline, probably from an angry restaurant owner not in the loop, caught Perkins' attention. Following a nice dinner at one of the restaurants, Gene determined the abalone definitely came from illegal fishing. The large steaks looked nothing like the puny little commercial morsels raised in tanks and sold to restaurants.

Gene Perkins spent many fruitless months of frigid nights and damp, bone-chilling mornings watching, listening, checking licenses and talking to fishermen to get nowhere. But the restaurants kept offering nice sized slabs of abalone, so Perkins persisted. Finally, a few caustic remarks from annoyed abalone fishermen gave Gene a tip. Complaints about some way too successful fishermen set Perkins' sights on three locals. Two lived in a trailer park and one lived in a small granny house behind his parents' home. It didn't take Gene long to determine these three idlers maintained no permanent employment or steady income. When fishing, they all limited out every time and they seemed to accomplish the feat easily. Perkins watched them, checked them, questioned them, but they were always legal and agonizingly cooperative.

In desperation, Gene finally snuck to the rented trailer and, not so legally, poked through their garbage. He found no evidence that they ate any of their abundant harvest. They consumed mostly fast food and drank beer, a ton of beer, expensive beer. How do out-of-work slackers support such a lavish indulgence?

The bloodhound in Gene told him he'd found the poachers, but how did they pull off the theft? It wasn't until the next abalone season and another two months of wasted time that Perkins quit following the three when they fished for abs. Instead he started tagging along, in surveillance mode, at other times. At long last, he discovered the secret to their success. Turns out these three had a boat and scuba gear stored at another buddy's house. The day before a fishing trip, usually two of the three would take the boat out spear fishing. With binoculars Gene could tell they were actually illegally scuba diving for abalone. The diver dislodged three nice limits then moved into shallow water. At a prearranged location, the diver lashed and weighted down a small wire basket holding their illegal harvest in the rocks and kelp. The next day, the three snorkeled at that very beach and banged out three nice limits. Once the previous day's scuba diver found his cage, he just divvied up the catch. They'd swim around free diving and surfacing just like legal fishermen and, once it appeared they had fished long enough, would return to the beach.

Once Perkins knew how the poaching took place, the department set up surveillance and eventually found the middle man, the restaurant's go-between. The time involved to build a case and catch everyone from poacher to market tortured Warden Perkins. Week after week these low life scumbags continued to strip abalone from the California coast and drink their expensive micro-brews. Eventually, the word came down that the D.A. had his evidence and ordered the arrest of the whole operation. Perkins personally nailed the poachers. Adding to the satisfaction of reading the three losers their Miranda rights and cuffing them, Gene personally confiscated their two-and-a-half cases of microbrews. Gene enjoyed every one.

But past performance doesn't count for squat at a new assignment. Perkins hoped to quickly prove himself to his new supervisor and fellow wardens. Gene loved his work and, just as passionately, hated poachers. He wanted a quick slap down, someone flaunting the Fish and Game codes, a poacher who felt like he could do so with impunity.

Walking into his new boss' office, he shook hands with Lieutenant Dalton and met the other two wardens assigned to the office.

Lieutenant Dalton did the honors. "Gene Perkins, this is Warden Dennis Chan and Warden Frank O'Dell."

After introductions and too much strained small talk, Perkins moved right to the point. "Which local would you guess is the biggest poacher who hasn't been caught yet?"

When his supervisor and the other two wardens didn't respond Gene added, "In other words, who would make the biggest splash in the community, if caught, to send a message to other poachers?"

Lieutenant Dalton gestured to his other two wardens with a questioning nod. They looked back like deer caught in headlights. Exasperated, he raised his left hand, palm up and asked, "Well?"

After not an utterance from either one, Dalton said, "Since my wardens appear brain dead," shaking his head and turning his gaze to Perkins, he continued, "the worst local poachers are probably the Jameson brothers."

"But," Dalton paused for effect, "the guy who would make the...biggest splash, as you say, would be a guy named Benjamin Whittingham. Whether Whittingham poaches or not, I honestly couldn't say; but safe to say, he bends our game codes. And he's categorically no friend to us or any of the other regulatory agencies. He lives by his own rules and definitely has a following of locals who...tend to dislike us."

Gene asked, "Why does Whittingham have a bug up his ass for the department?"

"He hammers us but spreads his assaults to the other agencies, too. To get a sense of this guy, check out some of his editorials—letters to the editor or opinion pieces in the local paper—or check transcripts at county and state board meetings and public hearings. He makes us all look pretty inept. The problem being, he's smart and picks his battles. So, Warden Perkins, bust his ass and you'll make your big splash."

Warden Perkins asked, "I'm a little confused. Do you think he's breaking our regulations and other agency laws, or is this just personal?"

Dalton leaned forward. "I don't like living in a community where the residents question our integrity, think my people are incompetent, and cause me problems upstairs. So yes, it looks personal. But, if you can prove Whittingham breaks the law and can nail him on a clean bust, no way will it look personal. Whittingham's arrest will go a long way to restore our credibility in the community."

"What's his background?"

"Look, he's born and reared here. Whittingham knows the back country well, plus he's well educated. He has a biology degree and a forestry degree. He knows plants, animals and their habitats well enough to be dangerous. You can't bullshit this guy; and when regulators try—for lack of a better term—to push him around, he fights back."

Gene had dealt with some wardens, policemen and regulatory agency inspectors who tried to use the power of government to bowl over ranchers, farmers, and the public, and he didn't like it. Confused, Gene said, "I'm still not following. Is he a bad guy or just a pain in the ass?"

"Let's say both; plus, he just happens to be Logan County's sheriff's son."

"I see." After a few seconds, Gene added, "Well, so what if his daddy's the sheriff; nobody's above the law. If he's breaking our regs or codes, I'll nail his ass."

Lieutenant Dalton leaned back and looked above his glasses at Perkins. "If you can bust him on a good case, be my guest; but don't get bogged down with this guy." For emphasis Dalton added slowly, "One more thing...don't let the guy get into your head."

Gene thought that last statement a bit odd; *Don't let the guy get into your head? What the hell does that mean?* He figured he'd just let it go. He nodded to everyone and left the office for his rig.

Just as Gene started to pull out of the parking lot, one of the silent wardens exited the building and raised a hand for Gene to wait. Walking up to the driver's side window as Gene rolled it down, the Warden said, "Just so you know, this Whittingham guy...it's personal with the lieutenant."

"Warden Chow, right?"

The Warden smiled and said, "Chan, Dennis Chan."

"Sorry. Okay, Dennis, I'm listening."

"The Warden you're replacing—Sandy Welker—well, Whittingham got to her. Somehow, he turned her against the lieutenant and the department. It was an embarrassment to Dalton that one of his own wardens questioned his authority and department policies and procedures. Being a woman, it made the situation dicey. You know how it is now if a male supervisor and female subordinate clash. The situation found its way to Sacramento; the lieutenant received a black eye out of it and a letter in his file."

Gene put up his hand and Dennis stopped. "Not buying it. You're pulling my leg, right, Dennis?" When the Warden gave him a sour look, Gene put his truck back in gear and said, "Sounds like a new guy bullshit story to me... a little too hard to swallow."

Taking offense Dennis said, "No bullshit, just information, but if you don't want to hear it, fine. No sweat off my balls."

Dennis turned to walk away. Gene thought, *Goddamnit, there I go again. Way to make friends at the office, Gene.*

When Dennis Chan heard Gene's truck stop, he turned around. Gene rolled forward and said, "Sorry, Dennis; your information just seemed a little farfetched and caught me off guard. But I'm listening; try me again."

Dennis put his hand on the outside mirror bracket and continued. "Sure, no problem. Believe me, I get it. It's a little hard for me to believe, too. Sandy was a good warden; she targeted Whittingham just like you're doing now. She even staked out his cabin, waiting for him to screw up. But somehow, he messed with her head. After that stakeout, she started to change. Next thing you know she's asking where are the scientific studies and research to back up some of our codes and regs. Turns out many just kind of evolved over time or were adopted without proper research. It felt to the lieutenant like she took the bad guy's side over ours. Lucky for the boss, she just walked in one day and quit. I heard she went back to school."

"Were they intimate?"

"Sandy and Whittingham? We all suspected, but no one knows for sure. She never said, and Whittingham wouldn't say shit if he had a mouthful. He actually seems like an okay dude. It's not like he yells or swears at you; he always conducts himself professionally. You just get the impression, under the surface, he's holding back or suppressing a violent side. Plus, Whittingham just doesn't like authority. Well, that's not quite right either. If he disagrees with a requirement or mitigation imposed, he comes right at you. Plus, he's very private; hard to get a true read on the guy. He seems to only be close to his local buddies. Now you know what I know. "

Gene sat there looking forward, nodding his head slightly, absorbing what he'd just heard. Finally, he turned to Dennis and said, "Well, he's not getting into my head whether he uses voodoo, magic potion, or hypnosis. If he's poaching, he won't stop and eventually I'll nail him. If he's clean, I'll find someone else; there's always someone else. Thanks for the heads-up, Dennis, appreciate it."

They shook hands, then Gene put his truck in gear and pulled away.

Chapter Nine
Ain't Love Grand

Katelyn Summers sat at her desk staring blankly into her computer screen. Sharron Jensen, the other female reporter at Progressive Politics' Washington office, sat across the narrow aisle from Katelyn and shot Katelyn another quick glance. Sharron, forty-seven, was a little thicker than she'd like and envied her taller, leaner and prettier counterpart. A liberal's liberal, Sharron remained staunchly anti-everything illegal, except when it included her, and it was fun.

Sharron put her hands on the edge of her desk thinking, *let it go, Sharron; it's none of your business. Let Katelyn flounder a little longer and you'll be the congressional reporter. Isn't that what you want?*

Sharron's experience placed her senior to Katelyn and management chose Sharron as the White House correspondent; prestigious, but, as it turned out, boring...boring, that is, compared to Katelyn's congressional assignments. Katelyn seemed to go to endless functions; luncheons, fact-finding tours, formal dinners, impromptu events, fundraisers and all those wild congressional and private parties. With 435 legislators versus one President, the numbers spoke for themselves. Plus, any grand executive branch events, Katelyn always received an invitation anyway. *Could it be because she's so damn good-looking?* Sharron's analytical mind had to grace the point. Every man in the beltway liked to be seen with beautiful women. Absentmindedly patting her slight double chin with the back of her fingers, Sharron thought, *Well, damn it, I'm no slouch, and no prude either.*

The rumor mill whispered that party-hardy Katelyn had been more untouchable than ever...nun-like. Something was up, and Sharron's reporter curiosity wanted the scoop. Maybe one of Katelyn's parents fell ill; maybe Katelyn's pregnant. She shook her head while she pushed her perfectly ergonomically fitted chair away from her desk. *Screw this; I'm going to find out. Let's see, hmmm. I'll try the older sister approach.*

Walking across the aisle to Katelyn's desk, she plopped her rump on the corner. "Katelyn, no offense, but you've been…way out of sorts for months. It shows in your work, your appearance, your demeanor. What the hell is wrong? Is there anything I can do to help?" *Like help push you out of my way to those wild congressional parties.*

After a miserable twelve weeks of denials to every question of what's wrong, all pretenses gave way. "Oh, Sharron, it's crazy but I think I'm in love. In love with a—"

"Senator? Congressman? Is he married?"

"Worse, I think, I'm in love with a…a Republican."

"What?" Sharron blurted out way too loud.

They both looked around to see everyone in the newsroom looking their way.

In a whisper Katelyn said, "Oh, it's a long story." Then she corrected herself. "No, actually it's a very short story."

"Tell me you didn't sleep with it? A cold-blooded Reptilican? Katelyn?"

Katelyn's big sheepish eyes gave Sharron her answer.

"Oh-my—" *Sharron almost said God but chose not to mention the higher power she didn't believe existed.*

Standing up and looking around again to see everyone still watching, Sharron stated, "Honey, this is worse than I thought. We're getting out of here and you're going to tell me everything. Let's go have lunch somewhere where we can drink. You need an exorcism or lobotomy or…both. At the very least, you need an antibiotic douche to vanquish every vestige of evil poison that forked-tongued devil shot into you. If you don't, the next thing you know, you'll be kicking the homeless out of your way and defending indigenous people clubbing baby seals."

Smiling, Katelyn said, "Funny you should say that."

"What? He does?"

"No; geez, Sharron. He's not like that."

"Doesn't matter; I'm sure he condones it." Katelyn was about to protest but Sharron cut her off. "Sister, you are messed up; let's go. I know I can help."

Help me become Progressive Politics' next congressional reporter, that is. Hello, nightlife. "Come; I know just the spot."

Twenty-five minutes later they were sitting close together with their second glasses of wine between them. Katelyn recited the entire evening from when she walked up to Benjamin Whittingham at the Kennedy function to the next morning. She discreetly left out the details of most of their…acrobatics.

"When I woke, he was gone."

Sharron threw her hands up and said, "So the prick slips you the pickle then slips out without the merest pleasantries. Makes you feel cheap, right?"

Looking across the tables and sneering at a handsome well-dressed older acquaintance sitting with a Katelyn-type beauty, Sharron added dryly, "I know that species of subhuman. Did he throw some money on the counter to complete the insult?"

"That's the strange part. When I woke, I thought I smelled bacon. I sat up and, sure enough, it was bacon."

"Bacon? Pig fat? Hell, that's just what Republicans smell like after sex."

"No, Sharron, and you're not helping. It was real bacon."

"In your house? I've only seen you nibble at chicken and fish."

"Well, normally, but I was starving, and I have to tell you, it smelled great. I jumped up, ran in the bathroom and brushed my teeth while I peed. I fixed my hair, threw on my full-length robe and scooted downstairs. There he was making breakfast and offering me a glass of orange juice and a cup of coffee."

While Katelyn recounted the morning, she relived every second.

"Morning, sleepy head; coffee first or juice?"

"Hello…you…crazy…person. Um, coffee first, I just…." She smiled and made a brushing her teeth motion.

Nodding, Whit asked, "Black?"

"Please."

Whit slowly poured steaming coffee into a large white porcelain mug from one of her barely used shiny black pans. He handed it to Katelyn. She blew on the surface then took a sip.

"Hey, this is good. How did you make this without using my fancy coffeemaker?"

"I just boiled water in a pan and dumped the grounds in for about four minutes; you know, cowboy coffee."

With her eyes open wide Katelyn said, "You're kidding, right?"

Whit just shook his head.

"But I don't taste any grounds."

"Oh, you take the pan away from the heat and slowly pour a little cold water around the perimeter and the grounds settle out. You know, cowboy coffee."

"You said that twice and, no, I don't know cowboy coffee."

Whit smiled and said, "Comes in handy." Pointing to Katelyn's shiny black coffee/expresso maker he added, "Not too many of those out in the woods." Whit turned back to the stove.

"I see that or taste it. This is really good. And what else are you fixing and where did you get it? I don't keep much food."

"Well, I woke up early, you were snoring and—"

"I don't snore!"

Chuckling, Whit said, "Okay, I woke up early and you were...breathing loudly." Whit looked over his shoulder for a response.

Katelyn nodded and replied, "Better, thank you."

"So, I decided to make coffee and find something for us to eat. I came downstairs and after checking your refrigerator and cupboards, decided to go out and forage for sustenance. With what you put me through last night, I was famished...and dehydrated."

"What I put you through? It takes two to tango, mountain man."

"Shit Howdy, ma'am."

While laughing, Katelyn asked, "And you took my car?"

"Yes, I did. You made it easy by leaving the keys on the end table by the front door. Since I don't know where the hell you live, I had to ask directions from numerous puzzled but nice people. I finally found a store with what I needed and came back here hoping you were still snor...I mean sleeping."

"Which I was."

Whit made a snoring sound.

Katelyn gave Whit a cross-eyed look and stuck out her tongue. "How did you get past my home security system without the code?"

"Oh, that; well, I temporarily disabled it."

"How did you do that?"

"Necessity is the mother of invention; well, in this case, hunger and dehydration."

"Okay, so what are we eating, Mr. Electronic-Wizard-Slash-Smartass?"

"Bacon, French toast made with sourdough French bread dipped in whipped eggs, cinnamon and a little cream. We can smother them with real butter, real maple syrup, and blackberry preserves."

"Sounds delicious, but how are you cooking the French toast, in butter?"

"No, bacon fat."

"Ah, gross! I can't eat that. I might as well inject poison directly into my veins."

"Katelyn, have you ever tried French toast made this way? My dad cooked it for the family almost every Sunday when I was a kid…at least when he wasn't working or taking me fishing or hunting. Look at me; I'm not dead yet."

Something about this guy, truly a stranger really, but so damn open and…nice. Plus, the effort he willingly put out for her made her decide to just drop the standard pretenses and go with it. "Okay, Chef Ptomaine, I'll take a bite."

"That's the spirit."

After what Katelyn finally had to admit turned out to be an outstanding breakfast, Whit washed the dishes while Katelyn dried them. She didn't even question why he didn't stack them in the dishwasher. He'd probably just say, "Not too many of those out in the woods."

Katelyn wanted this moment, this day, this feeling, to go on and on. Unfortunately, the reality of where this little interlude headed made her anxious. She really wanted to find a way to make this new relationship last somehow. How could it? She had no clue, but she wanted to try. Katelyn needed hope that love at first sight was real and true…and here and now. They fit so well; doesn't true love work that way…love conquers all? *Come on, Katelyn, think of something.*

But she couldn't. They both became quiet the closer they came to the last few dishes. Katelyn actually called reject and put their coffee cups back in the soapy water. Whit actually slowed his washing to a crawl, trying not to finish. Painfully the moment of truth arrived; awkwardly they both started talking at the same time. Then they both stopped. The casualness and the natural rhythm they shared earlier became jerky and stiff. It was Whit that mercifully broke the silence, but what he said cut like a knife.

Standing in front of Katelyn, looking nervous and pathetic, Whit said, in a flat lifeless voice, "Katelyn, Kate, I have to go and…I…you see…we…."

This wasn't going in the right direction. His stammering voice and his body language said, this is the end.

Backing away from Whit and crossing her arms she said, "So we're back to that, are we. Well, just come out with it. I'm a big girl; I mean, woman."

Whit closed his eyes, rocked his head back then looked up at the ceiling. He took a deep breath, then dropped his gaze directly into Katlyn's eyes and let it fly, "It can't work, so why try? We are so different, you and I, and so far apart, it's crazy to think we could...." That's as far as he made it before he couldn't continue.

She just looked at him with stoic silence. But he could see the hurt and sadness.

"I'm sorry, I'm sorry, Kate. I feel it, I know you feel it too, this connection...bond...whatever we have...had. It feels, felt so right with you. But, Jesus, we just met, what, fifteen hours ago?"

In a much gentler voice Katelyn asked, "Can I at least have a phone number?"

"I only have a landline, and I just don't think that's wise."

"I see." *Damn you! Damn you, Benjamin Whittingham.*

Whit could tell she didn't mean it, was extremely upset, and getting madder.

"Katelyn, I'm not trying to hurt you. I don't like to see anything hurt. The toughest and saddest part of my job is running into injured or suffering animals in the woods. One way or another I make their pain go away. But this—"

"What do you do, kill them?"

"Most of the time, yes, I end their suffering quickly and as painlessly as possible. That's what I'm trying to do with—"

"I'm not an injured wild animal!" Katelyn shot back. Softer, she said, "I'm a woman, you entered my life, and you...you know this is real."

"I know, I know, Kate, I do. I just don't see how this can work. The least painful solution is to leave."

Why? Katelyn's eyes asked.

As if he heard her, Whit said, "If we drag this out, you here and me out west, both with our demanding jobs, our different lives, politics, all of it, it will end up badly. I don't want to hurt you, Kate, but I don't want both of us to suffer a lingering decline and just end anyway. Maybe I see life too black and white, but there it is."

There was so much Katelyn wanted to say. How she had been looking for someone for so long who allowed her to be feminine, mischievous, fun, and an equal. Someone to make her laugh, feel so damn safe in his arms, to have total trust. And here he stood, all macho shit, brushing her off like she was a speck of lint on his ill-fitting borrowed suit. She vowed that he would not see her cry. She looked up at him and coldly said, "I'll call you a cab; please wait on the front porch."

Whit lifted his hands above his waist and opened them like he was going to try to hold her. "Kate, I want you to know I—"

"Please don't...just go."

He looked into her fiery eyes one last time, closed his hands and dropped them to his side. A helpless feeling overwhelmed him. But he said to himself, *Better to get it over with quickly, it's for the best for both of us; I know it...it just hurts now, it will fade...it always does.*

He turned for the door and didn't look back. At the door he reset her security system and heard Katelyn dialing for a cab. Her voice was pleasant and beautiful as he walked out.

"Katelyn, you're going to make me cry." Sharron, for the first time, truly felt empathy for Katelyn. Normally, jealousy, self-preservation and opportunism overrode any other Sharron emotion. "Did you ever try to find him?"

"What do you think? Of course I tried, but not at first. I reverted back to being tough, proud, independent Katelyn. Besides, he knew where I worked. I wanted him to call first. But as time went on and he didn't contact me, I gave it a halfhearted attempt. The Sierra Nevada turns out to be a big mountain range and I really didn't have much to go on. He pretty much lives off the grid. After a few dead ends, I quit. I figured he didn't really care or he would have found me, so I decided not to care. But Sharron, it's been months and I can't let go."

After a long pause, Sharron offered, "I hate to give a friggin' Republican any credit, but he was probably trying to be chivalrous and realistic." Surprising herself, Sharron added, "God, I can't believe I just said that. God, I can't believe I said God." Quickly she continued. "He's probably one of those religious nut balls with a dozen squalling little brats, a fat baby machine wife and a wandering eye.... Praise the Lord." Smiling, Sharron said to herself, *There, that sounds better; more like me.*

Katelyn said weakly, "Well, he told me his political view slanted heavily conservative; I just assumed he was a Republican."

"Good reporter's nose, Katelyn. If it walks like a duck and steps all over little people, it's a—"

"He's not like that," Katelyn said defensively.

You were with this guy for what, fifteen hours, and you know he's a Republican, with a heart? Do they even exist? Then a thought popped into Sharron's brain. "Didn't you say your country bumpkin came to Washington, D.C. because of a buddy? Someone who was trying to get a job at the Naval Yard?"

"Yeah, so?"

"Katelyn, if you're really hung up on this mysterious hick, help me help you. What was the buddy's name…think."

"Mikie, Mike." Snapping her fingers, she added, "And his wife's name is Janet. She talked Whit into going to the Kennedys' party." After a little more thought she said, "They have three boys." Katelyn could see where Sharron's lead took her and became excited. "Mikie just retired as a Lieutenant Colonel. Jesus, why didn't I think of this?"

"Honey, when you're in love, the brain doesn't function well. But listen, with your contacts in Congress, don't you think that if this Mikie guy just found a job at the Naval Yard, or didn't for that matter, they could find him? There's your link."

Reaching out and holding Sharron's hand, Katelyn said, "You're the best investigative reporter of all of us. That's why management gave you the White House, Sharron."

Patting the side of Katelyn's hand, Sharron said, "Thanks, honey," then thought, *I can already see all those congressional party invitations stacking up on my desk. Ain't love grand?*

Chapter Ten
The Inner Circle

As was customary, Steven Sliger entered his office without fanfare, small talk, or even a good morning. He silently slid into his cushy leather CEO chair and looked across the brilliantly polished, dark cherry wood desk at his three generals...the "Inner Circle." To acquire and maintain their undying devotion, Sliger merely gave them each what they desired most; solitude, power, beauty...it was easy. For bestowing these gifts, Sliger received blind obedience. Their loyalty rivaled Gobbles, Himmler, and Goering's subservience to Hitler.

Everyone hates something about themselves. Everyone craves for something unattainable. Some become so unhinged their obsession dominates their very existence. *"If only I was, or if only I could."* What if miraculously a benefactor with the means steps in, kneels down, lifts you up and grants you your wish of wishes. At that point he becomes your hero, your master, your God. So had Sliger become to the members of his Inner Circle.

The Inner Circle consisted of three individuals. One man and one woman, straight-backed and attentive; the third person, an odd fellow, slouched down in his chair staring intently through thick glasses at a small stack of crumpled papers on his lap. The slovenly man's head rocked back and forth slightly. These three devoted souls knew Steven Sliger's real name and his past...well, some of it. They also knew where the skeletons were buried...mostly because they helped dig the graves. Sliger had already told the Inner Circle about his plans to destroy the lives of his once close ex-high school buddies. He required information to be accrued by all three, and today they were summoned to reveal what they'd learned.

Lance Sliger sat in the middle. Only eleven years younger than his step-father, Lance was actually Steven Sliger's first wife's son. After the divorce, the older and far less wealthy Mrs. Sliger left. However, her psychotic son stayed. Lance's name was Larry Baker back then. The wiry 5'9" young man lived with the paradox of being both handsome and ugly to women, at the same time. Many women found him reasonably good-looking...from a distance. He possessed pleasant features, short, dark, straight hair never out of place, a small pointed nose and similar chin. Even his thick eyebrows and dark brown eyes centered evenly on his face. In fact, he always looked fine in a picture. But life doesn't stop at a single frame. Unfortunately for Larry, when speaking to people, especially women, he exuded creepy. Larry appeared to leer and frown at the same time when he spoke. He verbalized in short bursts while his eyes darted back and forth, giving him an almost rodent-like quality. With women, he often stood a little too close, and his initial conversation tended to be way too personal or suggestive. The art of seduction, all but lost in his desire to cut to the chase. He knew what he wanted; why play some stupid game? *I am in control, just yield to me, comply, give in.* Larry worshipped power and control, neither of which he remotely attained prior to knowing Steven Sliger. Now he had the means to match the will. Money talks and bullshit walks. Changing his name to Lance Sliger only added to his feeling of empowerment.

To Lance's left sat Jeff Bowman, a rather thin, pasty-white man in his early forties. His rumpled clothes, unkempt prematurely gray hair, and piercing body odor disgusted Lance to the tenth power. Oddly, it never seemed to be an issue with his persnickety, clean-freak stepfather. Lance was actually leaning slightly to his right trying to minimize the sharp assault of unwashed clothes, bad breath, and ripe human stink emitting from his left. Jeff Bowman didn't give much thought to his body; it was just a vehicle to move his brain from one place to another. He had little use for people or his life in general outside of the world he created inside computers. He'd spend all day role playing on some stupid game if not...properly controlled. Plenty of prior employers gleefully terminated the smelly anti-social nutcase, never understanding or appreciating the immense potential they chose to cast to the winds. About fifteen years earlier, just prior to graduating from college, a mutual friend introduced Jeff to Sliger. They met for a marathon roleplaying weekend of Dungeons and Dragons. Sliger immediately realized the hidden genius within the odiferous loner and kept in contact. If fantasy and reality were blurred and interchangeable to Jeff Bowman, Sliger knew the same would be true with legal and illegal. When the time came, Sliger offered Jeff his very own safe, isolated computer world, and Jeff accepted. To keep it, Sliger required Jeff to occasionally write a complex program or hack into someone's impenetrable firewall; for Jeff, no big deal.

To Lance's right sat Andrea Moran, Sliger's public relations specialist and human resource officer. Andrea represented the face of Sliger's empire to the public and press. The attractive, articulate and built-like-a-brick-shithouse spokesperson controlled completely what the world knew about Serpentine Solutions, Inc. Her title also covered all aspects of employer/employee relations, both legal and, well, not so legal. Nicknamed the Iron Madam, Andrea ran operations as a hardnosed, no-nonsense administrator. To stay employed at Serpentine Solutions you followed three simple requirements; play by Sliger's rules, work your ass off, and never ever question or bad mouth management. In reality and what the press, public and especially law enforcement didn't know was that Andrea Moran controlled all of Serpentine Solutions' finances and investments…again, both legal and illegal. The aboveboard business stayed clean and tidy; the payoffs, bribes, surveillance and worse…much, much worse…remained nonexistent.

Andrea grew up as Sheena Piper in a small town in the southern Sierra. Sharp as a tack, Sheena never did much homework but remained near the top in every class. Cute, smart, and athletic as hell, in baseball terms Sheena was destined to hit a homerun. Unfortunately, life and genetics cut into her bright future. Poor Sheena's permanent teeth continued to grow and turned crooked and uneven. Her parents didn't have the money for orthodontics; strike one. Her large, wide Betty Davis eyes developed into a bulbous, bug-eyed fish look; strike two. But the worst, the most crushing change hit at puberty: terrible, scarring acne; strike three. She lost her confidence and shrunk inwardly. Good and bad; on the flipside, from the shoulders down, Sheena's body developed into a well-proportioned, hard, muscular package which allowed her to focus on sports. Devastated to find out that "Sheena the Hyena" became her nickname, she was never asked out on a date in high school and couldn't muster the courage to go to dances or parties stag. By the time she reached college on a softball scholarship, her well-defined features exuded sexuality. Sheena wanted the passion and love she'd missed in high school. What she found was advantageous males that wanted her…for her body. Through one bitter lesson after another, Sheena learned the singular focus and cruel drive that afflicts all young males. They wanted to be with her...just not in public. They wanted to touch her...but mostly in the dark. By the time she graduated, her bachelor's degree in economics should have read: Bitter with a minor in hating men.

Looking for work, Sheena applied with numerous businesses and non-profits. After a lackluster eighteen-month career of unrewarding part-time work, she took her meager experience back to the marketplace to hopefully upgrade. Her third interview occurred with a strange little fellow she remembered from somewhere, maybe a night class. An older guy, maybe an upper-classman; she recalled often catching him looking at her but they never spoke. She had blown him off back then as just another horny dickhead looking for a quick meaningless piece of her ass. However, that interview and Sliger's proposition changed Sheena's life forever. Sliger offered her what she wanted most, what she needed most. Sheena surprised herself a little by quickly agreeing. Two years later and more dental work, teeth implants, pressure-releasing eye surgeries and skin treatments than she could remember, "Sheena the Hyena" morphed into "Andrea the Angel." Not the petite, fashion-plate Miss America type gorgeous, but more hometown girl, football-queen type pretty... strong features with a suggestive smile all situated nicely on a tight, well-defined frame. Many attractive women appear delicate like crystal; not Andrea. To most males, Andrea exuded, *"I work hard, play hard, screw hard...and look and feel good doing all three."* Andrea Moran could now date men as easily and singularly focused as so many did with her. The one big difference now, she was in the driver's seat and she relished the power. For this gift, she rewarded Sliger with the perfect and perfectly loyal PR woman and financial wizard. In a very dark and cynical way, poor little Sheena Piper finally hit her homerun.

Sliger started the meeting by addressing his nervous nerdy computer geek first. "Jeff, what have you found?"

"Uh, I have it all in this printout." Jeff held up the crumpled papers. "Can I go now?"

Calmly, Sliger said, "No, not yet, Jeff. Why don't you just give us the Reader's Digest version?"

Confused, Jeff said, "Huh?"

"Jeff, give us a summary of your report."

"Oh, why didn't you say so?"

Lance jabbed, "He did, you stupid piece of—"

Bang! The loud slap of Sliger's hand on his desk stopped Lance cold and made the nervous Jeff Bowman lose his glasses as he nearly leapt out of his chair.

Sliger glared at Lance while he calmly said to his computer genius, "Go ahead, Jeff."

Finding and returning his glasses to his face, Jeff looked at Lance over the rims with bugged-out eyes and stuck out his tongue. Lance turned away and looked at the ceiling, disgusted.

Jeff finally started. "Ned Penrose, thirty-eight, married twice, no children, though both wives had one child each from previous, ah...involvements. Financially, he's vulnerable; his stationery store just limps along. He gives away way too much money to his church and too many items for raffles and auctions. He's a sucker for any fundraiser or cause. Penrose's taxes reveal he hands out more of his earnings than he can even write off. Plus, his two previous wives soaked him; not too bad, but enough. Penrose's business hangs by a thread."

Still staring at Lance, Sliger said, "Very succinct, Jeff; thank you. Who's next?"

Looking at his notes, Jeff continued. "Greyson Milner, thirty-eight, single, no children, lives in a huge Victorian on his family's farm. He switched to organic farming after his mother died and the business took off. He also owns a gardening supply business. He's expanding and appears to be doing fine. Milner would be hard to mess with financially.

"Okay, what about Whittingham?"

"Benjamin Whittingham, thirty-eight, single, no children. He mostly pays in cash. I can't find much on him; not much of a paper trail. There are big gaps in his past; nothing notable in his college years that I could find. He fought fires for the State of California in the summers his last two years of high school and during college. He received a degree in Wildlife Biology and another in Forestry from the University of California at Berkeley. For ten years he worked for a large private landowner, but now consults on his own and has for the last six years. Whittingham pays property tax on a cabin in Logan County and his family home in Cedar Creek. His dad, a widower, is the sheriff of Logan County and lives in the family home. Benjamin seems very outspoken; I've found lots of editorials and opinion pieces he's written related to, you know, animals, wildfires, trees and stuff like that. He seems very critical of federal and state management practices and regulations."

"Okay, anything else, anything we can use against him?" Sliger asked while still looking sternly at Lance to make sure he kept his mouth shut. Lance slowly rubbed the left side of his nose but, in reality, he was pressing his left nostril closed. All of Jeff's nervous movement wafted around even more vileness.

Jeff continued. "The Whittingham guy got into some trouble with the Department of Fish and Game a while back, but it was dropped. I'm trying to get the incident report."

"Well, that could be useful; keep digging."

"Okay, so can I go now?"

"I think we can finish here without you. Give me…no, give Lance your printouts and send me the Fish and Game information as soon as you get it."

Jeff stood to leave and stuck his hand out to his right. Lance took the papers with his fingertips like being forced to hold the tail of a rotten fish.

Sliger's eyes followed Jeff as he scurried out the side door of Sliger's office. Jeff relished the safety of his computer room and computer-generated world. Sliger shifted his gaze back to Lance and said, "I will not have Jeff abused. He's an integral part of this operation and indispensable. Clear?"

"Why do you coddle that geek? He stinks to high heaven and he's—"

"An integral part of this operation and indispensable; do I make myself clear?" Sliger cut in curtly.

Lance knew he had pushed his mentor too far; he looked down and said, "Yes, sir."

Sliger bellowed, "Look at me when I speak to you!"

Lance snapped his head up and said, "Yes, sir, I, I was—"

"Shut up!" Sliger boomed again. In the silence that ensued, Sliger sat back in his chair and swiveled it sideways to avoid looking at his stepson. *Jesus; of the three, he's the weakest link…too emotional and vain, just like his mother. I thought he'd be an extension of me, someone I could trust to handle my…black ops. I get 95-percent cold steel; then this emotional, whiny, prissy, little dandy crap crops up. Shit; at this juncture, he's what I have and he will have to step up…or else.* Sliger let his thought trail off. He didn't want to think about making the decision to order his stepson's…disappearance. *We're too far down the road to stop; besides I can't wait. I want my dear old buddies to suffer. I'll just have to work with Lance harder; lead by example.*

Spinning his chair around, Sliger snapped, "Hand me Jeff's report."

Trying to man up, Lance grabbed the papers firmly, knowing he'd smear Jeff residue all over his hands. He'd wash off the man's filth as soon as his stepfather terminated the meeting. Lance leaned forward and slid the crumpled papers across the desk.

Sliger took the report and pushed it to his right. Changing the subject, he asked Lance, "Did you find our girl?"

"Yes, sir, you were right; she was in Brazil. She goes by Allyson Chandler now."

"And she's coming?"

"She should be here by the end of the week. I told her to call when she hits the States."

"And if the price is right she's up for another...contract?"

Confidently Lance said, "I'll make sure she does. I can handle a high-class hooker."

Mocking Lance, Sliger said, "Like the last time?"

While Lance turned red and sat silently stewing, Sliger smiled to himself and thought, *I shouldn't pick on him, but he deserves a taste of his own medicine until he stops the jabs at Jeff and toughens up.*

Sliger turned his gaze to Lance's right. "Andrea?"

All business, Andrea spoke up. "Some positive news; our realtor says commercial property is available and Office King is looking to expand in the foothills. With the migration of urbanites to the foothills, they forecast substantial growth in Cedar Creek. We can turn this with no trail back to Serpentine Solutions. If we want to bankrupt Penrose Stationery, we can pull the trigger; it's there."

Nodding slightly, Sliger asked, "And Greyson Milner?"

"As I told you earlier, his personal life can be exploited. Recently, in the last few years, he's turned into a cock-hound and a shmuck. He aggressively chases good-looking women. Greyson Milner has plenty of enemies; fathers, ex-husbands, ex-boyfriends and brothers of some of the women he's dated. There are plenty of angry women he's dumped too, if we want to use that angle. I assume you have an idea; that's why you've asked for Ms. Chandler?"

Sliger responded, "Yes, I'm thinking maybe a love triangle, something like that. We can use Ms. Chandler's...allure to drive a wedge between Penrose and Milner. Milner's lust for chasing tail and Penrose's lack of success with females gives us a friendship-destroying opportunity."

Sliger leaned back in his chair nodding his head. The two remaining Inner Circle members knew that would be exactly the course they'd direct Ms. Chandler to pursue.

Finally, Sliger leaned forward again and asked with thick sarcasm, "And what about my old pal, Whit?"

"As Jeff said, he's tough to read; very private for the most part. However, when it comes to his business…well, more accurately, issues involving forestry, biology or ecology, Whittingham has made plenty of enemies. Many of the field representatives for those state agencies that regulate Whittingham's forestry and biological consulting activities don't like him at all. Apparently, they can't bull him over or push him around. In an odd way, Whittingham forces them to do their jobs. As the manager of your workforce, I kind of respect that."

Sliger stood and angrily hissed, "Don't get mushy on Whittingham or any of them. This is personal and important to me and to the success of my business. And don't forget, these guys turned on me; their friendship was nothing more than a damn lie. Now it's my turn to get even…plus interest."

Calmly and professionally, Andrea responded, "You have my full support, sir."

Calming down a little, Sliger added, "Okay, good. Let's jump on Whit with both feet on that Fish and Game incident." Still standing, Sliger said, "There remains other classmates that need to feel the sting of my revenge as well, but let's focus on Penrose, Milner and Whittingham for now. Andrea, get Peterson to do surveillance on all three and to report directly to you."

"Yes sir. But Mr. Sliger, do you think bringing someone from outside the Inner Circle…appropriate?"

"I need up-to-date intelligence on these three, more than Jeff, Lance and you can provide. The better I know my enemy, the better I can exploit their weaknesses. This is a job for Peterson. Neither Peterson's employer nor any of the other private investigators are to know; only Peterson. He'll be extremely loyal and discreet."

Sliger thought, but didn't add, *Peterson has no choice; I know his real name, that he's AWOL from the Marine Corp, and whom he killed.* "I want to know everything about these three; who they see, where they go, what they eat and drink, what they drive, the floor plans of their homes, where they shop, everything. Tell Peterson to tap their phones if necessary."

Realizing they were finished, Andrea started organizing the paperwork in her lap. "Yes sir. I'll meet with Peterson personally."

"Then we're done. Be back in an hour for our regular business meeting."

With that, Stephen Sliger turned his back on his lieutenants and walked to his private office and quarters.

Chapter Eleven
Just Once More

The slender but curvaceous well-dressed woman strolled casually up to the Green Planet building. Claiming more aliases than manicured fingernails, today she happened to be Ms. Allyson Chandler. The structure she stood before, one of the first of a growing number of allegedly energy neutral buildings, occupied a prominent spot near the capital in downtown Sacramento. Ms. Chandler noticed as she approached, the Green Planet building actually did cast a pale green Mother Earth hue.

Allyson wore her shiny, black hair pulled straight back. Her hair and deeply tanned skin contrasted well against her v-neck white blouse. The slits up both sides of her heather gray mid-thigh skirt revealed lean, muscular thighs above well-defined calves. She looked like a long-distance runner, except for her breasts. No sports bra could sufficiently constrict her perky set well enough to avoid painful jogging. Not huge, but for her petite size, Allyson's set definitely were the type that bulged out of both sides of a bikini top. Minus the two-inch white heels, she stood a short 5'4". Her smooth skin, wide almond-colored eyes, slightly freckled cheeks, and slender nose made her look ten years younger and far more innocent than what lied beneath her vexing veneer. It made what she did for a living so...damn...easy.

The sole occupants on the top floor of the building consisted of the executive offices of Serpentine Solutions, Inc. In less than ten years, SSI had grown to be one of the state's top restoration and hazardous site reclamation companies.

As she approached the entrance, a whooshing sound of air pushing outward hit her as the door opened quickly. A pleasant but slightly flat mechanical sounding female voice said, "Please enter briskly to save energy." As her very firm behind passed an invisible sensor, the front door whooshed closed, followed by, "Thank you for saving energy."

She had to stop briefly before a second door as sensors checked to make sure no excessive heat had entered the building with her. The mysterious voice returned. "Welcome to Sacramento's very first certified energy-neutral building. Our solutions are global because we're all part of one Earth."

The second door parted in the middle. Walking into a large lush and slightly humid atrium, she looked straight ahead to a bank of elevators. The voice returned with a suggestion. "Using our stairs makes you healthier and ecofriendly."

Ignoring the eco-noxious voice, she walked to a smallish elevator adjacent to the three normal-sized elevators. She entered a four digit code on the keypad next to the mini elevator. The door quickly opened; she stepped inside. Using the second code provided her, she punched the digits. The only elevator to ascend to the top floor whisked upward.

Exiting the elevator, she moved briskly down the hall toward the tall, dark red and knotless redwood double doors at the end of the hall, the right door made an internal click and swung open automatically. Before she entered, she wiggled her upper body to make sure her square shouldered white blouse sat right and positioned the point of her V-neck top to center on her cleavage. Allyson slid her thin black purse under her left arm and walked forward.

The plush executive suite, far more opulent than the spartanly bland décor downstairs, stood out strikingly different than the image presented to the masses. The frugal and ecofriendly motif downstairs portrayed the company's image. The executive suite exuded excess and privilege with the squandering indulgence and exploitation of Mother Earth's resources solely reserved for the top brass. The lavish furnishings usually found only in the offices of high-end lawyers, lobbyists and the public's humble servants...the state's senators and assemblymen, screamed money, power, and the confidence to use both.

She walked around to the front of the huge desk and said to herself, *Ah, shit, the ferret...figures*. She thought she was going to finally meet her most lucrative and secretive employer, a man she only knew as Mr. Smith.

Gazing across the desk's polished finish, she stared blankly at the slender, fidgety, pointy-nosed man, Mr. Smith's creepy little...what, assistant, sycophant, lap dog?

He stood, and with an effort to be pleasant, offered his hand and said, "What a pleasure to see you again. What's it been, two years? Please sit."

Refusing to take his hand, Allyson remained standing and maintained a neutral expression. She said to herself, while looking into the self-absorbed and unstable twerp's beady eyes, *No, it definitely is not a pleasure to see you, you horny, spoiled, inept…. Why do you have to work for my richest client?*

The only job she'd ever turned down from the ferret's boss was $10,000 to sleep with this little creep. She wasn't even sure that Lance hadn't just tacked on his little fantasy bonus to the end of her last job without Mr. Smith's knowledge. That was almost two years ago after successfully destroying the marriage and business of one of Mr. Smith's competitors. Ronda Chase, as she was known back then, had simply disappeared after the pictures of the raunchy adulterous affair became public. The poor sap lost everything. *That's what you get when you think wealth and power gives you special privileges. If you can't keep your married little pecker in your pants, you better have a pre-nup. The dumbshit didn't, and hit rock bottom; too bad, so sad, asshole.*

Half-heartedly, Allyson answered Lance's question. "Yes, two years this summer; and the name is Allyson now…Allyson Chandler. Why are you here? I had the impression I was finally going to meet Mr. Smith."

Trying his best to ignore Allyson's insolence and maintain his composure, Lance offered, "Duties of a busy man; besides, I still take care of all of Mr. Smith's…special projects. So you will be working directly, ah, under me…so to speak."

In your wet dreams, asshole. "If I take the job."

"Oh, I think you'll like the terms and take the contract. Can I offer you a drink?"

Ignoring Lance, Allyson simply said, "What you can offer are the specifics of the job and Mr. Smith's top negotiating price for my…services"

Frowning, Lance looked down for a second, then sat. *This cold bitch hasn't changed a bit. But, Goddamnit, she needs to learn who's boss. Once she hears the price, she'll come around.*

Looking up again, he calmly proceeded. "It's a little complicated and could take time to explain. It's not what you would consider one of our normal contracts. If anything, this job requires even more…delicacy. I thought we could discuss it over dinner."

With a stern flat voice Allyson shot back, "Look, you little shit weasel, playtime's over. I wouldn't let your boss buy me for you two years ago and—"

Allyson paused and backed away from the edge of his desk. She slid her right hand down to the slit in her skirt and lifted the flap up and to the left, giving Lance a bird's-eye view of what the front of a very fit woman looked like, without underwear.

She continued. "Take a good look, shit weasel, because you'll never get to see this again, get it? Now, you little perv, do you want to go jerk off, or are we talking business?"

Lance kept staring long after Allyson dropped her skirt. Eventually, he looked up to her eyes. He didn't say a word, but she could see his building rage. Keeping her expression neutral, Allyson thought, *This asshole needs to know his place, but poking a stick at a rattlesnake...especially this nut job...could be detrimental to my health and retirement. But if I don't slap the boundaries across his face, this crap won't stop.*

Too angry to talk, Lance's brain sizzled. *I'm going to have you someday, bitch, guaranteed. And you'll be begging for it and when I'm done with you, you won't be fit for any man.* The stare down ended abruptly when Lance stood up and hissed, "Someday you're going to—"

"Look, asswipe, I came up here to talk to your boss about a job. I find you sitting here playing, me Tarzan, you Jane. If this is how you manage your boss's special projects, I'm through with you." Opening her purse, she added, "This is my new contact number. Give it to your boss."

Allyson tossed a business card on the desk but left her purse open. Her Lady Colt sat handle-up, inches from her fingers. Allyson was confident she would prevail. Shit Weasel's boss needed her. What did Mr. Smith say about her? "You have a talent for male destruction." If Shit Weasel pushed too hard or went berserk, she'd pull her automatic and end the ordeal quickly and quietly or loudly and with extreme prejudice. It was his choice now how negotiations proceeded.

The next eight seconds ticked off in deafening silence. Finally, Lance's better judgment won over his manic and fragile ego. He broke the ice by returning to a calm manner and said, "Look, let's both calm down a bit. I apologize; I acted inappropriately. Can we start again?"

Lance waited, but Allyson said nothing. He finally spoke again. "Please sit down so we can be comfortable while discussing the job."

Allyson sat but kept her purse open.

Lance continued. "Pardon my poor manners. Can I order sandwiches and coffee?"

Allyson thought about saying, *I don't know, can you?* But she realized they were back to bland if not phony professionalism, and she decided she'd do her best to keep the little turd focused. She said, "That'll work."

Allyson already knew she would take the job. Whatever it was, it would pay well and she would bring down another faithless sleaze ball. In her mind she provided justice in a way few could. Her body destroyed egotistical scumbags who thought with impunity they could cheat on their wives, step all over little people, or use their position to treat women like sex toys. Well, play away, you greedy, selfish sons of bitches; this sex toy bites back. Besides, Allyson reasoned, she needed the money. Her lifestyle and retirement plans demanded it.

Exiting the Green Planet building twenty-five minutes after entering, Allyson carried a large folder. The door slid open with a whoosh of air pushing her out into the afternoon heat. The same metallic female voice thanked her for being a noble warrior for Mother Earth. Allyson flipped the location of the sound of the voice a quick middle finger as she turned east at a brisk pace.

She thought, *Double what I thought, plus an awesome bonus....not bad. Fifty Gs up front, fifty Gs upon completion, and all expenses paid, $100,000 plus I get to keep the Mercedes. Jesus, Mr. Smith must really need these guys to go away. No, not go away; destroyed, crushed and humiliated.*

Waiting at a crosswalk, Allyson tried but couldn't figure out the angle. What did these small-town hicks do? What could they have done to Mr. Smith to be a threat? Maybe they're just in the way of something Mr. Smith wants to do, but what would that be? Something doesn't quite fit here. This stationery store owner seems harmless. The information in the file Allyson carried revealed nothing more than a twice-divorced, community-oriented, rural town, small businessman. Not the arrogant, pushy, full-of-themselves types she normally hired out to destroy. The other guy owns an organic farm. He's a skirt chaser but, big deal...he's single.

Waiting to cross the street, Allyson absentmindedly smiled at a guy also waiting for the light. As he uncontrollably stared and admired what he saw, her mind remained on the job, *Hells bells, this job will actually be easier and less dangerous. Shit, I already know exactly what to do to pull it off.*

When the guy started to speak, Allyson cut him off by sticking her tongue between two of her fingers, and declared, "You're wasting your breath; I'm lesbian."

As she crossed the street, Allyson left the guy standing frozen in place with his mouth wide open. How many times had she used that line to cut a conversation off? She couldn't remember. Only once did a guy have a comeback that made her laugh. He asked, "Oh, how are things in Beirut?"

Chapter Twelve
Comes with the Job

Periodically giving her boss a blowjob wasn't the end of the world. Andrea just figured it was a small price to pay and part of the deal she'd made to become... awesome. If not for Sliger, who would she be...nobody; what would she be... nothing; and where would she be...nowhere.

It wasn't like it took her long to make him climax; she'd perfected the right grip and stroke. If only all those men she mercilessly teased, who wanted her lips wrapped around their little worms knew how well she performed her duty. Too bad, so sad, suckers. In fact, the only issue with the whole process was the fact that Sliger liked her to take it all, clean and tidy. Clean and tidy for Sliger maybe. That was the problem. It wasn't even the taste so much—kind of a combination of sweet and bitter, or maybe sweet and salty if she had to guess. The damn consistency just grossed her out. *Nothing like slithering down a warm load of egg whites and snot to make your day.*

Andrea worked very hard to control her gag reflex, and why not? The man who rearranged the stars for her, made her the desire of so many pathetic souls, and gave her the power over them, needed servicing. So what's a brief little inconvenience compared to the overwhelming power she now possessed?

Even though Sliger was married when she initially came to work for him, they had indulged in regular sex during her reconstruction years. In between doses of corticosteroids, minor plastic and reconstructive surgery for her eyes, teeth removal, implant surgery, and acne treatments, Andrea and Sliger banged out a merry tune. In fact, their trysts finally gave wife number one the leverage to get the hell out. It cost the ex-Mrs. Sliger dearly financially, but she cared only for freedom.

However, as Andrea's incredible beauty developed, Sliger's interest seemed to wane. Sliger finally revealed it wasn't the sex; he still needed the release. No, it was the time involved and the mess. An obsessive compulsive to the extreme, his fastidiousness required being clean before and after sex. The necessity for both to shower, have sex, then shower again took a lot of dedicated time. Sliger's solution—blow jobs; clean and quick, the act done with little time wasted. Since Sliger had little sexual imagination and always shot his wad quickly, it wasn't like Andrea was missing a good roll in the hay anyway.

Andrea rocked back on her high-heels and stood up from her kneeling position. She grabbed the towel she used to rest her knees as she rose. Andrea looked down at Sliger and said, "I'll be right back." With her lips tightly closed, the words came out more like, "Hm, hm, hmmm, hm."

Sliger just nodded as he was already busy cleaning himself with handy wipes. Heading to the large washroom at the side of Sliger's office, she only gagged once before pushing through the door. Scurrying to the first sink, she dry heaved into the basin. While flushing her mouth out with tons of water, she thought, *Jesus, what the hell was that, a load and a half? Ever since we started this "old gang" operation, he's been…excessive. It's like their impending pain arouses him. I haven't seen him this happy in years…not since we destroyed the owner and CEO of Reynolds Environmental Restorations, Inc. Damn, that was grand. With Ms. Chandler's assistance, I think our best operation. First, his self-righteous denials of an affair to the press, then those pictures, those gloriously raunchy pictures. After the very ugly and very public divorce, plus our syphoning away of some of Reynold's best people, came declining profits. Finally, the stoic resignation as he crawled away in disgrace. We picked up most of his contracts, clients, and contractors; bingo bango, another competitor swept aside. Well, I don't know what Steven's high school classmates did to him, but they hurt him terribly. We'll just bring them down a notch or two…or three. Maybe when we're finished crushing their lives we can look up some of my dear old college lovers. That would be a lovely dish best served cold; hmmm.*

Realizing she was fantasizing and Steve was no doubt impatiently waiting for updates, she thought, *Better blow off taking a pee; oh, no pun intended. I'll just quickly brush my teeth.* When she finished, Andrea looked at herself in the mirror and smiled. She liked very much what she saw. Then she quickly rushed out.

Even before Andrea sat down, Sliger barked, "I want to know about Office King first."

"Fast-tracking since the City Council will approve the project next meeting. If Jeff hadn't found the kiddie porn on that councilman's city computer, we were heading for denial. We'll get a 3-to-2 approval now. Since its only superficial changes of a recent renovation, the permit process will be fast-tracked and quicker for the contractor. A little longer for the rest of the project, but who cares; they start minor alterations to the old Logan County Mercantile building in maybe two weeks. Office King could start moving in inventory in another four."

Sliger just bared his teeth like an angry dog and shook his head up and down.

Andrea tried to ignore Sliger's grotesque expression of joy by thinking about the councilman caught red-handed with some pretty explicit child sex act material. She finally asked, "Is there any firewall that's safe from our Jeff?"

Sliger replied, "Probably, but none so far; definitely not that councilman's, what's his name?"

"Hal Beldon; he rolled over while peeing all over himself. We'll receive nothing but cooperation from him. We're lucky to have Jeff and his skills."

Sliger shot back, "Luck had nothing to do with it, Andrea, only me…. I saw Jeff for what he was, the potential of his genius. I drew him in, I created and cultured him. Now I sustain him."

"Like me?" Andrea asked feeling suddenly vulnerable.

"No, Andrea," Sliger lied. "Not you. You were just a flicker away from brilliance; I just added a little spark. You blossomed into who you are all on your own. I just gave you a little nudge."

Andrea blushed and said in sincere admiration, "Thank you, Steven."

Sliger sat back in his chair assessing what had just transpired. *Know your disciples and how to stroke each one accordingly…that's the key; how easy. She kneels before me and sucks my cock then thanks me. Jesus, humans are so gullible, so weak… so trainable.*

Leaning forward, he asked, "Is Ned feeling the pinch of impending doom…drinking more, not sleeping? Have you heard anything?"

"So far no; many locals have dropped by to express their support. His routine has not changed. But that will not last."

Disappointed and impatient for signs of suffering, Sliger sat back making a dour face. "Well, what about the information Jeff found out about Whittingham and that deer incident that was dropped?"

"Our scheme to ruin Whittingham happens to be moving along quite well. I contacted Earth Wild's lead attorney, Luna Waxman. She's a velociraptor when it comes to cases like this. She's a fanatical wild animal lover and has already spoken to her like-minded friends in the state senate and assembly. They've kneeled hard on the neck of the Fish and Game director and her minions. Through some snooping, arm twisting, pressure from superiors, a little hacking by Jeff, and a subpoena from Ms. Waxman, I have a copy of the warden's initial incident notes, list of violations, a copy of the dispatch backup tape, the unfinished initial report, incident number and the names of all the players."

Andrea continued. "Apparently, the initial warden changed his mind and fought to have the charges dropped. Without him, the case stalled, then died. To a man, and woman, all the Fish and Game bigwigs feigned ignorance of the whole incident; what's new? Jeff discovered emails that prove at least some of them knew. But they've agreed to get the case reviewed. Ms. Waxman called the Fish and Game director and told her nothing less than prosecution would do. Plus, we own the eyewitness in the case, a realtor named, Alan Barbou. Our private investigator, Peterson, with a little help from Jeff, found out our shyster realtor is cheating on his wife and his taxes. Plus, he maintains a recreational use of cocaine. He's scared shitless of losing everything and will say and do anything we tell him. Whittingham is going down on this one, three years behind bars…maybe more. Plus, I almost forgot; if he gets a felony conviction…no more guns, no more hunting."

Sliger went into that bared-teeth, mad-dog grin again and silently started shaking his head up and down. Andrea flashed on the thought that Sliger looked like he was crapping his pants. She shook her head to erase the image, which caught Sliger's eye.

Sliger stopped abruptly and asked her, "Now what?"

"Oh, nothing, sir," she lied. "Just clearing my thoughts for the next subject."

Sliger asked, "Before we go on, who looks like they're going down first?"

"Currently, as it stands, Whit heads to prison, possibly soon. Ned survives on a wing and a prayer; it won't take long to bankrupt his business. We'll pull the scheme to destroy Greyson and Ned's friendship on Ms. Chandler's schedule."

Sliger stepped in. "I'll catch you up on Lance and Ms. Allyson Chandler's meeting. She's agreed to our contract, but she's shrewd. She must sense I really want this; she pitched Lance for a lot. Plus, if all goes as planned, she gets to keep the Mercedes." Without addressing Andrea, he added in his head, *She fell for keeping the Mercedes without any prompting from Lance. She demanded the car as a bonus. The greedy bitch walked right into my plan.*

Returning to Andrea, Sliger added, "A small price to pay, because if all goes as predicted, Ms. Chandler will soon have everyone hating Greyson Milner… especially his best friends."

Andrea just said, "Yes sir." She already knew about Allyson's contract and the Mercedes but worried about the deal. *Anything Lance does for Steven, I need to know. They are working on something and don't want me involved, or don't want my input. Why? Because they know I'd probably find a reason or reasons to say no, that's why. This is not good.*

Chapter Thirteen
My Fault, not Yours

Returning from marking bark beetle-infected pine trees on a small salvage timber sale, Whit pulled into the Central House parking lot at 2:00 sharp. Not wanting to be late, Whit didn't have time to clean up. Whit caught his reflection in his pickup's rearview mirror. The spray and ricocheting marking paint bouncing off of the dead and dying trees left Whit's face dotted with blue spots and gave his complexion an overall bluish hue. He quickly glanced at his right hand and the end of his long-sleeved shirt; they looked the same.

Even though Warden Gene Perkins had set up the meeting, Whit didn't see the dark green Fish and Game truck. Driving around to the back of the building he found the vehicle parked hidden from the highway. Whit added up the possibilities. *Gene's working but doesn't want the public or his office to know he's here. That means he doesn't want anyone to know he's meeting with me, or he's drinking, or both. Though drinking this early would be very uncharacteristic for Mr. Straight Arrow, but I'm betting this meeting goes way beyond the reason he asked me here. Besides, Gene could have just told me over the phone the details of catching the bear poachers.*

The use of the Central House site started long before the Gold Rush. For thousands of years, a clan of California's Indians, known as Maidu, made temporary summer camps at the location. The clean cold spring near the top of the long, rounded ridge heading up the Sierra made a perfect stop for the indigenous people as they foraged upslope in the spring and downslope in the fall. This stable pattern of nomadic life began to erode in the first half of the 1800s as a growing number of easterners began migrating west. Even before the Gold Rush, this main ridge became one of the favored emigrant trails for settlers descending the Sierra. The emigrant trickle turned into a torrent after the discovery of gold in 1848. During the massive influx of fortune seekers, an enterprising sole named Evert Coldwell built a waystation at the spring. Later, following a heated argument and Evert's sudden and violent demise, a man named Strand took over the enterprise and added a stable. All beasts of burden needed periodic rest, plus food and water. All were available by Strand, for a price. As time passed, the site became a stage stop, including a hotel. Since the location resided ten miles east of Cedar Creek, the name Central House took hold. Following the invention of cars, another owner added a gas station and restaurant. By the 1970s the gas station disappeared and the restaurant turned into a popular red-meat roadhouse and bar. Central House became a perfect meeting spot for Gene Perkins and Whit for two reasons. The bar and restaurant happened to be exactly halfway in between Cedar Creek and Whit's cabin; and it was far enough out of town to avoid prying eyes or eavesdropping ears for two guys who weren't supposed to meet, talk or—for that matter—even like each other.

The small windows, sparse overhead lighting, and dark red tongue-and-groove Douglas fir heartwood walls made for a dimly lit bar. It took a while for Whit's eyes to adjust to the darkness. Whit liked quiet bars where a man could talk without yelling or asking someone to repeat what they had just said. Due to the smooth wood walls, the acoustics were terrible; but not a problem when only two people sat at the bar. Whit walked up to the familiar guy wearing green pants and a white t-shirt.

From about ten feet away, Gene looked up at the mirror behind the bar. He heard the tall, dark figure heading his way say, "Hey, Gene."

"Hey yourself, Whit."

Whit pointed to Gene's beer glass and asked, "So what are we drinking?"

"Not a lot of choices on tap. Coors Light."

Whit made a face, scoffed and said, "You know this place carries lots of your favorite high-octane microbrews in bottles."

Gene nodded and said, "Yeah, I know; but I'm still on the clock. An ice-cold Coors Light seemed safe." Turning toward Whit, Gene added, "Hey, I didn't screw up your work today, did I?"

"Na, I finished."

"Where?"

"Jesse Ray Bean and his kid Alex; down on their ranch, a small salvage sale."

"He's the big guy, right? One of the guys in your gang?" When Whit nodded Gene asked, "What do you call him, Sasquatch?"

"Tiny."

"Jesus, Whittingham, you and your nicknames. What do you call me behind my back?"

"Warden Perkins, of course."

"Bull."

"No, really, I haven't figured one out for…Mr. Clean yet; but I'm working on it. How about Pope Perkins?"

Gene groaned, but before he could respond, a heavyset bartender with a huge handlebar mustache came puffing up the stairs behind the bar with restocking supplies. He said, "Hey, Whit, sorry; I didn't know anyone came in except," he tipped his head toward Gene, "the fish cop."

"No problem; I just walked in." Mocking Gene, Whit said, "Can you fetch me one of them there tasty Coors Lights on tap?"

Putting down the cardboard box full of various bottles of embalming fluid, the huge handlebar mustache moved up and down, "Coming right up; frozen glass?"

"That's probably a must."

After delivering Whit's beer, Igor the giant Mustache, actually his name was Butch, said, "Yell if you need anything." Pointing to the office he added, "I need to do some paperwork."

As he wandered off to the equally dimly lit office, Whit said, "Will do; thanks, Butch."

After a big gulp of his own beer, Gene said, "That heads-up you gave me on the bear poaching went down last night. You were right; it was the Jameson brothers, with the full blessing of that attorney, Amed Azeradi. We took telephoto shots of the brothers receiving money from Amed at his front door, right on cue, before the bust. The dogs found the gut pile near the property line you ran for that adjacent landowner. The bear, a two-year-old, was right there also…minus its paws and gallbladder. We found those in Amed's freezer. With the rifle and bear blood still in the brother's truck, and the contraband in Amed's freezer, they're all going down. Hopefully if we make it ugly enough on Azeradi, he'll give up who and how he transfers the bear parts to the Orient."

"Nice; you do good work, Pope Perkins."

Pointing a finger at Whit, Gene shot back, "Do not give me that nickname; I mean it."

Whit put his palms up and with a big bluish grin, crossed his heart and said, "Promise."

"Okay. Anyway, if you hadn't found that gut pile, chances are the killing would have gone on. Azeradi's property can only be accessed through the gate near his house. All his property backs up to the national forest land except that one property line you flagged. All in all, a pretty safe operation for poaching a bear or two a year. Thanks, Whit."

"My pleasure. Like I said, I hate poachers as much as you."

They sat in silence for quite some time. Whit waited for Gene to cough up the real reason he'd arranged the meeting. Obviously, the ice-cold Coors Light was not a celebratory beer. Gene was making little funny faces like he was trying to figure out how to start. Whit decided to end Gene's torment. "You better start before your insides blow up."

"That obvious?"

"You have a one-word neon sign over your head flashing 'Guilty.'"

Gene turned to Whit and let it fly. "That incident on the highway with you, that guy and the dead doe and fawn? It cropped up again."

After a long pause, Whit said, "I thought you had that...shelved?"

"I thought so, too."

They both fell silent as Gene spun his beer glass in slow circles. Gene saw his participation in the incident reel off clearly in his mind.

The chubby polyester-suited guy, a realtor named Alan Barbou, excitedly spilled his guts out to the newly transferred, very dedicated and hardnosed Fish and Game Warden, Gene Perkins. They were standing off the south side of the highway at the scene of the accident.

Mr. Polyester flapped his arms and babbled endlessly about the crazy killer that went berserk.

Warden Perkins interrupted. "Mr. Barbou, slow down. I can only write so fast, and you're bouncing all over the place."

"Sorry, Officer; it's just the guy went nuts, crazy. I'm lucky to be alive."

"Yes sir, and it's Warden, Warden Perkins. So he was tailgating you?"

"Yeah, right on my ass; I wouldn't have hit the thing, the deer, ah black-tail, otherwise. I was watching my rearview mirror when it ran out in front of me."

"Go on."

"So I stop, and this guy stops and he's all crazy and like, happy I hit the deer."

"Happy? Really? You'd call his mood happy?" Gene pressed.

"Yeah, yeah; ecstatic."

Looking at his notes, Gene asked, "Right; and that's when he kills the doe with the ax, then goes back to his truck and pulls out a rifle and shoots the fawn?"

"Yeah, that's right; he didn't say nothing just...wham."

"And he shot across the highway?"

"Wham," Mr. Barbou said again for effect. Then he pointed and added, "From his truck right over there."

"Did you notice if he loaded the rifle, or just took it out of the truck and shot?"

"He just pulled out his rifle and...wham."

Warden Perkins said to himself, *Plenty for an arrest now.* To Mr. Barbou he asked, "Then he—"

"He grabs this big knife and, and starts walking toward me, but I pick up my tire iron, so he stops. Then he turns and heads over to the deer and cuts a big chunk off, puts it in his truck and drives away."

Perkins puts a question mark behind the last statement, then asks, "Okay, I think I've got everything. But tell me...if he didn't assault you, how did you get that blood on your suit?"

"Oh, ah, that, well, it was, ah...oh, when he sort of attacked me. I forgot to tell you that part. Before he left he walked up to me and poked me in the chest and told me not to tell anyone about cutting up the deer and shooting the little one."

Warden Perkins finished writing then added three large question marks on his notepad. He thought, *I'm smelling some serious bullshit now, but I have a chopped-up doe and a shot-to-shit fawn. Sure as hell this city slicker didn't do it. Some homeboy just screwed up but good.* He asked Mr. Barbou, "You said the guy was tall, in Levi's and a white t-shirt. He had dark hair under a baseball cap. Do you remember any logo on the baseball cap?"

"No, but I remember his eyes; they were blue, really blue."

"And the truck, you said it was older and a dark color. See if you can recall the truck and tell me what color?"

Mr. Barbou put his hands over his eyes like his eyelids didn't work. He rocked back and forth a little then dropped his hands and said, "Blue, dark blue, and it had room behind the seat."

"Like an extended cab?"

"Yeah, because he reached in the back part to get the gun."

"Rifle?"

"Yeah, I mean rifle. Wham; it was loud."

Perkins had a pretty good idea he knew the truck and the owner. Warden Perkins wrote down, Benjamin Whittingham and circled it twice. "I think I have what I need. You have my card and I have your contact information. Call if you can think of anything else."

"Thanks, Officer, and thanks for bending my fender back so I can drive."

"No problem, Mr. Barbou…and it's Warden."

Warden Perkins walked back to his truck and sat in the driver's seat with the door open. One of the two sheriff officers at the scene came up to Gene and told him to expect Sheriff Whittingham in about five minutes. Gene thanked him, then took off his hat and rested his head on the headrest. Gene thought, *If it's Benjamin Whittingham, I'm about to arrest the county sheriff's son. This could turn out really good or really bad.* Perkins turned his head sideways and watched the white Volvo with the dented front bumper and fender pull away.

"Gene?" Whit tried a little louder. "Gene?"

Gene slowly said, "Yeah?"

"Christ, my dad does that. You just went blank. Where the hell did you go?"

"Oh, sorry, Whit; flashed on the deer incident and what that realtor, Barbou, said at the scene. How long was I in a stupor?"

"You went blank for about a minute or so. I thought you may have been stroking out; but like I said, my dad does that sometimes."

"Okay, sorry; where were we?"

"You tell me."

"Right. Some bigshot San Francisco animal rights attorney has the transcript of the initial report I radioed in to dispatch, as well as my notes at the scene. Plus, my official report later. As you know, they don't match. You ever heard of a Luna Waxman from Earth Wild?"

"No, but I sure as hell have heard of Earth Wild. They're deep ecology types. They give equal value to all of nature's creatures, except humans and domestic livestock, of course. Good intentions gone haywire. Many of the clients they represent take in wounded or abandoned wild animals to rehabilitate them. The dirty little secret...predators nail rehabbed critters soon after those bleeding hearts let them go. Abandoned young and injured birds and mammals stuck in a cage, coddled and dependent on human contact stick out like a sore thumb in nature. Predators look for nuances, a tipoff that something's not right. A deer with a slight limp, a bird not flying quite right, a nice fat pen-fed animal, slow and out of shape, makes an easy meal for observant hungry killers. The only good coming out of Earth Wild's client's programs...they provide high-protein meals for animals higher up the food chain."

"Nice diatribe, Whittingham."

"Don't give me that, Gene. You know most of those animals don't live long after they're freed."

"Yeah, so what? Hell, Whit, most young in the wild don't survive their first year either...Wildlife Population Dynamics 101. You know that, I know that," Gene pointed over his shoulder, "but most of the public doesn't know that and, more importantly, they don't want to hear it. For me or anyone in the department to acknowledge that point amounts to political, social and career suicide. Why step in it?"

"The truth will set you free."

"Bullshit, Whittingham, and you know it. This is a Bambi-educated and dominated country. Everyone loves their pets and the image that nothing suffers. The average person knows more about astrophysics than they do about life and death in the wild." Taking a sip of his beer, Gene asked, "Can we park this discussion for another day and get back to—"

"Why you asked me here?"

"Jesus, you interrupt worse than your dad."

"I was not interrupting; I just finished your sentence."

"It's the same damn thing and you know it."

"Geez, Grumpy, got a turd stuck sideways?"

"I do not have, I am not...you Whittinghams could piss off a saint." When Gene saw Whit smirking, he turned away and exhaled heavily. "You're dicking with me again, aren't you? Damn you, Whittingham; this is serious stuff."

"I know, I know; hey, it's my ass hanging out here...not yours. It's just that you can't get over your guilt; it makes you too easy to tease and get all worked up. I'm going to tell you for the last time; it's not your fault. If I had dealt with that issue differently, better, or as my dad said...properly, this whole mess would never have happened."

"Okay, okay, no more guilt trip; I got it. Now listen. Earth Wild has pull and keeps pressuring the DFG's bigwigs in Sacramento to pursue prosecution. This Luna Waxman has the ear of some senior state senators and assemblymen too. Our 'appointed' DFG director wants action. Waxman threatens to sue the department if it doesn't act."

Whit stayed quiet for some time, then said, "Well, water under the bridge at this point; I did it."

"Yeah, but not the way I initially called it in. When I transferred here I thought if I nailed a local, a real rebel, I'd put poachers on notice, make them think twice. Because your name is mud at the office, I figured you were my target. I jumped at the chance to nail your ass without...all the facts, or really knowing you. I blew it and now...." Gene's voice trailed as he shook his head and looked down at his beer.

"Gene." No response, so Whit said, "Hey, Warden Perkins."

"Yeah, I'm listening."

"How did some bigshot San Francisco animal rights attorney get a copy of that initial report, and why?"

Gene responded, "That's a good question. Don't know, but someone wants your ass, that's for sure."

"Fish and Game?"

"No. All the way to the top they just want this to go away. No, it's someone else, someone with the muscle to get Earth Wild involved and make the department's brass sweat fear and shit purple bricks. They're judge-shopping right now, and they have my notes from the scene and the statement of that dickhead civilian that hit the doe. He swears his version of the incident fits exactly with what happened. I heard his taped statement; it came off rehearsed and he sounded scared to death. Someone got to him, threatened him. I'm sure of it."

"So how will this go down?"

"If they get the local superior court judge to bow out, due to you being the Sheriff's son, they'll push for a Bay Area superior court judge, a guy named Jerry Franklin."

"Never heard of him. What's the bottom line here, Gene?"

"You remember when the Berkeley city council passed civil rights for pets inside the city limits?"

"Sure. I was going to CAL at the time, but it was overturned. Animals don't have human rights, not in our Constitution; sane minds prevailed."

"Right. But one superior court judge did side with the city council. Can you guess his name?"

"Holy crap."

"No; Jerry Franklin."

Only the occasional clicking of Butch's chubby fingers on an old adding machine pierced the silence. The beer kept getting warmer, but no one drank.

Finally, Whit asked, "So Franklin takes over. What's the worst-case scenario?"

Gene turned and looked Whit straight on. "Best case, plea bargain down to misdemeanors, if possible, so you can keep your guns and continue to hunt; shoot for reduced fines and probation. Unfortunately, that Waxman gash wants jail time."

"Screw that and screw her; I'll go to trial."

Incredulous, Gene shot back, "Shit, Whittingham, you nearly decapitated a wounded doe and shot a goddamn fawn. You will not survive a jury trial. The judge, the jury, Earth Wild, the press and the public will crucify you. They'll lock you up and throw away the key."

Whit stared at the bar for a full minute then stood up. He put a fiver on the bar then turned and put his right hand on Gene's shoulder. "I'm heading back to the cabin. I need to think. How much time do I have?"

"It's on the fast track; weeks…a month, tops."

Whit smiled at his friend. "Thanks for the heads-up." As he turned and walked out, he said over his shoulder, "At least now I know why you're drinking at two in the afternoon."

From the office Butch asked, "Need another beer?"

Whit said, "No thanks, Butch; catch you next time."

Gene downed his beer and slid Whit's barely touched beer over.

Butch asked, "How about you?"

Gene said, "No, I'm good." Looking at himself in the bar mirror, he shook his head and said to himself, *Shit, I'm a long way from good.*

Chapter Fourteen
Nature's Dark Side

After leaving his fish cop buddy at the Central House bar, Whit drove east and north toward his cabin without seeing one deer. However, deer were definitely on his mind. Whit's brain churned in turmoil. Warden Perkin's revelation that the Fish and Game would very likely bring multiple charges against one Benjamin Whittingham caused him to take seriously what he had up to this point figured would just fade away.

Whit needed to switch gears and focus on finishing a quick and dirty 20-percent cruise to estimate volume of the salvage timber he'd marked earlier this morning. The only problem, Whit could not apply his mental energy to anything other than his impending court case.

Finally reaching his cabin, Whit backed in to his parking spot and killed the engine. Walking to the cabin and up the porch, Whit looked for his pet but didn't see her. He sat down on his covered porch swing. Leaning over, Whit pulled an oatmeal stout out of his kindling box by the front door. Whit believed dark beers tasted better cool, not cold. Rocking slowly, Whit thought about Gene Perkins. Back then, the day of the deer incident, Whit didn't even know the warden, not by sight anyway. Peripherally, he'd learned a new hotshot fish cop had recently transferred to Logan County. That all abruptly changed with their terse introduction, volatile encounter and Whit's subsequent arrest...well, sort-of arrest. Whit remembered clearly, Perkins personified a high-collared, holier-than-thou, by-the-book, grade-A, number-1, Iowa corn-fed royal pain in the ass that day. *So much for first impressions.* Shaking his head, Whit finally gave in, closed his eyes and let the whole miserable stupid event slowly play out.

It was early summer and prime killing season. Most animals higher up the food chain give birth in late spring or early summer. They evolved to bear young early enough in the year to allow their offspring enough time to take advantage of as much maturing as possible before winter. Black-tail deer fit right in with this scenario. Nearly all of the black-tail doe, especially in the foothills, had already dropped their fawns. As spring advanced, forbs and brush species flushed with tasty new shoots and leaves. The does and their little followers moved up elevation as the plants progressively broke bud up the west slopes of the Sierra. Bob cats, coyotes, mountain lions and occasionally an opportunistic bear took advantage of individual deer in this annual migration as they, too, knew the drill well. Domestic dogs, often packs of them, also ran down and killed fawns and even older deer. *The predator/prey cycle of life and death, advancing through another year.*

But there was another killer waiting for victims and, just like domestic dogs, in ever increasing numbers. The explosion of people fleeing LA, the Bay Area, and other urban centers to take refuge in "the mountains" inundated the narrow foothill and mountain roads with more and more vehicles. Just crossing roads became a game of Russian roulette for wildlife. The blood splatters, carcasses, and all too common smell of rotting flesh permeating the air gave evidence to the success of these killers. In nature, predators of black-tail always focused on the weak, sick, young, old and dying. Their success and ultimate survival depended on expending as little effort and energy as possible for maximum gain; therefore, easy kills always took precedence. *Natural selection at its finest and cruelest, but that's the system.*

To the terrified individual critter dragged down and violently slain, nature provides no compassion, mercy or remorse. To the black-tail as a whole, the cropping of the inferior and easy-to-kill continued to promote genetic superiority and the best chance for the continued survival of the species. Cars, on the other hand, kill and maim indiscriminately. The healthiest doe or the fittest buck dashing across a road reverted instantly to one of the weak or dying after an encounter with rolling steel.

Whit knew this well as his main wildlife biologist at UC Berkeley drilled that stark reality into all of his students' heads. He spent decades conducting experiments, leading research projects and just observing the interaction of animals in the wild on every continent. An eloquent speaker and educator, he passed on the knowledge of the cycles of life and death. His most fundamental point: You cannot revel in the beauty and majesty of nature without knowing and understanding completely how it works. And to do that, you must accept, in nature, what appears to be cruel and savage as well. You can't have one without the other. *Razor sharp claws, dagger-like fangs, powerful bone-crushing jaws, body-puncturing talons and toxic venom evolved for a reason.*

Once you get it and see how perfectly it fits, you can never go back. That was Whit's mindset then and his mindset the day he pulled his truck around a sweeping left turn on the highway heading toward his cabin. He first noticed a white Volvo partially in his lane and partially off the road. A rather plump man, about Whit's age, stood in a polyester suit next to his front fender. A female sat in the passenger seat stoically looking forward. The heavyset guy had a tire iron and kept trying to pry his crumpled bumper away from his left front tire. As Whit pulled off of the highway, to the right and about fifty feet behind the Volvo, he noticed movement to his left. The other half of the accident, a young doe struggling to rise, lay in the ditch on the opposite side of the pavement. Her desperate attempts were pointless as her shattered left hip and hind quarters painfully refused to respond.

As Whit exited his truck, the guy said, "The stupid thing just ran right out in front of me. It crunched my fender into my tire." When Whit didn't respond, he added, "Now I'm going to be late for my conference in Tahoe."

Whit heard the guy but kept looking at the deer. Walking toward the man, Whit said, "It's not a stupid thing; it's a black-tail deer. Can't you see it's suffering?"

Polyester responded with, "Oh, you're breaking my heart. Look what it did to my car."

Pointing at the deer but looking at the man, Whit said, in a far-less-than-friendly tone, "Why didn't you put it out of its misery?"

"With what?" The man held up his right hand. "This tire iron? I'm not getting blood on my suit."

Whit glanced back at the struggling deer. Polyester said, "Hey, man, you going to help—"

The guy never finished his sentence as Whit snapped his head around and pointed his index finger at the man's face and said, "Shut up."

In the brief pin-dropping silence that ensued, Whit spun his boots around and walked back to his truck. He reached back into the pickup bed and pulled out his falling ax. Polyester dropped his tire iron and scurried around to the front of his car. But Whit didn't head his way; he walked briskly across the road and over to the doe.

She quit thrashing, almost like she knew her fate. The ground around her was torn up for quite a distance, and Whit realized the poor creature had been struggling and squirming for a considerable amount of time. As Whit reached the deer, she slowly and deliberately looked away from Whit toward the woods she would never reach. Whit just whispered, "Sorry, girl." He raised his ax and viciously drove the blade into the top of her neck. The blow nearly severed her head. At least her suffering had ceased. As Whit turned to leave, he noticed movement at the top of the cut bank.

Ahhhhh, hell, Whit's mind sadly registered. There stood a little fawn staring down at the whole scene. All it knew was to wait for its mother, but she wasn't coming. Whit could tell in an instant the pretty little bugger was too big to catch but too small to make it alone. With its survival tied to its mother, as soon as the car crushed her hip, the fawn's brief experience with life had ended, too. Starve, maybe; more likely a cat or coyote would find it and… Whit thought, *I hate witnessing the dark side of nature and being forced to deal with it. I know life-and-death struggles like this go on countless times every day. I accept it; I just don't like being the one to…end it.*

Whit's mind flashed to a few years back when he was cruising timber. He came upon a little fawn following a wild turkey. Obviously orphaned, the little four-legged beauty had attached itself to the bird. What was odd, the fairly young female turkey didn't seem to mind. The poor little lost soul stayed about ten feet behind the turkey the whole time Whit watched. It too was dead but didn't know it. Turkeys roost in trees at dusk to avoid night predators, not an option for the adopted young. Of course, it didn't make it. A profound sadness overwhelmed Whit.

The tubby guy said something, but Whit barely registered noise. He focused on listening for traffic then sprinted back to his truck. Whit popped the glove box and grabbed a 30.06 round. Then he reached under the back seat of the extended cab and pulled out an old cracked brown leather gun case. Sliding the zipper most of the way down, Whit grabbed his well-used Remington 700 rifle. As he stepped out of his truck, he pulled back the bolt and guided the bullet into the chamber. Sliding the bolt forward and locking it down, Whit raised the rifle to his shoulder and released the safety.

The guy started yelling again but Whit ignored him. Checking for cars and hearing nothing coming, Whit took aim. He lined up the open sights on the fawn's chest. Right before pulling the trigger he said, "Tough luck, little one." Whit knew it died instantly. The only consolation for Whit, he delivered a quick death, a far less terrifying end than what awaited its brief motherless future.

"What kind of coldblooded psycho are you?" Whit heard Polyester clearly yell. Whit's profound indifference toward the creep turned to anger. *You clueless jerk! You race through the woods totally unprepared to deal with anything other than your own selfish self-interests. Then you hit an animal and have no problem standing by and letting it suffer. And I'm the coldblooded psycho.*

Whit was just about to march over to Mr. Polyester and explain in no uncertain terms who had really killed the two deer when he thought of something else. *You want psycho, you ass, I'll show you psycho.*

Whit ejected the shell and picked it up. Leaning into his truck, he tossed the shell onto his bench seat then set the end of the rifle barrel on the floorboard of the passenger side and leaned the rifle against the door. He then reached up into his glove box and grabbed his skinning knife. He walked straight to the doe and skinned back a large chunk of hide. Cutting the back strap off of the undamaged hind quarter, Whit stood up and listened; still no traffic. He sprinted back to his truck, popped the tool box lid and rested the venison on top of his rain gear. He closed the tool box and marched over to the now completely terrified driver. Polyester tried to get in the driver's door, but the scared-to-death woman in the car had locked the doors. The guy just froze at his driver's door with his hands up, palms out.

Whit walked up to Polyester only stopping when one foot separated their faces. While staring eye to eye, Whit poked Polyester in the chest with two bloody fingers. Whit hissed, "Next time you come driving in the woods, make sure you carry something to humanely kill an animal if you hit it. Got it?"

The guy's eyes were huge as he nodded his head vigorously.

With that, Whit walked back to his truck and pulled a rag out of the driver's door cubbyhole. He poured water from his canteen onto the rag and wiped off his hands. After hopping in his truck and starting the engine, Whit slowly pulled out and drove past the Volvo.

The guy held up his hands and mouthed, "You just going to leave me here?" Whit just looked forward as he drove and gave Polyester the finger.

Whit could still smell the deer's blood as he drove. She was a young but very healthy doe; her little frantic fawn also looked in good shape; how sad.

Still sullen when he reached his cabin, Whit scanned his premises looking for his pet, Stinker, the ring-tailed cat he had rescued as a kitten. She was nowhere in sight.

Whit's mind mulled over the dichotomy of saving a kitten and killing a fawn. Most people like "Mr. Polyester" wouldn't understand the difference. But in Whit's world, he knew he could save the ring-tailed cat; he also knew he couldn't do the same for the fawn. In both cases, Whit intervened and disrupted a little part of the natural process. His wildlife biologist at Berkeley would have disapproved. *Let the dark side of nature take its course, Whittingham, you hypocritical pussy.* In reality, Whit should have just walked away from Stinker and the fawn, but he couldn't. The difference wasn't saving Stinker; hell, most people would have done exactly the same. Whit knew what separated himself from nearly everyone else was the fact that, knowing the ultimate fate of the fawn, he could line up the sights and squeeze the trigger.

Pulling the venison and rain gear out of his toolbox, Whit walked over to his faucet beside the front porch steps and twisted the shutoff. The iron pipes were old, and Whit let the rusty red water run until it cleared. He rinsed off the rain gear and threw it over the railing. After washing off the meat, he climbed up the three steps to the porch and entered his cabin.

Finding the biggest plate he owned, he folded the meat in half and put it in his propane refrigerator. Outside again, Whit brought in the food and supplies he'd purchased along with his rifle and skinning knife. After putting the food and supplies away, Whit cleaned and sharpened his knife, then grabbed his cleaning kit and a beer. Sitting at his wide plank table, he drank his beer and cleaned his rifle. Whit became madder and madder. Every time Whit lost his temper, eventually, he'd kick himself for losing control.

Whit's dad always told him, "*Use your brain, not your brain stem; your mind is stronger than your fists. When you blow up and start swearing or swinging, you've already lost.*"

Whit slammed the table and almost upended his beer. Something about that guy just lit Whit up. Whit didn't care much for the guy being out of shape, wearing that stupid-looking suit or his fancy car, but that wasn't it. It wasn't even the jerk's selfish concern for himself. It was his cavalier indifference toward a suffering animal that sent him over the edge. But scaring the crap out of the guy and ruining his jacket fixed...what? Did it bring the two deer back or change the guy's narcissism?

Hell, I didn't even get his car off the road. No, I just embarrassed the guy in front of his wife, girlfriend...maybe his hooker? Whit concluded she had really poor taste. But that still didn't give him any reason to act the way he did. *Way to go, Whittingham; you just proved there were two jerks out there on that bend of the road. Well, maybe we both learned a lesson today...or maybe not.*

Walking out to his front porch, Whit returned to the present just long enough to take another swig of his beer and stuff a canvas pillow behind his lower back. He set back into his swaybacked two-seater porch swing. Comfortable again, Whit started thinking about the ring-tailed cat. She definitely didn't need any help surviving now. When he was at the cabin, they just happened to occupy the same space. As Whit so often did, his memory took him back to the day he found the baby ring-tailed cat.

While out working, this time down in the foothills, Whit stopped walking and listened. He swore he had heard a faint cry. Eventually, he heard it again and slowly walked in the direction of the noise. Next to a small hole in a rotten white oak stump he found a little pile of fur.

Whit knew it was a ringed tail, but ring-tailed cats usually denned in rotten pockets or cavities up in trees. This little one's parents chose a hollow cavity in the stump. Something must have happened to the male because the female was forced to leave the den to feed. She, too, probably became someone's dinner, a great-horned owl or bobcat maybe, who knows?

The ring-tailed cat's young had dehydrated and withered away. The fuzz ball was the only one left alive and in desperation had exited the den. Too weak to be frightened, she drank a little of Whit's water, then a little more. All Whit had to eat was an apple and a peanut butter and jam sandwich. Whit waited until she drank again, then started sticking little specks of peanut butter on her nose. Eventually, she slowly licked each dollop away. Since one common name for ring-tails was pole cat, Whit decided if she lived, he'd call her Stinker.

Cutting the day short, Whit drove back into town and stopped at Pete's Place. As he walked up to the bar he asked Stacey, "Hey, Bar Keep, how about a draft of Moose Drool and a saucer with a little half and half."

Stacey gave Whit an inquisitive look until he held up the little lint ball in his hand. When the dish hit the bar, Stinker's little tongue went to work; but after about a half-dozen licks Whit took the dish away, much to Stinker and Stacey's consternation.

Stacey barked, "Why are you being so cruel to that…whatever it is?"

Whit responded, "It's a ring-tailed cat and I'm not being cruel; she's very weak and dehydrated. This stuff is rich. We have to control how much she consumes so she won't overload her system. We're trying to save her, not save her to death."

Looking sideways at Whit, Stacey wrinkled her nose and gave his response some thought. Finally, she nodded and said, "Okay, Whittingham, I'll buy that. And, I'll buy that beer, too…if you let me keep the kitty."

"Stacey, she's a wild animal and not really a cat. Ring-tails are related to raccoons. She'll grow up to be one vicious killing machine and she'll stink. She has scent glands in her, near her…ah…butt area. If she's startled, threatened, or just wants to mark her boundary, this little girl will raise quite an odor."

"Like a skunk?" Stacey asked.

"Close enough to be unpleasant."

"Oh," Stacey responded, then added, "Well, hell, then you keep her and you can pay for your own beer…two and a quarter."

Stinker's lucky day took place not quite two years ago, and she'd lorded over Whit's cabin ever since. Not seeing Stinker in the daytime was common. Being a nocturnal predator, she probably dozed off under the cabin or maybe in a tree near the pond where she could stay cooler and feel safer. Stinker could leave anytime she wanted, but she didn't. Whit guessed she'd move down elevation to her home range the first winter, but since the bug, rat, mice and vole population around Whit's cabin made hunting fairly easy, she stayed. Plus, her natural competitors and predators seem to give Whit's place a wide berth. Miners during the gold rush domesticated ring-tailed cats for the same reason…rodent control. That's what gave Whit the idea when he found Stinker. Unfortunately, her scent glands developed, and she did a fine job of marking her territory. Though she came indoors, she preferred outside. When in the cabin, Stinker kept her odiferous tendencies in check, for the most part, which Whit appreciated.

Whit felt an almost imperceptible movement. He opened his eyes and observed Stinker had slipped up beside him without making a sound; she barely made the swing shift. From two feet away she warily watched him. He slowly leaned forward and found her tuna can under the swing. Sliding it forward, Whit poured a little of his stout into her dish. Stinker hopped down and, after checking her surrounding, moved in. She quickly recognized the aroma and started licking. Whit realized he was daydreaming again and that made him angry. *I need to figure out what the hell to do about this court case and my mind just drifts off. I need help; this is way out of my league. I have to talk to my dad.*

Chapter Fifteen
No Bull, Warden

Exiting the Central House bar after finishing Whit's warm Coors Light, Gene squinted at the bright afternoon sun. His stomach felt sour, and he knew it wasn't because of the two beers. Regardless of what Whit said, Gene felt guilty for Whit's predicament. *I pushed for a big bust, didn't add up the evidence properly and walled off that little voice in my head that said Barbou's statement amounted to bullshit. I created and dumped this shit storm on Whit...damn.* Gene unlocked his truck, reached in and grabbed his shirt. After buttoning and tucking it in, Gene hopped into the driver's seat. He dropped his head back on the headrest and closed his eyes. Now it was Gene's turn to relive the mess he created that day.

Hearing a throaty cruiser pull up behind his truck, Gene knew the sheriff of Logan County had just arrived. Gene put down his notes and the list of Fish and Game violations he figured Benjamin Whittingham violated. He'd already called dispatch requesting the State codes for discharging a firearm across a state highway and willfully leaving the scene of an accident. Gene thought, *Well, it appears the sheriff's son has just handed the department a clean bust on a silver platter; time to see how Daddy will take it.*

Sliding out of his dark green truck and walking back to the sheriff's sedan, Gene Perkins watched Sheriff Bill Whittingham exit his vehicle. He figured the sheriff to be around sixty, tall and lean with a slight belly. Gene observed the sheriff exhibited a small but detectable hitch in his gait. When they were a couple of feet apart, Gene noticed the veins on the sheriff's nose and cheeks. *Looks like a certain county officer likes his cocktails.*

The sheriff spoke first while sticking out his hand. "Good afternoon, Warden."

Taking the sheriff's healthy grip Gene replied, "Gene Perkins, Sheriff."

"Call me Bill; I apologize for not stopping by your office and meeting you before now. I'm usually more prompt to visit new peace officers assigned to…my jurisdiction."

With the sheriff's emphasis on "my juristiction", Gene thought. *Well, the pissing match begins; okay.* Gene replied, "I'm sure as a small, rural county sheriff, you perform many mundane civic duties and community functions that keep you quite busy."

Prick, Bill Whittingham thought, then said, "Oh, you're right; this little detour to meet you took me away from a very important PTA meeting."

"Good one, Sheriff."

Sheriff Whittingham responded, "You're not so bad yourself, Warden. I tell you what, let's cut the bullshit and get down to killing snakes, shall we?"

"Fine with me. I have pretty clear evidence that—"

"I know this has something to do with my son, Sheriff Whittingham cut in. "One of my officers heard the description of the…person of interest."

Exasperated, Gene said, "Sheriff, I'm going to try very hard to work co-operatively with you. But I have to tell you, I hate being interrupted."

Another stare-down; Sheriff Whittingham thought, *Well, at least he has balls.* Finally, he offered his most sincere grin and said, "Okay, Warden, you have the floor."

"I have an eyewitness who says that the, ah…person of interest drove an older pickup, was tailgating and—"

"Not my son."

Pursing his lips and looking up, Warden Perkins fumed, but remained silent.

Sheriff Whittingham offered, "Sorry; bad habit, but not my son."

Staring at the sheriff for a few seconds, Gene tried again slowly and deliberately. "The individual, a Mr. Barbou, stated he was focused on the tailgater in the rearview mirror and didn't notice the deer crossing the road. The deer's hind quarters drove the Volvo's fender into the front left tire forcing him to stop. The person of interest did also. Mr. Barbou said the guy acted excited and ran across the road with an ax and killed the doe." Pointing to the dead doe, Warden Perkins emphasized, "Right over there. After the individual killed the doe, he looked up and saw the fawn. He ran back to his truck and pulled out a loaded rifle. He shot and killed the fawn from this side of the highway. The fawn's body lies on the top of the cut bank."

Gene waited for a response, but Sheriff Whittingham remained silent. "Then the guy took a big knife and cut a hunk of the doe's back strap. After putting the venison in his truck's toolbox, he approached Mr. Barbou and threatened him. I saw bloody smudges on Mr. Barbou's jacket. The person of interest told Mr. Barbou not to mention a word about what he'd done to the doe or the fawn. Then he drove off without helping Mr. Barbou. The description of the person of interest matches closely to your son; so does the description of the truck. Does what happened here sound like your son?"

Sheriff Whittingham thought, *How in the hell does this new transfer know what my son and his truck look like? Sounds like the Fish and Game had their sights on Ben before today. I better store that little tidbit for later.* Looking at the warden, Sheriff Whittingham replied, "Well, some of it; putting the doe out of its misery sounds like Ben. And shooting the fawn, if it was too big to catch, does too. But he doesn't tailgate; his truck's older and very low geared. He couldn't tailgate if he wanted to. And Ben never leaves any guns loaded in his truck; never. Are you sure about all this?"

"As sure as I can be with the evidence and the eyewitness," Gene replied.

Sheriff Whittingham rubbed his chin a while then said, "Okay, Warden Perkins, let's go have a look at the doe and fawn, then go visit my son."

"Oh, you're not coming with me; no way. These are Fish and Game violations."

"Think about it, Warden; your victim claims Ben…or the person of interest, shot across a state highway, threatened your witness, left the scene of an accident and didn't leave any identification. Those are not Fish and Game violations. So, I'm in. Besides, there are two other very good reasons why you need me along."

"And what would those be, pray tell?" Gene asked sarcastically.

"Ben's locked gate resides about three-quarters of a mile from his cabin; I know the combination."

"I get it that you're not going to tell me the combination. So, what's the other reason?"

"I know my son. You're acting like you're ready to make an arrest. If Ben thinks he's in the right, your encounter could get...ugly."

"Don't you worry one little bit about me, Sheriff; I can take care of myself."

"It's not you I'm worried about, Warden."

Gene Perkins stood there staring at Sheriff Whittingham, not sure how to proceed. Weighing the pros and cons, he decided that angering the local sheriff any more than he already had would cause too much future bad blood between their offices. Plus, arresting the sheriff's son, which he already planned to do, with his truck and radio contact three-quarters of a mile away, seemed far less than optimal. Looking down, then back at Sheriff Whittingham, Gene shrugged and said, "Okay, Sheriff, but before we go, let's look at those deer. I'm curious to see how old and developed that little fawn is."

"Was," Sheriff Whittingham corrected Gene as he turned to head across the road.

Oblivious to his dad's and Warden Perkin's surly confrontation and impending visit to his cabin, Whit realized Stinker must have smelled venison as she showed up in the cabin just as Whit started a fire in the stove. Whit retrieved the venison from his propane refrigerator and cut off a nice dark red slab. Stinker climbed right up Whit's pant leg and grabbed the meat. Fortunately, she only used just enough of her pointy hooked claws to grip the denim and left most of Whit's leg puncture-free. Stinker backed her way down his leg and took her treat to the hearth. About halfway through her meal, she popped her ears up then snapped her head around toward the front of the cabin.

"What do you hear, you little piglet?"

Stinker responded by grabbing the rest of her dinner and darting for her tiny little door, exiting onto the back porch. Whit made the opening so that Stinker could just barely squeeze through. Anything bigger couldn't get in, and anything smaller Stinker could handle.

Finally, Whit heard what his little furry early warning system detected. It was a vehicle; no...two vehicles. *Who the hell is this?* Whit grabbed his .45, pulled back the receiver to make sure a round was in the chamber, and checked the safety. He guided the automatic inside his pants and covered it with his t-shirt. The cold metal rested in the small of his back. Opening the front door, Whit walked to the end of the porch.

What's my old man do….ab, crap, Fish and Game. Okay, be cool, Whittingham. Whit backed into the house, slipped out his automatic, and put it in the wooden box just inside the door he used for muddy boots. Whit took a jacket off of a hook beside the door and dropped it in the box. Walking down the steps and out the walkway, he watched his dad step out of his patrol car. Whit knew his dad's mannerisms well; his dad's body language conveyed trouble, concern, apprehension. The Fish and Game guy, Whit did not know; then he thought, *Oh, the new guy.* The warden was standing outside his truck talking on the radio. Whit's dad didn't wait for the warden and walked up to his son. Just as Sheriff Whittingham reached his son, the warden signed off and started heading in their direction. The warden's gait appeared upright and stiff; Whit thought he walked like he had a 2x4 stuck up his ass. Whit guessed, *Stuffed shirt.*

"Hey, Pa, am I in trouble again?"

"Appears so, Ben; the deer incident?"

"Yeah, that was me."

Bill Whittingham tightened his lips and looked down. Whit hated that look; it meant he let his dad down. But Bill just said, "Figured; we're here, I hope, to listen to your side." Whit's dad stuck his thumb backwards and added, "Then we'll see what stuffed shirt wants to do."

Whit smirked at his dad's last sentence.

Whit's dad added, "There's nothing funny about this, Ben. This guy seems like a hard ass."

"I lost my cool a little, Dad, with the guy; but I didn't do anything to those deer you wouldn't have done. Probably no different than ole stuffed shirt heading this way would have done."

"Did you threaten the guy?"

"Poked him in the chest and told him to carry something to humanely kill a wounded animal, if he ever hit one again."

Whit's dad just closed his eyes and shook his head. He heard the warden approach and turned to make introductions. "Gene Perkins, this is my son, Benjamin Whittingham."

Gene could read the concern in the sheriff's voice. He thought, *I need to take control right now and end this quick.*

Gene and Whit nodded but didn't shake hands or speak. Bill stepped back and sideways to allow the two combatants to face off.

Gene started. "Were you the guy in the truck who—"

"Yeah, that was me."

Whit's dad half whispered out of the side of his mouth, "Son, he doesn't like to be interrupted."

"You killed the doe?"

"No; Mr. Polyester did."

"You know what I mean; you used an axe on its neck?"

"Yes, I put it out—"

"You killed the fawn?"

"No," Whit replied. "Mr. Polyester did."

"You shoot the fawn?" Now Gene was raising his voice.

"Yes, I—"

"From across the road?"

"Yes, but—"

"You cut the back strap off that doe?"

"Yes, but that's because—"

Gene cut in. "You're under arrest for numerous violations of the California Fish and—"

"Whoa there, hotshot." Now it was Whit's dad jumping in. "Talk about interrupting; you're not even listening and jumping to conclusions. Let Ben finish a sentence."

Turning slightly toward the sheriff but keeping his eyes on Whit, Gene barked, "I don't need his statement for the violations under my jurisdiction. I have enough evidence and an eyewitness. He can give his statement in your jail because that's where he's going. If you interfere anymore, I will charge you with obstructing the lawful execution of my duties."

"Execution is right, you little…. I heard about you when you arrived; Big Bust Perkins, the super warden. You're making a very big—"

"Dad."

"Don't interrupt me, son."

"Dad," Whit raised his voice.

"What? Damn it, Ben."

"It's okay. I did it, but it's not what it appears. We can fix this, but not here and not now."

Gene Perkins cut in. "I wouldn't bet on it, Whittingham. I haven't lost a case this cut-and-dry yet."

Whit's dad turned and put his face right up against Gene's. "Well, you're going to fucking well lose this one."

Inching forward, Whit took his dad's arm and pulled him back. "Back off, Dad; you're not helping." Turning to Gene, Whit asked, "Can I talk to my dad, in private? We'll stand right here, then I'll come to your truck when we're done. What do you say?"

"No, you're com—"

The next instant Gene saw a flash of movement. Whit charged and slammed into Gene hard. Gene didn't have time to reach for his gun or even set himself defensively. Whit caught Gene around the chest in a bear hug driving him up in the air and slammed him painfully to the walkway. Just before Gene hit, Whit put his right hand behind Gene's head to cushion the blow and prevent a possible concussion. Whit heard the wind gush out of Gene's lungs as his body crashed on top of the warden's. Whit felt his own measure of pain as his knuckles and the back of his hands took the brunt of the impact with the ground. Regardless, he held on tightly. He looked down at the warden's waist and yelled to his shocked father, "Get his gun!"

Numbly, the sheriff of Logan County complied. Kneeling close to his son, he whispered, "Jesus, boy, what have you done?"

Climbing off the doubled-up and still gasping Fish and Game warden, Whit looked at the back of his bleeding hand and flicked off some partially imbedded gravel. Whit turned to his still stunned father. "Dad, I'll go with him, but not until he hears me out. He can have his big bad arrest if he's truly that big of an ass."

"Christ; you're putting me in a damn precarious situation here, boy. You assaulted a peace officer right in front of the sheriff of Logan County. By all rights, I now have to arrest you."

"Hold on a minute, Dad; let me play this out. I know guys like this; I doubt he'll tell anyone about me getting the drop on him; his ego won't let him. That leaves you off the hook."

Shaking his head, Bill Whittingham scolded, "You can't just go through life making up your own rules. If your mother was still alive she'd—"

"She's not; a moot point, Dad. Just let me say my piece and we'll let stuffed shirt here decide what to do. Okay?"

Sheriff Whittingham looked down at the gagging warden and said, "Okay." *My son's getting worse; living by his own code, never backing down. His mother saved me; stopped my fall...changed my life. Jesus, I hope there's a woman out there somewhere who can save Ben.*

They had to wait another minute until Warden Perkins could breathe, sort of. Still unable to speak, Whit lifted him up and grabbed the warden's belt as they walked toward the cabin. Gene stumbled at the base of the porch, so Ben grabbed his waist and basically carried him up the steps, then half dragged the warden into his cabin. Sitting Gene in a chair at the kitchen table, Whit's dad brought over a glass of water.

Bent forward in the chair, Gene, still in pain, finally wheezed through short breaths, "Assaulting...a peace officer...you're going...to prison....asshole." Turning his head sideways to glare at the sheriff, he added, "I'm gonna...have your badge."

Calmly, Whit said, "Warden Perkins, you're not really thinking this situation through. It's not going to be all your way or all my way; we're going to meet somewhere in the middle. I'm more like you than you think or know. Drink some water and let me at least say my piece."

The humiliated Gene Perkins finally started taking deeper breaths and was about to say fuck you but stopped himself. *I have to think how I play this. This is nuts; either these guys are crazy or I'm missing something huge here. They're like wild animals, docile one second then lashing out the next. I need time to think, get back in control.* Finally, Gene Perkins sat up, still holding his midsection. Looking at Whit he stuttered, "I'm listening...but it won't...make any difference."

"Thanks for being so open-minded, Warden."

For the next twelve minutes, Whit recited his version of the deer incident in great detail. Coming upon the damaged Volvo made more sense than the tailgate story. Gene had to admit his witness' version was self-aggrandizing and inconsistent now that he heard Whit's side. When Whit explained Polyester's indifference toward the doe's extended suffering, it triggered a mental image. *How could that doe have torn up so much ground in such a short time if Whittingham was right there during the accident? Barbou lied; that's not going to sell well to a judge.*

When Whit said he used the ax to put the doe out of its misery, he asked Gene, "You saw her shattered hip. What would you have done?"

Gene thought, *Shit, I would have killed it, too, but I would have had to shoot it.* Finally, Gene grudgingly admitted, "Same."

When Whit realized the fawn was too large to catch but too small to survive alone, he asked Gene, "Be honest, Warden, what would you have done, knowing its fate?"

Gene said, "I'd have left it to its fate…or shot it too, if there were no witnesses."

Whit said, "You and I both know I didn't have the luxury to wait. More than likely, that fawn would have spooked and finally wandered off. If I was going to prevent the poor little bastard from suffering a terrifying end, I had to take the shot right then and you know it."

Gene turned his head away from Whit to collect his thoughts. *Shit, my case is going down the tubes.*

When Polyester called Whit a cold-blooded psycho, Whit chose to scare the guy shitless instead of pummeling him. Besides, the doe was carrion at that point anyway; might as well teach the guy a lesson and use some of the poor critter to feed his pet. Whit asked Gene, "What would have been worse? That's what I thought at the time. Probably not the smartest move, but Polyester had gotten to me by then. That's why I didn't fix his car either and just drove off."

Gene sat there silent for quite some time, his mind buzzing. *Goddamnit; if I was in his shoes, knowing what I know now, I probably would have done pretty much the same. Shit, I should have heard him out. I assumed, or maybe I just wanted so badly to make Whittingham my big arrest. It seems like I was way off base about this Whittingham guy. I was too eager to prove myself; make a big splash. Now what do I do? I already called in the incident. Well, he still jumped me.*

"You still assaulted me and took my gun."

"Check your holster."

Looking down in amazement, Gene said, "Oh." Then he recovered enough to say, "Well, you still jumped me and took me prisoner."

"Do you want everyone at your office and our little town to know how easily I got the drop on you? And a prisoner, really? Were you tied up? Don't you have your gun?"

Sheriff Whittingham stepped in. "Warden, you gave Ben no choice." Then, looking at his son he said forcefully, "Though I don't condone tackling a peace officer to get his attention." Looking back at Gene, he continued. "You were bullying Ben, asking questions but not waiting for answers. You were forcing an arrest using very poor policing…and you know it. You had jumped to conclusions with only one side of the story. I can tell by the look on your face, you know I'm right."

Gene remembered what his lieutenant said: *"Don't let him get in your head." Well, damn it, I guess I don't have to try and figure out what the hell the lieutenant meant now. I have to keep them talking. I need time to think; these two have me all turned around.*

While Gene sat there absorbing, pondering, assessing, Sheriff Whittingham added, "You have a crappy witness to the deer incident and me as your only witness to Ben and your…altercation." Without saying it, but letting Gene know, if push came to shove, the sheriff would side with his son.

As Gene continued to stare blankly forward, Whit hit him with the pitch. "Look, Gene, I know you're a good fish cop and you care. But I'm not your enemy; neither's my dad. We can be your best allies going forward, or your worst nightmares. It all starts right here, right now."

Gene thought of something to buy more time and piped up. "Before I agree to anything, I need to know something. What happened to Sandy, the warden before me? How did you get to her?"

"You really want to go into that now?"

"Indulge me."

Whit said, "Okay, I'll try to go through this quickly. Sandy decided to come to the defense of your department's local environmental scientist; her name was Serine. I worked Serine over pretty hard on some pre-harvest inspections for logging plans and a few of your lake and stream alteration permits. Serine's a nice enough gal, just green. She's still packing more spots than that poor little fawn I shot, but she wears the badge. Serine tried to push her weight around without the knowledge, experience, or background to back up her demands. When she quoted a study or some research, often the work took place in ecosystems other than ours, or she'd cherry picked only parts or completely misinterpreted the results."

"Keep going." Sarcastically, Gene added, "I'm riveted."

"So, Warden Sandy figures I'm a bad guy and that I need my dick slapped. Without knowing me, she also figured I was a sexist for picking on a woman in a male-dominated field. Sandy decides to periodically stake out my cabin hoping to find a doe hanging in my shed, shooting ducks off my pond out of season, something illegal."

Gene hissed, "I hate poachers."

Whit nodded his head and said, "See, Warden, there you go; common ground, me too."

Whit's dad cut in. "Hey, you two, focus a little here. Let's resolve this so I know how to proceed. I still have the rest of the county to protect."

Whit continued. "Sorry, Dad." Turning back to Gene, Whit continued. "Okay, so being a local guy, I catch wind of Sandy's plan."

The cop in Gene jumped in and he asked, "Loose lips from someone in the department?"

Whit smiled and said, "Let's just say a little bird told me. So every morning just before light I'd walk out on my porch and yell, 'Good morning, Sandy. Kind of cold; you might as well come in for a hot cup of coffee.' It took about two or three weeks. I don't know how many times she actually hid out there, but she finally gave up and walked in, pissed off, just like you are now. We had coffee, I fixed her breakfast, and we talked. She found out I care about plants, animals, and their habitats just as much as she did. We became friends."

No one spoke for quite some time. Sheriff Whittingham stared at Gene and his son, anxious for a resolution. Finally, Gene Perkins stood up fairly straight but still held his middle with his left hand. He started toward Whit. Whit, leaning against his kitchen counter, knew he should shift forward and square himself at the approaching warden but didn't. Staring at each other from about five feet apart, Whit tightened up when Warden Gene Perkins stepped forward and uppercut Whit in the stomach. Due to his bruised chest, the blow struck with more gesture than force. Whit doubled over, but when he straightened up he gave the warden a slow grin. Gene tried to hold his stare but eventually cracked a little smile also. He said just loud enough for Whit to hear, "Asshole."

Whit replied, "Guilty." Then he asked, "So where do we go from here, Warden?"

Looking back and forth between the father and son, Gene finally said, "Okay, you two...good old boys, here's what we'll try. I'll squash the report, if I can. You're not very popular at the office, so no guarantees; but adding your side of the incident and leaving out the part where you tackled my ass will go a long way. Oh, by the way, I did feel you cradle my head so you didn't crack my skull. I didn't get it then, but I understand now."

Whit held up the back of his hand showing off his scraped knuckles and wrist. No one spoke for quite some time as it looked like Gene was not finished.

Finally, he added, "This is kind of new ground for me. If I find out you're bullshitting me, Whittingham, I'll ream you a new—"

"No bull, Warden." Whit put out his right hand and said, "And its Whit, to my friends."

Chapter Sixteen
Three to Two, Approved

Grey and Whit sat in Pete's Place nursing their first drinks. They met later than usual, knowing Ned planned to arrive late. Ned needed to attend the Cedar Creek City Council's regular, second Tuesday of the month, public meeting. The city planned to take an important vote on an issue that could negatively affect Ned's business.

Whit often stood, but tonight, sat in the last barstool to Grey's right. Whit called it the "assassin's corner." Grey called it the "paranoid's corner." Sitting or standing at the very end of the bar, Whit maintained a commanding view of the entire bar and both the front and back door. No one could approach without being observed. Whit's unreasonable wariness exceeded Grey's own, and Grey viewed that as excessive and unwarranted. But Whit grew up being that way, just like his dad.

Whit's stout and Grey's Captain Morgan and Coke were down to the last swallow when Stacey came by to ask if they were ready or wanted to wait for Ned. She addressed them by name, kind of. "Hey Moe, hey Curly, where's Larry?"

Grey put the fingers of his right hand together like saluting, turned to Whit, and placed his index finger against the bridge of his nose. Whit pretended to poke Grey in the eyes as Grey said, "Nyuck, nyuck, nyuck!"

Stacey crossed her arms, and without smiling said, "My lucky day, graced by a couple of real comedians."

Whit turned his head sideways, listened and said, "Speak of the devil; I hear Abe walking up to the back door."

Grey said, "Ah, bullshit, Whittingham."

Whit told Stacey, "You better pour him a stiff one, Stace. Something didn't go well at the meeting."

Stacey asked, "How can you tell?"

Whit said, "Abe's damn near dragging his feet."

When they heard the back door open. Grey looked at Stacey and whispered, "You know, it creeps me out when he does that."

Ned trudged in from the back room, nodded at his two buddies, checked out Stacey then sat to the left of Grey. When he landed, Ned gave out an audible huff.

Grey looked at Whit and reiterated, "You really creep me out when you do that."

Whit nodded at Stacey as she placed another pint of stout on the bar. He turned to Grey and said, "You just have to pay more attention to your surroundings. All your senses talk to you, you just don't listen."

Stacey came over with three ounces of Maker's Mark in a highball glass and one ice cube.

Ned smiled, tipped the glass to Stacey and took in a healthy mouthful. He closed his eyes as he felt the liquid Advil burn all the way down.

Whit said, "Might as well make room for that whiskey by getting out whatever's bottled up inside you, Abe."

After a deep breath, Ned said, "I'm mad as hell at the city council for approving the re-renovation of the mercantile building. An Office King's representative testified that if approved tonight, in phase one, his store's inventory could start arriving in as little as four weeks. With all the new people moving up here using chain stores, by the end of the year Penrose Stationery will be just a memory."

Grey said, "The scuttlebutt around town universally agreed that the council planned to deny the proposal and ask for more review."

Ned stared into his drink and said, "Hal Beldon flipped."

Surprised, Grey asked, "Bay Area Butthole Beldon, the guy who never approves anything?"

"Yep. He seemed super concerned about environmental impacts, traffic, parking, the lack of infrastructure mitigations, the impacts on small businesses like mine, everything. Then bam, they vote, he switches, and three-to-two, it's approved. The council, on Butthole Beld…damn it. Now you have me saying it. The council on Hal Beldon's recommendation approved fast tracking the permitting and forgoing nearly all of the mitigations."

Grey added, "Something about that Beldon. He gives me the creeps."

Whit interjected, "See, Milner, you can pay attention to your senses, if you try."

"No, it's not about sixth sense, understanding wild animals, hearing voices from the beyond or any of that crap." Whit just sipped his beer so Grey continued. "But something about him isn't right. How in the hell does a guy who moved up here, what, three or four years ago, get elected to city council?"

Ned took another hit of high octane medication then replied, "He did it the old-fashioned way, knocked on doors. He talked the talk to the constituents and spoke to nearly every club and organization in the incorporated area. The incumbent he beat thought he was popular enough that he didn't have to do the leg work. Beldon squeaked in by nineteen votes."

Grey backhanded Ned lightly on the shoulder. "Hey, look at the bright side; if your business goes down, you can work for me. You can add organic farmer to your resume."

"Why, need another scarecrow?"

Ned normally personified Mr. Sunshine. This new pattern of Ned's poor-pitiful-me alter ego concerned Whit and Grey.

Whit stepped into the fray. "Look, Abe, we know and understand you as well as anybody. You haven't cut back on your time and financial assistance to all your clubs, organizations and church. Maybe it's time to scale-."

"How do I do that, Whit? We all help people in a lot worse shape than me. I just can't cut them off."

Grey added, "Not cut them off; scale back. You can't help them long term if Penrose Stationery goes tits up."

Ned just stared into his drink and murmured, "Like I said, this all may be a moot point. Office King will send a rep to each school district and large business and undercut my prices. They can even absorb a loss at this new outlet until I'm gone. That's how it works."

Neither Whit nor Grey spoke, not knowing quite what to say.

Ned solved the issue by slamming his drink and turning to Whit and Grey. "Man, I'm a downer tonight; sorry, guys. Let's try it again next Tuesday." With that Ned stood up.

When Ned reached for his wallet, Whit said, "My treat tonight."

A little too loud, Ned shot back, "I can still afford my own drink."

Whit leaned forward and replied sternly in a low tone, "That's not what I meant or implied and you know it. I'm offering to buy my lifelong buddy and one of my closest friends a drink, nothing more." A little softer Whit added, "As to what happened to you and your store, we'll get through it together, like always, whatever happens."

Still standing, Ned shook his head and said, "Man...I am sorry; I guess I needed that. Jesus, I just turned into a little pussy back there."

Whit and Grey made identical hand gestures signifying Ned had turned into a big pussy. They all laughed as Ned walked behind his two friends and held their shoulders. He asserted, "Attitude adjustment complete, thanks guys. I think I'll let you two buy me another drink."

As Ned sat back down, Grey balked, "Hey, don't include me. It's all on Whit; I was fine with you leaving."

As Whit and Ned stood and turned on Grey, before they could attack, Grey put up his hands in surrender and said, "Okay, okay, I'll get the next round, geez."

Sitting back down, Whit asked Grey, "Tell me again, how many times?"

"How many times what?"

"How many times, when you were a baby, did your mom accidently drop you on your head?"

Ned laughed loudly. Whit and Grey smirked at each other; they knew they had their buddy back.

Chapter Seventeen
Hi, Can I Sit Next to You?

Ned didn't have a sale or even anyone enter his stationery store since three, so at four-thirty he closed early and headed for Pete's Place.

As he entered the bar, he noticed Stacey beside her cash register chatting it up with a muscular, tattooed guy in a tank top leaning hard over the bar. Ned exhaled audibly, closed the door, and headed for his usual barstool. Inexplicably and for unknown reasons, his barstool remained empty on Tuesday evenings until he filled it. Once he asked Stacey if she saved it for him. She dropped her head and gave Ned her patented dagger stare and replied, "In your dreams, Abe."

Ned plopped down and after Stacey turned away from the guy in the wifebeater t-shirt, said, "Hey, Stace."

While she dropped one ice cube into a highball glass and added a healthy load of Maker's Mark, she responded, "Hey yourself, Mr. Penrose Stationery. It's not Tuesday and you're earlier than normal. Close shop early?"

"Slow day. I called Grey; he's coming by too."

Knowing Ned's angst about the impending loss of business due to the new Office King opening in the old Logan County Mercantile building, she decided to change the subject. "Rumor has it Horn Dog has a date tonight."

Before Ned could answer, they both heard a loud slap on the bar. Obviously, Tank Top didn't like Stacey wasting his time while she talked to some local yokel. Unbeknownst to Tank Top, he had just broken rule number one at Pete's Place: Never, ever slap the bar, bang your glass, or rap your knuckles to get Stacey's attention.

Stacey looked rather tense but calmly said to Ned, "Excuse me a moment."

Because Tank Top was new and didn't know about rule number one, he might have survived; but then he opened his mouth. Pointing at Ned with his beer, Tank Top asked, "What's so interesting about the freak?"

As soon as Tank Top put his beer back on the bar, Ned heard Stacey say, as she grabbed the half-full glass, "The beers on the house…if you leave now."

Their conversation heated up then died when Stacey grabbed the phone. She held up her index finger and said, "I'm guessing you already have issues with the police. What's it going to be?"

Tank Top flipped up his middle finger and said, "How about you suck on this." But as Stacey hit the speed dial button, he turned and left.

Ned focused on Stacey, marveling at her boldness. Stacey obviously faked hitting speed dial as she just put the phone away. She moved down the bar, checking on the rest of the patrons. Ned forced his thoughts back to Milner. *Stace is right; Grey and I do argue too much about his women. It's not like the subject's new. For the last three or four years Grey has fed his voracious appetite for beautiful women with an endless parade. It all changed soon after Mary, his mother, died suddenly. Somehow, he morphed. Milner inherited the family farm which included the huge, beautiful Victorian home. Thrust into running the family business, instead of just being "Queen Mary's" kick puppy, seemed to be the difference. Mary could be intense, demanding, and cut you to the quick with a few well-placed and caustic words. Grey always seemed to get the worst of his mother's verbal assaults. We all thought the new role as agro-businessman with all its responsibility would mature Grey, give him confidence…and it did. Grey changed the business to all organic farming just as the trend took hold. He did well. Too bad his mother wasn't around to see. But the maturity that he developed did not include respecting women. In that department, Grey flipped the other way. His self-assured confidence turned into selfish self-interest. It seemed like he had to make up for all the nights we went to parties or the bars and either ended up going home alone or wound up with someone, later, he wished he hadn't. We all hit the party scene pretty hard back then. God, what a bunch of geeks. But unlike the rest of us, his ability to appeal to attractive women went from zero to sixty overnight. Well, actually, it occurred over one summer. How the hell did he do it? He left the rest of us wondering if he had taken a secret course, Womanizing 101 or Latin Lover 1A. He changed his looks, attitude, and demeanor, too. Grey was always good-looking, but all of a sudden, he took even better care of his body and started dressing well. He became more assertive...no...aggressive toward very attractive women. He came across as confident, funny, interesting, knew what to say and when to say it. The gang figured running a successful organic farm attracted women, but it was more than that. It wasn't just earth muffins, organics and nature babes. His women truly spanned a cross-section of the females in our community; waitresses, attorneys, grocery store checkers, realtors, nurses, teachers...you name it. But the two common attributes possessed by everyone: good looks and nice boobs. Milner was a tit man, first and fore-most. Maybe his mom didn't breastfeed him enough. Maybe she breastfed him too much. Whatever the reason, Milner liked a nice rack.*

He's always stayed two steps ahead of any woman in his crosshairs. But soon after he rounds third base and slides into home, he moves on. And with Milner, it was a target-rich environment. Our little town and county happened to be experiencing a growth spurt. It seemed Grey found new talent or, as the gang referred to them, vic-tims, all the time.

Ned spun his barstool back forward, giving Stacey another quick glance, then thought about Janie, Grey's latest dumped woman. She was hot. Pretty, buff, friendly...and way out of Ned's league. Maybe that's why he was so miffed. Grey just casually and callously tossed another one away like she was Christmas wrapping on December 26.

Ned felt a slap on the back causing him to jump. For a second, he thought Tank Top had returned. Greyson Milner hopped up beside his buddy and said, "Hey, Abe, a little jittery, aren't you? Didn't you see me come in?"

"Oh, yeah, well, no, I was daydreaming and—" Ned's voice trailed off as did his train of thought because Stacey had returned.

After giving Grey his drink and trading nods, she bent over to wash glasses. Ned couldn't help staring down at her impressive cleavage. She looked up and once again caught Ned checking her out.

Stacey stopped washing glasses long enough to give a disgusted look at Ned, then Milner. Shaking her head, she said, "You two adolescents will never grow up." She flicked water on both of them, grabbed a towel, and walked back down the bar.

Grey asked, "What's that all about?"

"Oh, she just kicked a guy out and I think she's still amped up."

Grey observed Stacey and thought about his poor lovesick buddy. *Stacey had the look. You know; how tons of women turn your head, but some just have that* look. Ned's was tall, slender women with strong features. Grey guessed Miss Stacey stood about 5'10" or a bit taller and was built kind of like a swimmer. Not as muscular, but fit, with wide shoulders and narrow hips. Not beautiful, just damn pretty. Her brown hair, just under shoulder length, seemed always in place. He wondered if she looked that way after some serious muffin buffin'. Barring a miracle, Grey knew poor Ned would never find out.

Stacey came back with more dirty glasses. Her succinct admonishment aimed at Ned and Grey, the first of the evening, had only sliced a little flesh. She could dish out much worse. Stacey looked at them both, shook her head and returned to washing, trying not to show a slight smirk. Deep down inside, she liked them. She actually looked forward to their visits. If nothing else, they were entertaining and always tipped well.

As Stacey scanned her bar, she saw the drink in front of a new patron down to fumes. The guy sat alone near the front door. Everyone marveled at Stacey's situational awareness. Rarely did anyone run dry before she checked in. That's why she hated people banging on her bar. In fact, just about the only time she slipped up occurred when she stayed too long yacking it up with some tatted, baseball-hat-on-backwards, jock-looking moron. She dried her hands and headed down the bar again.

Milner leaned over to Ned and said, "I think ole Stace is warming up to us. Adolescents seems way less caustic than what she called us last week."

"Oh, yeah; that beats the hell out of jerkoffs, pin heads or whatever she called us Tuesday." Ned pointed to his somewhat underdeveloped chest. "I know she'll never be this desperate."

Milner ignored Ned's self-deprecation and tipped his head toward the guy Miss Stacey left to check. "That guy look familiar to you?"

Ned brought his gaze up from Stacey's behind and watched the interaction between Mr. New Guy and Miss Perfect. He sighed then said, "No, I don't think I've seen him before."

Grey acknowledged, "Yeah, me neither, I guess, but he sure as hell spends a lot of time glaring at us. He makes me nervous."

"Why, you bone his old lady?"

"No, you bonehead," Grey shot back. *Shit, at least I don't think so.* "He just looks crazy. Look at him fidget and glance around with those nervous little beady rat-eyes."

Ned looked at Milner and said, "Sure, he's creepy; put his face to memory then forget him. Now, let's get back to your women."

"Ahhhh. Abe, come on. I thought we were past that."

"No, we're not. I know you're going on a date tonight with a new victim."

"Maybe she'll turn out to be Miss Right, and all your anguish and concern for my poor lost soul will be over."

Ignoring Grey's sarcasm, Ned said, "How long do you think you can go through life being so totally base? You never used to be this way. One of these days, Milner, some little, screaming hot number will come along and tear you a new assho—"

"Holy shit!" Grey half whispered looking past Ned.

Ned snapped his gangly head around and scanned across the bar toward the front door. Not seeing anyone warranting Grey's version of an accolade, Ned said, "Where? Goddamnit, Milner, if this is another one of your deflections…."

Finally, Grey said, "Stop craning your head around like a damn owl. I said she walked by the front window. Come in, come in, come in, please come in."

"Do I need to remind you about your date tonight?"

Across the bar from Ned, Stacey cut in and said, "Hey, ladies, you want another round?"

Ned turned to Stacey who had pulled her top down, exposing about two thirds of her breasts. "Aah," Ned stammered.

Stacey snapped her top up and grabbed Ned's glass. While fixing another drink she smiled and shook her head. "Shit, Ned, you're hopeless."

Milner hit Ned on the thigh and said, "She's coming in, she's coming in; don't be a dork."

Still embarrassed and tongue-tied, Ned wasn't paying attention. He nodded and smiled at Stacey when she handed him his drink. Finally, Ned registered what Grey had said. *"Don't be a dork." Dork…that would be me. Every damn superhero, macho cop or cowboy stud on TV or in the movies has a "dork" for a sidekick. Who the hell applies for the part of the dork? No one, that's who; it just goes automatically to guys like me. I was born for the part.*

All of a sudden, out of the corner of Ned's left eye, an absolutely gorgeous face came into view not two feet from his cheek. She said, "Hi, can I sit next to you?"

Fortunately, Milner didn't see Ned's bugged-out eyes as he stammered, "Aaah, shuure."

He gestured toward the barstool to his left and recovered a little by saying, "Please, have a seat."

She was stunning; maybe 5-5ish, wide dark brown eyes below perfectly shaped eyebrows, a delicate straight nose, white even teeth, and a sturdy chin. Her skin looked smooth as silk. She pulled her thick, shiny, dark hair straight back tightly into a ponytail. Not many women have the type of hair and shape of head to pull off that look, but she did masterfully. To contrast her dark complexion, she wore a tight-fitting white summer dress.

As she situated herself on the barstool to Ned's left, her dress pulled up slightly revealing smooth shapely calves. Ned slowly rotated his head back around to Milner and silently mouthed, *Who's the dork now?*

When he turned back, the goddess was looking straight at him. *Good God, what an incredible face; she even has little freckles on her nose and cheeks. I'm guessing some significant Mediterranean ancestry; could be southern Italian, but not quite that dark-skinned. Maybe she just tans well. And no makeup other than a little reddish gloss on those voluptuously full lips.*

Ned brought his right hand up, but just before he said his name she beat him by saying in a low milky voice, "Allyson, Allyson Chandler."

He awkwardly left his hand dangling in space and said "Hi, Ped Nen… Ned Penrose."

While shaking her hand, Ned heard Grey whisper, "Jesus, Ned, Ped Nenrose?"

After letting his hand go, she said, "I saw a stationery store down the street with the name Penrose."

"Yeah, that's me; Penrose Stationery."

"Small world, Ned Penrose; nice to meet you."

From beside Ned, he heard Milner clear his throat. Ned straightened up and leaned back slightly. He turned his right hand toward Grey and said, "Allyson Chandler, please meet my ex-friend, Greyson Milner."

"Pleased to meet you, ex-friend Greyson Milner."

"Ditto, back at you…and it's Grey."

She nodded and smiled. "How long have you been Ned's ex-friend, Grey?"

"This time? Oh, about five seconds."

"I see." Allyson turned to Stacey and said, "Maker's, neat."

Ned thought, *twice while flying business class, a gorgeous woman had sat next to him, but they were assigned the seats and had no clue ole Honest Abe would be their traveling partner. This stunning beauty chose to sit by him, even though Greyson had an empty seat to his right. He knew this didn't make sense or compute in his world. But, what if…maybe?*

Ned just stared at her while she watched Stacey fix her drink. *Jesus, her profile's perfect, too, and she likes whiskey. I've died and gone to heaven.* She looked back at Ned and lifted her glass.

They touched glasses and Allyson said, "Salud y peseta y muchachas con buenas tetas y la fuerza en la bragueta."

They both sipped their whiskeys then Ned said, "I'm sorry, but I don't know to what we just toasted."

Allyson smiled, but Ned could tell she felt a little embarrassed. "Oh, it's awful. It's a naughty toast my father favored. It just popped out. I shouldn't translate."

Ned said, "You must now."

From behind them they heard, "Salud y peseta y muchachas con buenas tetas y la fuerza en la bragueta. An old Basque or Spanish expression, if I'm not mistaken."

They all spun their barstools around to see Benjamin Whittingham saunter up and stop in front of them.

Ned pointed toward Whit and said, "Allyson Chandler, this is another buddy, Benjamin Whittingham."

"My pleasure," Allyson said. "Are you Ned's ex-friend too?"

Looking at his two buddies, Whit replied, "No, I think I'm still on the active list."

Allyson eyes met Whit's. "If I may ask, how do you know that old saying?"

"Oh, I work in the woods, and on occasion run into old Basque sheepherders. They run flocks in the higher Sierra Nevada on summer federal grazing leases. Sometimes I stop to visit, have a drink and chat."

Grey asked, "But what does it mean?"

Whit looked at Allyson.

She smiled, shook her head slightly and said, "Oh, go ahead."

"To health and money and girls with big breasts and the force behind the britches. I think I'm close."

Allyson said, "Close enough," then chided, "Men, from time immortal, you're all the same."

Grey said, "Hell, I can drink to that. How about you, Whit, have time?"

"Love to, but I'm hooting owls tonight. I need to be in place an hour before sunset and have to get going. I saw you bums in here. I just stopped to say hi."

Allyson asked, "What do you mean you're hooting owls?"

"Before a timber sale, someone like me goes out in the area proposed for harvesting to conduct a biological survey to make sure no species of…concern, shall we say, live there. Tonight, I'm surveying for spotted owls. If I find any, protection mitigation must be provided. It's the same with sensitive plants and archaeological sites, which I also survey."

Allyson asked, "Is it dangerous?"

Pointing to his two friends, Whit said, "Not nearly as dangerous as hanging around this bunch of scallywags; watch yourself."

"I sensed that when I sat down."

"I really have to run." Tipping his baseball cap toward Allyson, Whit said, "Mucho gusto, senorita."

Allyson nodded and smiled. "El gusto es mio."

As Whit walked away, he waved at Stacey. In the awkward silence that ensued, Ned kept screaming to himself, *Say something, you fool.* But before he could think of anything she spoke first again. Only what she said shattered his world. The damn dream didn't even last five minutes.

She leaned forward smiling and asked, "Ned, do you have any quarters? I just parked out front and didn't realize I would need change for the parking meter, especially at this hour."

Greyson piped in over Ned's shoulder, "The city fathers, well, three are actually council-women, think they can squeeze a little more revenue out of tourist's right through dinner hours."

Ned couldn't believe it. *What a setup. She pegged me for a sap from the start. Stace would have given her quarters, but why would someone who looked like Allyson Chandler ask for change from Stacey? She had a perfectly willing stooge to step all over himself to help her.* Then it hit him; his mind leaped forward about five chess moves. *She wants my barstool, next to Milner. She couldn't just sit on the other side of Milner and have Grey split his attention, turning right toward her and left toward me or just ignore me all together. No, the better play, the smarter move, she needed to end up on my barstool. And when I return from putting quarters in the damn meter, she'll be in my seat and my drink will be in front of her barstool. Greyson would be looking at both of us and I'll be staring at the back of her head. Well played, gorgeous.*

So, doing his part like the good little dork sidekick, he sighed, "Sure, I'll get it; no problem. Which car is yours?"

"You're such a gentleman, Ned. It's the black sports car with the Texas plates."

Not looking at her anymore, Ned smiled, swiveled his barstool around, and stepped forward to begin…dork duty. Walking down the length of the bar, he heard Milner start in. Everyone in the entire place seemed transfixed on Allyson, except the new guy at the end of the bar, by the door. He stared right at Ned and he looked pissed. The guy held Ned's stare for about two seconds then looked down at his drink. *What's your problem, asshole?* Ned felt tempted to go ask but decided to just blow him off. It wasn't Rat Eyes' fault. Ned knew he was mad at himself for being so gullible, again. When he exited Pete's Place he looked right, and there she sat…a jet-black Mercedes, shiny as hell, with Texas plates. Bingo.

When Ned returned, he made a point to check out the asshole by the door. The guy was gone, but not his drink. *Hmm, maybe he needed to take a leak.*

When Ned looked down the bar, oh what a shock, Allyson was sitting on his barstool and his drink sat in front of where Allyson had been. *Oh, gee, there I am in deep left field; two's company, three's a crowd…checkmate.*

Stacey watched Ned sit down and gave him a shrug and smile. *Will you look at that; even Stacey feels sorry for me. Well, that's something. Okay my cue. Time for the dork sidekick to bug out.*

Ned stood and chugged his drink. Unfortunately, along with the whiskey, the last little speck of his ice cube shot down his windpipe and decided to detour with some whiskey into his lungs. He immediately fired off an involuntary cough, sending a spray of whiskey all over Stacey.

Stacey yelled, "Ah, gross, Ned! Now I have to change my ice tray." Glaring at him she snapped, "Don't you ever get tired of being a dork?"

His eyes watered and drops of burning whiskey dripped off the end of his substantial nose, making quite a spectacle. *Jesus, Penrose, can you embarrass yourself any worse than this? Just let me slink out of here and crawl under a rock.*

To Ned's surprise, Allyson stood beside him patting his back while asking for a tissue. Stacey gave her a napkin, and Allyson smiled while holding it to Ned's nose. In a cheery voice she said, "Not only are you chivalrous, but you're kind of a comedian." She ordered Ned another drink. Turning to Grey, she said, "Let's the three of us sit at a table so we can talk more comfortably."

A half-hour later, with Milner getting nowhere and acting uncharacteristically sullen, Allyson asked Ned if he could show her where she could find a clean, upscale motel.

Caught off guard again, Ned could only muster, "Shuuure."

Ned and Allyson stood to leave. Ned, in a daze, walked toward the door. He didn't even say goodbye to Grey or Stacey.

Allyson stood in front of the still-seated Grey, smiling.

Grey leaned forward and said flatly, "Tell me, Allyson, what's Ned got that I don't?"

Allyson slowly walked up to within six inches of Grey and leaned forward. At first Grey thought she was going to kiss him but she moved her lips past his face to his left ear and whispered, "Isn't it obvious, handsome? Ned has me."

Then she ran her right hand up Grey's chest, across to his shoulder and squeezed his bicep. "You're in damn good shape, Mr. Milner. It's been a pleasure."

Rising up, she followed Ned to the front door. With the silence in the bar nearly absolute, the only noise came from Allyson Chandler's high-heels clicking on the well-worn Douglas fir planks. She passed through the door that Ned held open and they turned right. Arm in arm they strolled down the sidewalk toward the black Mercedes with the Texas plates.

Greyson interlocked his hands on top of his head and watched them stroll past the large front window. Once they disappeared, he pushed his chair back and walked up to the bar. Sliding back into his favorite barstool, Grey noticed Stacey still staring toward the window with her mouth wide open.

"Stace? Stacey?"

She snapped her head toward Grey and said, "Jesus, did you see that?"

Nodding his head, Grey said, "Barkeep, I think I'm going to break my two-drink policy. Set me up, and anyone else in the bar who wants a drink… on me."

When Stacey returned with Grey's drink, she held a shot of Patron for herself. They touched glasses and Grey said, "To our woefully innocent friend." *Oh, Ned, old buddy, she's going to eat you up and spit you out.*

Stacey put her shot glass on the bar and asked Grey, "Hey, Romeo, forget something?"

Grey looked a little perplexed then reached for his wallet. "Oh, sorry, how much do I owe?"

"No, dumbshit, we can square up later; your date, the new victim."

Grey jumped up looking at his watch, "Oh, Christ!" He chugged the last two-thirds of his drink then set it back on the bar. As he turned to leave, he said, "Thanks, Stace."

To Grey's back, as he headed for the door, Stacey replied, "I certainly didn't do the woman, whoever she is, any favors."

Chapter Eighteen
Thousand to One

Katelyn couldn't believe her good luck. Passing through Cedar Creek just to get her bearings, she saw Pete's Place. She remembered Whit mentioned a bar called something like that during their pillow talk and recuperation time in between uninhibited, breathtaking, fantastic sex.

She could still remember his distinct masculine scent. Not strong like overpowering, strong like opposite sex…like arousing. Whit had mentioned the same point to her that night. He said she smelled like a woman should. She became a little self-conscious and gave him a concerned look until he explained. Whit told her in nature the opposite sex attracted one another through a myriad of ways. Some attract one another by sound, others visually or by elaborate displays, but many by scent. Humans are similar, but it's not perfume or aftershave; the true attraction boils down to compatible body odors. Whit told her that her feminine scent acted like an aphrodisiac. He wasn't aware of her scent when they initially met but he believed it was there, signaling, beckoning, drawing him in.

A long, loud honk from the truck directly behind her made Katelyn jump in her seat and yelp. Startled back to the present, she looked in the rearview mirror. A very agitated twenty-something threw his hands up above his steering wheel in a "What the hell, lady" gesture. She quickly pulled over at the nearest parking space and heard the driver yell something about flatlanders as he roared by. *Nice friendly folk here in Cedar Creek.*

Katelyn, feeling a little excited, decided to stay parked and quickly meander around, maybe take a look in the bar. She checked the side mirror to see if any more of Cedar Creek's finest barreled down toward her before opening the door. *Don't want to cause a scene or anger any more locals.*

As she twisted in the seat to climb out, Katelyn noticed two men across the wide main street walking in her direction. Something about the taller man's walk and appearance caught her eye. When the realization hit, she quickly snapped her head back forward and grabbed her chest. She thought her heart had stopped; her breathing surely had. There he was, Benjamin Whittingham, walking down the other side of the street with a shorter guy. *Oh shit, oh shit.*

She slid over to the passenger side and slunk down and watched as they sauntered by. Her vaginal muscles contracted then released, punctuating her elation. There he was not sixty feet away. He looked the same, only better, in his outdoorsy work clothes. *What to do, what to do?* Her reporter instincts told her, *Ambush him, catch him off guard, and don't let him have time to think.*

Opening the passenger door and getting out, she admonished herself, *You're a grown woman; stop acting like a little schoolgirl. Okay, so you're not prepared, but this is what you came to do…now do it. Just be totally cool and see how he plays it.*

She skirted the traffic and sprang onto the sidewalk behind her prey. Katelyn wanted to get closer, then say, "Hey, Country Bumpkin," but she froze when she noticed Whit abruptly stop, like he had hit an invisible wall. His friend stopped, too, and turned to Whit with an inquisitive look. Whit raised his head and turned his body sideways to slowly scan across the street.

Katelyn distinctly heard the other guy say in a raised voice, "Jesus, what is it this time, Whittingham; you hear a hummingbird calling for help?"

Whit ignored Grey and slowly turned his head back in the direction they had just come.

Katelyn had just enough time to put her hands on her waist and cock her hips to one side.

When Katelyn saw the astonished look on Whit's face, then that slow grin she loved so much, Katelyn had her answer. All pretenses lost, she couldn't help herself and ran.

Grey stepped back as he caught sight of a gorgeous sandy-haired blonde running toward them. He could tell she was looking at and heading directly at his buddy. She jumped into Whit's arms and he spun her around. She held his cheeks in her hands and they kissed.

It was obvious to Greyson Milner by the way the normally reserved and private Benjamin Whittingham embraced this beauty…right out in public… that Whit had a serious connection with Miss Gorgeous. Whit finally let her down and she stepped back looking straight into Whit's eyes. If she noticed

Grey or anything else in the entire world at that moment, Grey doubted it. Greyson knew that look; he'd seen it many times on many different women. This gal was batshit crazy in love. But who the hell is she?

Greyson Milner and Benjamin Whittingham had been friends since… kindergarten; best buds. No secrets between them, well, except for Grey's torrid relationship with Veronica. But that was different, right? Whit had never mentioned this awesome creature, not once. Obviously, they knew each other, and it was clear to Grey that they knew each other in…that way. Grey thought, *So, this is why Whit's been in such a funk and acting like a sad sack. I should have connected the dots.*

While holding her hands, Whit finally addressed Miss Gorgeous in his characteristically formal way. "Hello, Katelyn Summers."

She responded, "Hello, Country Bumpkin."

They both started laughing and hugged again.

Grey had no clue what the inside joke meant. Finally, Katelyn noticed Grey standing next to Whit and smiled.

Grey felt that all-too-familiar tingle and said to himself, *Holy shit!*

Whit finally let Katelyn go, turned sideways, and introduced Grey. "Katelyn Summers, this is my buddy Greyson Milner. Grey, this is Kate."

Katelyn took Grey's hand and spoke first. "Nice to meet you, Grey. Are you a country bumpkin, too?"

Tilting his head toward his friend, Grey said, "I tend to think of myself as being a little worldlier than the hermit, but yes, guilty as charged."

"Katelyn works for a news magazine in Washington, Progressive Politics."

"Did work in Washington."

"What?" Whit blurted out.

"I quit."

Whit remained speechless as he tried to process the news.

Grey picked up the surprise and interest in Whit's face, but tactfully kept his mouth shut and let this revelation play out.

"Didn't a certain someone tell me that there's a huge beautiful world outside of The Beltway, a real world full of life and adventure? Well, I took your advice, found a reporter job in Sacramento, and here I am."

All Whit could do was reproduce that slow grin and nod his head.

With open outstretched hands and a look of concern, Katelyn asked, "Well?"

"Oh, I think it's great, fantastic; but I thought The Beltway was your life, your passion."

"Maybe I found a new passion."

Again, she stunned Whit and left him speechless.

Finally, Grey broke the silence. "Well, I see you two have some significant catching up to do so—"

"Oh, don't leave; I'm actually on assignment and have to go. I took a slight detour through Bumpkinville with the one-in-a-thousand chance of running into Whit; and who do I see walking toward...the watering hole."

Whit quickly asked, "How did you find me?"

"Mike and Janet. A friend, she actually took my job, remembered that. Mike interviewed for a job at the Naval Yard." Katelyn stopped and became serious and angry. "I was so mad and upset with you, I just went blank on your connection to Virginia." Softening again she continued. "Fortunately, my friend drew it out of me when I spilled my guts about you. With my contacts, I found him."

"I know Mike; he would have checked with me first. This sounds like Janet."

"In fact, it was. I figured any woman who could talk you into going to a party at the Kennedys' held significant power and sway. I went straight to the top."

Grey put up his hands to get their attention and said, "Wow; you're saying this Benjamin Whittingham, standing right here, went to a Kennedy function?"

Whit just shrugged and said, "That's where we met."

Incredulous, Grey just shook his head and said, "Holy crap; and you think you know someone."

Then, remembering how their brief affair had ended, Whit turned to Katelyn and said, "I'm sorry, Kate; I really thought at the time and...and, I'm really glad you're here."

Slugging Whit in the arm, she said, "You stoic jerk, you knew where I worked; you could have called me."

"I thought about it a hundred times but—"

"But what?"

"I already said I'm really glad you're here."

Looking at Grey she asked, "Is that as good of an apology as I'm going to get out of this...oaf?"

"I'm afraid so; his apologies come few and far between."

Katelyn stared back at Whit, but he just smirked. She said, "I guess it will have to do...this time...because I have to go."

Taken aback, Whit asked, "What do you mean you have to go?"

Katelyn said, "Because I'm on assignment; you know, like work."

Whit stammered, "You can't go; when will I see you again?"

Looking at Grey, Katelyn said, "Now he wants to see me. Four months ago we have a wonderful evening together, he fixes me an incredible breakfast, then drops me like a, like a...."

"Rock, hot potato?" Whit offered, then added, "Old shoe?"

Slowly turning to Whit, Katelyn pointed her finger and said, "Don't you help me finish my sentences." She slapped his arm and added, "That's for calling me an old shoe, and I was talking to your friend."

Whit zipped his lips shut realizing she was entitled to her pound of flesh and seemed to be enjoying herself.

Turning back to Grey, Katelyn continued. "Oh, he gets what he wants then wouldn't even give me his phone number."

Grey looked at Whit, then shook his head and said, "Ah, the cad, the scoundrel, the lowdown scum; he's not worth it. Then again, in a sad and pathetic sort of way, someone could find him a teensy weensy bit lovable, maybe, I guess."

Ignoring Whit, Katelyn focused on Grey and said, "I'll have tomorrow evening free and just may come back and let him buy me dinner." Holding her hand up and rubbing her fingertips together she asked, "Where do you think we should go, Grey?"

"If I get your drift, some of the priciest meals in town can be purchased at Miner's Diner. It's that nice steakhouse right across the street."

"Please tell the lout I will be back Tuesday around 7:30. I'll check Pete's Place first, then the diner for my date. He better not ditch me again."

Whit said, "I'm standing right here."

Continuing to ignore Whit, Katelyn put her hand out to Grey again and said, "It's been very nice to meet you, Grey."

"Same," Grey said, after shaking her hand and giving her a half-salute.

Katelyn finally turned to Whit, hugged and kissed him again, and whispered in his ear, "I'm just teasing. I'll make it worth your while."

With that, she winked at Grey, turned and sauntered away. Whit and Grey watched intently.

Finally, Grey said, "Shit Howdy, Whittingham."

Katelyn yelled over her shoulder, "I heard that!"

Waiting a little longer until Katelyn walked across and up the street to her car, Grey turned to his lifelong friend. "Lucy, ju gat sum splanen ta du. I can't believe you'd hold out on me about a woman like that. Spill it."

"Look, Milner, it was a chance encounter; a fluke, an anomaly in my life for sure. I figured she was there, I was here, you know, worlds apart, different people on different paths, briefly in, then out of each other's lives. There was no point in dwelling on it or even telling anyone, you know…keeping it alive. She was like a warm beautiful evening, there one night, then gone forever."

"Well, I'd say you're heading for a long Indian summer full of many warm beautiful evenings, big guy. I don't know about you, but I really need a drink now, knowing a buddy of mine can keep something like Katelyn Summers a secret. I need to hear the whole damn story and start with this Kennedy business. Inquiring minds want to know."

Already formulating a PG-rated response for Grey, Whit began at the beginning of the fifteen-hour affair that gripped his heart. Lost in the Katelyn revelation was the reason Whit had called Grey. Whit needed to tell Grey that the Fish and Game incident had resurfaced, and Whit floundered in it waist deep.

Chapter Nineteen
99-Percent Sure, Grey Ole Buddy

Greyson Milner slid onto his usual barstool at Pete's Place just across from Stacey's serving station.

Stacey grabbed a highball glass, added ice cubes, and then reached down for the Captain Morgan. She finished the drink with a splash of Coke. When Stacy looked up at Milner she asked, "Hey, Gigolo, where's your clones?"

"Whit's across the street eating dinner with that East Coast angel. Ned said he would be here tonight. Of course, he said that last Tuesday. Has he been in at all?"

"Nope, not since he left here with that…call girl." Placing a coaster then Grey's drink down on the bar, Stacey added, "What's her story? And why in hell would a woman like that walk into this bar and latch on to a guy like Ned?"

"Abe Lincoln fetish?"

Straightening up and frowning, Stacey scolded, "Not funny, Milner." Softening a little Stacey offered, "I'm serious, Grey, she's going to hurt him."

"Look, Stace, I can only tell you what she told Ned and me. Her name's Allyson Chandler; she's recently divorced from some high-end developer in Texas. Basically, to avoid a very public and very messy split, her ex dumped a bundle of cash on her to simply disappear. She bought a new Mercedes and just started driving west and north. She heard the name Cedar Creek from another developer that does business with her husband. Apparently, he's the guy that fast tracked the Office King as part of that old mercantile building renovation. That would be the very same guy and the very same Office King that's putting Ned out of business. The developer dude told Allyson about Cedar Creek and she thought, what the hell. With money and no plans, she came to check out our little old mining town. When Ned told her he was the sole proprietor of Penrose Stationery, she truly seemed intrigued. Actually, meeting a small local businessman, the type her husband and his cronies crushed with their big chain-store developments, fascinated her. She seemed to take a real interest in ole Ned. Take it or leave it, pretty much that's—"

"Bullshit, and you know it, Milner," Stacey cut in. "That black widow doesn't care a lick for Ned. She's up to no good, can't you see that?"

"Whoa there, Miss Cummins, do I detect a little trepidation, some worry, maybe even a smidgeon of concern for my buddy, the guy you so thoroughly castigate on a weekly basis?"

Greyson received his answer by her silence and the immediate flush on Stacey's face. With a smirk, he added, "I'll be damned; you actually do care for my poor lovelorn mate?"

Stacey finally looked at Grey sternly, then held up her index finger and said, "Hold that thought."

She walked down the bar checking drinks and picked up an empty glass with a ten-dollar bill underneath. After slamming the cash register and tossing the tip portion in her jar, she walked back to Grey. Putting both hands wide apart on the bar she leaned forward and said, "Look, cockhound, I think it's sweet that a super nice guy like Ned would be infatuated with a…damaged flower like me. It means to me maybe there's someone decent out there somewhere for me, yet. You two are characters…goofballs and often a pain in the ass…but you're harmless and entertaining. I look forward to my Tuesdays, and you two are a big reason. And even though I doubt it will ever happen," she straightened up and cupped her hands under her breasts, "Ned has a far better chance of playing with these than you ever will."

Laughing, Gray said, "Stace, you're a treasure. I think deep down inside—"

"Deep down inside, we both know how the romance between Ned and Ms. Floozy will end."

Grey nodded as he leaned forward. Talking softly, he said, "That night when she left with Ned, she leaned over me and—"

"Shush, here he comes." Sticking her right index finger in Grey's face, she stressed, "This conversation never happened."

Ned sat down, and for the first time that Grey could remember, Ned didn't smile or at least nod at Stacey.

Grey said, "Hey, Abe, missed you last Tuesday. You usually call if you're a no-show."

"Sorry, Grey," and then with a little smirk added, "I've been a little pre-occupied."

"I missed my old sidekick."

Side geek is more like it, Ned thought but didn't say. "It's not like you don't disappear often enough when you're on the chase for a new victim. And how often do you call me?"

"Ouch," Grey responded. *Jesus, ain't we a tad moody tonight.* "Duly noted, old buddy. I'll be more responsible in the future, Scout's Honor."

Stacey brought Ned a Maker's Mark with one ice cube and smiled at the two of them. She waited for Ned's customary thank-you and small talk. None came, so she frowned and moved on a little down the bar, but still within earshot. Grey thought, *Geez. What the hell? Old Ned almost never acts this crabby. Well, might as well get it over with.*

But before he could speak Ned asked, "What were you two talking about when I walked in?"

Stacey snapped her head around and stared at Grey.

Grey responded, "Oh, you know Stace, she wanted to know what happened when Whit told Katelyn about his impending court hearing."

Ned shook his head and said, "Jesus, I forgot that was coming up. What a good friend I turned out to be. How did Katelyn take it?"

Grey said, "Don't know. Whit's supposed to tell Katelyn tonight. She's crazy about the big buffoon, but who knows? It's got to be a shock after dropping everything and coming to California to find him. And you know Whit; he told me if they really ream him with a long sentence, he didn't want her to waste her life waiting for him."

"And?" Ned asked.

"And I'm guessing that won't sit well with Katelyn. We'll find out soon enough." After a pause Grey switched gears and asked, "Speaking of relationships, how are you and ah…Ms. Chandler doing?"

"Wouldn't you like to know?" Ned quipped.

"Oh, for Christ's sake, Ned!" Grey snapped. "That's not what I meant. Get off your high horse, will you? I was just asking how you two are doing."

Realizing he was way out of line, Ned offered, "Ah, sorry, Grey; let me start over. Okay, to answer your question…great, incredible, amazing…but…."

Grey could see there was much more coming and decided not to respond. Ned continued. "Well, you see, it's too good. You know what I mean; she and me, it's just unreal. I'm trying to believe it's happening—can happen—to a guy like me."

After some dead time, Grey said, "Look, Ned, there's nothing wrong with you; well, nothing an anti-gullible pill can't fix."

Ned rolled his eyes at Grey's little joke but kept staring into his drink.

Finally, Gray offered, "Everything's going swimmingly, but?"

"But, I can't stop worrying, fretting over…the future. My business is going down the tubes, and now with Allyson. I'm waiting for the other shoe to fall, the bubble to burst, my dream to evaporate right in front of my eyes."

They both drank in silence for quite some time.

Finally, Grey offered, "Wasn't it your dad who always said if it seems too good to be true it probably is?"

"You're not helping." After another pull of his drink Ned continued. "And I apologize for acting so short and smug. I think I'm stressing out here a little. Allison seems sincere and even talks about me shutting down the store and going into some other business with her. But then out of the blue she'll ask me questions about you and…then I think, here it comes."

Ned stopped talking and uncharacteristically drained his whiskey. He equally uncharacteristically tapped the empty glass three times on the bar, the worst annoying gesture that Stacey absolutely hated. When she snapped her head Ned's way, he wiggled the glass signifying it was empty. That was Stacey's second-most hated gesture for requesting another drink.

"Jesus, Ned; Stacey's going to bite your head off."

Unaware of his actions, Ned continued. "I'm a little…concerned that…that Allison will move on." Then almost to himself he added, "Maybe in your direction."

Stacey came and snatched Ned's glass off the bar. She realized Ned remained oblivious and didn't verbally assault him for his classless bad manners. Ned did notice her nasty glare and leaned over to Grey and whispered, "What's her problem? Why's she so mad? Did I do something?"

Looking perplexed, Grey replied, "Geez, Ned, I have no idea."

Ned's drink came and he said nicely, "Thanks, Stace."

She looked at him blankly then said, "You're welcome." While taking her hand away she drew it across her neck like she was slitting his throat.

Ned looked at Grey with enlarged eyes and mouthed, *What the hell?*

Grey thought about what Ned said about Allyson. He was going to say, *If I was in your shoes, I'd just ride that pony as long as I could stay in the saddle,* but decided that was advice he'd give to himself, not Ned. Finally, he said, "Look, Ned, she may move on and that's a possibility you just have to accept; but she will not be moving on to me. No matter how hot the twat, I would never do that to you."

"Deep down inside I know this crap is all in my head and, thanks, just the same, for saying so, Grey." *Well, I'm 99-percent sure Grey, ole buddy, but Allyson is just so incredible, and you've turned into such a womanizer. Could you really kick her out if she came on to you...really, Grey, really?*

Hoping Ned believed him, Grey wanted to change the subject. "We come here Tuesday for pressure relief—not pressure. Let's think about possible business ventures, maybe even something you can put right in your stationery store? It's a good location. With all these foothill wineries popping up all over, what about a wine shop? Or maybe a...."

As Grey droned on, Ned half listened. The other half of Ned's mind drifted back to Allyson and then a scene in *The Wizard of OZ*. The Wicked Witch of the West, played by the actress Margaret Hamilton, turned a giant sand dial upside down. Ned heard the green hag's cackle and felt anguish and dread. Deep down inside he feared that the sand dial signified his time with Allyson relentlessly sifting, filtering, draining closer and closer to...the end.

Chapter Twenty
One Truism about Sex

One truism about sex, even bad sex, 99.9 percent of the time, once you start, you see the process through to its logical conclusion. After going through the motions of unremarkable lovemaking, Whit rolled left and Katelyn scooted right. Great sex or not, both were conscious to avoid the wet spot that soon would turn cold.

Neither spoke for quite some time. Finally, Katelyn offered, "It's finally reached the bedroom. Are you going to talk to me now?"

"Sorry, Katelyn...I, ah—"

"I'll tell you what, you ah." Katelyn turned on the battery-powered end table light and sat up.

Whit recognized that tone and knew not to interrupt. He also knew his procrastinating only made the inevitable worse. He put his arms behind his head and stared forward as she started. "It began at our dinner at Miner's Diner. You were just a little off kilter; you think I can't tell? You kept up the façade, keeping me oblivious, in the dark, out of the loop. But I know something's wrong in your life. I've been patiently waiting for you to tell me; you haven't." Crossing her arms under her breasts for emphasis she demanded, "Whit, it's time."

Rolling over on his left elbow to face Katelyn, Whit found himself at eye level with...the twins. With his eyes glued to Katelyn's huge nipples reacting to the cool bedroom, he said, "Okay, you're right. I have to tell you about something, something bad. It occurred before I met you. It has nothing to do with you, far from it. But it's going to affect you...us."

"You have a child. I knew it." Her eyes grew large. "Or children? Is that it?"

"No, Kate, geez, not even close. But, it does pertain to something I did. Look, before I tell you, can you cover those two? I can't focus or concentrate with—"

In no mood for humor, Katelyn wanted answers. She grabbed the sheet, pulled it up under her armpits, then clamped her arms down.

Whit decided to sit up, too. He took a deep breath. Reaching to his left, Whit tucked his hand under and around Katelyn's back. She accepted his gesture then grabbed his hand in hers and squeezed hard. He began. "Last spring, while driving up here to the cabin, I came upon an accident. This guy hit a doe. Worse than that, she had a fawn in tow and…."

Twelve minutes later Katelyn knew all about the incident; that Whit killed the two deer, accosted the guy who hit the doe, tackled Warden Perkins right in front of his dad, the deal they'd struck and the squelching of the incident. Then, from left field came Earth Wild's attorney, Luna Waxman, the indictment, and the cherry-picked judge.

A very upset Katelyn asked, "So why didn't you tell me sooner?" Before Whit could answer she slapped the bed. "Why do you keep your life so goddamn secret?"

"Kate, I didn't, don't know how this will turn out and didn't know how to bring it up. What should I have said? 'Oh hi, my true love; so glad you're back in my life. Oh, by the way, I mutilated a doe, shot a fawn, accosted the guy, tackled a peace officer and will no doubt go to prison'?"

Looking up blinking, Katelyn tried to stop tears from forming and running down her cheeks. She asked, "Three years? Are you sure?"

"My attorney and pretty much everyone else stresses I cannot go to trial. My side of the incident comes off cold, unfeeling, brutal; the other side…sensitive, bleeding heart, compassionate. Even my dad says, in a trial, I'll die on the vine. Basically, we're trying to broker a deal with an activist judge and a wacked animal rights attorney. We're pushing for one year of probation or house arrest and misdemeanor convictions. But I did break numerous criminal and Fish and Game laws, codes, and regulations. The other side holds most of the cards and plans to take a hard stance. Hope for the best but prepare for the worst; that's why I'm looking at three years."

"But if they railroad you, you can appeal, right?"

"Sure, but that costs money. I don't have it. My dad said he'd take a second out on the family house, but my attorney said Luna Waxman asserted Earth Wild would fight any appeal until we're all broke."

Katelyn offered, "I have money. You can't just give in."

"Kate...thank you, but no. Earth Wild has assets up the kazoo just for stuff like this. It's a stacked deck; they'll string this out and bankrupt you too. I'll probably be out before I could even get another hearing. Besides, I did it; my responsibility...not dad's, not yours."

Shaking her head, Katelyn asked, "Why are they doing this?"

Whit shrugged. "Don't know. Warden Perkins says it's not his agency. But, if not Fish and Game, then who out there wants to bring me down? I just don't have a clue."

Still shaking her head, in a voice so quiet Whit barely heard, Katelyn said, "Whit, I love you. What's going to happen to us?"

Whit almost said, *we'll always have Virginia*, but knew better. He just couldn't get past forcing the repercussions of his actions on Kate. Whit had already decided what to say. Katelyn needed to move on and not sit idly by with her life on hold waiting three damn years for a guy rotting away in prison. And they'd nail him for three years minimum, he knew it. He also knew what Kate would say. She would wait or try to. But she'll think the same guy that went into prison would emerge. *Not true, Kate. I don't want you to see what I'm afraid I'll become. They're going to slap a felony on me, too; the judge and that attorney are fanatical and vindictive enough. I'll be gutted like a fish if I can't carry a firearm and hunt. No, Kate, you won't even recognize me after a thousand days locked up like some zoo creature, then forced to return as an emasculated, neutered, half-man.*

Katelyn had seen that look of finality on Whit's face at her apartment in Virginia. This time she would not allow him to say it. Right before Whit started his "you have to move on" speech, Katelyn let go of Whit's hand, rolled toward him and placed her hand over his mouth. She ordered, "Scoot down."

Whit complied, and Katelyn slid on top of him, then pulled the covers up. "I was getting cold." She hugged him and he squeezed her in his arms.

With her head on his chest, her upper body rose as Whit took in a huge amount of air then slowly exhaled. With her head sideways just under his chin she said, "I know what you were going to say. I won't let you say it. No ultimatums; not yet."

Whit took in another huge breath. "Okay, Kate, okay." *My court date's to-morrow; not much time left. Maybe something will change? Maybe we can do this? Hell, I just can't see how.*

As if reading Whit's mind, Katelyn raised her head and slapped Whit hard on the chest.

Whit yelled, "Ouch! Jesus, woman, what are you doing?"

"Stop thinking. Let it go for now. You have a very naked, very willing, and very unsatisfied woman lying on top of you. What are you going to do about it?"

For the first time in weeks, the pent-up tension in Whit's shoulders relaxed. *Better ride this feeling for as long as it lasts.* He grabbed Katelyn under her arms and slid her up so they could kiss. Into her ear he said, "For the moment, I'm going to try like hell to show how much I love you."

Katelyn wiped, she vowed, the last tear from her cheek for the rest of the night. She put on her best game face, wiggled her whole body and said, "That's more like it."

Chapter Twenty-one
Judicial Tyranny

Fish and Game Lieutenant Dalton and Warden Perkins stood as the San Francisco attorney entered the lieutenant's office. The large clock on Dalton's wall revealed just two hours left before the plea-bargain hearing in front of Judge Franklin in the Benjamin Whittingham case. Knowing Warden Perkins and the lawyer had only spoken on the phone, Lieutenant Dalton made introductions.

"Ms. Waxman, this is Warden Gene Perkins."

With no handshake or even a nod, Luna Waxman flatly asserted, "To make the proper impression before the court and ultimately, the press, we need a unified front. That means you need to get on board with this case, Warden."

Gene shot back, "If by getting on board you mean your version, you'll get no corroboration or collaboration from me."

"Make no mistake, Perkins; Whittingham is going down with or without your assistance. However, your stubbornness could result in a career-ending move on your part. You better think about that and come to your senses. I sway considerable leverage with your agency's brass, all the way to the top."

Gene stepped forward and was half a second from exploding in Luna Waxman's face when Lieutenant Dalton stepped between the red-faced warden and the smug animal rights attorney.

"Let's calm down. Gene, we both know if this goes to trial you will be considered a hostile witness and under oath you will only be allowed to answer questions you are asked. Judge Franklin and Ms. Waxman will not allow you to elaborate. No cross examination will repair what the judge and Ms. Waxman lay out against Whittingham. You know how it works. And this plea-bargain gives Whittingham his best option."

Perkins didn't move his eyes off the arrogant attorney. Finally, Lieutenant Dalton blurted out, "Damn it, Gene; if you fight this, it only gets worse…for everyone."

Luna cut in. "Something happened between your initial report to dispatch and your confrontation with Sheriff Whittingham and his son. Care to elaborate, Warden Perkins?"

Gene refused to respond.

Luna attacked further. "That's it, isn't it? You took a bribe."

Gene snapped, "Not even close, you—" Gene exhaled and looked away. "I made a mistake. That Barbou guy lied through his teeth. Whittingham ended both animals' suffering. It wasn't pretty, but humane and quick."

In a raised voice Luna Waxman fought back. "By nearly decapitating a doe and shooting a fawn without even trying to save either one? You're as sick as Whittingham."

Gene shot back, "What's the difference; the truth doesn't matter. Whether I'm on board or not, your witch hunt is complete. You have your handpicked judge; the fix is in."

"Yeah, but Whittingham doesn't know the half of it. He's cooling his heels in prison for three years minimum and getting a felony to boot. That means no guns, no hunting. He deserves no less."

"That wasn't the deal."

"Well, isn't that just too bad. It appears Judge Franklin feels the seriousness of the crimes requires serious restitution; his prerogative. But, if you play ball, I'll recommend Whittingham gets, umm, two weeks to arrange his personal affairs before incarceration."

"You unethical, conniving bitch."

A satisfying smile came to Luna's face. She finally forced Gene to crack. "I'll take that as a compliment, but that's not an answer."

"What do you think?"

Shaking her head, Waxman remarked, "You're naive and pathetic, Warden. Have it your way." Deciding to twist the knife a little farther, she dug into Gene. "So, back to my other unanswered questions; tell us, Warden, what really happened at Whittingham's cabin. He's toast in about an hour and a half anyway, so it makes no difference."

Gene, angry at himself for swearing, just looked away and said, "You have my report and statement."

"I have your bullshit."

Gene ignored the caustic woman and walked to the window. What really occurred during the arrest attempt at Whit's cabin definitely didn't make it into his report.

Luna Waxman, fuming at Perkins' stubbornness and Lieutenant Dalton's lack of taking charge, turned to Dalton and asked, "How long are you going to just let that idiot stare out of the window?"

"As long as he wants."

"Dalton, we're running out of time; do your job. Remember, you're not immune to my Sacramento contacts either. Think about that."

Lieutenant Dalton took a deep breath then asked his subordinate, "Gene, Ms. Waxman needs you to engage. You know it's not just your ass hanging out here?"

Gene turned and looked with disgust at one, then the other seated individuals. He started walking toward the chair in front of them and said amiably, "Okay; go right ahead, Ms. Waxman."

As soon as she started to speak, Gene turned and walked to the door. Ms. Waxman yelled at his back, "You get back here, asshole, and I mean right now; or I guarantee you, your career will cease to exist."

Gene opened the door, spun around and bowed slightly. Now it was his turn to smile; he'd gotten the old hose-bag to swear and lose her cool. As he straightened up, he flipped her off with both hands and said, "Engage this." With his finger still extended, he sharply saluted his lieutenant then walked out.

Exiting his department's office into the sun, Gene expressed his anger by kicking a rock sticking up a little higher than the rest in the gravel parking lot. The tip of his boot launched the projectile like a bullet about thirty feet, bam, right into the back fender of the lieutenant's sedan. *Oh, shit.*

Gene instantly looked around to see if anyone saw. He caught Whit's profile leaning against the door of his pickup, laughing.

Whit said, "Impressive."

Whit and Gene walked over to the lieutenant's car and bent over. They noticed not only a little dent, but no paint in the center.

Whit remarked, "Nice shootin Tex; you couldn't do that again if you tried."

Gene bemoaned, "Why? Why does it have to be you to see me do that?"

"I'm like your guardian angel, always watching."

Gene gave Whit a sour look and said, "Well, I'm not yours. And that attorney Waxman is the biggest—"

"Whacked-out, fanatical animal rights attorney you've ever met?" Whit offered.

"That's not what I was going to say." Gene stared at Whit and added, "You know, I certainly won't miss you—"

"Finishing your sentences?" Whit cut in.

"No; interrupting me. Jesus, you can be so damn annoying."

Whit responded, "Sounds like I won't get the opportunity for quite some time."

Shaking his head Gene said, "How can you act so cavalier?" Pointing toward the building, Gene said, "She's in there right now gloating over your demise."

"Ah, hell, Gene, I'm just getting into my game face. I don't want to blow up, swear, or show them any emotion. That's the only play I have left. I'm not going to give them the satisfaction."

Gene grabbed Whit's shoulder. "Jesus, Whit; I'm sorry."

They stood silent for quite some time. Then Whit said, "I better get over to my dad's house; he gets to sit in. Besides, don't want anyone to see us…colluding."

Gene shook Whit's hand and said, "I think you'll get two weeks under your dad's supervision before your incarceration. We'll talk, and I'll help you any way I can from the, ah—"

"Outside?" Whit said with a grin.

Gene nodded, but Whit had already turned around, heading for his truck.

Exactly one hour and thirty-three minutes later in the Logan County Superior Court Judge's chamber, Luna Waxman's handpicked judge lowered the boom on Benjamin Whittingham. True to Luna's word, Judge Franklin took special glee in handing down the harshest sentence he could levy.

Whit stood before the bench with an impassive expression, not wanting to give the judge or the Earth Wild attorney a smidgen of satisfaction.

Judge Franklin finally asked Whit, "Since you chose not to make a statement before sentencing, do you wish to speak to the court now and possibly atone or apologize for your unspeakable acts and reckless behavior?"

Whit cleared his throat and, while staring at Luna Waxman, said, "In nature, often predator becomes prey, even those ostensibly that sit at the top of the food chain."

Judge Franklin made a comical look of confusion, then turned to Luna Waxman with his arms up, as if asking, *What the hell is he talking about?*

Luna understood and angrily pointed at Whit and said, "How dare you threaten me."

Still confused, Judge Franklin asked, "What's this?"

Whit replied, "Two species cannot exist in the exact same niche or habitat; the weaker of the two species always dies out."

Luna shot back, "You're going to prison, not me. I'm not the weaker one."

Looking at the still bewildered judge, Whit said, "Nature demands excellence and tends to promote the best specimens of each species...as in...the cream rises to the top." Turning to Luna, Whit added, "But with humans, sometimes turds float to the surface."

Luna yelled, "How dare you speak to me like that!" Turning to the judge she demanded, "Do something! Didn't you hear what he called me?"

Judge Franklin, in frustration, said to Luna, "I don't even understand what he's talking about; it's just a bunch of babble to me." Looking down at Whit from up high, Judge Franklin asked Whit, "Mr. Whittingham, are you quite done?"

Turning his slow grin toward Luna Waxman, Whit said, "Yes; I think I made my point."

Luna demanded, "I want him taken away in chains, now."

Judge Franklin finally took charge and said, "I've already remanded the defendant to the local sheriff for two weeks. The sheriff will return the defendant to this court no later than 10:00 A.M. two weeks from this day for transport and incarceration at the State medium security facility in Lancaster. My ruling stands." With a bang of the gavel he concluded with, "Clear the courtroom."

Chapter Twenty-two
Don't Taunt Me, Bitch

Allyson, dressed for business, her kind of business, walked into the oldest hotel in Cedar Creek, The North Star. She checked her watch; the dials confirmed two o'clock, straight up. Allyson thought the old brick and stone building looked beautiful. Someone spent some serious bucks restoring the old girl. In a display case near the entrance to the bar, Allyson saw two old registers; one with Samuel L. Clements' signature and the other with President Grover Cleveland's. She could imagine the old stage coach pulling up right outside… the hard-drinking Mark Twain stepping down and heading immediately up the steps and into this very bar to lubricate his travel-weary, parched throat.

Moving on, Allyson thought about the person who summoned her here, the man she despised most in this world. Allyson had to admit, Lance Sliger definitely bypassed the longtime leader in that category, her father. As she walked past the reception desk in her low-cut gray blouse and mid-thigh black skirt, the eager freckle-faced young man behind the counter jumped up. Dressed in a vintage turn-of-the-century style suit, he asked if he could be of assistance.

Allyson thought of saying, *A whole twelve rooms, I think I can find it*. Instead, she smiled pleasantly and asked, "Room number 7?"

Unable to stop himself from scanning her from tits to toes and back again, Freckle Face flushed as he answered, "The room at the end of the hall on the right, at the top of the stairs. It's the honeymoon suite."

Figures, Allyson thought as she walked past the ancient elevator to the stairs. She distinctly heard scuffling on the polished hardwood floor as Freckle Face scurried around from behind the counter. Grabbing a broom and dustpan, he found an urgent need to sweep up imaginary dust bunnies at the bottom of the steps.

Allyson smiled to herself. *Okay, Junior, you want to watch, I'll give you a show.*

Allyson slowly ascended the stairs. At the last step, she stopped. Allyson put her right foot on the landing then bent over. Placing her purse in her right hand, she lowered her left hand and grabbed her left ankle. Sliding her hand up the back of her leg, she reached the bottom of her skirt and paused. All sounds of sweeping stopped. She let her hand move up a little farther revealing the left half of her round, firm, and very bare ass. Allyson gave herself a loud spank. She heard the dust pan hit the floor with a bang. Alyson stepped up to the landing and straightened her skirt. Without looking back, she turned right and walked out of Freckle Face's view.

Allyson saw the tall, thick door to room number 7 open, and the beady-eyed Lance poked his head out. Seeing Allyson, he said, "You're late. What was that noise?"

"Mr. Smith call?"

Lance had to admit, "No, not yet."

"Then I'm not late."

It only took five seconds for Allyson to anger Lance. He repeated, "What was that noise?"

Walking past Lance into the huge honeymoon suite, Allyson replied, "I think the kid at the front desk must have been distracted; he dropped his dustpan."

The room smelled like old wood, old furniture polish, old dust and just plain old…but not unpleasant. As she scanned the room, Allyson thought, *I'd love to get my hands on that marble-topped dresser and matching bed with the cathedral-like headboard.* Not ten feet from the bed, on a tile platform, sat a large clawfoot bathtub. *Two could easily soak up to their chins in that monster. For Lance's health, I hope the ferret doesn't pursue that thought.* Coming back to the present, Allyson moved over and leaned against a little writing desk. She thought it must have been made for a child but then realized maybe not. A century and a half ago most people were much smaller.

Lance pointed to a loveseat. "You can sit. I don't bite."

Allyson thought, *Sighed the snake.* Just then Lance's cell phone rang. It rested just to her left on the writing desk. Allyson moved as if she was going to pick it up.

Lance leaped toward her yelling, "No!" He snatched it away while passing her a nasty look. He answered, "Yes, Mr. Smith," as he scurried off to the other side of the room.

Speaking with a hint of excitement in his voice, Stephen Sliger, aka Mr. Smith, asked, "Lance, do you have Ms. Chandler there with you?"

"Yes, Mr. Smith; we're both here as you requested."

"Whatever the game plan, I want to hear it from Ms. Chandler."

Dejected, Lance walked back to Allyson. Allyson put her hand out and received the phone without looking at or even acknowledging Lance.

Allyson said, "Mr. Smith, how nice to be able to speak directly with you."

Pleasantries, protocol, manners; Jesus, women can be so annoying. "Yes, yes, nice to hear your voice, too, ah, Ms. Chandler." Lying, Sliger added, "I'm a little pressed for time. I understand you are ready to spring the trap. How will it go down?"

"As you suggested, a straightforward love triangle. I'm showing up at Grey's Victorian unannounced this evening. If all goes as planned, we'll do something…very naughty. I'll then show up at Ned's an hour or two later. I won't shower, and I'll look and act flushed; he'll know. I'll do the guilt trip, a sobbing mea culpa, and tell Ned what Grey did to me. I know Ned; he'll internalize it, then slowly get madder and madder."

Sliger couldn't contain his excitement. "Do you think he'll become suicidal? Homicidal?"

"No, not Ned; he's way too grounded and too much of a straight arrow. Easy to say, though, the love triangle will ruin Grey and Ned's friendship. At some point I'll get up and tell Ned that I need a drink. I'll fix him one too, spiked of course. When he passes out, I'm gone."

Mr. Smith must have turned his head or partially covered the phone because Allyson could barely hear a muffled chuckle and Mr. Smith say, "Absolutely delicious."

He cleared his throat, then spoke into the phone again. "Well, we were going for the breakup of their friendship; anything beyond that will be icing. Okay, Ms. Chandler. If all goes as planned, the remainder of your payment will be transferred."

"Including the pink slip for the Mercedes." Allyson's inflection made it a statement, not a question.

More than a little perturbed, Mr. Smith responded sternly, "Yes, yes; and the Mercedes." Curtly, he finished with, "Is there anything else?"

"I do have one question."

Wearily, Mr. Smith asked, "What is it?"

"When I've worked for you in the past, I've helped you bring down powerful men, men that stood in your way or interfered with your business. They also happened to be pure scumbags. Ned doesn't have a pot to pee in and he's a very sincere, giving person. What the hell did he ever do to you?"

Sliger's voice shot back, "You do not know his past or what—" He caught himself and immediately switched to measured words in his Mr. Smith tone. "You are being paid to do a job, not to ask questions. You are in fact being paid double, including, as you so rudely reminded me, the Mercedes. I suggest you do your job and leave the why to me."

"Certainly, Mr. Smith. It will be done."

"Put Lance on the line."

Allyson held out the phone for Lance. As he approached, she lifted it in the air holding the phone high over his head. Frantic to avoid keeping Sliger waiting, he half jumped and grabbed it away from Allyson. Lance glared again at her. Allyson simply smiled impassively.

Lance said, "Yes, sir?"

"You are my eyes out there; you know what I expect and what to do. Keep it tight and clean."

"Yes, sir, Mr. Slig-Smith." *Shit.*

Sliger angrily slammed down the phone. All giddiness lost.

Lance pretended the conversation continued. "Yes, sir. Yes, sir; I'll tell her right now, Mr. Smith. Yes, sir."

He put his phone away and snapped his head around at the still-smiling Allyson. *You're one snide remark away from my wrath, bitch; just push me once more.* Trying to throw his weight, Lance addressed Allyson. "You are to inform me when you get to Grey's house, when you leave, and when you arrive at Ned's."

She calmly asked, "Whose Mr. Slig-Smith?"

"Nobody; shut up."

"Steven Sliger, maybe, you fuck-up."

Squaring off in front of her, seething, Lance hissed, "Don't taunt me, bitch, or I swear I'll—"

"You'll what?"

Charging straight for her, Lance yelled, "This!"

Instead of retreating as Lance anticipated, Allyson stepped forward and, with a vicious left jab, popped him in both eyes with bent knuckles. His head snapped back, then he dropped to his knees. Pain and frustration made him scream like a wild animal. He reached into his jacket for his switchblade. Before he could snap it open, she kicked him hard in the head, and he flew backwards. Still blind, he struggled to get up. The cold steel of Allyson's Lady Colt pressing hard against his temple froze any further movement.

He didn't twitch a muscle, and she didn't speak. In the growing silence he remained too afraid to breathe. *She's going to pull the trigger.* Finally, he broke with a squeal, "Don't shoot me, just calm down, we—"

"Shut up, shit for brains," Allyson shot back. Calmer, she continued. "I don't know what Mr. Slig-Smith sees in you, but you're not right in the head. As far as I'm concerned, this is my contract and I require no further contact with you. I work alone; get that through your psychopathic little mind. You stay clear of me and my operation or I promise you I'll shove this pistol up your scrawny little ass and empty the magazine." Pressing her pistol hard enough into Lance's temple to produce a nice circular indentation, she reached into his jacket and took his gun. She stepped away and picked up his switchblade and phone. "I'll call your boss when it's done." Turning away, she calmly walked out of his hotel room and gently pulled the door shut.

Lance sat up holding his handkerchief over his slightly bleeding nose. *Fucking bitch. Maybe I won't get the luxury of abusing every one of your filthy orifices before you die, and you'll never know it was me that killed you; but, goddamn you, I'll know.* He still couldn't open his eyes. Finally, he forced one eyelid open enough to follow a blurry path to the bathroom. Lance needed to get squared away enough to call Sliger back. Cold compresses over his eyes seemed to help. After about five minutes he struggled to his oversized briefcase and fiddled with the combination numerous times. Through watery eyes he finally lined up the numbers and popped it open. Inside, next to a large canister with a timer attached, Lance found his satellite phone.

He dialed and Sliger picked up immediately. "What took you so long?"

"That gash poked me in the eyes. I did everything you said and didn't provoke her or nothing; she just—"

"I don't give a shit," Sliger cut in. "Did she buy it?"

"Oh, she bought it; she still thinks she's in control, getting her money, car, everything. Only she won't call me when she gets to Penrose's place, so I'll just have to hide out and wait until she returns from screwing Milner."

Testing Lance to make sure he'd paid attention to detail, Sliger asked, "Are you going to have time to affix the monoxide canister and set the timer?"

Annoyed, Lance replied, "I've preset the timer. The holder for the canister and the wire running to the odometer are already under the passenger seat. Twenty-five seconds max to unlock the door, slide the canister in place, plug in the odometer wire to the timer, and back out."

"And you're sure she's heading straight back to Texas?"

Confidently, Lance responded, "Absolutely positive; she lives in Texas and she wants that Mercedes so badly, what else can she do?"

"What if she doesn't leave directly?"

"Doesn't matter; the timer only works when the odometer runs. If she decides to find a motel, the timer stops. In six hours of driving she'll be screaming across the Nevada desert, probably doing 90. The monoxide will slowly put her to sleep and...it's single-car accident time. She'll die."

"What if she lives?"

Lance started getting angry. *Why does he always second guess me? Shit, he never frets about that stinking computer geek or Andrea's work...just mine.* Hiding his irritation, Lance reminded Sliger, "We already disabled her airbag, and one of the seatbelt bolts has been stripped. She will not survive."

"Good; just wanted to hear it all again."

Lance couldn't resist. "When are you going to trust me?"

"Don't start, Lance; do not start. You better keep your mind clear and deal with what's in front of you. Do not fail me." After a long pause, knowing Lance remained too mad to speak, he added, "Keep me posted."

After a big exhale loud enough for Sliger to hear, Lance said, "Yes sir, I—"

But the satellite connection had terminated.

Lance sat back on the huge hotel bed. Feeling a little dizzy, he lay down and closed his damaged eyes. All alone he felt a twinge of apprehension. Lance had never actually killed anyone before, though he had tortured animals as a kid and—of course—slapped around a whore or two. He'd also witnessed the death of that disgruntled employee at Sliger's warehouse. The idiot had gone to the press. Though their head of security, Ron Townsend, not Lance, had broken the dumbshit's neck; it didn't bother Lance in the least. Lance helped place the dead body in the car and drove it to the spot where they faked the single-car accident. But tonight would be different. Tonight was his biggest test to date; he was alone. He had no one to lean on for help and worse, no one to blame if something went wrong. A little nervous but more than a little excited, Lance thought, *Before the night ends, I'll be the executioner of not one but two.*

Chapter Twenty-three
I Wish I Could Hear

Lance turned off the headlights of his rental car in a small public parking lot three blocks away from Ned's house. The lot resided one block over from the main street that bisected Cedar Creek and four blocks from the onramp to the highway. Lance could make a hasty escape, if need be. He grabbed the plastic bag holding the monoxide canister, locked the doors, and started walking. The houses along the street were mostly two-storied, boxy older homes with either wood or asbestos siding. Most were well-kept, as were the yards. However, as Lance ventured off on side streets leading to Ned's house, the roads became noticeably narrower. Any cars parallel parked on the road made the width only one lane. The houses tended to be small and one-story. Lance guessed the largest ones contained maybe twelve hundred square feet. They must have been mostly rentals now as the houses and yards showed far less upkeep. Many yards were nothing more than parking lots or torn up fenced-in areas used to pen barking dogs...lots of barking dogs. The yapping must occur all the time as no one peeked out of a window or came out to investigate. Lance proceeded down a skinny but drivable alleyway to the back of Ned's house, completely unnoticed by anything with less than four legs.

The front of Ned's bright white stucco house exhibited pride through periodic maintenance. The trim bordering the windows and door matched the dark gray composition roof. The skinny little front yard contained thick, dark green grass, minus dandelions or brown spots. The three-foot metal fence surrounding the lawn kept out the neighbor dogs and, more importantly, their deposits.

The back of Ned's house displayed more wear, or definitely less maintenance. The stucco appeared less white, and the three steps and landing to the back door badly needed painting. With more and larger older trees in the back, piles of leaves and other debris collected. Lance could tell Ned maintained the front of the house for show but slacked off elsewhere.

Walking slowly past Ned's house, Lance suddenly froze in panic. The blinds covering the large back window rolled up. There appeared the gangly dork. It took Lance a few seconds to realize with lights on in the house and no lights on outside the house, Lance could see in well, but Ned couldn't see out at all. Lance watched Ned pace around from his kitchen to the living room and back again. He thought, *Allyson's running late and freaking out Penrose...perfect.*

Lance slowly moved to an old, leaning one-car garage about seventy feet from Ned's back door. Fortunately, a large tree caught the sloping garage's decline and prevented its entire collapse. Though it appeared to leak in some places, someone—probably Ned—stored firewood on its spongy wooden floor.

Backing farther into the doorless opening, Lance waited. As if he needed another reminder, Lance closed his eyes and gingerly touched his eyelids. Allyson's knuckle shot to his face left one more memento of how much he loathed the woman. He put the plastic bag on a pile of kindling, moved a splitting mall and ax, and sat on the chopping block.

After an hour and fifteen minutes of sheer boredom, Lance saw distant headlights and heard plenty of barking as a slow-moving car approached. His red, swollen eyes watched as the Mercedes glided around to the back of Ned's small one-bedroom home. From his vantage point, Lance realized that if Allyson and Ned stayed in the living room, he could watch and witness perfectly the confrontation about to ensue.

With a pang of jealousy Lance wondered, *What the hell did you do with that Milner guy, whore; something raunchy no doubt?* He had to admit, the bitch could act. As she slid out of the car, Allyson looked guilty as hell. Everything appeared just a little off; the gait, the mannerisms, even her clothes and perfect hair looked slightly ruffled and out of sorts.

Now he wished he'd thought about bugging the room so that he, and then later Sliger, could hear the volatile exchange. Lance mused, *Our well-orchestrated cascade of events to destroy Sliger's old buddies keeps falling into place. Benjamin Whittingham heads for prison tomorrow and, very soon, Greyson Milner will be hated by his closest friends, his family, and probably everyone else in this inbred shithole com-*

*munity. And this pathetic Ichabod Crane's looming bankruptcy and impending be-
trayal by yet another woman will provide the stress to end it all...with a little help.
We destroy the old gang tonight and, around six hours later, the bitch goes down, too.*

Lance's only regret, something he wished he could change, would be just
one night with Allyson; that would be icing on the cake. The encounter, for him,
would produce a slow, measured and very pleasurable terminus to their relationship; for Allyson, well, quite frankly, a painful and most disagreeable evening.

Realizing once again that daydreaming over what he wanted to do to
Allyson's body left him unfocused, he shook off the images and looked back
up at the living-room window. It had only been maybe five minutes, but the
silent movie taking place before Lance appeared to shift into high gear. Allyson
and Ned's calamitous end really heated up. Watching, fascinated, Lance
thought, *I wish I could hear.*

Thinking Allyson's destruction of Ned and Grey's relationship proceeded
along as planned, Lance would have definitely crapped his pants in panic if he
knew the truth. Initially, Allyson tried to complete her contract and bury her
feelings of regret, remorse and shame for breaking her personal code of right
and wrong. Two events shocked her to the core and derailed those plans. First,
Grey refused to sleep with her. That had never happened before, ever...with
a man anyway. While pushing the narrative to Ned that Grey did sleep with
her, the second event—more like a revelation—struck. Allyson couldn't go
through with it. The lie would have worked, too; but she only half tried, then
quit. To seal the deal, she would need to become what she hated most in the
very type of greedy, heartless, venal assholes she relished destroying. She just
couldn't do that to Ned. Poor Ned—the epitome of a gentlemen and decent
man treated her with the utmost respect and kindness. Unfortunately, stopping
the lie and telling the truth to get out of her predicament proved far more difficult than she imagined.

Allyson tried again. "Ned, it's far more complicated than you know; I just
need to come clean, then I'll leave."

"Did you or didn't you sleep with Grey?"

"No!" she yelled, then more softly, "No, I lied to you. If it's any consolation, he wouldn't sleep with me...because of you. Now will you please let
me explain?"

While thinking how impressed Sliger would be to have a taped recording
of the downfall of one of his hated classmates, Lance realized, *Holy shit! I forgot*

to place the monoxide canister into the Mercedes; damn it. Scurrying back into the woodshed, he grabbed the plastic bag. Even though the darkness concealed his movement, Lance inched forward to the vehicle. He unlocked and slowly opened the passenger door of the Mercedes. Lance checked that no one noticed the dome light. When satisfied, he examined the six-hour setting on the timer, then secured the canister in place under the passenger seat. The last function took only a few seconds as he plugged in the preset wire, hidden under the carpet and connected to the odometer. The timer would count down as long as the odometer operated. Little endorphins fired off through Lance's body as he stuffed the plastic bag in his pocket and turned to head back to his observation post. Lance stopped when he realized he could hear muffled voices coming from inside Ned's house.

"What's there to explain? Jesus, Allyson; you went to Grey's for no other reason than to screw one of my friends. I should have known." Ned hit himself on the temple with the palm of his hand three times. "Stupid, stupid, stupid."

"What? You think a guy like you isn't good enough for someone like me, is that what you're thinking? Believe me, if anything, it's the other way around."

Ned just shook his head and stared at her with sad, humiliated, embarrassed eyes. The way she had just devastated this truly harmless man, made Allyson for the first time in a long, long time, feel appalled at her actions. "Will you please stop pacing and let me explain? Nothing is as it appears…not by a long shot."

Angry and in a raised voice, Ned replied, "Again, what's there to explain? You're just like all the others."

Squatting down behind the Mercedes, Lance thought, *I can pretty much hear every word. If I sneak up next to that open window, I'll hear it all clearly.* Scanning for a way to approach the house without being detected, he made a quick decision. Lance figured if he walked slowly up behind the large ugly tree next to Ned's living room, he wouldn't be seen or heard and could listen in on everything. Casually but deliberately, Lance strolled forward, keeping the big tree between the two combatants in the living room and himself. When he reached the tree he leaned his back against the trunk.

Lance reacted with a knowing smile to himself after hearing Allyson say, "What I did, as it turns out, is far worse than you can imagine."

Lance thought, *Well, at least the slut isn't pulling any punches. Sounds like she's really tearing the ugly guy down. Sliger will be so impressed when I can give him an actual blow-by-blow account.* Suddenly, something nasty and acidy assaulted Lance's nose. *What the—?*

The sensation of dozens of insects racing from Lance's jacket to his neck and head drew sheer panic. The black locust tree that Lance leaned against emigrated as a seedling from the southeastern corner of the U.S. Some settler or miner brought the young tree to California in hopes of using the wood someday. The dense, hard, and slow-to-rot tree made excellent fence posts. Now, over one hundred thirty years later, the decadent tree contained many rotten pockets. Protected from the elements, these cavities of advanced decay made perfect homes for large colonies of ants. The locals called them piss ants due to the sharp, caustic, chemical smell they emitted during an attack. Their standard defense of the colony and their queen consisted of rushing out in mass, finding flesh, and clamping down hard with large mandibles. Anyone growing up in the foothills of the Sierra learned at a very young age that leaning against or climbing old trees often turned into a very bad idea. Of course, none of this was known to Lance as he high-stepped away from the tree, tearing off his jacket while emitting frantic little squeaky sounds and slapping himself silly. Retreating behind the old garage, Lance finally bested the last of the insects. Sweating profusely with his heart pounding…slowly, eventually, he calmed down.

Peeking around the garage at Ned's house, Lance was relieved to see Allyson and Ned still arguing. Yet again, Lance found another reason why he hated leaving the city. But at that very moment, Lance's minor encounter with nature was not his biggest problem. Had he just stood behind the large tree instead of leaning against it, Lance would have stayed long enough to hear something very different than what he assumed was taking place. Enough so to radically change what Sliger ordered him to do.

Allyson, in an uncharacteristically pleading voice, said, "No, no, I'm not; I'm worse, much worse. Look…I was hired to destroy your friendship with Grey."

That stopped Ned dead in his tracks. He was pacing and looking away from her. After hearing the word "hired" he spun around and stared wide-eyed at her.

Allyson thought, *Well, at least he stopped pacing.*

Putting up one hand, she said, "Okay, I was supposed to hurt you, too; but I couldn't. Well, I did; but I couldn't go through with it. It's like this; I was paid to get involved with you then sleep with Grey to destroy Grey's relationship with his friends, his buddies. He wouldn't sleep with me, but I still wanted the money, so I told you he did sleep with me. I was just being a greedy bitch, thinking only about myself. Besides, who would believe Grey anyway, with his reputation? But I couldn't—"

"But you couldn't what?"

"When I lied to you about Grey and me, I…I couldn't go through with it. You're nothing like the type of guys I've brought down in the past. They were scum. I—"

"You've done this before?"

"Yes. Jesus, Ned; that's what I'm trying to tell you. This is what I do; just not to nice guys. I bring down bad men; selfish, greedy, men that crap on others. I took this job thinking Grey and you were filth." Calmer now, Allyson continued. "Grey fit the profile I was given more than you. I would have enjoyed knocking him down a peg or two by treating him like he treats women. But you turned out to be completely different than I was led to believe. You're kind and gentle and giving. At first, I thought the money would override my feeling…my feelings for what's right…why I do what I do. You have been such a gentleman; no one's ever treated me the way you have, not honestly anyway. And just in the brief time I've spent with you I've seen so many people who care about you and look up to you in this community. You fit here like a glove. I was destroying someone good, noble and special. The type of creeps I bring down step all over guys like—"

"Stop, Allyson, just stop." Ned finally turned away from her, holding his head. Pacing again, he said, "You're talking crazy. You were hired? Who would want to do this to Grey or me? I can't make any sense out of what you're saying."

Taking her cue from his perfect lead in, Allyson said, "Look…okay, Ned, you sit here and try to calm down. I'll fix us drinks. This is very difficult for me, too; I know it's hard to believe. Just be patient, please, Ned?"

She walked toward the kitchen to the cupboard where Ned stashed his alcohol. As she passed, he put his arms out to her, but Allyson put up her hands and said, "Drinks first, okay?"

"Sure, sure," Ned responded. He watched her walk into his kitchen. Ned took a huge gulp of air and exhaled hard. Shaking his head again he said to himself, *Why am I so damn gullible?* He moved to the couch, turned, put his hand on the arm and dropped heavily.

Lance saw Allyson heading into the kitchen and figured she left to make drinks. He knew he'd better get ready. The bitch wouldn't tell him what she decided to use to spike Ned's drink. Since he didn't know how long Ned would be incapacitated, he needed to act fast.

Allyson needed maybe fifteen minutes to a half-hour, so she sprinkled what she guessed was enough Gamma-Hydroxybuyrate into Ned's glass. Previous to tonight, Allyson had used the date rape drug twice before to extricate herself from the end of…not-so-beautiful love affairs.

Allyson returned to the living room and casually handed Ned a healthy four fingers of whisky. She had poured two fingers for herself. After watching Ned take a long pull from his drink, he licked his upper lip and made a face.

"What?" she asked.

"Oh, nothing. I must not have rinsed this glass well; tasted a little soapy."

"I'll get you another."

"No, it's fine. No more delays. Let's wade into the muck. How much were you getting paid?"

Allyson put her drink on the coffee table and held up one finger. She grabbed a dining room chair and scooted it up to the couch next to Ned. If she sat on the couch Ned would tower over her. In the chair they looked at each other more or less eye to eye.

Allyson said, "Would you believe $50,000 up front and $50,000 if I succeeded?"

"Jesus, who hates Grey and me that much; what the hell did we do?"

Well, even if Ned remembers this conversation, my career with Mr. Smith terminates tonight anyway; what the hell. "Do you know a guy named Mr. Smith in Sacramento?"

"Smith? No."

"How about a guy named Stephen Sliger?"

Ned shook his head again.

Allyson continued. "I'm sure Smith is an alias, but he also has a dark-haired little weasel that handles his…dirty work. He calls himself Lance; a shifty-eyed little creep."

Ned snapped his finger. "He was at the end of the bar at Pete's Place drinking by himself the night you walked into the bar."

Impressed, Allyson said, "Very perceptive."

"Yeah, right, except when it comes to women."

Frowning, Allyson continued. "Lance was my go-between with Mr. Smith. I've been used by Mr. Smith in the past to destroy...individuals, in his way. The first was an investigative reporter looking into the mysterious death of a disgruntled employee. He was married to a Sacramento city council woman. I seduced him and it made quite a stink in the local papers and news outlets. His paper shipped him to a sister newspaper two states away, packing divorce papers. His fact-finding fizzled as no one else picked up the investigation."

"The second contract involved an arrogant bully and business competitor. Due to some very graphic pictures, the scandal that followed destroyed his marriage and eventually his business. They were both not nice men; screwed around on their wives...they deserved what they got."

"But why Grey and me; what did we do?" Ned's head dropped slightly then popped back up. He looked around the room, squinted, blinked a couple of times then took another sip of whiskey.

"I don't know, Ned, honestly. I thought you were just another jerk to bring down. That's the impression I was given. I want to retire and this job would have made that possible. They paid me double to rip you and Grey apart. I wanted the money; I tried, I tried hard to ignore my feelings, my...personal sense of...," Allyson paused, then added, "now don't laugh; my personal sense of right and wrong. Until you, I viewed myself as kind of an avenging angel."

Ned's head dropped hard this time and came up slowly. He leaned forward and stared hard at Allyson. He looked at his drink then it slipped out of his hand. In a slurred voice he asked, "Wha, wa di?"

Allyson rose from the chair, and gently pushed Ned against the back of the couch. She turned sideways and sat on his lap. Ned's arms lay at his side like lead, and he had a hard time holding his head up. She placed Ned's head between her hands and smiled. "Ned, I have to go; you will never see me again. It's for the best. I want you to know, I've never met someone so wonderful. You've changed me—forever—in a good way. I wish we had met under different circumstances. I'm so sorry."

Whether Ned heard or could comprehend what Allyson said, she couldn't tell. She sat up and slowly rolled Ned's body over on his side; his gangly legs dangled off the couch. Looking down at the tall slender figure Allyson sighed heavily. *You cost me fifty Gs and the Mercedes, you big...naive, gentle soul. And, so much for retirement.*

Gathering the glasses, she washed, dried and put them away. Picking up her purse and scanning all the rooms for any trace of Allyson Chandler, she blew a kiss to Ned and walked out the back door.

As Allyson pulled away, Lance watched and thought, *So long, you greedy slut; just drive six hours.* He could see her speeding down some long, lonely, straight stretch of highway at 90 miles per hour. Maybe she'd be on Highway 58 passing over the Tehachapi's or way down 395 past Lone Pine. He imagined Allyson's head flop forward as the Mercedes drifted off the road to the right. As the front right tire dug into the loose desert soil, the car turns sideways briefly then starts flipping over and over, eventually violently exiting its battered ragdoll occupant. He fantasized Allyson's destroyed brain briefly registering pain and the image of his face. *Yes, bitch, yes.*

Lance's gaze eventually focused on Ned's house. *Shit, what the hell am I doing? I have to get to work.* Putting on gloves, Lance looked around and listened. He assured himself no snoopy neighbors were watching. To build up his own confidence, he thought, *He's out cold; the bitch saw to that. You're safe for now, so get to it. Prove to Sliger, and Andrea for that matter, who has the balls to be the heir apparent. After I kill Ned and Allyson, maybe I'll get my own inner circle to do my bidding.* Smiling to himself, he added, *And I won't have to sit next to that putrid geek anymore.*

Checking his pocket, he felt the case with the needle and the small vial of Propofol. *I just need to find a vein someplace where no one would normally look or could overlook during an autopsy. But why do an autopsy when Penrose obviously hung himself? I'll let the drug take effect, setup the suicide, wait fifteen minutes or so until most of the drug has cleared his system, then let his own weight finish the job.*

Just before he turned the door knob and entered Ned's house, Lance slowly checked his surroundings. *All clear.* His canvass of the area ended at the large black locust tree near Ned's open window. *Fucking ants.*

Chapter Twenty-four
He's Dead, I Killed Him

Nearly two blocks away from Ned Penrose's house, Lance walked with a noticeable limp way too fast to appear like someone just out for a casual stroll. He didn't care; Lance could only focus on getting to his car and driving the hell away. The fear of someone yelling for him to stop forced him to emit little squeaky sounds as he kept looking back over his shoulder. If not for his banged-up knee, he'd have run. Finally, his rental car came into view. Gasping, Lance reached the driver's door, unlocked it and jumped inside. Banging his bad knee on the steering column, he emitted a pain-derived shriek. "Ahhh, goddammit, shit, shit."

At last, seated in his car, Lance regained enough composure to look quickly around then start and drive his rental car away with a measure of control. Feeling more confident, Lance glanced less and less in the rearview mirror. After driving another block, he said to himself, *He's dead, he's dead, I killed him.*

Lance's instructions were to call Sliger as soon as he returned to his car. He decided to get the hell out of Hicksville first. The way their simple plan fell apart; self-preservation over road orders, escape and distance from the scene became top priority. As he pulled out onto Main Street, Lance heard sirens. Looking ahead about two blocks, he saw a patrol car shoot across the intersection, heading north...toward Ned's. *That bartender must have called right after she entered Ned's house. Shit, that was close; too late, bitch.*

Lance veered left a block earlier than the most direct route to the main highway. He decided to use back streets. As he pulled up to a stop sign, he slapped the steering wheel and yelled out loud, "Jesus, that was close."

Turning right and seeing the onramp, Lance felt elated. *I'm going to make it.* Picking up speed, he reached for his satellite phone. Suddenly, Lance dropped it like it seared his hand. *Okay, so it didn't go as planned. The end result turned out the same. But, I didn't have time to do a walkthrough. What if I made a mistake…left evidence, dropped or overlooked something in my haste. I better think through what went down before I call Sliger.* Panicked, Lance reached down to his jacket pocket and thankfully felt the plastic case holding the syringe and the near empty vial of Propofol. Exhaling loudly, Lance forced himself to relax. *Okay, just go over everything that took place inside the house.* Lance did just that.

After putting on gloves, Lance scanned the dark backyard from the stoop. Canvassing the area, Lance's search ended at the large black locust tree near Ned's open window. *Fucking ants.* He turned the knob and entered.

Lance quickly moved over to Ned sprawled across the couch. Ned hadn't moved a muscle since Allyson left. Lance turned Ned's face from side to side; nothing. Then he gave Ned a vicious backhand. *Good, out cold.* Lifting the unconscious man's head, Lance searched the hairline and found what he needed. Just at the base of Ned's short sideburn, Lance saw a small razor cut. Sliger's head of security, Ron Townsend, told Lance to take off Ned's shoes and socks and find a mole or blemish. If none then just use a spot in between two toes. Lance knew when he'd heard Townsend's advice that that wasn't going to happen. Taking out the plastic case holding the vial and syringe, Lance popped it open. Sticking the needle in the vial, he withdrew a good load of Propofol. Lance turned the needle up and pushed the plunger until fluid came out. He didn't know why but had seen actors in lab coats do it on TV. Lance stuck the tiny needle into the razor cut and depressed the plunger slowly. Lance's instructions required him to carefully use 15 ccs, but he figured, *screw it; close enough.* How much Propofol had he actually drawn; how much had he administered? In reality, Lance had no clue nor did he care; just as long as he set up the suicide quickly, it didn't matter.

Lance moved off to the kitchen to find the liquor cabinet for the Maker's Mark and to grab a knife. As he passed through the living room toward the bedroom, Lance opened the whiskey bottle and tipped it over on the coffee table. In the bedroom, he pulled out a long segment of drapery cord, cut a good eight feet free, then moved to the bed. Lance took off his shoes and leaped up in the middle of the huge, spongy bed. When he looked up to the light fixture above, he panicked. *Shit!* Lance couldn't tie off the cord; he was too short. Frantic, he leaped from the bed and grabbed a chair, but the soft bed made it too unstable. Lance put the chair sideways but that didn't work either. *Shit, shit, shit; what's with these old houses and high ceilings? Nice plan, Townsend. How am I supposed to dangle Ned's upper body off his bed if I can't reach the damn ceiling fixture? Shit!* He leaped off the bed, retrieved the chair and grabbed his shoes. Feeling panicky, to calm himself Lance sat in the chair and forced himself to slowly and deliberately retie his shoes. It didn't work; his anxiety grew as he shot to his feet and bolted from the bedroom.

Racing into the living room, his beady eyes frantically scanned the ceiling. He focused on the fan above the couch and figured he could use it. Lance straddled Ned on the couch, threw the cord into the fan blades and pulled the fan's chain. When the cord wrapped around five or six times, he pulled the chain again. But the fan started turning faster. *Shit!* Lance pulled the chain again and the blades slowly churned to a stop, but not before the fan took in too much cord. *Shit!* Lance pulled on the cord but it didn't budge. *Shit. Think, goddammit; you're running out of time.*

Lance sprinted back into the bedroom to get more cord but couldn't find the knife. *Shit!* Lance noticed a tie on the floor by the chair he'd used. *I must have knocked it off of the chair. Mmm, perfect…a silk necktie.* Lance picked up the tie, found another one in Ned's closet, then scurried back to the couch. With great effort, he pulled Ned's body to the edge of the couch. Lance twisted and tipped Ned's chest, shoulders and head over the back of the couch. Ned flopped down like a rag doll. Lance tied one tie around Ned's neck then knotted the two ties together. Ned made a moaning sound which caused Lance to leap backwards and nearly fall off of the couch. *Shit; he's coming around.* Lance nudged Ned in the head and waited, but Ned remained still. Lance stood on the couch again and tied a loop in the cord. Putting his fingers under the knot around Ned's neck, Lance pulled Ned up high enough to put the second tie through the loop in the cord. Now sweating, Lance pulled up on Ned's neck and down on the second tie. His effort straightened Ned somewhat upright on his knees but still left Ned leaning off the back of the couch. Ned's hands dangled about eighteen inches off of the floor. Lance let go of Ned and held the second tie with both hands. Pinching the tie where it passed through the loop in the cord, Lance fought to wrap two half hitches without Ned's body dropping too much. Finished, he stepped back, exhausted from the effort. Backing up to admire his work, Lance decided to push the couch forward a bit to pitch the now suffocating Ned Penrose further over the back.

As he gripped one side of the couch, Lance heard dogs barking. He turned his head toward the backyard. Growing headlights and the sound of crunching gravel made Lance turn hollow inside. *Shit, shit, shit!* Frantically, Lance fast crawled over to the nearest wall and worked his way to the edge of the large back window. An older car pulled right up to the back stoop and stopped. Lance could see the bartender from Pete's Place in the driver's seat. *Shit; what's she doing here? She doesn't even like this guy.*

Stacey's beater rattled to a stop and she quickly stepped out. Obviously worried, she marched up to the back door. Lance nearly had a heart attack as he backed away into the kitchen. *Oh shit, oh shit!*

Stacey knocked and called out, "Ned? Ned, it's your favorite bartender."

Lance maneuvered as quietly as he could to the front door. The lock produced a slight click. He slipped out through the door and just before he pulled it closed, Lance heard the back door open.

The bartender said again, "Ned?"

Letting go of the door, Lance turned and raced across the short lawn and leaped over the small fence, but his front foot clipped the top. Lance fell awkwardly onto the sidewalk with a thud. Dog barking erupted as Lance stood up grimacing and clutching his knee. *Shit!*

From inside Ned's house, Lance heard Stacey scream, "Ned!"

As Lance hobbled his retreat, his thoughts returned to what became the theme of the evening's effort...*shit!*

Not quite what they had planned; Lance needed to think through and sanitize before talking to Sliger. Ignoring Townsend's recommendation to try a few dry runs and to discuss contingencies would definitely become a huge problem...if the whole story came out. That's why Lance had to get his version down pat before calling Sliger. Bottom line, distraught Ned successfully killed himself and, in five hours plus some change, Allyson will join him.

Twenty miles south of Cedar Creek, Lance dialed and waited. On the first ring Sliger picked up and yelled, "What took you so damn long? What went wrong?"

Chapter Twenty-five
The Last 24

For the two weeks following Whit's sentencing, Whit and Katelyn remained inseparable, almost exclusively at his cabin. Not a clinging, desperate two weeks but an intimate, almost casual fourteen days. Whit kept his phone unplugged and only activated it when Katelyn called in to work or when he periodically checked in with his dad.

Katelyn stepped up and maintained a positive and defiant attitude. She refused to give in to mounting sadness or impending despair. If Whit became quiet or started simmering, she stepped in and pulled him out of the slightest melancholy.

She proved to be so great that a little piece of Whit's brain told him, *I can do this. I can come out in three years and start again where we left off.* The rest of his brain wished to believe the dream, too. But serious doubts continued to rise to the surface and refused to recede. The guilt of leaving Katelyn in limbo, the doubt that his self-reliant, independent, free spirit could survive intact, and the knowledge that he could never possess a gun or hunt again welled up anger, screamed failure, and foretold…a meltdown.

Time never relents, and eventually their last full day together arrived. Whit woke early, started the fire, showered, then began making coffee and cooking. Either on purpose or by coincidence, Katelyn woke up to the smell of bacon. She knew in an instant, Whit planned to prepare French toast. Was Whit subtly reminding her by coincidence that the end was near or just fixing her one of her favorite breakfasts? She chose to think the latter and slipped out of bed.

Katelyn threw on one of Whit's flannel shirts and buttoned it down the front. She snuck up to the bedroom door and peeked out to watch Whit.

Whit had his back to her and appeared oblivious but then he said, "Hey beautiful; ready for some cowboy coffee?"

Frustrated, Katelyn walked forward and asked, "How did you know I was watching you?"

"In my line of work, you develop eyes in the back of your head."

Katelyn started running toward him and said, "Your floors are cold as ice…catch."

Whit barely had time to drop his spatula, turn around and step away from the stove before Kate flew into his arms. She wrapped her legs around his waist and hugged him tightly.

After they kissed, she asked, "Really, how did you know I was peeking at you?"

Smiling, Whit said, "I caught a glimpse of Stinker out of the corner of my eye. She popped her ears up and looked your way. I didn't hear you, but she did."

"In touch with your world, aren't you?"

Whit slipped his right hand under his borrowed shirt and right up the crack of Katelyn's ass. He said, "Very much in touch."

"Oh, mmm, warm-hand cowboy; but this cowgirl wants coffee, a shower, coffee, breakfast and ahh, coffee. If you take me on a picnic, though, I'll definitely be in the mood for…warm hands."

Whit bit her lightly on the chin and said, "Deal."

She released her legs and Whit gently let her slide down to the floor. Whit poured cowboy coffee into a mug, which she eagerly accepted.

Whit said, "The stove should have the water hot by now." Then he pointed at a linear wet spot near the bottom of his t-shirt and said, "Snail trail."

After taking a sip of coffee, Katelyn smiled and said, "I told you I needed a shower. As she walked toward the bathroom, Katelyn pointed at Whit's t-shirt and said, "That's mostly you, by the way."

Turning back to the stove, Whit replied, "Guilty."

After he heard the bathroom door close, Whit shook his head and said to himself, *three years; guilty as charged.* His defeatism lasted a whole two seconds before he thought, *stop the self-pity, Whittingham; it's Katelyn's last day. Make it special for her like she's done for you the past two weeks.*

After way too much breakfast, they sat on the front porch couch swing with the last of the coffee. After the early-morning chill, the mid-morning temperature and lack of breeze informed Whit the day would turn quite warm. He told Katelyn, because of the heat, he knew the perfect place to picnic. She seemed excited about their adventure. After draining their coffee, they washed the dishes together, changed the sheets and made the bed.

While making peanut butter and jam sandwiches for their picnic lunch, Whit told Katelyn to use elderberry jelly.

Katelyn said, "Okay, and why?"

"Elderberries contain lots of natural pectin. The jelly congeals very firm. If you use the boysenberry jelly, by the time we get to where we're going, our bread will be soggy and purple."

Katelyn nodded. "Gotcha."

They placed the sandwiches, two apples, a small bag of chips and two large stouts into various pockets of Whit's cruiser vest. Whit put on his web belt with two-quart canteens filled with spring water.

"Does this reporter get an itinerary?"

Whit said, "Sure. On the way we'll stop by an open mineshaft. It's about six feet in diameter and drops straight down, probably over one hundred feet. We think it's an air shaft for the Red Ledge Mine, so it could bottom out even deeper. Then we'll mosey through a healthy mixed conifer forest I thinned about ten years ago. If we have time we can check out a section of Rock Creek, catch some grasshoppers and feed the rainbow and brown trout. Eventually, we'll walk through a large hydraulically mined diggings and on the far side we'll end up at our lunch spot."

"I'm intrigued, mountain man; lead on."

Over the next two and a half hours Katelyn received a crash course in historic hard rock mining, placer mining, basic forestry, plant physiology, fire ecology, wildlife biology, fresh water aquatics and how the indigenous people used the land prior to the gold rush. Katelyn allowed Whit to ramble on. She only brought up questions to get clarification on a point. As they walked by the stacked rocks, old rusty, riveted pipes, scraggily brush and stunted pine trees in the bottom of the huge clay and gravel diggings, Katelyn felt overwhelmed.

As they walked toward a large reddish clay dune, Katelyn put her arm through Whit's and said, "So much to know and retain."

"We're not done yet," Whit said. "Hear that noise?"

Katelyn listened for a second then said, "Frogs; lots of frogs."

Whit said, "Tree frogs." He tipped his head for Katelyn to look forward.

As they rounded the dune, a deep blue pool about one hundred feet across came into view.

Katelyn said, "Whoa, that's beautiful. It's so clear."

"We call it Blue Hole. There's an upwelling of water that keeps it clear, as long as wind, bears, or swimmers, like us, don't disturb the banks."

"Bears?" Katelyn asked while looking around.

"Sure; they get hot, too. In the spring, bears get wet, then wallow in mud. When the mud dries, it helps pull off their winter coat. Today they'd just hop in to cool off, but we have priority today."

Whit and Katelyn walked up to the water's edge where Whit had fastened together some oak pallets, gray with age. Whit took off his cruiser's vest and web belt. He grabbed the full canteen and handed it to Katelyn. He drained what was left in the other one then sat down. Katelyn drank, then handed the canteen back to Whit and sat next to him.

Katelyn said, "I can't see the bottom."

"That's because it's damn deep. Lunch?" Whit asked.

Katelyn started unbuttoning her shirt and said, "Swim first; I want to cool down."

Whit nodded and said, "Deal," as he bent forward to untie his boots.

When undressed, they stood side by side. Katelyn stepped in front of Whit, held his hands and leaned forward. She stuck her foot in the water and said, "Kind of warm."

"There's a warm layer on top, but don't go too deep."

Katelyn noticed something small dart off under the water. She pointed and asked, "Was that a tadpole?"

Whit said, "Oh, I forgot to tell you; someone planted some tiny little Asian catfish in here. If you keep moving though, they won't bother you."

"What do you mean if I keep moving?"

"I guess these little buggers can be aggressive. If you're a woman and you don't keep moving, these fish have been known to swim up orifices. They have spines on their gills that make them tough to get back out."

Katelyn backed into Whit who didn't budge. Shaking her head, she said, "I am not going in there."

Whit cupped his hand around her crotch and tipped her forward, "I'll keep them out for you."

Inches from falling in, Katelyn yelled, "Whit!"

Whit held her firmly and calmly said, "Kate, I'm pulling your leg."

Slapping his thigh, she said, "You scared me."

"The only fish in here are bluegill; your orifices are safe…from them."

Whit sidestepped her and hopped in. She stood on the pallet watching him with her arms crossed. Finally, she gave up trying to be mad and dove in. When she surfaced, her eyes showed surprise.

"Geez, you weren't kidding; it's cold down there."

Whit said, "That's why I jumped in." While treading water, Whit added, "During one particular dry winter and hot summer, this pond dropped about twenty feet. As clear as it was, we still didn't see the bottom. It must be more than one hundred feet deep."

Whit swam backwards and pointed to the far side. "See that log, Kate?"

She swam over to him and said, "Yes."

"It's called a brow log. We place them on the bank next to a filling station. When I logged that timber stand we walked through, the logger's water truck drafted water from there. He sprayed it on the roads to keep the dust down."

Looking concerned, Katelyn asked, "Don't you suck up the little frogs and fish?"

"We put a gunny sack over the intake screen, but yeah, we sucked up a few."

"Doesn't that harm the…population or genetics or something?"

"Ah hell, Kate; you ought to see the carnage when the mergansers arrive. That's a frog-and-fish-eating duck. Between mergansers and King Fishers—that's a smaller fish-eating bird—most of the frogs and a good number of bluegill become lunch."

Katelyn replied, "Oh, I see. That ties in to your wildlife population dynamics talk earlier, doesn't it?"

"I see you were listening." Whit tipped his head toward the pallets and said, "Speaking of lunch?"

They both turned and side-stroked back to the pallets, Whit said, "One more point; the clay on the banks feels like talcum powder, it's so fine. It really sticks to you. Try to hop up on the pallet when you get out."

Katelyn said, "Now you tell me. Well, it would serve you right if a bunch of mud stuck in my…parts."

"Well, for self-preservation's sake, I'll help you out."

Whit swam over to the pallet, grabbed the edge and pulled himself up while twisting. He spun around and dropped his butt on the edge of the pallet.

Katelyn said, "I don't think I can do that."

While leaning back and placing all their clothes in a pile, Whit said, "You don't have to. Just give me one of your hands, put your feet on the pallet. Give me your other hand and I'll lift you out."

She did as she was told, and when Whit held both of her hands, he started to pull her out of the water. In a squatting position with her butt just out of the water, Katelyn said, "Stop for a second."

As Whit suspended Katelyn over the water, she spread her knees apart and said, "All clear?"

Whit grinned while looking between her thighs. "Nice vertical smile there, Kate, and yes, all clear, no little fish or mud."

"Thank you, kind sir."

Whit lifted Katelyn forward, then sat back on the pallet. He drew Katelyn to him and she straddled his lap. They wrapped themselves together and kissed. When their tongues touched, Katelyn put both hands around Whit's shoulders and, with her legs spread wide, started grinding her crotch into his pelvis. Whit put one hand back to support them. He moved his other hand to the base of her ass. Each time she pressed against him he pulled her to him and up slightly, forcing more sensitive contact. She pulled her left hand down and under herself to find Whit's balls. Katelyn cuddled them in her hand, pulled on them slightly and scratched under each one gently. She could feel Whit responding, growing. "Mmm" she said, wondering how making love on a pallet could feel so good, so comfortable. Then she realized, *that's why Whit put all our clothes together*.

Katelyn put her lips to Whit's ear and whispered, "I thought I was initiating this, but I see you already had this planned."

"Shit Howdy ma'am, no splinters."

Katelyn kept rocking and grinding against Whit. Eventually she rose up slightly, drew Whit's member back a little then sat back down. She used her hand to press him against the crack of her ass as she moved up and down slowly. He became very hard and slippery which pushed her to the limit of her patience and willpower. She took her hand away and stopped moving. Whispering, she said more to herself, "Wait, wait; not yet."

They sat motionless for maybe fifteen seconds, but Whit could tell any movement would be too much. He grabbed Katelyn's ass with both hands and raised her up. They lined up instantly. Katelyn slid back down enveloping him. She could tell by Whit's breathing she had only seconds, so she started half humping and half wiggling wildly. When she felt him explode, she pulled back-wards until his head rested just inside her vagina. She could feel him pulsing as her muscles squeezed around him. As she drew him back in, her body shud-dered too. Whit's head fell forward while Katelyn's rocked back. They held each other focusing only on the sensation. Finally, Katelyn dropped her head on Whit's shoulder. They remained panting and sweating.

Finally, Whit said, "Wow."

"Wow, indeed," Katelyn responded, while wiggling gently.

Whit and Kate eventually decided they were starving; but first, they helped each other up and jumped back in the water. After they rinsed off, Whit hopped out and pulled Katlyn out, the same as before. They sat back down on their clothes, straddling each other's legs, crotch-to-crotch again, and ate their lunch. By the time they finished their stouts, the sun had dried them and a good portion of their clothes.

As they headed back, Whit hoped the memory of this perfect day with Kate would hold him steady, somehow sustain him, maintain his sanity during the long hours, weeks, months, years without her. Deep down inside he knew it would be just the opposite.

They bee-lined straight back to the cabin, but still took their time. When they could, they held hands, but most of the walk back they spoke very little. Obviously, the weight of the looming forced separation could no longer be pushed away.

At the cabin, Whit and Katelyn shared another stout on the front porch swing. Stinker, obviously more comfortable with Katelyn around, came by for her cut. Katelyn poured the beer into the ring-tailed cat's tuna can and Stinker actually allowed Katelyn to stroke her tail. Stinker left to prowl her domain while Whit and Katelyn rocked and held each other. As long shadows started forming in front of them, they moved indoors.

A light dinner of salami, cheese, grapes and apple slices seemed appropriate. After eating, they decided to take a bath together in Whit's cast iron tub. Whit started a fire to heat the water in the coils woven back and forth in the back of the stove. At the last minute, Katelyn wanted popcorn. Whit just grinned and nodded his head. He heated oil in a pan, tossed in the kernels and covered the top. When the corn started popping he shook the pan vigorously until the pop-ping stopped. Whit dumped the hot popcorn in a bowl and added a little salt. They took it in to the bathroom with them. With too much on their minds, at this point, bathing together was not sensual or erotic, just intimate. They were connecting together in love; not sexual love, just plain, no-one-else-in-the-world love. They didn't verbalize it, but it remained foremost on their minds.

Katelyn assumed Whit had agreed to try out the future, her way…he on the inside and she on the outside, waiting. In Whit's mind, he agreed to try; that's all…try. They actually drained the tub and filled it again. Katelyn rested against Whit's chest and Whit wrapped his arms around her. They let the water fill slowly to avoid steaming up the place too quickly. Finally, with their behinds getting sore, they gave up.

After brushing their teeth, Whit and Katelyn climbed into the clean sheets they had changed earlier. Whit decided to reenter the world and plugged in his phone. He lay on his back while Katelyn snuggled up against him. Katelyn loved her hands massaged, and Whit held her right hand in his left. As he rubbed and squeezed her fingers, the phone rang.

Katelyn complained, "What the hell? You can't stop now. You have to do both hands or I'll be uneven."

Whit grinned at her and said, "I need to take this; it could be my pardon."

"Not funny, Whittingham. Besides, we both know that's not going to happen."

As Whit reached for the phone, he replied, "I know. Bad joke; but this late, it's probably something important."

Whit picked up and said, "Whit here."

After a two- or three-second pause, Whit heard Grey say, "Ben."

Ben…not Whit…something's wrong; maybe something's happened to my dad. Whit sat up and said "I'm here, Grey."

Now Katelyn sat up and leaned into Whit so she could hear. Whit moved the phone between them.

Grey finally said, "It's Ned; he hung himself tonight."

The shock created a huge emptiness in Whit's chest. Katelyn grabbed Whit's shoulder for support and put her other hand up to her mouth.

Whit asked in a low even tone, "Hung as in dead or hung as in tried?"

"I don't know; your dad called me because he couldn't get you. I did hear your dad yelling to someone to bring the ambulance around to the back of Ned's house."

Throwing the covers back, Whit said, "Kate and I can be there in twenty-five."

Grey replied, "I'll be right—" realizing Whit had already hung up. Grey lowered his phone and said to himself, *behind you.*

Chapter Twenty-six
If You Don't Mind, Sheriff

When Whit and Katelyn arrived at Ned's, Whit noticed no coroner and no ambulance. He hoped Ned rode to Sutter Memorial, code three, instead of to the morgue with no lights and siren. Seeing his dad's cruiser, Whit pulled up alongside the sheriff's sedan. He noticed the passenger door open and someone inside. He walked around to the passenger side with Katelyn at his side. Stacey Cummins sat half in and half out of the front seat. She jumped up when she noticed Whit. She wasn't crying, but her puffy face and red eyes proved she had been. Stacey grabbed Whit tightly, letting him support nearly all of her weight. When she backed away, Katelyn stepped forward and they hugged.

Whit tried to wait for Stacey to speak first but couldn't. "How is he?"

"I don't know, Whit; unconscious, non-responsive. The paramedics had him on oxygen when he left. His heart and lungs were working on their own, but Jesus, Whit, he looked terrible."

"Brain damage?"

"No way of knowing, but quite possibly."

"What happened, Stace?"

Before Stacey answered, Bill Whittingham walked up and put his arm on his son's shoulder and squeezed Katelyn's hand. "Benjamin, Kate."

"Dad, what the hell happened here?"

"Apparently, Ned hung himself. Stacey found him. I was just going to take her statement, that is, if you're ready, Miss Cummins?"

Stacey shook her head affirmatively.

Sheriff Whittingham offered, "Let's run down to the station and get you out of the cold."

"If you don't mind, Sheriff, I'd rather go to the bar. I'll make coffee, but what I really want is a drink."

Nodding, Sheriff Whittingham looked at his son and asked, "Ben, can Katelyn and you take Miss Cummins? I'll be along shortly, after I line out my men. I've sent one of my officers to the hospital. He'll call with any news."

"Okay, sure. Can you tell one of your officers to tell Grey, when he shows up, that we're at Pete's Place?"

Sheriff Whittingham nodded as he walked back to Ned's home.

Fifteen minutes later, Stacey brought a pot of hot coffee to Whit's table along with a bottle of Bushmills Irish whiskey. Katelyn set down five mugs just as Sheriff Whittingham came through the front door. Bill and Whit added a splash of Bushmills to their coffee. Katelyn and Stacey added a splash of coffee to their Bushmills.

Katelyn looked toward the front door and asked, "Shouldn't we wait for Grey?"

Bill replied, "No; by all protocol, you two shouldn't be sitting in on this either, but under the circumstances...." Bill's voice trailed off. He turned to Stacey and asked, "If you're ready, Miss Cummins?"

"Sheriff, it's Stacey or Stace, okay? 'Miss Cummins' sounds way too young...and innocent."

"Fine, take your time and please start with your conversation with Allyson Chandler." Bill saw his son's reaction and stopped Whit before he spoke. "Ah-ah, Ben!"

Stacey took a big gulp from her mug, closed her eyes and swallowed. When she opened her eyes, she was ready. "So, since it was a weeknight, slow night, I closed early...I think around 10:30. Just as I had everything about wrapped up, that hooker—"

"Allyson Chandler," the frowning Bill Whittingham corrected.

"Okay, Sheriff, I'll try to avoid editorializing." Stacey recited the encounter verbatim, just as it unfolded.

Stacey looked up as the front door opened, and coldly surveyed Allyson as she entered the bar. Allyson appeared upset and a little bent over as she closed the door.

"Good evening, Stacey," Allyson offered.

Stacey shot back, "You look like shit, Cruella; one of those little Dalmatian puppies bite you in the snatch?"

Ignoring the insult, Allyson asked, "I need you to do a favor for me."

Something's wrong. "Why should I do anything for you?"

"It's not for me, really; it's for your, ah, friend Ned."

Stacey thought, *she's dumping him*, but asked, "What?"

"Can you check up on him tonight, please? The sooner the better; he's kind of upset."

"You dumping him?"

"It's not like that."

"Are you dumping him?"

Looking away, Allyson said in a slight voice, "Yes, but it's not—"

"Fuck you! Get out!"

Allyson yelled back, "If you give a shit about Ned, do it. If not, then fuck you! You're no better than me." With that, Allyson turned, walked to the door and yanked it open.

Stacey offered, "Hey, Cruella." When Allyson stopped, she added, "I'll do it."

Allyson didn't look back but said, "Thank you."

Bill held up his hand at his son and asked before Whit could, "Did Allyson explain why she dumped Ned, or say where she was going?"

"No, she just walked out; but she was very upset, too. If I had to guess, she felt badly and either didn't want to leave or she had to leave."

Whit asked, which got a nasty frown from his dad, "What the hell does that mean?"

Katelyn cut in. "Men; Jesus. It means she cared for Ned but couldn't stay."

Exasperated, Whit asked again, "But, what the hell does that mean?"

Bill yelled, "You two shut up; sit there like church mice or you're gone. Got it?"

Katelyn and Whit looked at each other then back at Whit's dad and nodded.

Stacey said, "I turned out the lights, locked up and beat feet to Ned's. I drove around to the back and saw Ned's car parked there, that's all. I walked up to the back door and knocked; nothing. I yelled his name; nothing. I didn't hear any movement in the house so I turned the knob. It was unlocked, so I walked in, calling his name. I could smell booze, lots of booze. That's when I saw the cord hanging from the ceiling fan and Ned dangling over his couch. I screamed his name. He must have tossed the cord into the fan then turned it on long enough to jam it tight. But then the cord was too short so he tied two ties together to the end of the cord. He wrapped the lower tie around his neck, got on his knees on the couch and just leaned over the back."

Whit couldn't stand being silent. "I've known Ned all my life. I just can't imagine Ned doing that."

Bill offered, "Hell, Ben; could have been a combination of issues. We know how heavy the pressure of losing his family's business weighed on his shoulders. Maybe being dumped by another woman became just too much for him."

"Not my Ned; he was tougher than that. Besides, he still had his buddies, his religion, his community. There must have been something more."

Just then Grey walked in. He scurried over to the table and asked, "Any word on Ned?"

Everyone just shook their heads.

He poured whiskey in the last mug and sat down. "I have some very bizarre infor—"

"Quiet, Peckerneck. Miss Cumm…I mean Stacey…isn't finished with her statement."

Grey tried again. "But it's really—"

Sheriff Whittingham slapped the table which made Grey jump. Under Sheriff Whittingham's glare, Grey decided he better sip his whiskey. The sheriff turned to Stacey and said, "Please continue."

"Okay. So I ran around the couch and found him bent over the back with his head touching the floor. He still had a tie around his neck. Ned's weight must have pulled apart the knot holding the two silk ties together. I grabbed his belt and yanked him over the couch. The couch flopped over, too. I rolled him over on his back and tried to get the tie off his neck. I couldn't, so I pulled my Swiss army knife out of my pocket and cut the tie. I slipped the knife in beside his Adam's apple and, well, kinda cut his neck pretty badly." Looking around the table she added, "But he was bleeding; that's good, right?"

The sheriff patted her hand and said, "You did incredibly well, Stacey, really. Go ahead."

"I checked, and he was breathing, but very shallow. I quickly called 911." Pointing to Bill, Stacey said, "The sheriff beat the ambulance, checked Ned's vitals and loosened his shirt and pants. When the ambulance arrived, they took over. I tried calling you, Whit; so did your dad. Then he called Grey. That's when I walked out and sat in the sheriff's car."

No one dare utter a word.

The sheriff wrote for quite some time. Finally, he asked Stacey, "Did you see or hear anything during the entire time—anything, no matter how insignificant."

"No."

"Just go over the chain of events in your mind."

Stacey put her elbows on the table and rested her chin on her folded hands. Finally, she turned to Bill. "I heard a bunch of dogs start barking, soon after I entered the house, out in the front. That's it."

The sheriff responded, "Excellent, Stacey; thank you. If you think of anything else, let me know." Turning to Grey he asked, "Now, Peckerneck, what's your pressing revelation?"

Grey stunned everyone when he said, "Allyson came over to my place tonight, alone. She came on to me."

Whit clenched his fists and closed his eyes; he couldn't suppress his growing anger. *I knew there had to be something else.*

Stacy jumped in. "Cock hound, you didn't—"

"No! No, I did not touch her, I swear."

Katelyn asked, "Why would she do that?"

"I have no idea; it doesn't make sense."

Whit couldn't hold back. "It sure as hell does."

Taking offense, Grey snapped, "What the hell are you implying?"

"I knew there had to be something else. Something terrible that pushed Ned too far."

"I did not sleep with her!" Grey yelled.

"Doesn't matter if Ned thought you did. Your pathetic treatment of women bothered Ned, you know that. He knew you were better than being a womanizing gigolo. Maybe he was jealous or a little envious, too. Who the hell knows at this point? But, if he just thought you slept with his woman, how would that make Ned feel...devastated, let down, screwed over by a friend. What else could push Ned over the edge? Nice going, Milner." Whit pushed his chair back and stood up. "I can't stay here. Dad, can you take Katelyn to her car?"

Before Whit's dad could answer, Grey jumped in front of Whit and yelled, "Don't you dare walk away and try to put this on—"

A vicious left jab caught Grey's throat and blocked his next word. Grey staggered backwards and fell, holding his neck, gasping. His eyes turned huge as he made little gagging sounds. The table emptied as they rushed to Grey.

As Whit reached the door, he heard Katelyn yell, "Whit! He's really hurt."

Whit kept walking but thought to himself, *Maybe I did hit him too hard. Hell, what's the difference; I have to turn myself in tomorrow anyway. I'll have plenty of time to sort this all out...in prison.*

Chapter Twenty-seven
What the Hell

Heading across town and eventually east, Allyson wanted to get to Reno as soon as possible. A small meal in an expensive suite, a shower, and then a long sleep seemed in order.

But first Allyson needed to deal with Mr. Smith, a call she dreaded. She knew to play him...delicately. Mr. Smith would not be happy. Allyson knew to direct the conversation toward the half-assed profile of Greyson Milner and the out-and-out false profile on Ned Penrose if she hoped to salvage any part of her contract beyond the initial $50,000. Even the loss of the last $50,000 she could accept, but her fallback position centered squarely on keeping the Mercedes. Possession being nine-tenths of the law, after all, and she still really wanted the car.

Other oddities about this contract, beyond the bullshit profiles, kept buzzing around in her head, but she just couldn't pull them out into the open. Overriding it all, a first for Allyson, she had failed miserably. The fact that, eventually, she couldn't follow through with crushing Ned wasn't the only problem. Being turned down by a man, especially a cock hound like Greyson Milner, well, that hit hard. Pushing forty-one, Allyson pondered, *Am I losing my touch?* After some self-reflection, Allyson decided, *No, this operation turned out to be far more complicated than just the attraction of a man for a woman. These local boys possess some type of incredible connection, bond, brotherhood, and...loyalty it seems, at least when it came to each other.*

Allyson had dealt with unprincipled men for so long, maybe she just lost perspective. *Is that it?* If it is, that doesn't bode well for the future of Ms. Allyson Chandler's employment. *Shit. Okay, Allyson, park this crap for later and focus on the call. It needs to be done soon, before Lance gets wind of the whole truth.*

Driving down Cedar Creek's main drag, Allyson slowed down as she passed Pete's Place. She didn't see any patrons at the bar, and Stacey appeared to be closing up early. The old Allyson said, *We're done here, don't do it.* The new Allyson slowed down the Mercedes even more. Old Allyson jumped in, *Shit, just get the hell out of here, drive…wait, wait, why are you parking?*

Allyson said out loudly to herself, "Shut the hell up. Jesus, I'll only be a minute."

Pulling into the exact same spot where she parked the first evening she walked into Pete's Place, Allyson thought about chivalrous Ned and the quarters for the parking meter. *Well, at least he's still the same guy…I hope.*

While twisting and lifting herself out of the car, Allyson gave out a quick yip. "Ouch." Grabbing her lower back, she bemoaned, *What the hell, you old bag, there it goes again.* Massaging her lower back, she marched up the sidewalk and into Pete's Place. Would Stacey check on Ned? Allyson didn't know but felt compelled to try.

Twenty-two minutes later Allyson glanced at the dash. *Twenty-four miles, not bad; soon I'll hit I-80.* Allyson figured to be about as prepared as she would ever be; time to call Mr. Smith. Pulling over just before the interstate, Allyson grabbed her satellite phone and made the call.

After the first ring, Mr. Smith said, "Ms. Chandler."

"Mr. Smith."

A long pause ensued, until finally Sliger pushed the issue. "I'm a busy man, Ms. Chandler."

Yeah, right, you liar; not if you picked up after one ring.

Just when she parted her lips to start her selective report, Mr. Smith cut in again. "I've already heard from Lance. He was at Ned's house and said he heard everything."

Oh, shit; I'm sunk. That little weasel bastard; I should have done more than poke him in the eyes. Salvage mode, Allyson. "Look, Mr. Smith, I think you set me up with those profiles; they weren't exactly—"

"What is this?" Sliger cut her off. "Don't you dare play games with me, Ms. Chandler. We have a contract; you will not get a penny more."

A penny more? What the hell? Allyson stammered, "I'm a little confused here."

"Did you take some of the drug you gave Penrose? There is no confusion here. We had a contract, you fulfilled your end and I will meet mine, period. I'll transfer the money, but it won't happen until Monday. You take 'your' Mercedes back to Texas and we're done. Are we clear?"

Allyson thought, *anything but clear,* but said, "Clear as a bell; nice doing business with you, Mr. Smith."

They both hung up, but Allyson just stared at the phone. *What the hell just happened? I failed...but Mr. Smith thinks I didn't. How can that be if Lance heard Ned and me?*

She crested the summit when it hit her. It had to be. *Damn! That blowhard Lance must have been at Ned's watching but didn't hear what went on. He told Mr. Smith everything worked as planned. Well, Ferret, you just screwed your boss out of a Mercedes and $50,000. That is, unless they figure out the truth before Monday. I'm betting the $50,000 doesn't show up.*

Allyson drove for another five minutes before deciding she was in deep shit. Pondering that odd phone call from Mr. Smith, the other anomalies about the contract suddenly boiled up. *Why did we meet at that eco-building? It was obviously part of Mr. Smith's empire, not at a neutral location as before. The firewall separating me from any connection to them went out the window...why? They must have known I'd check who owned Serpentine Solutions. Lance all but confirmed Mr. Smith is Stephen Sliger when he slipped up and called him Mr. Slig-Smith, over the phone, at the hotel. So why meet me at Sliger's executive suite? Initially, the contract didn't appear to be that hard; yet when I asked for double my last job's price, Lance barely scoffed....why? And they tossed in the Mercedes as a bonus...incredibly out of character...why? There appears to be no connection between Mr. Smith/Sliger and these country boys. The previous contracts included men presenting a direct threat or potential danger. Why take the risk to destroy the lives of individuals with no apparent consequence or peril to you or your business? And why involve Lance and keep him birddogging my every move? Even the transfer of money in a few days instead of immediately just adds one more quirk. Of course,...I'd have to be alive to collect.*

Allyson let all those issues swirl around in her head as she drove on. Descending down the east side of the Sierra, some answers started to emerge.

By the time she passed the town of Truckee, Allyson wondered why she remained alive. *I know too much. Maybe Lance was supposed to kill me at Ned's but chickened out. No, killing me there would be too messy and would prompt a se-rious investigation. But, what if I died somewhere else, far enough away to eliminate any connection?*

The contract to harm Ned and Grey involved a personal attack, not for gain, but revenge…very emotional and personal. Allyson realized she knew too much, was a loose end, and a serious liability. The fact that she had failed and sooner or later they would know made it worse; but now she realized they were going to kill her anyway…but how? The two remaining connections between Allyson and the job involved the money transfer on Monday and the Mercedes. The money transfer seemed safe enough, but she already knew now Sliger never intended to send the $50,000. Why send money to a dead woman?

That left the Mercedes, the prize they knew she couldn't pass up. They were going to use the Mercedes to kill her, but how? A bomb? No, too dan-gerous; and a significant murder investigation would ensue. Plus, that would include the FBI. Probably run her off the road on a lonely stretch of desert heading for Texas. The car was easy enough to find and follow, especially if bugged. But it would have to look like a single-car accident, wouldn't it; no sideswipe damage, no paint or parts from another vehicle at the crash site. Well, whatever that little prick Lance had in mind, he'd stuck around Cedar Creek to set it up, sure as hell. Allyson had to ditch the Mercedes and disappear fast. Paranoid of every vehicle near her, she pushed on.

Instead of heading to one of the nicer Reno casinos, she drove past them all and turned south on 395. Allyson took the off-ramp for the Reno Interna-tional airport. Taking a ticket at the long-term parking gate, she placed it on the dashboard then drove to the back of the lot. Allyson backed into a well-lit parking place near a large light post. She took her time wiping the car clean of prints. Exiting the vehicle with her personal items, Allyson locked the door and dropped the keys on the ground. She scanned the parking lot as she walked to the terminal keeping a firm grip on her Lady Colt. Allyson needed to ditch the gun, but not until she entered the terminal. She'd use the bathroom, wrap the pistol in toilet paper and drop it into a waste basket. Allyson turned and looked one last time at the Mercedes. *Too bad, but if that car stays in this lot twenty-four hours, I'll be surprised. Hopefully, someone isn't right on my ass…track-ing, watching, stalking. If I can get out of here, Lance and his goons will be chasing after some dirt bag car thief all over Nevada. Have fun, asswipes.*

Entering the terminal, Allyson located the closest departure display. An Alaskan flight heading to San Jose in twenty-two minutes. Perfect; she'd just make it. Well, not perfect when you're running from an employer trying to kill you, but perfect in the sense of starting the disappearing act. At least Sliger thought she lived part-time in Texas when in the States and the rest of the time at her South American home in Brazil.

In reality, she lived in a nice flat in the French Quarter of New Orleans, and at a beach villa in Dangriga, near the Melinda Forest Reserve in Belize. Allyson thought, as she headed for the Alaskan counter, *Smoke and mirrors right back at you, you pricks.*

Chapter Twenty-eight
Loose Ends

Pulling into the basement garage at the Serpentine Solution's building in record time, Lance bolted from the car. He wanted to change his shirt and rinse his hair before the Inner Circle meeting. He kept finding and stripping bits of dead ants off of his body and clothes. Every time he did, he'd smell his fingers, grimace, and wonder when their vile little dead bodies quit stinking. After entering the secure code outside the elevator to the top floor, he took off his light jacket and snapped it in the air. He brought it to his nose and cussed. At the top floor, as soon as the elevator doors started to split, he shot through the gap. Hurrying down the hallway heading for his office, Lance saw Andrea up ahead, walking toward Sliger's office. He realized if he detoured, he'd be late. He cussed again. Walking briskly, Lance caught up with her at Sliger's huge double doors.

As one of the big doors swung open, he whispered, "Any news? The geek died, right?"

Andrea just glanced back at Lance with a blank stare. When she didn't respond, he tried to bypass her through the door. She bumped his hip forcing his shoulder into the closed door with a thud.

Lance yelped and snapped his head back toward hers but said nothing. Something in Andrea's eyes told Lance not to confront her and to just keep walking. That's exactly what he did.

Andrea wrinkled her nose and spoke to Lance's back as he moved toward his chair. "New cologne, Lance? Eau de Bug Guts?"

Lance slowed briefly while she spoke, but he didn't stop, turn around, or respond out loud. *Funny, bitch.*

Though not showing any anger, Andrea remained mad as hell at Steven Sliger. Earlier that evening, after one of her kneeling sessions with Sliger, he'd informed her about his and Lance's ongoing scheme to kill Ned Penrose and Allyson Chandler. They neither asked for her input nor informed her prior to activating their plans. Andrea certainly could guess why. She'd have walked them through a hundred pitfalls that would have forced them to back down. Lance knew how much Steven loathed his ex-high school buddies and how uplifted and animated Sliger became as the Inner Circle's actions against them turned fruitful. In yet another power play, Lance must have approached Steven with the proposals. How devastating to the old gang if the geeky beanpole, Ned Penrose, killed himself due to Greyson Milner's sexual prowess and betrayal.

Andrea shook her head as she thought, *Steven's analytical mind, free from guilt, morality or concern for the rule of law, managed to pull off an ever-growing string of high-yield calculated risks, all to the betterment of his empire. However, every one of those decisions came devoid of emotional attachment. Well, all that certainly changed with this ex-high school buddy project. Sliger's ability to clearly analyze and accept risk for a desired outcome now excluded good judgement due to personal hatred driving his decisions. Allowing Lance to attempt to kill Ned Penrose and do whatever they planned to Allyson unnecessarily jeopardized Sliger's entire empire. Their stupid stunt put them all in jeopardy.* Andrea reminded herself, *that's why I need to culture my Sean Peterson exit strategy, just in case. I better date him again and accelerate our bond a little closer.*

Andrea's deliberation continued. *Why is Steven risking all he...and we, created on this quest to destroy such peripheral, non-consequential people? Why keep me out of the loop? Why let a slacker like Lance, who never pays attention to detail, try to conduct 'black ops'? Steven has his head of security, Ron Townsend; he could pull these ops off blindfolded.* Grudgingly Andrea had to admit, *Well, Ron's worn out knee definitely restricts his ability to function.*

Andrea reached her chair, maintaining a neutral outward expression. She turned to Jeff Bowman, nodded and sat down.

Lance, still fussing with the back of his head, just sat down as Sliger entered from his private office. Jeff's stench overwhelmed Lance. Obviously, due to being forced to conduct extra research and attend this meeting on such short notice, Jeff couldn't control his nervousness or sweating.

Sliger walked around to the front of his desk and slowly looked at each one of his Inner Circle; his eyes refused to blink. Even Andrea felt a twinge of angst. He finally set his gaze back to Lance. Suddenly, he bellowed, "What the fu—" then caught himself and put up his hands.

Jeff leaped backwards so hard the heavy chair he sat in actually slid backwards nearly two feet. Sliger shook his head, then walked around his desk and sat. He caressed the back of his head with his left hand for a long time then looked at Andrea. "I apologize for keeping you out of the loop. Lance came to me with a proposal that I thought would wrap this whole operation up in one final maneuver. With Whit going to prison and Ned perceived as killing himself due to Grey's indiscretion, I thought the whole project could be successfully completed in a grand cataclysmic final act." Looking sternly at Lance, Sliger finished with, "Apparently, that's not the case."

Andrea just nodded her head in acknowledgement, portraying the dutiful trooper. But something she detected in Sliger's expression made her think; *there must be more...more problems.* She immediately thought of the other loose end and asked, "And Ms. Chandler?"

In a rare, awkward pause by Sliger, including a quick glance toward Lance, Andrea knew her instincts hit pay dirt.

Sliger sat back and tried to sound matter-of-fact, "Yes, well, the uppity Ms. Chandler signed her own death warrant when she arrogantly demanded double her fee and the Mercedes."

Andrea felt fairly certain Sliger was fudging the timeline, but asked, "So, she's dead? If so, how?"

Sliger sat back again into his chair and replied, "Not yet." He lifted his left hand toward Lance.

Lance cleared his throat and said, "Ingenious, really." Checking his watch, "In about four or five more hours of driving, somewhere in the desert west of Las Vegas, a carbon monoxide canister will go off under the passenger seat of the Mercedes. Her seatbelt and airbag will fail; Ms. Chandler will die in a single-car accident. She's as good as dead."

Andrea deadpanned, "Just like Ned Penrose?"

Afraid Andrea's insolence could turn the meeting against him, Lance bolted out of his chair, turned to her and yelled, "That was not my—"

"Sit down!" Sliger yelled. "We're getting way off point. What's done is done. This meeting will determine whether we continue or move to damage control."

When Lance sat down, Sliger turned to Jeff Bowman and asked, "What do we currently know?"

Jeff, feeling more at ease knowing Sliger's wrath focused elsewhere, sat forward and stated, "The last dispatch to Sheriff Whittingham stated Ned Penrose remains unconscious. Though he's breathing on his own, he's on oxygen."

Sliger told Jeff, "That will be all for now, Jeff; thank you. Monitor everything. I want any news on Ned Penrose and anything pertaining to Allyson Chandler's demise, immediately."

Watching Jeff scurry off and close the door to his computer world, Sliger finally turned to Lance. "What the hell happened?"

Lance recited his well-rehearsed version of the events that occurred at Ned's house. He conveniently left out the ant attack but stressed his quick thinking when he couldn't reach the light fixture over the bed and moved the suicide attempt to the couch. He of course left out winding too much cord into the fan, or the need to use two ties. Lance finished by bragging that his decision to use the fan over the couch instead of the light fixture over the bed actually allowed Ned to dangle longer before the bartender interrupted the op. That was why he determined Ned suffocated.

Obviously, with Lance's torn pant leg, slight limp and disheveled appearance, his report left out much detail. But Sliger remained more concerned about their exposure and asked, "No one saw you?"

"No, sir; not anyone. Even when I snuck up to hear Ned and Allyson argue, you know, to make sure the bitch wasn't double crossing us, they were oblivious to my presence."

Sliger already knew from Sean Peterson's monitoring of the Logan County sheriff's radio frequency and Jeff's hacking into the hospital computer system that, as far as the sheriff was concerned, the incident remained an attempted suicide.

Sliger continued. "And no evidence that you ever entered Ned's home?"

Lance reached into his pockets and retrieved his gloves and the plastic container holding the Propofol and syringe. Holding them up for proof, Lance responded, "Nothing other than these entered with me."

Sliger sat back with his fingers interlocked on his chest. He looked up but remained silent for quite some time.

Andrea finally asked, "Sir, may I make a suggestion?"

Sliger pivoted his chair toward Andrea and pulled his hands apart as a gesture for her to speak.

"As I assess our operation...and exposure, I see pluses and minuses. Benjamin Whittingham turns himself in tomorrow to be caged in Los Angeles for three years...a major coup. Grey's reputation with family, friends and his community just hit the toilet. Most certainly it will also negatively affect his business. We hit our minimum goal with respect to Grey...another success. Regardless of Ned Penrose's physical condition, he's soon to be financially wiped out. Since Lance assures us that Ned remained unconscious the entire time during his, ah...attempt to fulfill your wishes, no exposure exists toward us. For this operation, all in all, we've met our minimum objectives."

Lance, angered by the slight, began to object, but Sliger's glare stifled any rebuttal.

When Sliger turned his attention back to Andrea, he asked, "Minuses?"

"If for some reason the sheriff requests a toxicology report and finds trace elements of knockout drugs, we could have a problem. But, more than likely, though, Ms. Chandler becomes their primary suspect. That leaves what happens to Ms. Chandler as our only...loose end. I assume since you think she will die soon, you don't plan to transfer to her the final $50,000?"

Lance piped in. "Why pay a dead whore?"

Ignoring Lance, Andrea asked Sliger, "When were we to transfer the money, sir?"

Sliger told Andrea, "I told Ms. Chandler the money would be transmitted first thing Monday morning." More than a little annoyed, Sliger asked, "Why?"

"Because, sir; if for some reason the canister fails, someone steals the Mercedes, she gets in a fender bender and can't drive or one of a dozen other scenarios, Allyson will remain with the living. If the money does not arrive as promised, she'll know...or strongly suspect...that we knew she wouldn't be around to collect."

Those thoughts had never entered Lance's brain. By the look on the normally meticulous Steven Sliger's face, neither had he. They overlooked too much counting solely on Lance's complicated scheme.

Sitting up now, a far more concerned Sliger asked, "Suggestions?"

Andrea said, "If we do not receive 100-percent confirmation of Allyson Chandler's demise by early Monday morning, we better transfer that money. Potentially, she represents a very knowledgeable and very danger-ous adversary."

Sliger started to buzz Jeff Bowman, then changed his mind. Turning to Lance, Sliger said, "Go to Jeff's office. Tell him to monitor all emergency traf-fic from here to Las Vegas."

Lance made a sour face, aggravating Sliger, who yelled, "Move!"

When Lance left to enter the putrid computer room, Andrea said, "I pulled Sean Peterson, our only remaining footprint in Cedar Creek. He should be here shortly. I'll debrief him and come to you if he has anything new."

Sliger, lost in thought, waved her away; obviously, meeting adjourned.

Andrea stood up and turned for the door, more convinced than ever that their house of cards could crumble at any minute. *Dollars to doughnuts I bet Allyson smells a rat. She'll survive and show up to collect the transferred final payment. Best case, she just takes the money and disappears. Worst case, she'll know Sliger and Lance tried to kill her. No, she'll think I bought off on killing her, too. That woman will turn on us to reap serious revenge. Damn it to hell. Okay, Andrea, you know what to do. Play Mr. Sean Peterson like a fiddle tonight and have your disappearing act in place at the first sign of trouble.*

Chapter Twenty-nine
The Author Takes a Break

Finishing Chapter 29, the author—known as Sam Lund to everyone except Katelyn's agent—took a break. Katelyn sat back from her computer. She rolled her head around slowly. *Jesus, it's late and I need to pee so bad I can taste it.*

Shaking her head, Katelyn realized she'd done it again…one of those stupid sayings of Whit's had crept back into her head. She protested, *stop saying those things, stop keeping his memory alive.* "Get out of my head, damn you." *I thought coming back to the East Coast would help me forget you.* In a whisper she begged, "You're gone; go, just go."

The more she shook her head, the madder she became. Angrily, she vowed, "I'm done." *I will no longer think or repeat "Harder than a whore's heart," "drier than a popcorn fart," "hornier than a three-peckered billy goat," "slicker than shit through a tinhorn's ass," or any other of his stupid metaphoric comparisons.*

Looking at her clock she exclaimed, "Christ; I've been typing for six straight hours."

When she left her condo's windowless computer room to head for the bathroom, she entered the hall without turning on the light. Her mind quipped, *Darker than a well digger's ass in here.* "Oh, goddamn it."

Sitting on the toilet, she leaned forward and put her head in her hands. Even though the Benjamin Whittingham she thought she knew never really existed, the damn man remained locked in her heart. The power of his influence and hold over her just kept beckoning. *Why the hell did I start this damn book? Benjamin Whittingham, that's why. Why can't I move on…with anyone? Benjamin Whittingham, that's why. Why don't I just go back to my previous reporter life? Benjamin Whittingham, that's why.* Her hope beyond hope centered on the finality of the book. Maybe, just maybe, the completion of the book will end this…obsession. Hell, she had no clue. Or was it just the fact that, in some way, writing this book kept their relationship alive, breathing, somehow real? Exhausted and whispering through her hands, she sighed, "Ah, hell."

After splashing water on her face and walking down the hall back to her computer, Katelyn realized she wasn't tired anymore and decided to push on. She also recognized she had reached a gap in the book…a dead zone…a period of time when nothing happened.

She sat back down. How would she write through this lull in the real lives of all those people? The almost six-month hiatus had her flummoxed. Katelyn finally thought, *Well, what if I just list it, summarize what occurred and come back to it all later?*

She sat forward and started typing about, who else, Whit.

Whit left for prison without even saying goodbye…so like the stoic ass. Katelyn stopped for a second, hit backspace to eliminate the last three letters and wrote "bum." For the first month of incarceration Whit couldn't receive visitors; orientation they called it. Finally, when Katelyn could visit Whit, their meeting ended disastrously. He told her watching her walk away to freedom while he returned to his controlled, state managed, caged life nearly destroyed him. Seeing anyone or even hearing from "the outside" soured him, angered him, depressed him so much he started getting into trouble. Whit told her over their final phone call not to come anymore, not to write, and, if she could, just move on. For both of them that would be best. Whit said he knew of no other way to survive, to cope, and not go completely crazy. Katelyn felt devastated, but Whit refused to see her or even open her letters. Whit told his dad the same. Except for any news about Ned, he just wanted to live out his "dead time" with absolutely no contact from the outside.

Katelyn chose next to write about Ned Penrose. Poor Ned did recover… mostly. To this day, his oxygen-depleted brain couldn't recall what the hell happened that night. He never knew for sure that what he did remember was anything more than what he'd been told. He knew that Allyson and he fought, but maybe that was because Allyson visited Stacey at the bar that night. Allyson said she left Ned very upset and for Stacey to go visit him. Apparently, Stacey saved his life. The docs told Ned to expect about six weeks for his brain to recover, reroute, and mend whatever damage had occurred. After that, he could expect little additional improvement. Fortunately for Ned, his personality and most of his memory and physical abilities returned. He left the rehab facility with a cane due to bouts of light headedness and poor equilibrium. The cane stayed as part of his new life and, even after almost half a year, he still wasn't allowed to drive. To this day, though, he adamantly stressed he would never try to kill himself. The one plus for sad-sack Ned Penrose—Stacey Cummins stepped in to help. Stacey brought her sister down from Portland to work the bar during the day while Stacey kept Ned's store open. Stacey said she'd stay until Ned recovered and finished rehab. Whether the community felt sympathy, guilt, support, or just by coincidence, his business actually picked up under Stacey's management.

Greyson Milner felt the sting of his small, fairly close-knit community. After Whit punched him in the throat at Pete's Place, his personal and social life spiraled downhill. His antics with women—never popular—exploded with the rumors, half-truths and innuendos floating around about Grey's alleged involvement with Ned's woman. He stopped going to Pete's Place and, generally, out in public all together after Sheriff Whittingham pulled him over twice for chicken-shit traffic violations. The last time, Bill Whittingham told Grey, "Can't say since your mother died you've been acting mature enough to gain my or anyone else's respect, Peckerneck. You've lived off of the community and treated…certain citizens like shit long enough. You better act like Jesus Christ himself in my county. If you don't, I will personally make your life one miserable existence. Sign here and get the hell out of my sight."

Grey spent as much time as work allowed with Ned, though Stacey remained too irritated at Grey to allow him to help much at Ned's stationery store. To his great relief, Ned said he knew that nothing happened between Allyson and Grey. Ned didn't know exactly how he knew, but he was sure that was the truth. Ned also told Grey, "The doc says I can start having a drink or two. We better start going to Pete's Place on Tuesday evenings again. The more everyone sees us together, the sooner the community and Sheriff Whittingham will back off."

Katelyn eventually learned much of what happened to Allyson during this time from Whit. Allyson, out of the blue, came to Whit's prison on visitation day and, uncharacteristically, Whit saw her. That was a real game changer. Katelyn felt sorry for Allyson; her life story, so sad. But what Allyson tried to do to repair the damage she created, Katelyn believed, demonstrated Allyson's true character.

Katelyn sat back from typing to ponder the largest information gap in her book. She knew absolutely zero about what Sliger and his Inner Circle did during this six-month period. Gaps in her knowledge of the actions of the evil players in this tragedy remained the biggest voids. She admitted to herself, *Well, I'm writing this as a fiction anyway.* She assumed Sliger and his disciples decided to run silent and let the situations they created play out. With loose ends like Ned's faulty memory and Allyson Chandler's disappearance, they must have been worried about exposure. *Why didn't they just take their successes and cut their losses? They probably could have gone on with their evil, narcissistic lives and I'd still have Whit. No...no, that's not true. Sliger couldn't stop. In his sick, pathetic mind, to survive, his old buddies had to be destroyed. And my Whit; Jesus, after they tried to kill Ned, Whit would never have stopped either. Once he learned the truth, Whit's personal sense of right and wrong and his brand of justice took over. Christ, he became as obsessed as Sliger.*

Chapter Thirty
It's Not What I Want Anymore

At an emergency meeting of the Inner Circle, Steven Sliger exploded at the messenger. "Six months with our thumbs up our asses, letting everything slide, and now this…a goddamn backstabbing betrayal. This better be a mistake or an exaggeration, because I am in no mood for bad news."

Andrea seemed unfazed by Sliger's outburst and the information Earth Wild's attorney, Luna Waxman, conveyed to her fifteen minutes earlier. That phone call prompted Andrea to ask Sliger to summon the Inner Circle. She stood and slowly walked back and forth behind Lance's and her chairs, always stopping well short of Jeff's. Andrea noticed Lance's smug look, enjoying that it was she who currently sat in the hot seat.

She spoke confidently. "Luna Waxman informed me this morning that Judge Franklin, at the request of his son, will revisit Whit's conviction. Upon his review of new evidence, I am told, Judge Franklin will reverse his decision."

Sliger threw his hands in the air and yelled, "Who in the hell is Judge Franklin's son, and why is he aiding Whittingham?"

"He isn't, sir."

Sliger looked like he would explode. "You just said—" He knew he was missing something, so he sat down and ordered, "Explain."

"Trial Lawyer Andrew Franklin runs a large legal staff at Franklin, Diamond, and Goldberg in the Bay Area. As to why he requested a review of Whit's case, we don't know. But for sure he's not aiding Whittingham by choice."

In a slightly calmer voice, Sliger said, "Well, then, find out what's going on and stop him and stop that damn judge."

"That won't happen, Mr. Sliger. Ms. Waxman will not contest the review."

Angry again, Sliger hissed, "Why the hell not? Who do these people think they're dealing with?"

"Sir, Ms. Waxman told me in complete confidence that Diamond, Franklin and Goldberg retains certain...sensitive information regarding Earth Wild. I assume that information constitutes illegal and unethical activities. If revealed to the public, the fallout would devastate Earth Wild's reputation, fundraising and political leverage; their hands are tied."

"Goddamn it; so, Whit walks?" Slamming his palms flat on his desk, Sliger bellowed in cadence with his banging, "Fuck! Fuck! Fuck!"

Andrea noticed Jeff Bowman, with huge eyes, look around wildly while pulling his arms up and in under his chin. Poor Jeff reminded Andrea of a little frightened mouse. Even Lance sunk down as deep as his chair would allow.

In her same even tone, Andrea continued, "Whit walks, plus his one felony count will be vacated."

Sliger reverted to his toothy sneer. He emitted a low growling sound while he shook his head from side to side.

Andrea thought, *He really does look and act like a rabid dog.*

No one spoke while Sliger progressed through his enraged, cornered, wounded animal faze. Andrea had seen this side of Sliger enough to know he was about done and that they could soon focus on a game plan.

Finally, Sliger asked in an eerily quiet manner, "Well then, Ms. Moran, what exactly do we know?"

"I have some bits, and a theory about what happened."

"Then share."

"The judge's son, Andrew Franklin, maintains huge political aspirations and someone caught him doing naughty. He, and I assume the judge, are being blackmailed. And whatever it is, it's really, really bad."

Sliger's voice rose as she finished. "Do you have a name for this soon-to-be-dead blackmailer?"

"I believe it's Allyson Chandler."

It was Sliger's turn to be stunned. "What? How? Are, are you sure?"

Lance cut in. "No way, I can't—"

"It has to be her," Andrea interrupted. "A woman fitting her description also accosted the witness to the deer incident, our Mr. Barbou. She put a gun in his mouth and said he needed to retract his statement and recant his sworn testimony. She implied that we sent her as a messenger, and that we now want

Whittingham set free. Knowing Ms. Chandler's…talents, I can only assume she's the one holding the Franklins' and Mr. Barbou's testicles and their futures in her hands."

"Why in the hell would she help Whittingham?"

"Well, you did try to kill her, and she ditched the Mercedes; plus, she never picked up the final $50,000. Either she knows or strongly assumes she's supposed to be dead. It would take a miracle for her not to figure that out."

Annoyed, Sliger asserted, "Yes, yes, I get all that; but what's she have to gain? She's a whore heading to be an old whore. Old whores don't give a fuck for nothing. I just don't get it."

Andrea offered, "She wants hush money."

Sliger mulled the point over then said, "Possibly, or she's up to something else."

No one else spoke but all eyes focused on Sliger. Finally, looking exhausted, Sliger raised his gaze. He stared blankly past the three. The Inner Circle waited patiently; this was not the time to interrupt Sliger's thoughts. Finally, his focus returned and he started nodding his head slowly as if he had completed the formulation of a profound decision.

Sliger's look of determination reappeared and he calmly explained, "What was it, almost a year ago? I found out what ate at me, infected my thinking, my psyche. We took on and completed stage one of my therapy…recovery… revenge, whatever you want to call it. We put Whit in prison, nearly bankrupted Penrose and—" Sliger stopped and glared at Lance. "And almost successfully faked his suicide. We set up Milner and devastated his relationship with the gang, especially with Whit. Everything fell into place."

In a very rare moment of conciliatory outreach, Sliger looked at his eclectic lieutenants and offered, "At that time, I was the happiest I've been since… I can't remember. Your loyalty and devotion to duty made that possible. The only loose end…what happened to Allyson Chandler? We never found her. Jeff discovered the police report and article in the Reno paper about the two dirtbags that crashed and died in the totaled Mercedes. But Jeff found no electronic or paper trail to her anywhere. Well, she's back and needs to be dealt with, permanently."

Obviously, the unexpected accolade surprised Lance and Andrea. They quickly glanced at each other and traded raised eyebrows.

Jeff fidgeted and looked like he wasn't paying attention, but then said, "Thank you." Looking over his glasses he asked, "Can I go now?"

Glancing Jeff's way, Sliger offered, "Go ahead, Jeff." Jeff rose to leave but before he took one step, Sliger said, "Thank you for your assistance with the secure phone call. I'll need you to set up another."

Jeff raised his left hand awkwardly in acknowledgement then scurried away.

Sliger turned to his remaining two lieutenants and said, "I've decided I'm through with scheming and manipulating Ned, Grey and Whit's affairs to destroy their lives."

Both Lance and Andrea felt instant relief. Though they had never spoken to each other about Sliger's vendetta, they both felt the risk too great. Their very existence remained tied to the man that resurrected their lives. Obviously, their mentor relished and mentally reveled in this quest for revenge, but at what cost? Well, at least it was over. They could go back to their regular hectic lives and return to their grant funded slice of the business world, or at least that was what they thought.

Sliger observed the almost imperceptible liberation in Andrea's physical demeanor. Lance's relief, however, stuck out like a sore thumb. Sliger thought, *Still the weakest link, wearing his emotions on his shirt sleeve. Well, time to pop his bubble and man him up.*

"I enjoyed the process, but the operation took too long, became too complicated, included too many players and left too many actions out of my control. Now, much of our work has collapsed. I'm done; this is not what I want anymore."

Lance leaned forward and started to get out of his chair thinking they were finished. He stopped cold when Sliger continued.

"I've decided I want them all dead."

Andrea just sat forward waiting for instructions. Inside she screamed, *No, no, no, Steven! Shit, I'm done. I need to tell Sean, we need to be ready at the first sign of trouble.*

Lance sunk into his chair, and Sliger heard a visible moan. Sliger leaned over his desk and asked, "Something wrong, Lance?"

"Oh, ah, no, nothing." Lance stammered, then lied, "We should have just whacked them at the start and been done with it."

"I'm glad you feel that way, because you're taking the lead to make sure that's exactly what happens."

In a far less than confident tone, Lance responded, "Yeah, good; um, but how? I mean, how would you prefer it to be done?"

"Easy. With Jeff's indispensable assistance, I spoke on a secure line to Johnny Ramelli. He's agreed to send a couple of his professionals. They'll be working under my direction, through you."

Turning to Andrea, Sliger said, "Andrea, put Peterson back on surveillance. Keep Lance current with his latest intelligence."

Looking back at Lance, Sliger added, "When a window of opportunity arises, come to me. I'll look it over and give a yes or no. Ramelli can send his two men within twelve to sixteen hours of when I say it's a go."

Relieved that someone else would do the actual killing, a more confident Lance answered, "Sure, no problem; any particular order?"

Sliger replied, "All of them at once would be nice, but impractical. After thinking a little longer," he said, "I want Milner dead first…then Whittingham. As long as Penrose can't remember shit, we'll put him on the back burner." Curious, Sliger turned to Andrea, "When's the soonest Whittingham can be released?"

Andrea replied, "Ms. Waxman says probably a month or so. Whittingham has no clue and probably won't for weeks, unless Ms. Chandler contacts him. I assume she will."

Ignoring Andrea's last statement, Sliger focused on Lance. "I want to know the best time and place to take Milner out. It must look like a random killing or a robbery gone badly, something like that. We don't want to alert the cops or trigger Whit's instincts. Better to take out Milner while Whittingham remains locked up. You got that?"

When Lance just nodded, Sliger added, "And Lance, make absolutely certain nothing…I mean nothing, blows back my way."

Chapter Thirty-one
Too Good to Pass Up

Knowing Lance would be annoyed; Andrea marched into his office unannounced. Lance leaped about six inches off his chair. Andrea could distinctly hear a woman's heavy breathing, until Lance slammed down his computer screen. "Damn it, Andrea; how many times do I have to tell you, do not—"

"That's not good for your computer, Lance." When Lance glared but didn't respond, she added, "Peterson called; says he's stopping by."

Flustered but trying to recover, Lance acted serious. "When?"

Knowing what he meant but unable to stop herself, Andrea said, "About an hour ago."

"No, not when he called; when will he be here?"

"He's in the hall right now."

Lance stammered, "Shit, why didn't you tell me sooner? Shit. What's it been, only a week?"

Even though Andrea knew, she replied, "He must have some time-sensitive information; that's my guess."

"Shit, this is too soon. I'm not ready yet."

"Well, you better be; we're all meeting with Steven right now."

Getting up, Lance grumbled, "Shit."

With a broad, knowing smile, Andrea turned and walked out.

Andrea and Lance met Sean in the hall. They arrived in Sliger's office knowing their boss would enter from his private quarters at any moment.

Sean Peterson had been in Sliger's private office before, so he knew never to sit or stand near the far-left chair. That stinky spot remained forever reserved for Jeff Bowman. Sean stood beside Andrea's chair and snapped erect when Sliger opened his door and entered. Peterson wasn't a big man; he was a thick man. Next to Lance, his 5'10" height and 220-pound frame, big thighs, huge chest, massive arms and no neck made Sean look like a Mack truck next to a Vespa. His expression remained placid, revealing no emotion; not even his eyes. But those penetrating eyes hid a terrible secret. In one violent outburst, Sean had lost his dream, his passion, his calling since childhood. Sean was on the run and living a lie. He also found himself stuck, trapped, blackmailed into working for the little man that had just entered the room...a man Sean did not respect. But that man knew Sean's secret and could destroy him with a single phone call. All because of a single punch; hell, Sean knew he'd taken harder hits. His name back then was Gunnery Sargent Olstrum...Swede, to his friends. Swede was known as a hardnosed, hardworking, hard-playing and hard-drinking no-nonsense Marine's Marine. But after that punch, Swede's world took a radical turn. The four biggest changes: Swede left his house forever, never returned to his unit, never again drank hard liquor, and left his rather distraught wife's boyfriend with a caved-in face. Somehow Sliger found out that Sean Peterson, four years earlier and three thousand miles away, had been Gunnery Sargent Olstrum. How, Sean had no clue. Such is life when your secrets don't stay...secret.

Sliger sat down and immediately turned to Sean. "Report."

Sean began. "Andrea and I stay in touch. I give her a daily briefing and, except for today, it's been fairly dry. I've been focusing on Greyson Milner at your—"

"Don't waste my time telling me what I already know."

"Yes, sir. I bugged Milner's phone and scoped out his house after he left for work. He doesn't even lock his doors during the day. Monitoring his phone calls, I've heard nothing worth reporting until this morning."

Impatient, Sliger barked, "Yes, yes; go on."

"Milner will be receiving a visitor—a female—tomorrow night. She told him to clear his calendar for that night and the next day. It sounded to me like a hookup."

Excited now, Sliger asked, "Can we exploit this rendezvous? What do you know about her?"

Sean Peterson said, "Not much; just a voice on the phone...a very assertive voice." Peterson put down his tape recorder and, before he hit play, said, "This is the meat of their conversation."

They heard Milner's voice. "Weatherman says possible thundershowers east of here; maybe the Harley isn't a good idea."

Veronica responded, "Just because I have a pussy doesn't mean I am one."

"No doubts on this end, V; just be careful. How early in the evening are you thinking?"

"How the hell should I know? You'll know when you hear my pipes; but probably not early."

"Well, then, I look forward to...hearing from you."

"Clever, Milner."

Sean turned off the recorder and said, "Like I said...assertive."

Looking at the two attending Inner Circle members, Sliger asked, "Any questions for Peterson?"

Lance asked, "We know the layout of his house, right?"

Sean said, "Yes, I know the layout. I mapped it out; it's in the file. Milner's bedroom is in the back of the house. If you enter the backdoor, it's just to the right." Lance just nodded so Sean continued. "I also took pictures as I walked through the house and around the outside. I was going to pretend to be lost if someone came by, but I never saw a soul. No neighbors close, either. It's all there in the file."

Sliger looked at Andrea and flicked his eyes toward the door.

Andrea stood up and said to Peterson, "That will be all for now. Thank you for coming, Mr. Peterson. I'll walk you out."

Once outside of Sliger's office, Andrea squeezed his arm and said, "Nice work, stud. We need to talk."

"Thanks, gorgeous; work or pleasure?"

Smiling, Andrea replied, "Patience, horn-dog; work right now. Since your other target isn't out of prison yet, you can return to watching Milner's place. Pass on any new information to me immediately and if we activate something, I'll contact you."

Since being blindsided by Sliger and Lance when they took it upon themselves to try to kill Ned and Allyson without her input, Andrea wanted to get back to the meeting.

Andrea could sense Sean wanted to talk and didn't want to shut him down. She actually realized she liked the mini-Hulk, even if he screwed like a Bengal tiger.

Sean's obvious interest in her worked well for her plans. *The poor bastard doesn't even feel the hook.* She said, "I'll call you later; I have to get back in there." Sean nodded. As he turned to leave, Andrea whispered, "Later big guy."

Hurrying back to the door, she entered to only find Lance. "Where's Steven?"

"He's with Jeff setting up a call to Ramelli to activate the hitmen."

"So, you decided to pull the pin without my input...again?"

"It's too perfect, with no downside."

"That's what you two thought when you tried to take out Ned Penrose and Ms. Chandler. How'd that work out for you, for us?"

Defensively, Lance flared, "You can't pin any of that on me. Everything worked as planned until that bartender bitch showed up at Ned's unannounced. And Chandler ditching the Mercedes...the way she drooled over that car, no way in hell would anyone guess she'd dump it."

Andrea shot back, "Faking a suicide or a fatal car wreck always fails due to anomalies, flukes, the unexpected. You can't just rush off and hope for the best. Jesus, Lance, and all that James Bond crap with the monoxide canister...too complicated. And why do you think Ms. Chandler bolted? She lives by her wits and felt threatened, you pinhead. I told you not to underestimate her. Now, she's out there somewhere, a serious Goddamn threat to us."

Dismissively Lance chided, "Now who's whining? Jesus, Andrea, take a chill pill. Besides, all this could be over soon. You missed an interesting exchange with Steve while you were flirting outside with Peterson. We knock off Milner and Whittingham and we're done. Sliger said he doesn't give a shit about the other three guys in the old high school gang. Since Penrose can't out think a turnip, he's not a target anymore either. We're close, Andrea."

They heard a door open and saw Sliger exiting Jeff's computer sanctum. Rubbing his hands together, Sliger said, "We're all set. The two hitmen will be here before noon tomorrow. They're flying into Stockton, renting a vehicle, and driving up."

Lance asked, "They coming here?"

"No. They'll call Andrea when they get close; you'll meet them somewhere en route to Cedar Creek. They have your number, too. Take Peterson's information; let them look it over, but you keep it. Do one drive-by of Milner's place, but that's it. Stay the hell away from Cedar Creek until night."

Confidently, Lance said, "We'll pop Milner tomorrow night then move on to Whittingham when he gets out of the joint. I hope Whittingham goes down as easy as Milner."

Andrea couldn't let that go. "Lance, don't get ahead of yourself. Focus on Milner. Go over every inch of Peterson's report, maps, pictures, everything. Make sure our…out-of-town guests do, too."

"Sure, sure; no sweat."

Erasing the image of looking through steel bars…from the wrong side, Andrea pressed, "Lance, do not get cocky or leave anything to chance. The devil's in the details."

Chapter Thirty-two
That's Got to Hurt

The Milner family's Victorian was really the old Porter House—or Porter Mansion. At least, that's what the old miners called it. The Milner's bought it from Gertrude Porter in the 1940s. The frontier carpenters built the seventeen-room, massive, two-story structure well, in classic 1850s style. The boxy rooms displayed spacious twelve-foot ceilings. Beautiful clear Douglas fir and sugar pine wainscoting resided below ornate, mostly floral designed wallpaper covered walls. A wide covered porch wrapped around most of the house's exterior, and dormers poked out of the steep shingled roof. Eastern hardwood furniture, including two red oak claw-foot tables, marble-topped maple end tables, and matching corner pieces filled the large rooms. The two-story structure consisted of two kitchens, two living rooms, three bathrooms, five bedrooms, a sunroom, a pantry/storage room, a washroom, a giant office, and a sewing room. The main kitchen, constructed for cooking, included big cupboards, wide counters and large flour and sugar bins including built-in sifters.

The Porters designed the back kitchen for canning and processing game. Old man Porter oversaw the construction of the house and outbuildings from start to finish. That included the terracing of nearly three acres of southern exposure, half for fruit trees and half for vegetables and numerous varieties of berries.

Somewhat ahead of his time, old man Porter took advantage of the free energy provided by the sun to heat his behemoth. With tall, wide, thick custom-made windows and a sunroom on the southern side, he tried to capture every free BTU. His sun room jetted out from the southwest corner of the house with rows of 9"-by-12" pane windows. On sunny winter days, the sunroom could climb to 20 or 25 degrees warmer than the other rooms. He even designed the covered porch to shade the windows on the south side of the house in the summer. However, in the winter, the sun's arc dropped low enough to bathe the southern windows and walls. To maintain this solar advantage, he removed all of the sun-blocking conifers. He replaced them with shorter, deciduous Pippin and Arkansas Black apples, Bartlett and Winter Nellie pears, and English walnut trees with black walnut grafted root stock. Even though well-built, the old structure weathered and required constant maintenance to replace dry rot or just well-worn boards.

All this was known, but currently oblivious, to Greyson Milner as he slept on his left side. Suddenly his eyes popped open in the black quiet. He raised his head slightly from his nearly flat goose down pillow. Grey realized he was holding his breath and slowly exhaled. They must not have been sleeping long as his right arm was still wrapped around Veronica's ribs, his hand still cupping her left breast. Had they just dozed off or was it longer…he couldn't tell. Sex—or more accurately, the workout—with Veronica knocked Grey out better and faster than a sleeping pill. Veronica liked to spoon after sex; she seemed to enjoy the closeness of passive physical contact after intense marathon intercourse. In a rare moment of openness, she once revealed cuddling with someone she could trust made her feel safe and usually kept the nightmares away. It wasn't easy or natural for Veronica to let her guard down. She had walls, thick walls, protecting her world, current and past. The only trouble with lying close to Veronica occurred soon after she fell asleep; she turned white hot. *How in the hell do women do that?* Grey always retreated away from her to avoid profusely sweating. So, they must have just fallen asleep, or maybe Veronica hadn't turned on her internal heater yet; either way he was awake now. Veronica changed her breathing slightly but did not stir as Grey slipped his right arm back to his side of the bed.

He lay on his back looking straight up. His wakening mind tried to process what his ears had just told his sleeping mind about five seconds ago. Had he imagined it, dreamed it, or actually heard it? As the fogginess cleared, he said to himself, *Hell, yes, it was real.* Someone or something had put weight on the third step of Milner's back porch stairs, the weakest step of the lot, with its all-too-familiar loud creak. Greyson stayed very still; he was holding his breath again. Then he heard it, another faint step. Someone was just outside on his covered porch. Grey shook Veronica gently and whispered her name just as the first blast of a shotgun shattered the quiet. Grey immediately grabbed Veronica's naked body around the waist and slid her off the bed and against the wall between the window and the bedroom door.

The force of the buckshot disintegrated the handle of the screen door and shattered the door frame holding the back door's dead bolt. Veronica distinctly heard the killer jack another round into the chamber. *A pump shotgun.* The screen was kicked out of the way with considerable force. Grey realized they only had seconds before the intruder would enter the back of his house. Once inside, all the assailant had to do was turn right to face the door to Grey's bedroom. Other than escape out the large bedroom window, about fifteen feet down the covered porch from the back door, they were cornered. Veronica, to Grey's surprise, did not utter a word, but her body language revealed she was instantly awake and alert.

Side by side with their backs to the wall, he whispered, "Help me pull the bed against the door."

They both leaned forward and yanked on the side board of the large antique bed. The combination of fear, adrenaline, and the legs of the bed resting on a hardwood floor allowed Greyson and Veronica to slide the heavy bed just enough to block the bedroom door from swinging inward. The edge of the thick, ornate, eight-foot headboard rested about a foot past the doorknob; it could take many rounds and not give in. They had just given themselves a little more time. With his eyes adjusted to the darkness, Grey could see Veronica looking right at him.

She said, in a matter-of-fact tone, "We are two very naked and very defenseless ducks in a barrel."

The assailant shoved against the back door, which pushed open about eight inches, then stopped. Another violent shove added another inch or so, but not enough room to squeeze through. Another shove with a loud grunt added little. Too professional to vent out loud, his mind screamed, *What the fuck is jamming this fucking door?* Just as quickly, he made a situational decision.

"Plan B," the gunman said into his mic.

"Copy," came the response.

Grey quickly realized the killer had not entered the house. Why? More importantly, what was the killer's next move? What should Veronica and he do?

Then Veronica leaned over toward her clothes. At first Grey thought she must not want to get shot naked. *Women...Jesus.* But Veronica didn't reach for her clothes; she reached across them to her backpack. She slid herself and the backpack back against the wall next to Grey.

Grey asked her, "Do you have a gun?"

"No," was all he heard before a shotgun blast blew apart the drapes and a large portion of the bedroom window.

Without access through the back door, the gunman's Plan B became apparent; just walk down the covered porch to the bedroom window. If he couldn't gain access through the back door, he'd enter through the blown-out window.

A thought hit the gunman. *Shit; this should have been Plan A; so much for good intel.* He had backed to the outer edge of the porch to gain some distance, raised the barrel of the Remington 870 to his waist, and squeezed the trigger. The glass and old wood-framed window flew into the bedroom and all over the bed. The gunman pumped the shotgun's action and made the mental note, *Three rounds left.*

Grey had the sinking feeling that he and Veronica had just outsmarted themselves. By protecting themselves from an attack through the bedroom door, they had just blocked their only way to escape from the gunman's new assault. With nothing to stop him, the killer could just walk up, point the gun into the bedroom and start making Swiss cheese.

The gunman shot once more as he stepped up to the window. *Might as well keep their heads down until I can find them and finish this.* He pumped in a new shell. *Two rounds left.*

The concussion of the near point-blank blast cracked deafeningly. Veronica, closest to the window, ignored her ringing ears. She waited a second then calmly pivoted onto her right butt cheek. As Grey was frantically trying to shove the bed away from the door, Veronica flicked back the depressor guard on top of a large canister and shot a three-second burst of orange propellant out of the splintered opening.

The gunman never expected or anticipated a two-foot diameter fog of pepper spray to come screaming his way. He gave out an involuntary exhale that sounded like a short bark. Right before his throat locked up, he uttered, "Mutha—."

The killer's driver, waiting patiently, became a little concerned when he heard his partner say, "Plan B." However, when he heard the additional gunshots, he relaxed. But then the cough, out-of-character garbled cussing made the driver sit up straight and ask, "Report?"

Through choking coughs, the driver heard, "Extract," or something close enough to set him in motion. He started the truck and quickly backed down the driveway.

Not a virgin to tear gas, the gunman emptied his final two rounds through the window—or at least in that direction, turned, and staggered down the porch.

Veronica, with both eyes closed, spoke through her cupped hands toward Grey. "That's got to hurt." Turning her head toward the shattered window, she opened her hands and yelled, "How's that feel, asshole?"

The killer knew he had to get to the truck before his body completely shut down and left him focusing solely on just trying to breathe. He ran quickly with both eyes shut tight and burning like fire. He reached the stairs but stumbled and fell down the entire flight. *Fuck!* his brain screamed as his shotgun hit the sidewalk with a loud metallic clank.

The killer willed his body up the back walkway. His feet told him sidewalk from lawn as he staggered toward the driveway. He hit and pushed through the old wooden gate leaving it dangling on one hinge. Hearing the sound of the truck, he struggled in that direction and banged against the side. Instantly realizing he had hit the truck bed, the gunman tossed the shotgun in the bed.

Out of air, he grabbed the side of the truck and, with the last of his strength, half leaped and half rolled into the bed. The truck roared off. The gunman rolled onto his belly then rose up on all fours. Ripping off the mask already wet with tears, snot and slobber, he faced straight down, trying to breathe and not vomit. He thought, *Shit; we are in serious trouble.*

Grey, wheezing from the tiny amount of pepper spray that drifted around them, gagged, "I can't breathe."

"That's the general idea, Milner. How do you think that asshole feels? That shit will knock down a grizzly. Of course, it takes about four seconds to stop one of those big bastards; sometimes that's about three seconds too late. Our lethal buddy folded in about a second; good thing, too. He still had the presence of mind to empty his 870 our way before beating feet." *She raised her middle finger to her temple in a mock salute to his professionalism.*

"Yeah, I know; I thought we were dead." When she did not respond, he said, "Hey, how do you know his shotgun is an 870?"

"I've heard them enough to know their signature pump action."

"Where?"

Veronica clammed up. Ignoring Milner, she said, "Don't you think we should get out of here? Help me shove this bed back; with any luck we won't step on a chunk of your window."

"I still can't see."

"Can you stop with the whining? You're still alive and, you're welcome, by the way. Now man up and help me push this damn bed."

Milner silently turned and helped shove the bed straight then gingerly got to his feet. Feeling for and finding the doorknob, he walked into the hall and thought, *Veronica Sanchez, who in the hell are you? You're all charged up, like you're high.*

Veronica carefully leaned over and grabbed her backpack and followed Grey out of what was left of his bedroom. As they walked down the hall to the kitchen, Grey veered off to the laundry room and grabbed a yet-to-be-washed pair of Levi's. As Grey entered the kitchen hopping and yanking on his pants, he saw Veronica and her backpack heading out the door to the driveway.

Milner said, "Hey V, where are you going? You're butt-ass naked, you know? What if they come back?"

She stopped long enough to lean back into the kitchen, look over her shoulder, and give Grey her best 'you dumb ass' look. "Milner," she began, "did you hear that vehicle tear out of here or not? Mr. 870 wasn't driving, that's for sure. They blew their chance and they're gone; trust me."

With that, she continued out. At her bike, she grabbed a group of keys out of her backpack and unlocked one of the bike's back compartments. Veronica pulled out her Springfield Custom Professional 1911A1, .45 caliber automatic. She opened the action to check that a live round was in the chamber, closed the action, and checked the safety. She learned a long time ago she could shoot a 9mm a lot more accurately, but 9mm rounds didn't deliver enough stopping power. Once Veronica became proficient with the .45, she stuck with it. Even if she missed center mass, the nearly half inch diameter projectile could knock someone ass-over-teakettle with just a leg or arm hit. Once a .45 round put you down, your chances of getting up were slim. She also grabbed a flashlight before closing the compartment then walked around the back of the bike. From the other back compartment Veronica pulled out a pair of socks, panties, pants, a t-shirt and a pair of tennis shoes. She closed the compartment and looked around. As far away as the nearest house sat, she figured no one had called the cops. Guns going off at night were not that uncommon. Ranchers and farmers shot raccoons, possums, skunks, coyotes and other night predators and pests all the time. Standing there naked to the world, she felt excited, invigorated. With all her senses acute as hell, she started flicking one of her erect nipples. The tingling sensation made the muscles inside her vagina contract. She turned and walked straight back to the house.

When Veronica entered the kitchen, Grey asked, "I need to know how to play this. Are you sticking around?"

"Hell no."

"That's what I figured. How do I explain the bear spray and everything else?"

"Your problem, Milner; you know our deal. No one knows about me; especially cops. Think about what you're going to say and stick with it."

Grey nodded then Veronica pondered, "I wonder why that gunman didn't just keep coming through the back door?"

Milner replied, "I think I know; come with me."

Following Grey toward the bedroom, they stopped at the back door and Grey pointed to the floor.

Veronica commented, "It's that thingy you put along the bottom of your doors. It wedged when the asshole tried to push the door open."

"It's one of my mom's door socks. It's just a cloth tube filled with rice. Most old houses are drafty as hell. This old place is no different. Door socks help reduce cold air drafting in. Between that, the throw rug and my unpolished hardwood floor, it jammed the door nicely."

"Good thing you didn't just add weather stripping."

"My mom would never modernize this house; she said it would lose its character. I guess I'm the same."

Looking at the hardwood floor in bad need of attention, Veronica said, "No, Milner; you're just a slacker."

She slipped on her tennis shoes and gingerly entered the bedroom to grab the rest of her stuff. When she came out she noticed Grey remained standing where she had left him, looking hurt. Heading to the bathroom, she leaned into Grey, kissed him, then said, "Cheer up, slacker; you excel in other areas."

At the bathroom door Milner said, "You weren't even scared? I was about to shit my pants…well, if I'd been wearing any. You were all business like you've been in situations like this before."

Veronica ignored Grey. "I smelled your fear, Milner; you were scared shit-less, but you did well. You dragged me off the bed and thought about blocking the bedroom door. That showed good mental control...thinking clearly when seconds counted." Changing the subject, Veronica said, "And yes, by the way, I do have a gun; but it was locked in a compartment on my Harley. I'm sure they knew or strongly suspected I wasn't packing and that you don't have a gun in the house."

"How would they know that?"

"Because that asshole came straight at us; he either knew or felt pretty damn confident he wasn't facing any lethal threat. I think someone has cased your place and probably has been watching you. That means professionals."

That stopped Grey cold. *Who the hell would put a professional hit on me?* Get-ting back to Veronica, Grey said to the bathroom door, "Maybe it has something to do with you. Maybe they've been casing you and followed you here."

"Fat chance, Milner. No one knows squat about me or where I go; I'd know."

Resigned to her point, Grey replied, "Hell, V, I don't even know anything about you."

"You know about my tattoos, and you have to get pretty close to see those."

"I'm serious, V."

Veronica exited the bathroom wearing a t-shirt and carrying her pants and panties. Again, she ignored Grey's interest in her past. Grey noticed her nipples were protruding hard against the t-shirt's fabric. Walking toward the kitchen, Veronica said, "Professionals, Greyson, professionals; someone wants your ass dead. And I bet they specifically chose when I was here." She stopped and turned around. Grey nearly crashed into her. She looked at Grey and asked, "Why?"

Milner looked at Veronica bug-eyed and shrugged his shoulders. "I...I don't know."

"Think, Milner." Another blank look prompted Veronica to continue. "Could be they wanted you dead while with a woman. Maybe they're trying to throw the cops off?"

They both paused on that thought.

Then Veronica added, "We have some homework to do, but first things first." Veronica dropped her backpack and clothes on the floor, pulled up her t-shirt, and pressed her chest against Grey's. She kissed him and slid her thigh between his pant legs. When she pulled her head back, she proclaimed, "Shit like this makes me horny as hell." She grabbed the top of his jeans and pulled him toward the kitchen table while kicking off her tennis shoes. Veronica pulled out a chair and turned it sideways. Putting her right foot on the seat of the chair, Veronica leaned forward and put her left elbow on the table. Looking back at Grey, she slapped her ass hard with her right hand and said, "My tattoo area needs attention."

Maybe four and a half minutes later, sweating again, Grey held Veronica around the waist. Spent, but still inside her, he backed her up, turned slightly, and slowly sat in the chair. Veronica continued to shift her legs back and forth on Grey's lap with her head down. Grey thought, *Shit, V, what the hell doesn't make you horny? You are one crazy-assed woman.*

After a few minutes, she raised her head and leaned back against Grey's chest. With a smile, she said, "Nice shooting, partner."

Grey brought his head forward and put his chin on the back of her head. He closed his eyes and thought, *We were seconds away from violent death, and fifteen minutes later she wants sex and makes jokes.* While exhaling, he whispered, "Jesus, V; you're crazy."

Grey immediately regretted what he'd just said as he felt Veronica stiffen.

Veronica said flatly, "Let go of me." When she stood, she added, "I need to look around outside before you call the cops."

Veronica moved over to her clothes and backpack. She bent down and grabbed her panties and pulled them up to her knees. Then she grabbed and pulled her clean socks apart. With one she wiped her legs and crotch. She wedged the other one up between her legs and pulled up her panties. She situated the sock evenly, then looked at Grey watching her. She said, "You can't believe how this stuff chafes on a bike, especially the loads you share." She slipped on her pants and tennis shoes then walked over to Grey. Leaning over, she cupped her right hand under Grey's jaw and gave him a tender kiss. "You're a good fuck, Milner. You know how to make a woman tingle." Locking her eyes on Grey's, she squeezed his throat hard.

Grey cringed but willed himself not to squeal.

She stated evenly, "I...am...not...crazy." Letting him go, she rose up and walked to the door. "Call the cops. I'll talk to some...acquaintances. I'm going to find out why your head's on the chopping block. Someone out there doesn't know it yet, but they just made a terrible mistake."

Rubbing his pinched Adam's apple, Grey asked, "Because they tried to kill me?"

"Hell no, Milner, I'm going to nail them because they tried to kill me." With that, she turned and walked out.

Slowly, Grey sat up, pulled up his jeans, and walked over to the kitchen window. Leaning against the wall, he stared numbly as he watched Veronica's flashlight lead the way to the back porch. Eventually, she made her way down the back walkway and out to where the killers had parked. He went to the sink and poured a glass of water. While drinking, he heard Veronica's Harley start. Grey thought, *maybe not crazy, V; but, holy crap, something in there's broken.* Then he remembered that old joke about rodeo sex. You mount your woman from behind and tell her she's the worst piece of ass you've ever had, then, try to hold on for eight seconds. With Veronica, it was all about strapping in and holding on. He put down his glass, walked to the phone, and dialed Sheriff Whittingham's number from memory.

Chapter Thirty-three
Set the Narrative

Donnie Sloane slowed down when he hit pavement. He tried to talk to his partner by saying his name twice, but Lamar Jackson couldn't stop gagging and writhing in pain enough to speak into his mic.

Donnie dialed on his satellite phone and waited. He heard a very excited Lance ask, "Is it over? Are they...hamburger?"

"I'm not sure."

Lance couldn't process what he'd just heard. *"I'm not sure." What the hell does that mean? They're either dead or not dead. Shotguns at close range don't leave room for ambiguity.* "What do you mean you're not sure?"

Donnie ignored the question and cut in. "Meet us where you did before in thirty." Donnie cut the connection. He'd already whiffed pepper spray, so he knew someone blasted Lamar. Donnie pulled over, hopped out and quickly hustled back to the truck bed. "Lamar, you okay?"

Lamar choked out, "Water."

Donnie turned back to the cab and grabbed four plastic water bottles from behind the driver seat. As he brought them back to Lamar, Donnie shook his head. *Damn it; why did I let Lamar talk me into switching places?*

Donnie handed one bottle to Lamar. He dropped the other three in the truck bed, then thought about their conversation in the pickup earlier that night.

"Come on, Donnie; it's a cake walk. Let me do this. How am I ever going to learn?"

"Lamar, you don't know what you don't know…believe me."

"And I'll never learn if I don't start somewhere. You have to admit; this hit can't be easier. They're like ten feet from the back door, they're unarmed and asleep. I'll be on them in seconds."

Donnie didn't say anything to his driver for a long time. The pluses were weak; he needed to think about the minuses. One, they only knew what they were shown and were told, and they didn't know who collected the intel. The guy that showed them the file hadn't conducted the intel and the little rat-eyed freak seemed…squirrely. Two, Donnie didn't like what he saw in the pictures…fresh intel handed to Lance earlier that evening taken with a telephoto lens. The second target, a dark-complexioned woman, looked hard. If Donnie had to guess, he'd say active or ex-military…not good. Arriving on a Harley, she looked extremely fit, walked with purpose, and appeared to continually scan her surroundings. Three, they were in rural California…not urban Illinois; Lamar and he were way out of their environment and comfort zone. Finally, Donnie's boss, Johnny Big Nose, told Donnie this hit was very important to Johnny's California associate, which made it very important to Johnny. *You will follow my associate's right-hand man's orders to the letter. Do it quick, do it clean, and get your asses back here.*

Lamar cut into Donnie's thoughts. "Come on, Donnie; haven't I been there for you? Don't I always cover your back?"

"Yeah, I know, Lamar. But like I said, you don't know what you don't know."

"Okay, then walk me through it again. You're one of the best, right? How can I screw up? Plus, we'll be in radio contact; I'll just be an extension of you."

Lamar knew not to say anything more. While driving, Lamar watched Donnie with his peripheral vision. He could tell Donnie struggled with the decision.

Finally, Donnie said, "Goddamnit."

Lamar hooted, "F-ing A, partner."

Donnie looked over at his driver and said, "Against my better—"

An empty water bottle hit Donnie in the chest. Lamar opened and poured the second water bottle over his eyes and tossed it, too. This time he missed Donnie. Lamar forced the third bottle into his mouth and crushed the bottle. The water blew back out of his mouth along with loud gags and coughs. He was able to swallow some of the fourth.

Donnie needed information. "They're not dead, are they?"

Lamar shook his head.

Donnie said, "Shit, Lamar; I heard the step creak from the truck. You didn't walk up the outside like I told you. You walked right up the middle."

Lamar just shook his head up and down, admitting he had screwed up.

Mixing idioms, Donnie said, "Spilled milk under the bridge at this point. We are in serious trouble." Easing up on Lamar, Donnie said, "Sorry, partner, can't let your stinking ass in the cab; you'll have to ride back here."

Lamar nodded again and Donnie added, "We'll meet Lance first...make him purchase a motel and get you cleaned up."

Donnie slapped his partner's shoulder then returned to the cab. He pulled up to the highway, turned south and powered the truck up to just over the speed limit. He hoped Lamar figured out why he couldn't get in the cab. They had to return the truck back in Stockton in about five hours. Your average everyday businessman doesn't return a rental vehicle reeking of pepper spray.

Donnie drove to the back of the motel's parking lot and found Lance sitting in his car. Lamar, obviously feeling better, hopped out of the truck bed and met up with Donnie outside of Lance's driver door.

Lance lowered the window and shot out, "What the fuck?" Then his nose and eyes felt the sting of the residual pepper spray. He made a face and said again, "What the fuck?"

Donnie jumped right back. "Bad intel, that's what the fuck!" Pulling out his automatic, he held it six inches from Lance's left eye. "I ought to cap your worthless ass right here!"

Lance froze, and Lamar, looking around frantically, said, "Whoa, whoa, whoa, partner, easy."

No one moved.

Lamar added, "Calm down, partner; it's cool. Let's get cleaned up and talk about this. We need to think this through before heading back."

The thought of facing Johnny's wrath registered hard with Donnie. He still opened Lance's door, grabbed him by the collar and yanked him out.

Lance jerked free and hissed, "You have no idea who you're—"

Donnie slapped Lance on the side of his head to shut him up then pointed toward the motel office and said, "Go wake someone up and get us a room."

"Get your own goddamn room!" Lance shot back.

Knowing Donnie would slap Lance again, or worse, Lamar held his partner's arm. Donnie snapped his head around to eye his partner. Lamar released Donnie's arm as they glared at each other. Donnie finally pursed his lips and gave a quick nod. He turned back to Lance and said, "What do you smell, asshole? Lamar reeks and I stink of residual pepper spray. That manager will definitely remember if either of us asks for a room. No, you're getting us a room. We need to shower and to change clothes. Then we'll have a little chat. Now move."

Pointing to Lamar, Lance finally figured it out. "You let him do the hit, that's why you failed."

"Shut your mouth, asshole. Something blocked the back door and that hellcat brought bear spray with her into the house. So, because of your incomplete intel, what happened to Lamar would have happened to me. That's your fault." Grabbing Lance's collar and shoving him toward the office, Donnie growled, "Now get us a motel room."

Lance quit protesting; he had to get rid of these two as soon as possible. He needed Sliger to call the killers' boss first and set the narrative. He wasn't taking the fall for their screw-up.

Chapter Thirty-four
Meet Mr. Hollow Point

Leaving Grey's house, Veronica normally would have driven straight through to Reno; but discomfort forced her to pull off at the Gold Creek rest stop. With the temperature heading down as she headed up in elevation, the drive required another layer of clothes. Plus, replacing the sock between her legs with a wad of toilet paper would decrease the chaffing which was starting to become an issue. When Veronica left the ladies' room, she stopped just inside the wide entrance...scanning, watching, listening. She quickly picked up the rattle as a poorly tuned engine died. Her gaze settled on the rust bucket, now two parking spaces away from her Harley. Two slovenly dressed, white trash punks opened both front doors. Quite a bit of smoke exited their junker with them as they slowly wandered toward her Harley. She registered and assessed the vehicle when she pulled in. *Forewarned is forearmed.* They had parked their idling rust bucket, an old purple Bonneville, in the far corner of the lot. Burning oil passing by well-worn piston rings created a distinct blue hue. The two occupants of the shit-mobile now stood on either side of her bike, smoking. Veronica checked her pockets and belongings to make sure everything remained in their proper place. When satisfied, she marched directly toward her ride.

Thinking they cornered a potential easy mark, the two didn't back away as Veronica approached her bike. She stopped about twenty feet from them and crossed her arms. The skinny one said, "Hey, sweetie, you want something for the drive? Maybe something to keep you awake?"

Veronica did not possess the gene for diplomacy but tried her best. "No, thank you. Please step away from my bike. I don't want any trouble and I know you two...gentlemen...don't either."

The big guy said, "Maybe trouble's our middle name."

So much for diplomacy. "No, Einstein; dumb-shit's your middle name if you don't move your fat ass."

Dropping her arms to her side, Veronica marched another ten feet closer to the two. She smelled marijuana and body odor. By boldly walking up that close, she observed surprise and wariness in their body language.

The big guy dropped his cigarette to free his hands and tried to regain some control. "Kinda lippy for a woman all alone, ain't you? Maybe your name is dumb-shit."

"Look, you strung-out white trash, back off. Your last chance; besides, I'm not alone."

The two started looking around like idiots. When their pea brains remembered that she came in alone, the skinny one said, "Maybe we'll take that chance; maybe we'll take you for a little ride, and maybe we'll have ourselves a little fun."

Ignoring the scrawnier of the two, Veronica took another two steps and squared off in front of the bigger guy. "Make your move, asshole."

Even though his brain labored under the load of a perpetually pot-induced high, his clouded mind registered aggression and sluggishly sent out warning bells. Now they both weren't so cocky. The boldness of this woman made them glance back and forth at each other; she had just put them on the defensive.

Skinny finally said, "What are you, nuts?"

"I'm done talking, shit-for-brains; fight or flight."

After a long stalemate of silence, the obviously more nervous Skinny broke first. He turned to his buddy and said, "Hey, forget her, man; let's get out of here. She's probably just a sloppy old whore full of old rotten spouse."

But the big guy tried to save face and took a step forward, pointing a finger at Veronica. He made it as far as, "You're one lucky—" before his blurry eyes focused on the ugly end of her .45, aimed right at his face.

They both froze as she said, "I told you I wasn't alone." Staring at the big guy Veronica added, "I'm betting I can send a bullet straight through that gaping pie hole of yours faster than you can move one inch closer. Want to try?"

Skinny put his arms up and pleaded, "Hey, hey, hey, man, no need for that; it's cool, we're leaving."

Watching the big guy but talking to them both, Veronica said, "How rude of me not to make introductions. Mr. Hollow Point, may I present Fat Ass and Slim."

Neither spoke.

Veronica tilted her head toward their vehicle and said, "Walk." Neither one moved until she yelled, "Move!"

She stopped them about ten feet from the driver's side door of their vehicle and told them to turn around. Veronica reached into her jacket, tossed four large zip ties on the ground, then said, "Slim; get your ass over here and pick these up. Put one around Fat Ass's ankles and another on his wrists, behind his back. When you're done, do the same to your ankles. Put the zip tie on your wrists, in the front, and pull it tight with what's left of your teeth." When Slim didn't move, she added, "You're angering Mr. Hollow Point."

Silently, Slim did as he was told. Fear kept them both quiet. Veronica walked behind them and pushed them hard in the back. They tumbled forward and hit the pavement painfully on their knees and stomachs.

She asked, "Any syringes in your pockets?"

They both shook their heads.

"Guns or knives?"

Slim said, "We both have knives."

After Veronica frisked them, she tossed their wallets and pocketknives out on the pavement. She said, "I said knives."

Veronica walked in front of them, reached into her jacket, and pulled out her switchblade. She knelt down and snapped it open. Two sets of bugged-out eyes stared at the six-inch blade glistening from the distant streetlight. She waved it in front of their faces and added, "For your information, this is a knife."

Instantly crying and pleading, they dropped off to whimpering when she stood up and walked over to their car. Keeping them in sight, she punctured both front tires.

As the tires hissed themselves flat, they watched her, wide-eyed and frightened to death. She walked back over beside her two captives and swiftly kicked Fat Ass in the head. His head rocked back then fell forward. His nose started bleeding, but he didn't move. Slim started pleading again, until Veronica yelled, "Shut up."

She finished dragging them both over beside their car just as an 18-wheeler pulled into the far side of the parking lot. Whether the trucker saw anything or not, Veronica wasn't sure; but it was definitely time to leave.

She leaned down to the cringing Slim and said, "Open your mouth."

When he did, she stuffed the sock she had wedged between her legs at the start of the bike ride into his mouth. It had accrued a certain level of ripeness that made Slim gag.

Veronica said, "You spit that out and I'll use my knife to stuff it back in."

Slim stared, breathing loudly through his mouth and gagging as she continued. "That's for calling me a sloppy old whore full of old rotten spouge. You were half right; too bad for you it wasn't the sloppy old whore part."

Enjoying her educational point for a bit and letting it sink into Slim's thick skull, she knelt down. "I'll only say this once. If I ever see you two again, I'll kill you…understand?"

Slim shook his head vigorously.

She continued. "You have no future the way you're going; dump that tub of lard next to you and make a serious life change."

Slim's muffled response came out. "Es, ma'am, es ma'am, ank you ma'am."

Veronica stood up and said, "And Slim, one more thing."

When he lifted his head and turned to look up, she kicked him. Slim mimicked his tubby buddy; his head snapped back, then dropped like a stone.

Veronica yanked her sock out of his mouth and pulled her knife. She cut off the zip ties and pocketed them with her knife. Walking casually back to her bike, she picked up their two wallets just for spite. While picking their wallets clean of way more cash than these two scumbags should be packing, she realized her nipples were hard as rocks. She was excited again. Veronica fired up her Harley and headed out the exit.

As she pulled onto the onramp to I-80 heading east, she tossed the wallets over the guardrail. Thinking about Slim thanking her profusely, she smiled, then laughed out loud.

Reaching Reno at around 5 A.M., she turned off West McCarron heading south. Veronica took a left onto Plum and a right onto Chantel. When she reached her home, owned by her employer, Veronica fished out her garage door opener and hit the button. Then she pulled her .45 and put it in her left hand. Throttling into the garage, she hit the garage button again. The well maintained 1960s vintage two-story, two-bedroom, two-bath house fit her needs perfectly. She checked her security system, which looked fine, but walked inside with her .45 leading the way. After a quick check of all the rooms and closets, she walked back to her bathroom and stripped off her clothes. While showering, she realized just how irritated the joy juice, sock, and ride had rendered her vagina and crotch. When she exited the shower, she lightly patted herself dry.

Lifting one leg to the sink, she checked out the damage. Veronica spoke to her parts. "Well, girlfriend, you certainly don't get red and raw by sitting around home." She found her jar of Vaseline and gingerly smeared on a layer. Putting on some sweatpants and a t-shirt, she headed downstairs.

Starving, she wanted to eat, but needed to make a call first. She went to her safe and retrieved her secure phone. Seeing the battery was sufficiently charged, Veronica dialed the number by heart. No stored or written down numbers in her profession. The receiver picked up on the first ring.

A male voice said, "Yes?"

She replied, "Es mio."

"Hey, Chiquita; nice of you to check in."

"What's shaken, Desk Jock; any work?"

"Maybe something very soon, but for now you'll have to survive on your retainer."

"Fine with me. Hey, I have a question for you."

"Shoot."

"Any hitman activity going on in California?"

"Not that I know of, but I'll check; you have any particulars?"

"Two guys...one shooter, one driver."

"How wide a search?"

"Make it wide but only domestic stuff...no foreign assassins; and specifically, two guys...no, make that two perps. The shooter was definitely a guy, but the driver could be a woman."

"Okay, Chiquita; you got it. Where can I reach you?"

"I'll be nesting for a while."

"If I get anything you'll be the first to know." After a little silence DJ added, "Are you in some kind of trouble?"

"Not me, but I'm looking into a situation for a guy."

"Sounds serious...and personal; you cheating on me?"

"Oh, no way, DJ; you know there's no one else but you."

"Yeah, right, you tease."

"I'll check in tomorrow if I don't hear from you." With that she hung up but left the phone by her bed.

Now serious hunger gripped her. Eat or sleep? She decided she better not try to sleep after eating. The bad dreams always seemed worse when she slept alone on a full stomach. She'd rest up. Tomorrow she'd eat a big breakfast, go get her mail; later, a run and a serious workout.

Chapter Thirty-five
You Saved My Life, Sarge

After an hour and a half with nearly every light on in his house, Grey grew tired of sheriff's officers in his bedroom, in his kitchen, on his porch, and up and down his driveway. Hoping it would all end soon, Grey sat at his kitchen table with Sheriff Whittingham. Grey's exhaustion stemmed from the combination of Veronica sex and the fatigue that hits you after a huge adrenaline rush. Sheriff Whittingham finally seemed satisfied with Grey's "official statement," a statement completely devoid of Veronica Sanchez's participation. Oddly, Grey sat drinking coffee. Not a good idea, but Sheriff Whittingham wanted some; so, what the hell. Grey never knew if Bill Whittingham ever really liked him or not. The last few years, the sheriff left little doubt that Grey had earned a spot on Bill's shit list, punctuated by his pet name for Grey... Peckerneck. But tonight, sitting at Grey's table, the sheriff remained professional, cordial, interested. However, that ended when the last officer said goodnight while exiting the kitchen door.

Hearing the door click, Sheriff Whittingham wasted no time. "You're a good liar, Peckerneck, but not good enough. Who was she?"

Holy shit. Mocking surprise, Grey tried his best to shrug and look baffled. When Sheriff Whittingham didn't detour his glare or even blink, Grey felt cornered, sunk, busted.

Grey opened his mouth to speak but the sheriff held up his hand and cut in. "Before you allow any more shit to exit your mouth, let me tell you what I know. Your covered porch, bedroom and hallway smelled like gun powder and pepper spray but not your kitchen. I was the first one here, if you recall, and when I entered this room I smelled sex. And don't tell me you were choking your chicken because that fragrance exuded pussy. You screwed some hottie in here just before you called me."

"Bill, I—"

In a booming voice that made Grey jump, the sheriff yelled, "Until you stop lying, you call me Sheriff Whittingham!"

"Yes, sir," instantly popped out of Grey's mouth. At sixty-one, Bill Whittingham still commanded respect. Grey sat there with his hands on his head like a prisoner of war. Finally, he collected his thoughts; *V's going to kill me.* "Bill, she's not underage, or even a local girl, if that's what you're worried about. She works for the Feds, I think, and she does undercover work for them…I think."

"I don't give a rat's ass what you think; tell me what you know.

"Bill, she's a mystery to me, too…honest. I met her a few years ago with Ned at Pete's Place. He'll back me up. She just pops in on her schedule every now and then; that's it, really."

In a much calmer voice Bill asked, "Does she think the shooter came after her?"

"She says no. She thinks they wanted me."

"Why would someone want to kill a cock-hound like you, Peckerneck? All you do is use women, then dump them."

That brought on a long period of silence.

Mad at himself for the unprofessional jab, Sheriff Whittingham needed Grey to talk. Trying to get back on track, he asked, "What else did your mystery woman tell you?"

Talking into his coffee cup, Grey said flatly, "She said they were professionals and they knew their business. They wouldn't have attacked head-on like that if they knew *V*"…*ah, shit,* "if she packed a gun. She does carry, but she locked it in her Harl"…*ah, shit,* "I mean vehicle. Obviously, the bear spray caught them off guard."

Sheriff Whittingham did not respond to Grey's attempt to conceal as much about his mystery woman as possible. Grey filled in the void with, "She thinks I was the target and she was there to make the murder look like a revenge killing or crime of passion."

Sheriff Whittingham had seen the bike tracks in the gravel driveway and wrote down "*V?*" next to "Harley" in his notepad. Looking up at Grey, he asked, "Definitely a logical assumption for investigators to pursue, if the shooting had worked. So, her bear spray?"

"Yep, yes, Bill, ah, Sheriff Whittingham. She's all business, focused; I don't even think she was scared."

"Tough."

"Oh, Shit Howdy. She saved my life."

All of a sudden, Sheriff Whittingham's mind left the building. His mouth opened slightly as he stared blankly forward, like in a trance. Grey knew the sheriff's little episodes were occurring more often. Grey remembered, while growing up, sometimes Whit's dad would lose his train of thought or just go blank for a few seconds, then pop out of it acting a little disoriented. Obviously, these bouts were getting worse because Bill Whittingham's mind definitely transported him somewhere else. Grey looked around his kitchen not knowing what to do. Finally, he stood and retrieved more coffee, thinking movement would bring the sheriff back. That didn't work.

Leaning against the counter by the coffee pot, Grey asked himself, *Where the hell did you go, Bill?*

"More coffee, Bill?" Grey asked loudly.

Looking up, Bill mumbled, "You saved my life, Sarge." He started looking around the kitchen with a puzzled expression, then tried to focus on Grey.

"More coffee?" Grey asked again.

"Oh, ah, no, I have to get back to the office. I think we're good for now, Grey."

Grey, is it? What happened to Peckerneck? I don't think ole Bill's quite all the way back yet. "You okay, Bill?"

"Yeah, yeah, fine." Sheriff Whittingham stood leaning forward, keeping both hands on the table for support. Eventually, he brought his head up straight as he finally fully returned.

"Sorry, Peckerneck; lost in thought for a second."

Yeah, more like a minute. Grey asked, "About the girl...can you keep her out of this for now, please?"

Thinking for some time, Sheriff Whittingham finally gave his official response. "Okay, for now she doesn't exist. But if the Feds get involved, no guarantees. You're putting me in a bind here, Peckerneck; withholding evidence, a witness and potential victim. To keep this down deep, at some point, I'm going to have to meet her and...chat. That's the deal."

Oh, shit, not good. "Okay; thanks, Bill." *V's going to kill me.*

Bill put his coffee cup in the sink and asked, "You want me to call or write and tell Whit about this?"

That question made Grey stop and think about the last time he'd seen his friend. Whit had viciously punched Grey in the throat. Reflexively, Grey reached for his neck and rubbed his Adam's apple. He recalled the intense pain and fear of suffocation. Whit left for prison still thinking the worst about Grey and his inadvertent involvement in Ned's near death. *Why prod a wounded bear?* "No, Bill; let's let this ride for now."

As Bill reached the kitchen door leading to the backyard, he replied, "Your call...Peckerneck."

Chapter Thirty-six
Yes, Sir

Sliger paced back and forth behind his desk. No one in the Inner Circle spoke. Eventually he was ready to address his minions. Stopping near the middle of his desk, he put his hand down and leaned forward. In a somewhat controlled voice, Sliger asked, "What is so goddamn hard about killing someone? It's not like we haven't done it before."

Jeff Bowman squirmed in his chair like he was about to wet his pants. The more nervous he became and the more he fidgeted, the more his body odor escaped into the room.

Andrea sat straight-backed and attentive. She could be sitting at a recital during a church social. Of course, she also knew where Steven chose to direct his ire, and it wasn't at her.

Lance thought he had manipulated his position pretty well by pointing the finger squarely at the two hitmen. Now he felt compelled to restate the high points. "The hitmen traded places. The rookie tried to kill Milner and his wench. He couldn't even enter the house, then—"

"I don't give a shit at this point!" Sliger yelled. "As far as I'm concerned, you all screwed up." Looking at Andrea, he asked, "What are the cops saying? What does the press report say?"

Andrea replied, "So far, I can find no mention of the woman. It appears she bolted before the police arrived, which means Milner never mentioned her. But the police are leaning toward the shooting stemming from rage; possibly a nasty warning by someone close to one of Grey's female throwaways. That's the reported direction of the investigation, and the press just regurgitates what the police report."

Sliger sat and processed the information. *First Ned, then Allyson, now Greyson; zero for three. Well, Ned's a vegetable; he can't remember shit. I guess that counts for something. But Allyson...I thought we had her. No way in hell did I think she'd abandon that Mercedes. But Grey; shit, that was a no-brainer. That fucker should be...gray. I'm not ready to pull the pin...not yet. If I can keep Johnny Ramelli from going berserk and sucking in his nuts, we'll keep going. I want—no, I demand—we finish what we've started; nothing short of a "final solution" for my dear ex-friends.*

Looking up, Sliger noticed no one paying attention. He slapped his desk. Jeff yipped; his eyes displayed huge white borders. The other two turned around and sat up straight. Sliger started, "You are failing me, and not just with our current operation. Your performance and focus toward the business sucks, too. We've lost two EPA bids to...asshole nobodies. We've come up short on the last large Department of Resources round of grants and the Sierra Conservancy wants to audit our Scott Creek cleanup project. I don't like out-of-state companies taking my EPA jobs; I don't like missing out on easy, long-term revenue projects from the state, and I hate fucking audits."

Pointing to Jeff, Sliger said, "I want you inside both of those uppity little out-of-state companies. Every fucking item they type into a computer, I want to know. This will be the last time either one of those assholes outbids Serpentine Solutions. Is that clear?"

Jeff leaped to his feet and ran toward his office.

Sliger yelled, "Christ, Jeff; not right now."

Jeff tried to stop but slipped and fell on his ass. Sliger shook his head and said much quieter, "Forget what I just said, Jeff. Yes, go; go now and see what you can do."

When the door accessing the computer room closed, Sliger turned to Andrea. "Fire someone in accounting, grant-writing and in legal. Let's put the fear of fucking God back into those damn departments."

Andrea said, "Yes, sir. I keep a running file on everyone; how strong of a statement?"

"Pick bootlickers, brownnosers...no, wait. Pick workers well-liked that have been around a while...all three departments."

"Yes sir."

"And Andrea, get Peterson working background on Whittingham. By now, Whit must know something's afoot to get his ass out of prison. I want intel on him as soon as he walks."

"Yes, sir."

"That will be all."

Lance and Andrea started to stand but Sliger pointed at Lance and said, "Not you."

Sliger could tell Andrea didn't like being excused. When she reached the door, Sliger said, "Stay in your office; when I'm finished with Lance, I want to speak with you."

"Yes, sir."

When the big outer door closed, Sliger pointed that way and said, "You need to be more like Andrea. That's exactly what I expect from each one of you. A goddamn 'Yes sir' and it gets done."

Lance knew better than to defend himself or even respond. When Sliger decided to chew ass, you let him.

Sliger sat back down. He knew Jeff would work diligently until he hacked into Sliger's newest competitors. Andrea would soon march three employees out the door. Control by fear definitely encourages the minions to buckle down even harder…or else. Now it was Lance's turn to squirm. But instead of yelling, Sliger took an almost fatherly tone. "You have to step up to the plate. We are hitting for the fence. Once Grey and Whit bleed out, we go back to solely… empire building."

Smartly, Lance said, "Yes sir."

"Mostly, mostly that is, I don't blame you for Milner's reprieve. I know the hitmen deviated from the plan, but it was still your operation. Opportunities will arise again; what I need are results."

"Yes, sir."

Sliger said, "Grey's a fool. He'll step into another trap easily enough. Whittingham's another story. He senses things, knows things, feels things; he's not normal. You must be very cagey with that guy."

"Yes sir."

Sliger stood up. Lance did also.

Sliger said, "On your way by Andrea's office, tell her to return here."

"Yes sir."

As Lance walked out, he mocked Sliger's comment. *"Why can't you be more like Andrea?"* *Shit; at least I don't have to give the old man blow jobs.*

Chapter Thirty-seven
Hope You Can Keep These

Walking through Pomodoro's, one of Johnny "Big Nose" Ramelli's high-end restaurants near Chicago's business district, Donnie saw the head bartender, Antonio, look up. Most of the lights were off; the chairs at the two-seat tables in the bar remained upside-down, and the strong smell of pasta sauce, stale beer, and red wine lingered in the musty air.

Antonio stopped wiping down wine bottles long enough to say, "Good luck, Donnie."

Donnie just raised his chin and kept walking. Heading to the far back office, Lamar, walking behind Donnie, received no acknowledgement. Lamar focused on Donnie's heels until they reached the end of the long bar, then he stopped. Johnny ordered Lamar to show up with Donnie, but to wait outside. Lamar peeled off to his left, grabbed a turned-up chair and pulled it off the small table.

Antonio grabbed a handful of watery ice out of the bar tray and flung it at Lamar. The splatter of water and small ice bits hit the black man's head and back. Lamar threw his hands up and snapped his head toward the bar.

Antonio scolded, "Not there, Dickhead; go to the back. Al and Milo got a spot for you."

Donnie stopped and turned around long enough to say, "Come on, Lamar...better put that chair back up."

They walked in silence through the main dining room, past the kitchen and down a long wide hallway. Alphonso stood at the end by the last door; he opened it and beckoned them in.

Milo, sitting behind a wide desk, stood up and walked around to meet the arrivals. Classic goombahs...big, fat but muscular, these two dark, curly-haired thugs mimicked twins; two peas in a pod. The only difference, Milo's right hand held a large automatic.

Pointing the gun toward Lamar, Milo said, "Stand right there, Darkie, where I can see you."

Alphonso walked behind Donnie and said, "You know the drill, Don."

Donnie lifted his arms and spread his legs. Alphonso thoroughly frisked Donnie's upper body. When he started below the waist, he nudged Donnie's balls and said, "Hope you get to keep these."

"That's not funny, Al."

When Alphonso finished with Donnie, he turned to Lamar. Lamar just stood there glaring at Milo for calling him Darkie. Alphonso slugged him hard in the solar plexus. Lamar coughed, doubled up, and fell forward on his knees.

Milo laughed. "Hey, Don; your partner's a dumb-shit."

Donnie didn't move a muscle, but said, "Hey, no need for that, Al."

Alphonso threw up his hands and said, "Your pal here shouldn't be pulling an attitude, Don."

Alphonso pushed Lamar forward, kicked his legs apart, and frisked him. When he was satisfied, he grabbed Lamar by the collar and threw him backwards into a chair. He told the doubled-over Lamar to stay put.

Alphonso looked up at Donnie and said, "Okay, let's go, Don; you first."

As he moved to the thick metal door beyond Milo's desk, Donnie said, "Be cool, Lamar."

He turned the metal lever down and entered; Alphonso followed.

Donnie and Alphonso walked into the dark room. Donnie moved over to the metal chair situated before the large cluttered desk and sat. A small light pointed down toward the far side of the desk. Behind it sat Johnny "Big Nose" Ramelli in his large leather chair. The other light's narrow beam pointed right in Donnie's face. Donnie didn't see, but sensed, someone else's presence in the room.

Donnie said, "Hey, Tony."

From behind, in one of the dark corners, Donnie heard, "Hey yourself, Don."

Tony "Two Tap" Bassetti received his nickname due to his signature method of terminating…problems. His attendance meant that Donnie's future remained in serious doubt. With Johnny's top enforcer sitting behind him, Donnie knew to not embellish, only tell the truth, and not get caught in a lie. The problem facing Donnie, however, was that he had no clue of what that hit-bird Lance told his boss or what his boss told Johnny. Donnie could tell the truth and it might sound like a lie.

Johnny finally spoke, "What the fuck, Donnie?"

What the fuck, what? How am I supposed to answer that? Donnie remained leaning forward with his hands on his lap. His eyes looked forward, staring just below the beam of light, a totally defenseless, submissive position.

For a long time, the only sound Donnie heard came from fat Al's breathing.

Finally, Johnny said again, "What the fuck, Donnie? You let the darkie try to do the hit?"

Okay, here we go; stay calm. Speaking a little too fast, Donnie said, "Yes sir, my decision and my mistake. It seemed like a no-brainer, in and out in forty seconds, tops. I thought I could bring Lamar along, he's good and—"

"Apparently not good enough," Johnny cut in.

"Yes sir. But I believe, had I been there instead of Lamar, because of some poor intel and unforeseen...circumstances, the end result would have been the same."

Another long pause and, in the stillness, Donnie heard Tony stand up and slowly start walking toward the desk. He tried to swallow, and finally succeeded after his third try.

Johnny asked, "So, what you're saying is, if I take out your partner, I only fix half the problem. That what you're telling me?"

Shit. "What I'm saying is, even if Tony tried that night...because of what we didn't know...it wouldn't have worked."

Donnie tried to control his breathing and heard an angry voice just behind his left ear. "That's bullshit."

The next sound Donnie heard came from the click, click of the hammer of an automatic locking into the firing position. The sound punctuated Tony's remark.

Donnie took another huge breath, sat up straight, and put his hands to his side. Donnie knew well Tony's style, one through the guts, or maybe a knee...some place really painful. When Tony tired of the game, or you begged enough, wham...one right through the eye...blackness.

Time passed excruciatingly slow in complete silence; not a sound, not even fat Al's breathing.

When Johnny spoke, Donnie exhaled heavily; he would live. Johnny lumbered to his feet and as he walked around the desk said, "You know, my associate in California took this failure on your part very badly; he's furious. But what's worse, what you done, it makes me look bad, like I got second-rate peo-ple working for me. I can't have that and remain…successful. You get me? Now, I'm a fair man. I understand nobody's perfect; shit happens, mistakes are made." Johnny leaned forward down to Donnie's face. "But never when we whack bums."

Johnny straightened up and started walking slowly back to his chair. "I got a reputation to uphold and need to make a statement, an example…show I mean business."

Johnny dropped his large frame back down into his chair and said, "So today…you walk. But I'm going to have Tony here make your partner disap-pear. That sound good to you?"

Shit! Just nod your head, get up and walk away. Walk away! But that's not what Donnie did. He looked in Johnny's direction and in an assertive voice said, "Johnny, he's a good man and loyal. That's why he wants to learn more and move up in your operation. It wasn't his—"

Tony stepped forward and placed the barrel of his gun on Donnie's left knee. "Shut the fuck up."

Alphonso moved forward and pulled Donnie's head back by his hair.

Everyone froze waiting for orders. Johnny made a grunt as he stood up and walked around his desk for the second time. He moved up in front of Don-nie, leaned back against his desk and crossed his arms. He stared at Donnie for a long time.

"Shit, Donnie, you got balls…but also loyalty. I like my guys that under-stand and respect loyalty." Waving a finger at Donnie, Johnny added, "But you need to learn a whole lot more about self-preservation." Johnny walked around a little more then said, "Let him go."

Alphonso released Donnie's hair then gave him a hard pat on the cheek.

Johnny looked at Tony and waved him away. Tony backed off into the shadows. They all heard Johnny take a big breath and exhale. "I must be get-ting old." He walked back to Donnie and said, "Get the hell out of here."

Donnie stood up and Johnny flicked his hand toward the door and added, "Take your boy with you. Lay low and stay out of sight until you hear from me."

Donnie followed Alphonso to the metal door and heard Johnny say, "And don't do nothing that makes me change my mind."

Chapter Thirty-eight
Good Old Max

After protecting a key witness at a safe house for ten muggy, uneventful, boring days in Biloxi, Mississippi, Veronica wanted more than anything to go home. Unfortunately, DJ diverted her to help on a one-week surveillance job in Safford, Arizona. Not quite her forte, but DJ said the team in Safford needed help when someone dropped out sick. Apparently, an attorney, with the help of a few correctional officers, decided to pad their incomes by smuggling drugs into the federal medium security prison. When Veronica's replacement came, she left not learning anything more about the perpetrators than when she arrived.

After getting a ride to Santa Fe, Veronica flew in a puddle jumper to Vegas before a commercial flight to Reno. She never flew from anywhere directly to Reno. Sitting in an exit row next to a very polite and very sinewy wrangler type, she decided he fit the mold of the quintessential cowboy. He didn't stop chewing but chose to swallow his tarry saliva rather than spit into an empty coffee cup. *Real proper western upbringing.* Veronica instantly liked him but only engaged in minimal innocuous conversation…walls up.

About halfway through the flight Veronica thought, *Two more or less legal jobs in a row; a first in quite some time.*

Legal in the sense that DJ subbed her out on occasion from a pool of "vetted" agents to other federal agencies like the U.S. Marshall Service and the FBI. The camaraderie and legal, on paper, assistance allowed DJ to acquire certain sensitive information about ongoing investigations, probes and surveillances.

Veronica finally trudged into her home, late at night. She thought, *I always seem to show up here in the dead of night or too damn early in the morning.* She knew half of her exhaustion stemmed from boredom, crappy food, and lack of exercise. After checking her house, she showered and crashed hard.

Four hours later, her tiny earpiece pinged. Veronica Sanchez snapped awake and quickly grabbed her automatic. Scanning the room and listening, she determined the alert had not come from one of the house's motion detectors. *No threat.* Her deeply shut down system misinterpreted the warning. The motion detectors buzzed; the sound she heard was definitely a ping.

Turning to look at the clock, she thought, *Shit.* The ping announced incoming information from her handler and, as usual, DJ called way too early in the morning. Since he was East Coast and she was West Coast, when at home, his calls often caught her sleeping. Oddly, even though she felt comfortable and close to DJ, she'd actually never met him. Her old handler, Max, was killed overseas a little over a year ago in some shithole in the Mideast... maybe Lebanon. Neither Max nor the asset he tried to save made it out; they simply disappeared.

Max was the devoted father, trusted teacher, demanding mentor; but most of all, the brilliant analytical psychiatrist Veronica Sanchez needed to survive. Manipulation, mind control, taking advantage of a damaged soul...maybe; but Max knew enough about her past to know, without intervention, her self-destructive behavior would land her in prison for the rest of her life...or dead for the rest of her life. Max also knew that not taking advantage of Veronica Sanchez's...special abilities, would result in a staggering waste. Operatives like Veronica came along once in a blue moon. Her psychological profile revealed a highly intelligent woman with an extremely aggressive behavior and obsessive personality. She possessed an innate, almost manic, drive to succeed...at all costs. Her assessment also revealed a high level of passion, self-righteousness and self-guilt. The dichotomy of self-striving and self-loathing tore her apart. She lived in a world of black and white with a paper-thin layer of gray separating the two. You were an ally or an enemy; cross her, and you paid. Ultimately, this lack of compromise brought periods of tremendous success at the cost of overwhelming failure. Veronica destroyed the relationship with her parents, her husband, her daughter, and eventually the military. By the time Max intervened, Veronica needed a letter from the Secretary of Defense to secretly release her from the Army's maximum-security prison for women in Leavenworth, Kansas. Based on Max's recommendation, the agency stepped in and added this highly volatile but potentially very effective asset to their arsenal.

To pull Veronica out of her nosedive and redirect her anger outwardly, Max taught her that redemption came in the form of retribution. She could never mend the damage she'd caused those closest to her, but she could make them proud by doing her nation's dirty work. If she could make the country safer, a better place, well...that counted for something. Max said someday those she cared for, and who once cared for her, would know and be proud. All bullshit for sure; Veronica's loved ones would never know; but what the hell, it worked. Once Max locked her in, she literally relished crushing bad guys. Of course, bad guys became a relative term. In reality, she let the agency determine who she targeted. In her mind, if they came under the agency's scrutiny, they chose the wrong side.

Too many times, assigning someone like Veronica to the wrong handler spelled disaster. That was why doctors like Max proved so invaluable. He not only evaluated and selected the operatives; he constantly observed and scrutinized the agency's handlers as well. Culling the herd of sadists, egomaniacs and disgruntled employees helped keep the agency out of the headlines and, just as importantly, out of congressional hearings. The bottom line, the agency's domestic operations constituted unconstitutional acts; however, to some bigwigs at the top...a necessary evil.

Max pushed every button that made Ms. "Hot Head" Veronica Sanchez want to succeed. Off the grid, illegal undercover work meant you had to rely on your training, wits, guts and instincts. There would be no rescue if caught... just a lot of pain and, if you were lucky, a mercifully quick bullet in the back of the head. Max marveled at how none of that seemed to faze Veronica; she thrived best when way out on the edge.

Max knew Veronica could never work undercover overseas because she couldn't control her explosive temper. Veronica's short fuse, in Max's mind, remained her one glaring flaw. Plus, all her tattoos screamed, "I'm American!" But domestically she excelled; the only problem, strictly against federal law. Veronica melted into the lower ten percent of society as a biker, druggy, drug dealer, hooker, migrant worker, truck driver, ex-con, or low-level thief, like a chameleon.

But good old Max was dead and gone, dried up and blowing around the desert like dust from some old forgotten Oklahoma farm. He tried to do what he said would never happen—come to the aid of one of his operatives. In the end, even Max, the stone, had a soft middle. He just couldn't sit by, detached, knowing one of his girls was blindly heading into a trap. But the bad guys were waiting for the cavalry. Poof...dust to dust.

Fortunately for Veronica, Max began grooming a replacement handler for his eventual retirement or, as it turned out, rapid decomposition. Desk Jock, or DJ, even monitored and ran one of Veronica's assignments before Max's exit. The operation went well, and they bonded; well, as well as you can bond with a voice on the phone. They were both very fond of Max, and their long talks helped them both cope and move on. Even though DJ knew what Veronica looked like, Veronica remained in the dark about DJ. Someday, she reminded herself; for sure, someday.

Putting her gun down, she grabbed her secure phone. Trying to hide her sleepiness and displeasure, Veronica said in a perky voice, "Good morning."

"Hey, Chiquita, catch you sleeping?"

Suppressing a yawn, she replied, "Nah, just making coffee."

"Oh, really?"

Realizing DJ knew she was lying, Veronica asked, "You checked the motion sensors, didn't you?"

"Yep; nary a whisper of movement in your entire house."

"Damn you; I'm fed up with no privacy."

"Hey, beautiful, not to spy on you or catch you blowing smoke up my ass, which of course you just tried to do. I watch your back...always. You sleep; I watch."

After a loud exhale, Veronica said, "I know; I know. I...appreciate your... ." An awkward silence ensued. Finally, she changed the subject. "Well, I'm up now, so go get a cup of coffee. I have to pee and I don't want you listening."

"Hang on; this will only take a second. I may have something for you...or maybe nothing."

"You talk; I'm still going to go pee."

"Okay. We found no intel on assassin activity in California, but we discovered an obtuse connection to some thugs in Chicago who aren't at home. They do dirty work for a guy named Johnny 'Big Nose' Ramelli. The FBI has been eavesdropping on the kingpin for quite some time."

"Go on."

"This guy's dirty but clean, if you know what I mean."

"Yeah, like two dozen arrests and no convictions clean?"

"Bingo. So, the FBI catches old Big Nose talking to a guy in California who says he needs two of Johnny's men; for what, we don't know. Like I said, it's sketchy. Johnny has a strong connection with this guy; but what, again, we don't know. The guy in California is the same person, a while back, who asked Big Nose to check about a psychiatrist named Dr. Ivan Zulov. Apparently, this California dude has a computer whiz that checked Zulov's voice patterns and inflections and thinks he might be from the Windy City. But the only Ivan Zulov we could find operates a private practice in San Diego."

"That's it?"

"Sorry, Chiquita."

Veronica thought for a while then asked DJ, "What's the timeline?"

"The timing of the thugs heading for California fits with your incident. I read the police report and found articles in some of the Northern California papers. They called it a revenge attack or shotgun warning, but not specifically a murder attempt. They also referred to only one person—a guy—as the potential victim. Were you there?"

After flashing on the close call, Veronica finally responded, "Those assholes had us, DJ; cold turkey, and they were professionals."

"They thought they had you; they don't know my girl." After a while, DJ asked, "So, why is the local sheriff and the paper downplaying the incident?"

"My, ah, date, kept me out of it." Trying to avoid revealing any more detail, Veronica asked, "Am I still off the clock?"

"Actually, I could use you for about ten days. We need to protect a witness, a woman who needs to continue to process oxygen, at least until she can testify."

"Geez, you're all heart, DJ. Can you get someone else?"

"Sure, okay, I think so, if that's what you want. What are you planning to do?"

"I'm going to give that psychiatrist in San Diego a visit. His name cannot be a coincidence. Besides, I have nothing else to go on. Did the FBI check out Zulov?"

DJ said, "Not that I've heard. But if you—"

Veronica cut in, "I know, I know, drive safe, no tickets, don't get arrested, stay out of the news, no pictures, blah, blah, blah."

"I was going to say, if you get any goods on Johnny Big Nose, the FBI will owe us big time."

"Oh," Veronica replied, "I thought you were going to give me the... mother hen talk."

"I would, Chiquita, but I know you know the drill. Oh, currently we have no assets down there so stay in touch, be safe and watch your back."

Veronica almost made a hen's bawk, bawk, bawk sound but dropped the thought. Instead she replied, "If Zulov knows anything about this Big Nose Ramelli thug, I'll find out. See ya."

Chapter Thirty-nine
Then I'll Snap Your Neck

Benjamin Whittingham lay on his bunk reading, as he did during most free time. Yeah right; free time, what a joke. Neutral time, limbo time, or dead time captured his predicament more accurately. But reading did let his mind escape...if only for a little while...even though his body couldn't. Not much else to do when you're rotting away in prison.

After the reality of being railroaded during the sentencing and before getting shipped to prison, Whit specifically requested his dad and friends not call, write, or visit. He didn't want to know what occurred back home; the only exception, he requested his dad to relay any changes in Ned's condition. Everything else seemed irrelevant and pointless. What in the hell could he do about anything anyway, good news or bad? Any information from the outside just made him feel more isolated, sadder, angrier and more alone than his incarceration already created. Whit relented for Katelyn the first time he could see someone from the outside. Seeing her, kissing her, holding her, then watching her walk away just about destroyed him. It hurt so badly his attitude crumbled, his short temper surfaced, and his ability to cope collapsed. He couldn't go through that again and survive. He later made one phone call to her. Whit told her it was okay to move on, if she could. *Katelyn, please find someone else. Be happy, live life to the fullest. Sitting around waiting three years for me is nuts; just crazy.* She didn't think so and took his rebuke badly.

Whit figured a few weeks or months of pain beats the hell out of three damn years. But it wasn't a few weeks or months; Katelyn kept trying. *Damn her anyway.* What the hell was she trying to prove...resilience, loyalty, love?

Obsession, insanity, and being downright unrealistic fit Whit's thinking more. But damn her to hell, she wouldn't quit.

He wasn't surprised when Officer Sturgis poked his head in the open cell and said, "Hey, Whittingham, someone to see you."

"I'm not going to see her. Tell her to go away."

"Oh, you'll want to see this one, unless you've crossed over to the dark side during your time in here…if you catch my drift."

Whit sat up and swung his legs over the bunk. "What are you talking about?"

"It's not the regular one trying to see you; Katelyn, is it?"

"If it's not Katelyn, then who is she?"

"How the hell should I know? I was just sent to get you; are you coming or not?"

Whit turned to Officer Sturgis with a puzzled look. Finally, Whit shrugged then creased the page with his thumbnail where he quit reading. Before he hopped off the bunk, he bent the corner of the page back and closed the book.

Whit stretched and asked, "What does she look like?"

The jailer offered, "Oh, she's a looker. A tad skinny, but a looker. You coming?"

Skinny? Has to be a mistake. He shook his head. Whit finally said, "What the hell, yeah, sure. It's not like my dance card's full."

The guard asked, "What dance card? What the hell are you talking about?"

"Nothing, it's just an old saying. Hey, wait a second; I want to brush my teeth."

It was a Wednesday, visitation day at California State Prison in Lancaster. As he walked down the hall, Whit asked, "What does she look like?"

"She's about, ah, 5'5", or so, nice rack, and dark hair that she pulls straight back."

"Nah, couldn't be."

"Couldn't be who?" asked the puzzled guard.

"Oh, nothing; just thinking out loud."

They walked on in silence. Officer Sturgis opened the door to the visitation common area. It looked like what in a public school would be called a multi-purpose room. Whit entered the visitation room and began to scan from right to left. He didn't get past the first person…Allyson Chandler. *Son of a bitch.* She looked as stunning as ever, but as he walked toward her, he noticed she appeared out of sorts. Gorgeous but pale, thinner, almost frail in her stance.

She put out her hand and said, "Hello, Whit; probably the last person you thought you would ever see again, right?"

Even though he hated this woman, out of well-ingrained manners, Whit instinctively shook Allyson's hand. "Yes, quite frankly; you disappeared rather quickly when the crap hit the fan."

"My job had been compromised; it was time to fade into the shadows."

Leaning toward her, Whit said in an angry, low voice, "You destroyed a good man, Allyson. Ned couldn't hurt a fly, but that didn't faze you."

Allyson's eyes started to water and she whispered, "I know; I know, but Whit, I—"

"Bullshit!" Whit said in a raised voice that made everyone in the room stop, turn, and stare silently at him. They all eventually turned back to their conversations, everyone except the two officers closest to Whit. Whit lowered his voice and said, "You knew."

Looking away, Allyson asked, "Can we sit? I need to sit. I want to tell you something; it's important."

Pointing toward an empty bench, Whit thought, *Something's not right here. Allyson escaped free as a bird. Why come back? Why hunt me down?* Then it hit Whit like a rock to the head. *Allyson must be ill; like, badly ill. She's hurting and acting way out of character. I get the feeling something huge will be revealed if I can keep my mouth shut long enough to let her spill her guts. I just can't figure out why... why now?*

Taking her elbow and walking her gently to one of the last remaining empty plastic picnic-type tables, Whit asked, "Can I get you some water?" Then added in his head, *"with a healthy dose of arsenic, you miserable money-grubbing black widow?"*

"Yes, please. You were always a gentleman to me; a good guy."

Whit shot back before he could stop himself, "Almost as much of a gentleman as Ned."

The look of sadness and guilt on Allyson's face made Whit regret venting. *Goddamn it, Whittingham; shut the hell up. She's trying to help somehow. Maybe she's trying to help herself, too. I hope she doesn't bolt for the door when my back's turned.* Whit quickly grabbed a pitcher and two glasses and hurried back. To his relief, Allyson hadn't budged.

He poured her and himself some water; she thanked him. Whit sat there in silence, waiting patiently, calm on the outside while his insides screamed for her to start.

"How's Katelyn?" she asked.

Whit almost said, *"Why the hell should you care?"* but caught himself. *Be cool and let this play out on her terms.* "I don't know; I've pushed her away. I only saw her one time following the sentencing. I told her to move on, to forget about me…us. I've refused to see her since and don't answer her calls or letters."

"How can you throw her away like that? A blind person could see how much she means to you, and you know she's crazy in love."

Whit blurted out in almost a hiss, "How in the hell will any of that work, Allyson, with me in here for, what, two and a half more years? Hell, I've already been in here longer than I knew Katelyn on the outside. And why should you care, especially after what you did?" *Goddamnit, control your damn emotions, you ass. Focus, find out why she's here.* After a long silence, Whit tried to recover by saying, "Sorry; that was out of line."

"No, it wasn't; I deserve it, I know. I wasn't even sure you'd meet with me. But don't patronize me. Guys like you can't pull it off. Milner could, but you can't."

Biting his tongue, Whit said, "You're right; I was patronizing. I'm just angry and impatient to hear what you have to say. I'll wait until you're finished, then I'll snap your pretty little neck. How's that?"

Allyson smiled. "That's more like it, more like you."

After a long pause, Whit couldn't help but ask, "Are you ill, Allyson?"

Allyson quickly tried to speak, but a lump welled up in her throat. She lowered her head and cried softly. Whit walked over to the main counter and plucked some tissues out of the box, returned, and gave them to Allyson. Crying women occurred often on the fourth Wednesday of the month in the Lancaster visitation room, especially toward the end of the day.

After a while she straightened her back, turned and looked straight at Whit and said in a sturdy, confident and strong voice, "I have stage-four cancer in my prostate and elsewhere. The sand dial is running out. All my money can't change the outcome."

Whit thought, *Prostate? She must mean pancreas and that's bad. She's probably heavily medicated and confused.* "Jesus, Allyson; I'm sorry. I hate seeing anyone or anything suffer, and I can tell you're hurting. But it doesn't change what you took part in doing. You helped severely damage one of my best friends, and I can never forgive you."

After another long pause Allyson finally said, "You are such an open book and such a conundrum. I can feel your anger, but I can also sense you sincerely feel sorry for me. How can you do that? How can you feel hatred and compassion at the same time?"

Throwing up his hands Whit said, "It's just the way I'm wired, I guess."

"But how? I don't know anyone like you."

Whit thought, *Good, keep her engaged.* "Maybe I can explain it this way. You're like a beautiful predator…let's say a bobcat. Bobcats are exquisite creatures but also one of nature's premier killers. Like you, they are gorgeous and deadly at the same time. You can't accept one part without respecting the other. One crosses your path and you admire such a sleek and graceful animal. Then another time you watch how heartlessly it incapacitates a jackrabbit or squirrel and toys with it. The squeals and cries of pain and fear do nothing more than entertain and excite the beast. You think, what a cruel, vile and evil animal. But it's the same animal, and that's what you have to accept about nature…and about some people. Does that make sense?"

"Yes, yes, I see your point. In a strange way, it makes me feel a little better about myself. But I can't leave this earth without clearing up what I did and did not do to your friend. Maybe it will help you, and you can make things right. Maybe I can redeem or fix some of the harm I've caused, but you have to listen and not interrupt. Can you do that for me, please?"

"If you're asking me for forgive—"

"No, damn it; I don't want forgiveness. I know what I did, but I also know what I didn't do. You don't; so can you please shut the hell up and listen?"

Whit just sat there, took his right thumb and index finger to his lips and made a zip motion across his lips. He turned to face Allyson more directly and gave her his full attention.

"I've made a very profitable business out of…selling my body to clients. These clients needed someone removed who stood in their way…interfering or blocking their path to success. Not killed; just disgraced, humiliated, their credibility destroyed. My talents work best on married men or individuals in positions of power where a sex scandal would destroy them. I receive a proposal; if I accept, I negotiate a price and go to work. What better way to ruin the high and mighty than a steamy, disgraceful, messy and very public sex-capade? I never felt like a whore or call girl. I believed I performed a service, like an avenging angel, a truth detector, a tester of someone's character. I'd show them a little candy and well, if they bit, they got what they deserved. Their lack of moral and ethical commitment to their wife, church, position in the community, whatever, brings them down. Everyone I destroyed lived arrogant, egotistical and shallow lives. I just made their weaknesses...public. But, you must believe me, not until Ned did I ever hurt anyone that didn't deserve it. Corporate executives, politicians, lawyers, even a reporter, all self-destructed, like sheep to slaughter. They all fell because they couldn't keep their dicks in their pants. After I washed off their filth, I'd feel good. Ned was completely different; I should have known something wasn't right. But I didn't know or care at the start. I was offered double my normal fee and that black Mercedes to set Ned and Grey up and selfishly accepted.

"How many times have you done this?"

"Ned was number nine."

Whit said nothing for quite a while. Finally, he had to speak. "But Ned wasn't that way; besides, he was single. If anything, he's too nice to even be a good businessman. Hell, with what he gives away to schools, charitable organizations and his church, he only pockets about half of what he should. So, why Ned? He doesn't fit the sleaze ball scenario."

"That's it, Whit; I don't know. The job never fit from the start. I shouldn't have taken it; greed dominated my decision. I couldn't say no. My actions ultimately help hurt your friend."

Whit wanted to know who hired her, but asked first, "What were you to do?"

"The job required me to get in between Ned and Grey; you know...a love triangle."

Whit's anger welled up again and he couldn't hold back. "Well, that wasn't too difficult a job. Poor lovesick Ned was a sucker for any female's attention, and Milner would screw a knothole or warm mud if it came with a nice rack." Whit looked away and slowly calmed down a little. "Why pay to hurt a guy like Ned?"

Allyson said, "Look at me, Whit." When Whit turned and looked straight in her eyes, she said, "Nothing is as it appears. It looks like the love triangle worked, but that's not what happened."

Cocking his head back, Whit asked in a surprised voice, "What the...what are you saying?"

"You were right about Ned; he fell hard, but I couldn't make Milner touch me."

Whit put up his hands. "Wait, wait a minute. You're telling me Milner didn't touch you?" *That's what Grey said. I should have believed him. But at the time, I thought it didn't make any difference anyway, as long as Ned believed Grey slept with Allyson. Christ, what a mess I've made.*

"Oh, he played along; right up to the act, then laughed in my face. He said, 'Sorry, darling; no matter how hot the twat, I will never cross a buddy.' I was stunned. Nothing like that had ever happened before."

Putting the palms of his hands to his temple, Whit said, "I'm such an idiot." He dropped his hands, looked back at Allyson and asked, "Then why in hell did Ned try to hang himself?"

"He didn't. I know he didn't. I just can't prove it."

Boom! There it was, like a thunder clap; the reason Allyson had come back. Whit instantly realized he believed her. But what she said stunned him to the core; his insides twisted into knots. Whit looked away from Allyson and stared unfocused. The difficulty to think enveloped him. His mind flashed back to the last time he spoke to Milner. *All those vicious accusations; the punch in the throat that could have killed him.* Then he remembered Ned lying in the hospital bed, and his overriding feeling of disappointment toward Ned for being so weak as to try and take his own life. *How could I have been so stupid?* But for the first time since Ned's...incident...Allyson's revelation began to fill in a clearer picture, more fitting to Whit's belief system. *I should have trusted Grey. I should have known Ned would never try to take his life. Why did I let my emotions take over and block out what I knew about my friends? Damn it all to hell; I destroyed the gang!* After what seemed like minutes, Whit's rapid-fire kaleidoscope of thoughts slowed down enough to start processing again. Whit realized he needed to rule out one more uncertainty.

He turned to Allyson and asked, "How do you reconcile the fact that whether Milner diddled you or not, poor Ned thought Milner did?"

"Oh, he did at first; but that's because I told Ned that Milner slept with me. It was my last-ditch effort to get the job done and get paid. Like I said, I was greedy. But Ned looked so sad, crushed, devastated; I couldn't go through with it. In the past when I took down a sleazy asshole, I'd feel good. With Ned, I felt cruel, cheap, filthy...so, I fessed up. I told him what I was paid to do and that I had just blown fifty grand and the Mercedes. I told him I'd fix us both a drink then tell him everything. You know Ned; even after I wrecked his life, he took it almost matter of fact…like he expected it. It made me feel even worse. But at least, I think, he actually understood that I cared enough about him to stop the scam. I hope so. Then I spiked his drink, he passed out, and I bolted. I swear on a stack of bibles, Whit, Ned was alive when I left and had no reason to kill himself."

Leaning forward with his elbows on his knees, Whit dropped his head and whispered, "Son of a…." *I have to get out of here. I've made a mess out of everything. I need to fix it…all of it.*

Allyson watched a pained look cover Whit's face. She raised her arm toward Whit, then hesitated. She put her hand down and quietly said, "There's something else you need to know." When Whit didn't raise his head, she shocked him again by saying, "Things have escalated while you've been in here. Do you know someone tried to kill Grey?"

Whit quickly turned to Allyson. "What are you talking about? No, no, no, that's crazy. My dad would have told me." When Allyson didn't respond, Whit added, "Well, unless Grey asked my dad not to tell me. But, Grey's alright, right?"

"Yes, he's fine. The county, state, and feds are looking into it. But Whit, it's best for you to focus on your situation."

"Jesus, Allyson; I've helped mess everything up and I'm totally useless, stuck in here."

She lightly placed her hand on Whit's shoulder and said, "I've come to help, to make this right." Allyson quickly added, "As right as we can."

"How? I've got two and a half more years in here, and you're dying of pancreatic cancer."

"Whit, I've been working on getting you out of here for quite some time. Believe it or not, it may happen soon."

Whit cocked his head to one side and asked, "What did you just say?"

Ignoring Whit's question, she added, "I'm not dead yet; I still have some time. And Whit, I don't have pancreatic cancer…I have prostate cancer."

Chapter Forty
Special Sessions

Dr. Zulov produced his most sincere smile as the nervous Mrs. Bernstein waited anxiously for his answer. Zulov had been gingerly walking her in this direction for the last two sessions. "Yes, I agree it's quite unusual and not recommended for virtually everyone under a doctor's care. But in a few complicated and special cases, as in yours, Mrs. Bernstein...Ellen, I believe it's quite appropriate. You see, your ex-husband has destroyed your faith in yourself and your trust in men. To regain control of your life and to prove him wrong, this is the right course."

"Thank you, Doctor." Then with a sheepish smile, she added, "Ivan."

Smiling, closing his eyes and tipping his head slightly to show his approval of Mrs. Bernstein calling him by his first name, Dr. Zulov affirmed, "I'll call on you Saturday; 8 A.M. sharp, not one minute late. From that moment on, you will be treated like royalty. I'll place your luggage in the trunk, open my car door for you, and we'll be off. At my cabin, for the rest of the weekend, you will learn how a woman with your inner strengths and passion for life should have been treated...and, will be treated."

"It all sounds so wonderful. I so appreciate the extra care you're giving me. You really are a good doctor."

"We all try, Ellen; it's just that I care so much about my patients...all of them." Dr. Zulov took a quick glance over his glasses at Mrs. Bernstein to see if he was putting it on a little too thick. *Nope, not even close.* "But when I see a proud, magnificent, majestic bird wounded and hurting, I can't help but go that extra mile. You're that wonderful creature, Ellen. *More like a dodo bird; a gullible, good-looking and very rich dodo bird. No wonder they're extinct.* "Now remember, you are under a doctor's care and this…special session, to help you, must remain in strict confidence."

Standing up and offering her hand, Ellen Bernstein said with a broad smile, "Oh, I completely understand. Thank you so much. I'm so looking forward to seeing you on Saturday. I'll be ready, eight on the dot."

Dr. Zulov released her hand and watched her psychiatrist-ordered, jazzercised-tightened ass sway out of his office. *You cad*, he said smiling to himself, *you lucky, soon-to-be-riding-Ellen Bernstein-like-a-racehorse cad*.

Sitting down, Zulov hit the intercom to the reception desk and asked, "Can you come in, please, Mrs. Atkins?"

Mrs. Atkins promptly entered, closed the door, and while walking toward the oh-so-professional doctor's desk said, "Mrs. Bernstein certainly left in a good mood."

Zulov just nodded while looking down as if studying his notes. He didn't know if, or how much of his little…special session…Donna Atkins knew, but he didn't want to reveal anything by his facial expressions. "Yes, yes; she's coming right along." *If all goes as planned, she'll be coming all weekend.* Zulov asked, "Any insight on the new patient?"

She replied, "Not much; Ms. Morales is pretty, and pretty vague with the answers on our questionnaire. She says she's forty, I'd say, a hard forty. She looks more American Indian than Mexican; and she's built…not hugely muscular, just badass fit."

Intrigued, Zulov said, "Well, we better not keep her waiting."

Mrs. Atkins nodded, spun on her heels, and left to send in Ms. Morales.

Thinking about the potential client, he thought, *I've never had a Latina; let's see how Ms. Morales shakes out and find out if I get the opportunity to check "south of the border" off of my banged list.*

Dr. Zulov was not disappointed with Ms. Morales. Dressed biker-ish, she marched right over to his desk and sat in the chair directly across. She wore black pants and a black tank top that revealed firm small breasts and nicely defined shoulder and arm muscles. She possessed a pretty face with strong features, short dark hair parted on the left, and a no-bullshit stare. Her midsection was not as hourglass-shaped as Zulov preferred, but that was due to her wide, flat muscular midsection. Ms. Morales crossed her legs, revealing shiny black leather boots with worn soles. The stare-down started.

Dr. Zulov had treated similar women, tough on the outside but marshmallows on the inside. They try desperately to act hard to hide their pain. He knew professionally he should initiate the conversation but decided to let this little power play go on a bit. With a pleasant but neutral gaze, Zulov locked onto the dark eyes of the attractive Ms. Morales.

Suddenly, all sexual interest in this beauty disintegrated in an instant. His mind registered a memory, a very terrible memory. Warning bells banged in his head as the hair on his legs stood at attention. Zulov found himself staring into cold, dead eyes...just like Steven Sligers. *She's not here for help, and she doesn't have a soft center. This woman is dangerous.* Her stare made acid in his stomach burn just like that horrible day with Sliger. He decided right then he didn't want anything to do with Ms. Teresa Morales. He broke eye contact, and asked as professionally as he could, "What can I do for you, Ms. Morales?"

"Answer some questions."

Oh, no. "Are, ah," he had to clear his throat, "are you from the police?"

"You're not that lucky."

"What's that supposed to—" *Okay end this quickly.* "Ms. Morales, if that's your real name, I don't know what this is about, but—"

"It's not."

"Excuse me? What's not?"

"My real name."

Another stare-down; Dr. Zulov broke eye contact again and looked frantically around the room as if someone was there he could summon for help. Finally, in a voice far too shrill, he said, "I'd like you to leave at once."

"I'd like to pull you over this desk and kick your pussy little ass."

Silence and that stare again. He stood up defensively and she did at the exact same instant. Now he became very scared. In an even more frantic voice, he yelled, "Mrs. Atkins; call the police at once."

Standing behind his chair to gain further distance from this crazy bitch, he said, "They're right down the street; you'd better leave."

Mrs. Atkins swung open the door and asked, "Is there a problem?"

Veronica Sanchez straightened up and said, in a pleasant voice, "Nah; in fact, I'm all better...for now." Looking back at Dr. Zulov she said, "Thanks, Doc; see you around." With that, Veronica walked past the stunned receptionist, who kept one hand on the doorknob and the other against her chest.

After they heard the outer door close, the still wide-eyed Mrs. Atkins looked at Dr. Zulov and asked, "My God, what was that all about?"

Still clutching the back of his chair, Dr. Zulov, too numb to answer, just shook his head.

"Does this have something to do with that Sliger guy and that monster that sat in the reception room?"

Finally, Zulov offered, "No; no, I don't think so." *I know she's not with Sliger; not his style, too confrontational, too public. Besides, I've been a good boy, haven't said a peep to anyone. Sliger has no reason to come after me. But then who in the hell is she? Maybe she's just a crazy. This profession corners the market for walk-in-off-the-street nut jobs. She wouldn't be my first. Thank God, I'm leaving this weekend. I need some rest, and sexual diversion. Well, maybe not rest; and Mrs. Bernstein will be a nice diversion. Still, that nasty woman came to me for answers about something, but what?*

Noticing Donna Atkins still wide-eyed, staring his way, Dr. Zulov said, "Mrs. Atkins, please call the Papola Bail Bondsmen's office. Have Papola send Stan or one of his other bounty hunters to my house this evening. I'd like someone to watch my place at night and the office during office hours, for, let's say, all next week. I'll give whoever they send a description of this Ms. Morales. You do the same."

Finally, taking her hand down from her chest and relaxing, Donna Atkins asked, "Do you think she'll be back?"

In a reassuring voice, Zulov said calmly, "No, no; she must be a nut case off the street. After that scene, I'm sure she's gone for good. We'll maintain the added security, just to make sure."

"Very good, Doctor, and thank you. I'll go call and set it up."

"Thank you, Donna. Please take off when you're done. Have a good weekend. I'll see you Monday morning."

With the last session of the day abruptly terminated, Dr. Ivan Zulov left work early also. He kept a sharp eye out for the Latina woman, even stopping before he reached his car to thoroughly look around again. He found no one even closely resembling the muscular troublemaker.

But Veronica was there and watching, from quite some distance. She had the listening device and tracker in Zulov's car, so all she needed was for Dr. Pussy to drive away. Veronica backtracked down the side street. She grabbed her helmet, straddled the bike, plugged in the earpiece and turned on the receiver. *Blinky, blinky, I'm right here, Doctor Ivan Zulov...or whoever. Now that I've nearly scared the crap out of you, the next time we meet, I bet you shit your pants.*

Veronica heard the car phone ring in her earpiece and Dr. Pussy timidly say, "Hello?"

"Ed Papola here."

Sounding relieved, Zulov said, "Ah, yes, Ed; I have another issue with a, ah, new client...a real whack job."

"Okay, no problem; same rate. You seem to like Stan; I'll send him. As long as things remain this slow, use Stan as long as you want."

"Great. I'm leaving early tomorrow for my cabin in the mountains and need Stan to stay at my place and—"

Veronica stopped listening intently after hearing Dr. Pussy's weekend plans; that was all she needed to know. How perfect. She'd track him home, then find a motel and go shopping. She needed time to dye her hair, find an office supply store, and a uniform shop.

Chapter Forty-one
Deep, Dark Secret

Sitting side-by-side on a bench in the visitation room at the state's medium-security prison in Lancaster, California, neither Whit nor Allyson spoke for a very long time.

Whit kept saying over and over again in his head, *Prostate cancer? Prostate cancer?*

Whit squinted his eyes and wrinkled his face. "But, that's impossible; how can that be, Allyson? You can't have—"

Whit stopped in midsentence, raised his head and shook it back and forth. *No, no, no…no way.* He leaned forward and scanned, in detail, Allyson's facial features. *No frikkin' way.*

Allyson returned Whit's stare with her killer smile.

Finally, Whit broke the silence by saying, "Allyson, you have to be kidding me."

Allyson just broadened her smile, showing off two rows of straight white teeth.

Whit put his palms to his temples, closed his eyes and started rubbing gently. He said, "Well, I'll be damned; I've been played and played and played."

"Don't feel so special, it's not just you. Nobody knows or has figured it out."

"Someone must know."

"Well, let's see; my doctor, my surgeon, my mother, and now you."

"Jesus, Allyson…what is…was…your real name?"

"Louis Escobar; Basque father and a French mother."

Whit asked, "How long ago did you…?"

"Eleven years ago."

"What were you, twenty?"

"Almost thirty."

"You're telling me you're forty years old? You don't even look thirty."

"Almost forty-one; good genes, small pores, fine features. But Whit, the journey from there to now is a long and personal story."

"Okay, okay" Whit replied, "no details; we're just going a little too fast."

Thinking, but not wanting to ask, Whit's curiosity finally got the better of him. "But, how do you pull off, you know, what you do…the intimacy stuff?"

Smirking, Allyson responded, "Think about it, Whit; my work occurs in short-term setups, not extended affairs. I always control the act. You'd be surprised how easy it is for me to direct the intimacy to a blow job or anal sex."

"Jesus, Allyson." Whit had zero experience in this realm and wasn't quite sure where or how to proceed. "Look, Allyson, I'm a hetero-dude with absolutely no knowledge of what you're telling me." Whit motioned with his hands rather abstractly. "How do you…what happens?"

"Okay, dinosaur; I get where you're going. I've been surgically altered; I have a nice little…tuck-and-roll, if that's what you're asking." Whit nodded, so Allyson continued. "I take hormones; needed my Adam's apple reduced and, of course, enhanced my breasts. But that's it. I was lucky to have a slight build, skin with small pores, delicate features and a rather high-pitched voice." When Whit didn't say anything, Allyson figured where he was going. "Okay my vagina looks and works fine, as long as you don't check it out too closely. I try to avoid using it during…work-related contact."

"Jesus, woman; you've got balls."

"Used to."

That made them both start laughing.

After a bit Allyson sighed, "Oh, God; I can't tell you the last time I've laughed that hard."

"Me too, for that matter. But I'm still a little confused; how can you have prostate cancer? Don't they take all the…male stuff out?"

No smile or trace of happiness remained on Allyson's face. "Bad luck, fate, karma or just plain sick irony, I don't know. The difficulty of the procedure normally precludes the additional complications involved in removing the prostate. The risk of damaging critical nerves and muscles can potentially ruin the whole operation. I chose not to and didn't think I needed to check my prostate until I turned fifty."

"But what does the doctor say?"

"Simple…stage four."

"Oh."

"It appears I made a fatal mistake."

Neither Whit nor Allyson spoke.

Finally, Allyson let out a long sigh and asked Whit, "Can we get back to—"

"Why you're here?" Whit finished her sentence then added, "You said you're working on getting me out of here; how?"

"The good judge who sentenced—"

"Judge Franklin is not a good judge."

"Whit, will you stop interrupting so we don't run out of time? I need to tell you what's happening. I think you may be out of here before next month's visitation day."

Astonished, Whit clammed up.

Satisfied, Allyson continued. "Judge Franklin's son, Andrew, happens to be a hotshot trial attorney with political aspirations. His firm specializes in lawsuits against big pharmaceutical, big oil, big anything with deep pockets. Little Andrew has the fashion-plate wife, two adorable daughters, and maintains a spotless image outwardly to the press and in all the right circles. He's touching all the right bases, greasing all the right palms, and continues to build a war chest for a run at State Attorney General. His otherwise spotless image took a shit when he met me. He's my kind of creep…a total cocksure, arrogant asshole…the type that feels entitled to engage in a little fun on the side."

When she paused, Whit lifted his hands as if to say, *and*?

"And, I sent Andrew's daddy, Judge Franklin a strikingly clear and crisp audio and video recording from a little device in my purse…strategically placed on the dresser in my hotel bedroom. The video clearly shows said trial lawyer riding me like a pony. I had a brief and cordial conversation with the judge, and he graciously agreed to accept your writ and revisit your case…and sentencing. The best part, he assured me that his son would gladly prepare and serve the writ, pro bono."

Whit shook his head and said, "But couldn't they just play the entrapment game, or fall back on the sex addict angle? You know, the dutiful wife standing by her man at a managed press conference. The guy blubbers and apologizes profusely. Then he says he has a problem and needs help. Presto-chango, he drops into some high-end sex addict clinic and pops out the back door two hours later completely cured. Then it's back to business as usual."

Allyson just stared at Whit for about five seconds. Finally, she said, "Jesus, Whit; you always this cynical or is it that you just don't trust my…abilities? I did say audio too, didn't I? The judge took particular interest in the part where his son kept slapping me on the ass while yelling, 'Take that, Renee, you naughty little bitch!'"

"Who's Renee?"

"Oh, that just happens to be Andrew's thirteen-year-old daughter and the judge's first grandchild."

Whit smiled. "Oh, oh, my…that's good; I mean that's bad. Well, you know what I mean. I clearly see now how your poignant and touching appeal for justice made the judge and his son decide to cooperate." Whit thought for a second then said, "But, they still have Barbou, that realtor's testimony of the incident; that's what they used to sink me."

"So negative, Whittingham, so negative." Pointing to her chest, Allyson said, "This girl does her homework. I went house shopping in Sacramento, don't you know. The horny and so predictable Mr. Barbou came to my aid and actually seemed to know the business quite well. We became quick friends. At our third stop, a lovely, large, one-story Spanish-style home, he felt comfortable enough to stick his hand between my thighs; I let him. At that point, I felt comfortable enough to stick my Lady Colt in his mouth; he let me. Right after he wet his pants, we chatted about his testimony and your sentencing. He whimpered that his statement and testimony were exactly as we told him to say, and that he hadn't talked to a soul about the incident since."

Nodding his head, Whit asked, "So he thought you were with the same people that set me up?"

"Yep; and I told Mr. Barbou, we now needed him to act very confused and guilty about lying in his sworn testimony. That will give Judge Franklin the leverage to reverse his decision, drop the charges, and your sentence."

Completely overwhelmed, Whit kept slowly shaking his head, lost for words. Finally, he turned to Allyson and said, "Allyson, I don't know what to say; I—"

"Don't say anything. What I've done for you will never make up for what I did…what happened to Ned, but—"

The loudspeaker cut into Allyson's words. "Let's wrap it up, folks; it's ten to five."

Whit and Allyson stood up and awkwardly looked around, not talking or knowing how to end their meeting.

Finally, Allyson said, "I'm pretty sure that, unless you do something stupid in here, you'll be out before this time next month, maybe a little longer. Tell Katelyn as soon as you can and apologize for shutting her out." Allyson could see Whit's mind churning and added, "Until you get out of here, there is no point in going any further. We'll talk later about moving into...revenge mode."

Curious as hell about who hired her but realizing Allyson's revelations and insights were done for now, Whit just flipped his hands up and said, "Okay, sure; just don't die on me." As soon as he finished, he regretted what he had just said.

Allyson looked into Whit's blue eyes and started crying again. Allyson cupped her left hand over her eyes and choked out, "I'm so sorry about Ned... everything."

Whit told her, "My dad wrote me about six weeks into my incarceration. He said Ned still doesn't remember anything about that night; otherwise, mentally, he's coming back...mostly. And Stacey stepped in and took over Ned's stationery store. She hired her sister to help at Pete's Place. It sounds like tons of locals drop by, keeping Stacey quite busy."

Allyson tried to smile and said meekly, "I knew she liked him." She pointed her finger in Whit's face and ordered, "Tell Katelyn."

Whit nodded as Allyson turned to leave. As she walked away, Allyson appeared even frailer than when she arrived. Whit watched her shuffle away and couldn't help himself from thinking otherwise; even after what she'd done, he truly felt sorry for the guilt-ridden, deeply troubled, dying woman.

Chapter Forty-two
Blunt-Force Trauma

The drive to Dr. Zulov's cabin took four hours; in Dr. Zulov's mind, about three hours and fifty-nine minutes too long. The confinement of the sports car made the whole trip worse than any session he'd previously sat through with Ellen Bernstein. She really did fit the definition of a sack of nuts. *How sad too; those luscious playthings, attached to a complete fruitcake. I understand old man Bernstein's attraction to this, twenty-years-his-younger, beauty. But, holy Jesus, now I know why the old fart bolted.* She cried four times and wanted to turn around twice in the first hour. Zulov finally suggested she take a sleeping pill, two actually, and she snored most of the rest of the way. After pulling into his driveway Zulov thought, *She owes me big time, even if I need to drug her a little; I'm getting some serious split tail.*

So focused was he on his end game, Dr. Zulov never noticed or sensed Veronica's presence. But then, she never gave him a chance. Veronica watched Dr. Pussy enter his cabin with an attractive but hunched over woman. Leaning against a small pine tree, Veronica's simmer turned to a boil; *it appears Dr. Pussy's pumping one of his patients.* Veronica watched Zulov return from the cabin for their bags. *Cabin my ass,* she thought. The two-story house had to contain at least three bedrooms. Situated at the end of a dead-end road, it looked to Veronica like the wooded area had been subdivided into around three-acre parcels. Southern Californian's version of a cabin in the woods included underground utilities and smooth thickly paved roads. Most of the lots sported homes, with the exception of the two parcels on either side of Dr. Pussy's hideaway. She surmised, *Maybe for a little privacy he owned them, too. Too bad for you, Dr. Pussy; in about a half an hour, you could seriously use a couple of nosey, watchful neighbors.*

Zulov scurried back up to his front porch. Suddenly, he stopped and scanned his surroundings while looking guilty as hell. When he ducked inside, Veronica checked her surroundings also. She'd give her prey time to settle in. While she waited, she changed her clothes.

After twenty-five minutes, Veronica silently moved up to the front door and knocked loudly. She wore dark blue pants, a blue shirt, and a San Bernardino County Fire Department logoed baseball cap pulled down over her face. She banged again on the door with the edge of her brand-new clipboard.

Dr. Zulov had just about calmed Ellen down. She'd chugged a full glass of wine and had started on her second. When she registered the banging at the front door, Ellen Bernstein turned into a deer in headlights. She dropped her wine and froze with her hands in tight fists under her chin. Her wide, un-blinking eyes locked on the door.

Putting his palms up toward Ellen, Dr. Zulov quietly said, "It's okay; everything's fine. Please calm down." He turned to the door and angrily yelled, "Who is it?"

When Dr. Zulov yelled, Ellen Bernstein jumped up yipping like a little dog and bolted for the bathroom. She slammed the door but continued her rapid high-pitched bark.

Veronica calmly answered in a low baritone voice, "Fire Department; is this a bad time?"

"Yes, it certainly is; uh, um, just a minute!" Zulov yelled at the front door as he walked to the bathroom. "Ellen, please calm down; it's just the county. I'll take care of them; it's no big deal. I want you to take another one of your pills. Can you do that for me?"

Zulov could hear her tearing through her toiletry bag, saying over and over, "Take a pill, take a pill, take a pill...."

"I'll be right back, Ellen. I'm just going to get rid of the county person. Now take your pill, okay?" Zulov heard the faucet running and relaxed. *With that wine, she'll be down for at least two hours. Jesus, I need the break. I need a drink.*

Shuffling quickly to the front door, Dr. Zulov stopped to regain his com-posure. After a couple of breaths and a quick glance at the bathroom door, he almost spoke...then stopped. Listening for any sound and hearing none, he leaned forward on his tiptoes and looked through the arched glass at the top of the door. The county employee stood too close to the door. All he could see was the top of a baseball cap with a San Bernardino County Fire Department logo, a little bit of blonde hair, and the shoulders of a blue work shirt.

Dropping back on his heels, Dr. Zulov shrugged and asked through the door, "Is this really important?"

"Yes, sir, the department conducted a fire safety inspection of your property and you passed. You just have to sign and retain a copy of the inspection."

Zulov figured just to deal with it now. He unlocked and pulled the door open. The fire department employee kept her head down as she wrote on the clipboard. In a much more pleasant voice, Dr. Zulov stepped forward and said, "Yes; of course, I'll sign."

Veronica slowly raised her head with a broad smile. After about two seconds of confusion, Dr. Zulov eyes registered fear. Veronica shot forward and punched him in the throat with her left hand.

A millisecond before Zulov could scream, his throat slammed shut. The force of her punch sent him backward and he fell. Veronica walked through, closed and locked the door. Though Zulov couldn't talk, in fact, could barely breathe, his eyes glared wide with fear. Veronica leaned down and calmly started duct taping his legs and thighs together. He meekly complied. She rolled him over to tape his arms behind his back, then rolled him back over and taped his mouth.

She sniffed the air and said, "You know, creeps like you think their shit doesn't stink. Well, I guess we disproved that theory." Calmly, she added, "After I check on your girlfriend, we're going to enjoy our second, and last, session." Zulov weakly tried to buck away from her. She just patted him on the head, which made him freeze, then said, "Be right back."

Veronica had to break down the bathroom door and found a less-than-elegant Ellen Bernstein passed out on the toilet. No reason to hurt this poor woman. Plus, Veronica didn't want to leave marks on Ellen; so, she put a towel around her bare legs and taped them shut. Then she laid Ellen on the floor, folded her arms in front of her, toweled and taped them also. Veronica decided not to tape Ellen's mouth. Veronica saw the sleeping pill box open and decided she had plenty of time to interrogate Dr. Pussy before this fragile woman woke.

Grabbing the wine bottle off the coffee table and taking a swig, Veronica walked over to the now quite smelly Dr. Pussy. "Nice Cab; I like good wine, thanks." Leaning closer, she continued. "Now, listen very carefully. First, I'm going to introduce you to blunt-force trauma because you're a miserable little prick." Shaking her head and pointing the wine bottle toward the bathroom, she added, "Taking advantage of pathetic, gullible, lost souls like...Mrs. Basket Case in there...unacceptable."

With a vicious left jab, she smashed the heel of her palm into the upper-right side of Zulov's chest. The impact cracked or separated two ribs. Veronica chose that area for maximum pain with minimal chance of a punctured lung or other internal injuries. His muffled screams and snorting took quite a while to subside.

When his screams turned into rapid shallow nasal wheezing, she continued. "Now we are going to have a little chat." Veronica pulled out a switchblade and snapped it open. Though Veronica kept talking, Zulov's terrified eyes remained glued to the razor-sharp edge of the shiny six-inch blade. "If I think...just think, you are lying to me, I'm going to filet your dick like peeling a banana. If I know you're lying to me, the last image you'll ever see on this earth will be your detached balls being smashed into your eye sockets." After a pause, Veronica asked politely, "Now, shall be begin?"

When Zulov didn't respond, Veronica bumped his damaged chest with the wine bottle. Zulov buckled in pain and closed his eyes. Tears rolled down his cheeks as he whimpered through the tape, "Yes, yes, yes."

He froze again when she moved the stiletto to his face. She ordered, "If I were you, I'd hold very still."

Zulov's huge eyes crossed and he watched her move the knife up to his face as she poked a one-inch hole into the tape across his mouth. After allowing Zulov to take a half-dozen deeper breaths, Veronica asked her first question.

Walking to her motorcycle twenty-five minutes later, Veronica felt satisfied. She knew everything Dr. Pussy knew. Unfortunately, Zulov knew nothing about Johnny Big Nose Ramelli, she had no doubt. Plus, the way she'd left Dr. Pussy and Mrs. Basket Case, she knew, no police would get involved. But over sips of the very nice Napa County Cabernet, Veronica learned who, she believed, ordered the hit that night at Grey's Victorian. The soon-to-be-dead man had a name...Steven Sliger. When the interrogation ended, Veronica stated the obvious to Zulov. Violent death awaited him, if he didn't disappear. She advised him to grab as much easy cash as possible and bolt.

At that point, Zulov remained on the floor, leaning sideways against the couch with the tape off his mouth and arms, but not his legs. While taking short breaths and lightly holding his damaged ribs, he asked, "Then, you're not going to kill me?"

Leaning forward, Veronica, in a menacing tone, asserted, "I don't know about this Sliger asshole, but you will never disappear from me...ever. If Sliger doesn't find and kill you, you may have a future. However, if you leave a paper trail, Sliger will find you. Don't go anyplace you've ever been before or see anyone you've ever known. Pay in cash, use buses, always wear a hat, and never look into a security camera. Change your name, appearance and career. That might keep Sliger off your ass...but not me. If you ever pull shit like you're doing now," Veronica tilted her head toward the bathroom, "well, we will meet again...briefly."

Looking around the cabin and thinking for a while, Veronica stood up and walked over to the stairs leading to the second floor. She hopped up three steps, turned around and side-kicked the banister. She kicked it again and the banister broke enough to bend out awkwardly. Then she walked into the bathroom and, after a bit, dragged Ellen Bernstein out.

Veronica laid her on the carpet then walked back to her wine and Dr. Pussy. Pointing to the banister she said, "That's how you broke your ribs." Opening her hand, she added, "I want you to take two of Ellen's pills and the dregs of this wine."

Nervously, Zulov asked, "What are you going to do to me?" After a fashion, he added, "And Ellen?"

Shaking her head, Veronica sarcastically responded. "Such concern for your patient; I'm so touched." Pointing behind Zulov, Veronica explained, "Look, butthole, you two will wake up in that bedroom...no duct tape. When you come to, tell Mrs. Basket Case whatever you want; but take her home and you disappear."

Dr. Zulov tried to salvage a little dignity and said, "I'm sorry; I'm very sorry. Things just spun out of control. I'm really not a bad person."

Dr. Zulov could tell he'd just heightened Veronica's anger. Veronica told him to open his mouth and dropped in two pills. Raising the wine bottle up to his mouth, she asked after he swallowed a few times, "Open your mouth and lift up your tongue."

He did, and she said, "Good boy." Slowly she inched the wine bottle down to where she was holding the neck. She added, "Oh, I almost forgot; you bumped your head when you fell from the banister."

Confused, Dr. Zulov asked, "I did?"

Veronica backhanded the side of Zulov's head with the wine bottle, hearing a satisfying clunk. He tipped over on his side like a felled tree.

Climbing on her bike, Veronica wanted to call Greyson Milner and tell him to clear his schedule, but she couldn't. She had to get back to Reno. DJ had another job for her first, and since he'd given her time to come to San Diego, she felt obligated. The news about Steven Sliger had to wait. Veronica decided not to wear her helmet for a while. She fired up her Harley and slowly wound her way to Hwy. 18 heading north. It was going to be a long drive, six or seven hours. Veronica swerved to the right and gunned her Harley. As she did, she recalled the last words Dr. Pussy asked when she told him that he bumped his head: "*I did?*"

A family of four, driving an SUV too slow for Veronica's liking, wondered why in the hell the crazy dark-skinned woman with blonde hair decided to pass them on the shoulder. They were even more puzzled—and the father backed off further, when they realized she was laughing.

Chapter Forty-three
They Will Beg for Death

An ecstatic Bill Whittingham flew to Southern California to pick up his son. Over beers at the airport in Burbank, Bill and Whit updated each other. Sheriff Whittingham filled his son in on the details, as best he knew, of the murder attempt on Grey and how Grey's mysterious girlfriend saved them both. Whit told his dad all that Allyson had done to procure his release from prison. Whit also explained what Allyson revealed about the night of Ned's...mishap. The fact that Ned understood that she hadn't slept with Grey proved Ned had no reason to try and kill himself. It definitely was a murder attempt. Whit purposely left out Allyson's personal life, medical condition, the details of her contract, other than for some unknown reason, she was hired to destroy Ned and Grey's relationship. He didn't want his dad or anyone else in law enforcement involved or interfering with his plans.

The first two hours of freedom in Cedar Creek, Whit spent with Ned. Both actually teared up as they shook hands. Whit avoided talking about Allyson or the night she left. Instead, they spoke about Ned's store, Stacey's unwavering support and assistance, and Whit's promise to fit more time in with his friends. Typical Ned worried about others first and expressed, more than once, his concern about Whit and Grey. Ned wanted Whit to repair their friendship as soon as possible. Whit promised he would, but first he needed to "mend fences" with Katelyn. Ned knew how Whit felt about Katelyn and decided not to try to alter Whit's timetable.

Katelyn drove up to Cedar Creek after work and met Whit at Ned's store. Before Katelyn arrived, a shipment came, and she found Whit and Ned opening boxes in the storage room and restocking shelves. After a monstrous hug and kiss, Ned told Whit and Katelyn "No sex in his store, bad for business, so get out." They took their cue.

For the rest of the next two days, Katelyn and Whit spent their time at his cabin avoiding the local press and everyone else. They both felt the need to reconnect. In between long and often serious talks, they continued to reconnect and reconnect. Katelyn scolded him for being a stubborn old bear who dealt with tough emotional issues by brooding alone in his cave. For them to make it, that had to stop. To Whit's credit, he admitted his emotional hardwiring needed fixing, some upgrading, maybe complete replacement. He told Katelyn that with her help and patience he'd improve, open up, allow her in. *Of course, that access didn't include...the darkest corners.*

On day three Katelyn left early to return to work. Everything between the two seemed back on track except for their difference of opinion on violent retribution for the individual or individuals who tried to kill Ned and Grey. Whit wanted justice; his version...no arrest, no trial, no witnesses. Katelyn adamantly opposed violence and told him if he pursued vigilante revenge, outside of the law, he'd be no better, no different, no more virtuous than the animals he sought. Whit eventually acquiesced and told her she was right, but those were empty words. Even though Katelyn seemed pleased, he wasn't completely sure he'd sold her on his new enlightened position. Whit hated to lie to Katelyn, but he knew when the opportunity arose how he'd react.

Since they'd ridden out to Whit's cabin in Katelyn's car, they rode back to town together. When they reached Whit's truck, Katelyn gave Whit a long kiss and even longer, almost desperate hug. Was she trying to reassure herself that they were really okay, that her love could vanquish the lawlessness that lurked in the recesses of the man she loved? Whit revealed nothing behind his blue eyes as he smiled back at her concerned gaze. He was already thinking about the prearranged meeting he'd soon attend.

After purchasing two cups of coffee to go, he drove Old Blue to the Cedar Creek High School parking lot. He pulled in next to an older, white Impala. Whit grabbed the two coffees and walked to the car's passenger door. Putting one coffee on the hood, he opened the door and offered the other one to Allyson Chandler. Allyson grimaced as she reached for the cup.

Whit asked, "You okay?"

"Yeah, fine; it's just my lower back."

Grabbing the second coffee, Whit climbed in the car and closed the door.

Whit asked, "What's going on…with you?"

Shaking her head as if to say, *Nothing, drop it*, she decided, *Ah, hell, what's the difference?* "The cancer is pinching off my urethra and giving me bladder problems. Next will be a goddamn drain and bag for my bladder; after that, well, not good." Not wanting to continue, Allyson changed the subject and asked, "Have you patched things up with Katelyn and Grey?"

"Kate, yes; Grey, no, not yet. First, I need to clear up some issues floating around in my head. I remember what you said; I just need to know Ned's frame of mind. Did he really believe you when you told him that nothing happened between Grey and you, or was he just saying he believed you?"

"The relief on Ned's face was genuine. Like I said, I think he was more relieved for his relationship with Grey than with me."

Whit asked, "What happened next?"

"You mean after I left?" Whit nodded so she continued. "Okay, sure." After collecting her thoughts Allyson started, "That's the weird part. I headed for Reno and along the way called the client, Mr. Smith."

Whit cut in. "You and I both know that's not his real name and I'm sure you dug around enough to find out Mr. Smith's true identity."

Allyson scolded, "All in good time; just hold your horses for a second, we'll get there." *Sort of.* "Okay, so I phoned Mr. Smith and just as I started to tell him I failed, he interrupted me and said I had fulfilled the contract and would be paid in full, including the Mercedes."

Whit turned and stared out of the car into the woods near the school for a long time. Finally, he turned to Allyson and said, "That doesn't make sense, unless drugging Ned and leaving him there for someone else to kill was the plan all along. They hoped to use your indiscretion with Grey as the impetus to kill Ned and fake it as a suicide. But that would mean you were a liability to their plans, too. Why didn't they just clean house and fake a murder/suicide to eliminate you both?"

After considering the point, Allyson said, "The guy Mr. Smith uses for his dirty work is a wiry little weasel named Lance. I met him in Cedar Creek earlier that day. I'm guessing he tried to hang Ned. Lance is a remorseless, narcissistic psychopath, but also a coward. He wouldn't dare confront me unless I was unconscious, too. His control requires his victims to be powerless. To take me out, I'm sure he did something to the Mercedes. I don't know what, but I'm sure of it."

Whit didn't respond, so Allyson continued. "They knew how much I wanted that Mercedes and assumed I would drive it back to Texas. Something was going to happen to me in that car. I ditched it at the Reno International Airport, flew to New Orleans, then Belize. When I realized I was ill, I came back to the states for treatment, and that's when I found out about Ned and your imprisonment. The more I thought about it, the madder I became. I knew I needed to clean up what I helped create. When I found out I had stage-4 cancer, the urgency went into high gear. That's when I started researching Judge Franklin, his son, and that realtor, Barbou. Well, you know the rest."

"Not everything. Who's Lance's employer?"

Allyson held up her left hand. "Hold on a second and listen. I did two previous contracts for Mr. Smith...Ned being number three. For the first two, I met Lance in a neutral location. For the third contract, I met in a building owned by Mr. Smith."

"Where would I find this building?"

Allyson continued. "Look, Whit, I can't tell you."

Perplexed and getting angry, Whit asked, "Why not?"

After a while, Allyson said, "Just hear me out. My oncologist will try a delicate and rather radical surgery, then radiation. A 100-to-1 shot, 1,000-to-1... who knows? It still doesn't look good, but it could add months, maybe a year or more. Sounds like possibly a return to a little quality of life for a while, too."

Still mad, Whit said, "What's that have to do with me? Who's Mr. Smith and where can I find his building?"

Sternly, Allyson fired back, "I've known men like you. If I tell you any more, you'll go after him, without me. That's not going to happen. I'm in this to the end. We do this as a team. That means you wait until I recover."

Finally getting it, Whit just pursed his lips knowing she wasn't going to budge. He replied, "Okay, okay, Allyson. What are we talking, time wise?"

"If everything checks out okay today, I go in next week. If all goes as planned, after surgery, I'm laid up for about another two, two and a half weeks. With no complications, I'm out. I'll need radiation, but that's outpatient. I can do it in Sacramento."

Nodding his head and knowing he really had no choice, Whit said, "I think you should try; we have time, I think. It depends on what this Lance guy and his boss have up their sleeves. But it's your call, Allyson."

"I'd like to try. I need the mental boost and some relatively good health to clean up some...lingering issues." When Whit didn't ask, she decided to continue. "I need to travel to Spain and talk to my mom...and, my dear, sweet, understanding father. And some other people in my past, too; you know, clear the air, make amends, set the record straight."

"Okay, Allyson. Do what you have to do, but what happens if you, ah...."

"Die on the operating table?" When Whit nodded, she said, "My lawyer will contact you and give you a folder with all the information I have on Mr. Smith, et al."

With a positive smile Whit said, "I'll talk to you in a few weeks and we'll take this up when you return. Deal?"

"Deal; I'm glad we're doing this. I really messed up and want to make this right. I want them to pay."

Looking out through the windshield, Whit spoke in a low tone. "They're going to beg for death."

"Whit, please don't talk like that." Shocked and truly scared for Whit's sanity, Allyson tried to sound maternal. "Don't get pulled down to their level. I've been there; it will destroy you." When Whit didn't respond, she added, "It will destroy Katelyn."

Opening the passenger door and grabbing Allyson's untouched coffee, Whit's casual voice returned. "You made it back from their brand of black hell; so will I. Good luck with the procedure, and keep in touch. I'm off to meet with Grey to see if I can patch up our friendship."

With a worried smile, Allyson nodded. "You guys are too close; I know you will."

Chapter Forty-four
That Was Not an Apology

After his meeting with Allyson at the high school parking lot, Whit drove to Pete's Place. Whit had asked Stacey to open a little early, so he and Grey could talk in private. She welcomed him home from prison and said she'd be there at 10 A.M.

Whit arrived and received a huge hug from Stacey. She gave him a peck on the lips and asked, "How's our pet?"

"Stinker? She stayed and survived fine without me but did seem glad to see me. But then, how can you really tell with a ringed-tail cat?"

Stacey asked Whit, "Something to drink?"

"Coffee would be great."

"I'll join you. You want a little magic, too?"

"It's a tad early for whiskey, but maybe a shot of Baileys to celebrate my return to freedom."

"Perfect; I'll get it going." She squeezed his shoulder and added, "Damn nice to see you home, Whit."

"Thanks, Stace."

Whit had time to sit and take a quick look around the familiar surroundings. It felt good to be back...in his world. All that faded away when he heard the front door open.

Whit saw Stacey lean backwards and look his way. She gave him a thumbs-up. Whit slid off the barstool and waited as Grey approached.

Grey stopped about six feet away and said, "You could have killed me with that punch."

Whit nodded and replied, "I hit you with an open hand. I didn't want to kill you; I just wanted you to stop talking."

At the far end of the bar, they heard Stacey scold, "Whit!"

The stare down continued until Whit said, "I should have listened to you...believed you. I knew better; I just...lost it a little."

They heard Stacey say, even angrier, "Whit!"

Whit gave a scolding look down the bar, took a deep breath, then turned to Grey and softly said, "I didn't handle the situation well."

"What?" Grey asked. "I didn't quite get that."

Louder, Whit repeated, "I didn't handle the situation well."

Grey put his right hand to his ear and said, "What?"

Stacey turned her frustration on Grey, "Grey, goddamn you!"

"I'm just trying to savor the moment. I've never really heard Whit apologize before; just wanted to make sure I heard it right."

Stacey walked down the bar with the coffee pot and three mugs. She put them on the bar and grabbed the Baileys. Before she poured, she glared at Whit and said, "That was not an apology."

Grey said, "Oh, Stace, for Benjamin Whittingham that was a huge apology."

Shaking her head, she ordered, "Then you two assholes shake hands or I'm not pouring."

Grey and Whit looked at each other and shrugged at the same time. They shook hands and Stacey poured.

Stacey held up her mug and said, "I think a toast is in order. Here's to burying the hatchet...in the back of the head of whoever is fucking with you guys."

"Perfect," Whit and Grey said at the same time, as their mugs clunked.

After they all took a sip of their cloudy, sweet drink, Whit turned to Stacey and asked, "Didn't I ask you to open early so Grey and I could talk... in private?"

"Oh, screw you, Whittingham. If it wasn't for me, you two would still be circling each other, growling, and pissing on the furniture."

"Okay, Stace." Enjoying her humor, Whit added, "You can stay. Hell, you'd listen in no matter where we sat anyway."

"Damn straight! Besides, when someone messes with my...um, preferred customers, they're messing with me. So, I'm in...whatever you need."

They tapped mugs again, and over two pots of coffee Grey and Whit compared notes. They both knew each other well enough to know when to stop. Some information they just couldn't reveal to Stacey. Even so, with each new tidbit of news previously unknown to Stacey, she'd exclaim, "Holy shit!"

Whit and Grey needed to talk again in a more private location. In the world of bars and bartenders, secrets flowed like water. Exiting the bar, they walked out of Stacey's view then stopped. Neither noticed the plumber's van parked across the street from Pete's Place. The pseudo-sophisticated listening device wasn't good enough to penetrate the walls of the bar but clearly picked up Whit's voice, now talking to Grey. "Let's head up to my cabin Saturday morning. We won't be bothered there. We can talk freely...digest what each of us know and plan our next move."

Grey asked, "Shouldn't we get your dad involved at this point?"

"No, not yet. I don't want anyone getting spooked or all lawyered-up. I think we still have the upper hand at this point and just need to figure out... our best option."

"I know you, Whit; you want to handle this your way, all by yourself."

"I do not; I just think it's too early."

"Bullshit, Whittingham." When Whit didn't respond, Grey added, "You just got out of prison; do you want to head back there with a murder rap on your head?"

Lowering his voice, Whit said, "Look, Grey, we'll go to the police when we know enough to nail tight whoever attacked Ned and shot up your Victorian. That's all Grey...honest. So, Friday I'll be staying in town at my dad's. Saturday, I'll pick you up at Ned's parking lot at seven."

"Seven's too early; how about nine?"

Shaking his head, Whit said, "I'll pick you up at eight."

"Eight? Okay, but we have to eat breakfast first."

Shaking his head, Whit chided, "Milner, you're a pain in the ass. Alright, eight for breakfast, but you're buying."

"Ugh, now who's the pain in the ass? Okay, tightwad; deal."

They started walking up Main Street to their vehicles. After about ten steps in silence, Whit said, "My dad filled me in on the murder attempt at your home. Now, I want to hear it from you, and don't leave anything out." When Grey gave Whit an inquisitive look, Whit added, "Yeah, Dad told me about your mystery squeeze, too. He also said it was your idea to squelch the fact that she was there. Talk about me being secretive, schmuck."

Almost to himself, Grey asked, "What's this all about...Ned, you, me? What's going on? What the hell did we do?"

"Don't know, but I'm going to find out. None of this is coincidence.

Someone has a nasty grudge against us, Grey. When I find out who, I'm going to make sure they really have a good reason to hate us."

"Whit, you just said you wouldn't go batshit rogue."

Slapping his buddy on the shoulder Whit replied, "Hell, Grey, how can I? My dad's the sheriff."

Grey thought, *Yeah, but you didn't promise.*

Chapter Forty-five
Celebrate

Sitting behind the driver's seat of the plumber's van, Sean Peterson hit speed dial. He heard a faint click. "Serpentine Solutions, Public Relations, Andrea."

"Andrea, Sean here."

Andrea replied, "Well, hello, Sean."

"I received information about five minutes ago that could be what you're looking for with regards to the, ah, the subject matter."

"Excellent. How time sensitive?"

"Later this weekend; you have a little over three days."

"Are we talking about the first subject matter?"

"Both, actually; same place, same time."

Andrea took some time to process this information, *Milner and Whittingham together, hmmm. Three days...it could fit, but probably no way in hell will it look like anything else but murder; hmm. How to play this? Do I tell Steven and just get this over with, or do I wait for something...better, safer, less risky; hmm. No, I can't keep this from Steven.* "Sean, we better meet in person; about an hour?"

"I'll be there."

Sixty-five minutes later Sean Peterson followed Andrea's perfect little rear end into the elevator. When they exited the elevator, instead of heading into Sliger's conference room, they entered her office.

A little confused, Sean asked, "Mr. Sliger busy?"

"No, I just decided we'd meet here. I'll hear your report first. If it's what we're looking for and fits schedule wise, then we can meet with Steven."

"I have the pertinent conversation taped."

"Just tell me what you know. We can save the tape for Steven."

"Okay. I parked across the street from that bar after I saw Whittingham go inside, later Milner followed. I caught them on tape when they exited. They both seemed to know something about what's been going on. They're going to compare notes on Saturday at Whittingham's cabin, just the two of them."

Trying to hide her growing apprehension, Andrea asked, "Did they say what they already knew?"

"No, but they both seemed pretty confident about knowing something. They both agreed that someone has a grudge or vendetta against them. Whittingham seems especially sure. He's the one to watch out for because he seems the type to take action…legal or otherwise. At least that's the vibes I get from that guy."

Shit, Andrea thought, *I don't like the sound of that. But even as sloppy as Lance has been, I still don't see how they piece this back to us.* "When are they heading to the cabin?"

"Whittingham plans to pick up Milner around 8 A.M., but they're going to breakfast first. I expect they won't get to Whittingham's cabin before 9:30 or 10:00."

Andrea stood in front of Sean, deep in thought. She interlocked her hands but extended both index fingers together and absentmindedly tapped her lower lip.

Sean thought at that moment she looked studious and exceptionally beautiful, like a little innocent librarian.

Her mind buzzed. *These guys are not as dumb as Steven led on. We have exposure if Ned somehow comes out of his memory stupor or Allyson resurfaces. Hell, she already has and must be in contact with Whit; damn. If Milner and Whittingham keep pressing, more likely than not, something's going to give. Their past connects them; it's their common link to each other. Sooner or later, probably Whittingham will connect the dots. Shit. I need to be prepared to extricate myself, maybe very soon.* Looking up at Sean, she smiled her killer smile and told herself, *Time to shoot another arrow into Sean's heart. He's my ticket to disappear. If Steven, Lance, and Jeff go down, who's going to come looking for Sean or me? No one, I hope.*

"Excellent work, Sean. What can you tell me about Whit's cabin?"

"Enough for what I think your team plans to do. It's isolated, no neighbors for miles, and surrounded by forest. That's good. Unfortunately, he set his gate over half a mile from his cabin."

Andrea frowned. "That's bad."

Smiling, Sean said, "That would be a serious problem, if I hadn't figured out the combination to his lock."

Andrea playfully slapped Sean on the arm and said, "Stop toying with me. How did you do it?"

Sean thought, *What the Hell? She really does like me. Okay; focus, play it cool, Peterson.* "The tumblers retain oil from Whittingham's fingers. But only one area on each tumbler registered the most oil, where he presses the most often while he matches up the right numbers. A little unscented talcum powder, some trial and error and click…it popped open."

Mocking admiration, Andrea nodded and said, "Impressive. We need to meet with the others and discuss this in detail. I think this operation can be completed soon. I'm sure Steven will approve. Your work has been invaluable; excellent, Sean."

"Thank you, Andrea."

Andrea stepped back and put one leg behind the other. She crossed her arms and looked straight into Sean's eyes and said, "After we finish with your report to Steven, I think we should get out of here and celebrate."

Taken a little off guard, Sean asked, "Celebrate?"

Andrea smiled but thought, *He can't be this slow.* "You've forgotten about our…debriefing…at my house?"

Sean finally got it and said, "Oh, hell no. So, celebrating is like debriefing?"

"Maybe not the same position, but yes."

Chapter Forty-six
Alex and Willy

Two tall, well-built men—one white, one black—walked toward the far left automatic doors nearest baggage claim at Reno International Airport. As they exited the structure, both observed bright blue skies; however, a dry cold bit at their skin. Dressed casually in Levi's, t-shirts, and light windbreakers, they looked more like professional athletes than businessmen. Donnie stood taller and leaner at 6'1". His physique and long-balanced stride exhibited the natural grace of a fast wide-receiver or agile tennis player. Lamar, stockier, one inch shorter and a few years younger, at thirty-one possessed the thick chest, muscular thighs and narrow waist of someone built to play halfback. The determined expressions on both men's faces said they took life seriously. Both carried small duffle bags. A new, gray, 1990 four-wheel drive, extended cab Ford F-150 waited for them right in front. A guy in a light brown cowboy hat, long-sleeved western shirt and brown leather vest just stepped out of the driver's seat and tossed Lamar the keys. No nod, wave, tip of the hat…nothing. He walked to a waiting SUV and slid into the passenger seat as the vehicle whisked away. When the two threw their gear in the bed of the truck, they scanned their surroundings slowly. Donnie opened the passenger door, then the smaller back door. He noted what he expected to see. Donnie could tell the shotguns rested inside the two soft leather cases. The smaller hard case held the semi-automatic rifle and the longer hard case secured the sniper rifle. On the front seat he found a smallish briefcase and a bigger, black nylon sports bag on the passenger side floorboard.

Lamar opened the driver's door, slid in, and fired up the compact but powerful V8. Donnie joined Lamar in the front seat. With seatbelts on, Lamar hit the blinker, and what appeared to be two law-abiding model citizens pulled away from the curb. They could claim many monikers, but law abiding and model citizens were not two of them. They worked their way to the Highway 395 onramp and headed north.

On the freeway, while checking his mirrors and making minor adjustments, Lamar spoke to Donnie for the first time since landing. "Let's check the inventory and see if we have everything we requested."

"I'll check the rental agreement first." Opening the glovebox, Donnie read the name on the contract: Alex Brown, Springfield, Illinois. *Perfect.*

Donnie put the paperwork away then grabbed the briefcase. Under the case he found two lightweight nylon shoulder holsters. Putting the case on his lap, Donnie popped it open. One at a time, he pulled out the Springfield .45 caliber 1911-A1 model automatics. He checked to ensure both safeties were engaged. The automatics carried full magazines, plus one, locked and loaded in the chamber. Two loaded mags for each gun completed the inventory.

Donnie leaned forward, grabbed for the nylon straps, and slid the heavy sports bag up over his left leg and onto his lap. He unzipped the side and took inventory. Donnie thought, *Jesus; boxes of size 6 shot, buckshot, and even slugs for the 20-gauge shotguns...plus enough .223 rounds for the AR-15 and 30-06 rounds for the Mouser to hold back an army. I guess Johnny wanted to eliminate lack of ammunition as a reason for failure.*

Donnie said, "We're good, if the long guns in the cases are correct. We'll check those when we sight in the rifles. We have enough ammo to start a war."

"Whatever it takes, right?"

"Shit, Lamar," Donnie replied. "If it comes to a shootout we're both dead anyway. Johnny Big Nose won't accept another screw-up." *Donnie hadn't told Lamar any details about his meeting with Johnny...especially the part about how close he and Lamar came to feeding fish. Maybe he should have.* "We're lucky to get another chance. Why the client asked for the two of us again...personally, I can't quite wrap my head around, unless...."

Lamar glanced over at Donnie and said, "Unless what?"

"Unless nothing." *Jesus, rookie; if your self-preservation hackles aren't sticking straight out of the back of your neck by now you're never going to last long in this business.* Lamar looked like he was still waiting for an answer, so Donnie finally said, "It's just that Johnny's associate went so ballistic when we didn't kill Milner and that...hellcat. Why would he ask for us back?"

After ten seconds of silence, Donnie figured Lamar wasn't catching on; so, he brought up a related point. "It doesn't matter anyway; Johnny put his guarantee on this hit. He made me sit in on the conversation. I heard Johnny assure the guy on the phone while he looked straight at me. He will not accept failure. This is serious shit, Lamar. I've seen how Johnny Big Nose deals with employees who disappoint him." Drawing a finger across his throat, he added, "It ain't pretty."

"Yeah, well, how in the hell did we know that bitch was packing bear spray? The client's right-hand man gave us bad intel. How was that our fault?"

"Because, Lamar, we changed the operation by switching places. Johnny sent us both, but I was to do the hit. Incomplete intel or not, it turned out badly and Johnny blames us."

"But you said you told Johnny it wouldn't have made any difference even if you had attempted the hit, right?"

"Lamar, you didn't walk up the side of the stairs; you walked up the middle. I heard the step creak from the pickup. Did that wake them up? Give them precious seconds? We'll never know. I grew up with door socks tucked against the bottoms of doors. I'd have figured it out. You push on the door high, it pinches; you push down low or kick the base of the door, they'll budge. Would that have made a difference? Again, we'll never know. Of course, Johnny doesn't know any of that and doesn't give a shit anyway. I'm telling you, this is our one and only chance. We can't mess this up."

Lamar remained quiet, realizing Donnie had kept critical information from Johnny about his poor performance during the hit attempt...information that probably saved his life. Lamar needed to change the subject, so he asked, "The client's a big fish; Johnny said to do what he says which means dealing with his punk kid again. So, what's changed?"

"Nothing. The Big Fish's son or stepson, or whatever the hell he's supposed to be, is an inept, lying, wannabe tough guy who takes shortcuts. I don't trust that turd. He's trying to be a hard ass to impress his old man, but doesn't have the balls, discipline or brains. He doesn't know shit but thinks he does, which makes him dangerous."

"What's the deal with Mr. Big Fish; why is he so special?"

"I hear he figures pretty high in Johnny Big Nose's operations."

"Where'd you hear that?"

After a long pause, Donnie said, "Maria."

"Maria, as in Johnny's niece, Maria?"

Defensively, Donnie said, "Yeah, that Maria. You have a problem with that?"

Chuckling, Lamar said, "No, no, not at all."

"Not at all, what?"

Lamar put up one of his hands and said, "Okay, take it easy, jeez, no offense; it's just that she's kinda—"

"Kinda what?"

Lamar couldn't hold back and blurted out, "Shit, Donnie, she's butt-ass ugly, that's what. Her beak's bigger than Johnny's. But I wasn't going to say nothing, honest." Smirking, Lamar took a serious tone and asked, "Hey, you weren't...poking her, were you?"

"Don't push it, funny man." Looking straight ahead, a quick flashback crossed Donnie's mind and he quivered. He finally said, "Look, smartass; you hang around long enough, you'll find out the really dark side of working for Johnny Big Nose. Sometimes you get stuck with...compromising assignments."

No one spoke for nearly a mile. Finally, Donnie added, "Let me tell you something. Sometimes those compromising situations can be tougher on you than just risking your ass whacking people. I done it as a favor to Johnny. He asked me to take Maria out, make her feel good. She was like...depressed or something." After another image and another involuntary shake, Donnie continued. "Actually, the fucking wasn't bad, especially because she was so hungry for it. But taking her out in public...man, that was tough. Guys look at you, smirking, laughing behind your back, kind of like you're doing now. I wanted to bust 'em up but good, but I couldn't. I had to pretend I was with Princess Di. Anyway, she's got some other sorry dude now, so I'm off the hook."

Trying to keep a straight face and failing miserably, Lamar offered, "Hey, man, no offense, really. Finish your point. What did you learn from the fetching Miss Maria Schnozzola?"

"Fuck you, Lamar!" Donnie shot back. Staring a long time at Lamar, Donnie finally had to smile and shook his head. He turned his gaze away from Lamar and continued. "Okay, smart ass. Maria told me Johnny's California associate retains some kind of computer genius. He figured out a foolproof program that accounts for most of Johnny's dirty money. Somehow it filters through Johnny's produce, trucking, restaurant, and disposal businesses. It automatically overbooks what gets produced, delivered, sold and hauled off to landfills. The program monitors tons of real and fake expenses, transactions and write-offs. It links together all the accounts somehow and it works. Not only does it keep clean books for the feds, but it also maintains a tidy accounting of the laundered money as well. It doesn't cover all the dirty money, but it safely legitimizes about 70 to 80 percent. The 20 percent or so that's left, Johnny uses as operating capital. Johnny keeps purchasing video stores, antique shops, bookstores, laundromats, more legit businesses all the time…so says Maria. He has to pay taxes on the dirty money but figures, what the hell; with all the tax write-offs, he retains almost 90 cents on the dollar. The best part, it keeps the feds clueless because they get their tax dollars and Johnny stays out of the courts and prison."

"Donnie, if Johnny finds out you know, you're a dead man. Me too, now."

"I ain't worried. I diddled Maria good; she ain't talking. Besides it doesn't matter anyway if we screw up this hit."

A gnawing thought finally surfaced for Lamar, so he asked, "But this California guy, what if he's hiding ulterior motives for specifically asking for us again. Like, maybe, us being his fall guys, right?"

Donnie looked at Lamar and smiled. "Crowded at the bottom with all the other expendable pawns, ain't it?" *Now you're starting to catch on, rookie.*

Lamar said, "So we watch our backs and keep a better eye on tough-guy Lance. But, if he's running this operation too, how is it our fault if the client's son fucks it up?"

Donnie pinched his temples with his fingers. "You're going around in circles, Lamar. Right or wrong, fair or not, it doesn't matter. If anything goes wrong, we die."

Donnie's statement lingered in the air like a musty fart. Lamar veered east on I-80 heading into the guts of Nevada.

Donnie asked, "You know how to get to where we sight in the rifles, right?"

Lamar said, "Big Nose's ranching buddy lives behind that whorehouse he owns, the Cotton Patch. I know how to get to the Cotton Patch."

"I don't even want to know how you know how to get to the Cotton Patch. And don't call the boss 'Big Nose.' You can call him Johnny or Johnny Big Nose but never just 'Big Nose.' You want to lose your tongue?"

"Roger that; I forgot."

Disappointed, Donnie scolded, "And how many times do I have to tell you, kill the military lingo; Jesus, Lamar." Donnie let Lamar stew for a while then finally added, "Maybe we better get our game on; names, aliases, the whole cover."

Lamar didn't like Donnie's reprimand but realized he was really mad at himself for slipping up. He wanted Donnie's job someday but would never get there if he didn't focus. Little slipups ended careers and other really important needs, like breathing. Finally, he said, "Yes, sir, Mr. Alex Brown, accountant, Andriotti Commercial Produce, Springfield, Illinois."

"That's better...Mr. Willy Jones, dock manager, Andriotti Commercial Produce, Springfield, Illinois."

Eventually, while working on their covers and when cars and endless strings of tractor-trailers weren't too close, Donnie, aka Alex Brown, went back to adjusting the straps a few more times until the shoulder holster fit perfectly. Donnie thought about what lay ahead. Because the hit was supposed to be two victims caught in the open and at fairly close range, Donnie chose a bolt action Mouser with a simple 3X scope for his kill weapon. His granddad brought one home, a Karabiner 98k version of the Mouser, after the war. The most common rifle in the German's arsenal during WWII, Donnie always liked its feel, precision, and accuracy. Plus, the hit was planned as an ambush in the woods; Donnie didn't want to waste time looking for far-flung ejected shells from a semi-automatic.

Chapter Forty-seven
Nothing to See Here

The new Ford pickup with California plates pulled away from the Reno's Big 5 sports store. Carrying two passengers, the vehicle merged into traffic on west-bound I-80. The two occupants looked like male models selling hunting attire.

Looking at his partner, Lamar used Donnie's alias. "Alex, we look like a couple of pussies."

"City slicker, pussy hunter geeks."

They both laughed. But that was exactly the image they wanted to project.

As they entered California, from the passenger seat Donnie said, "Let's go over it again."

"Roger tha—*ah, fuck!*" Lamar stammered. He glanced at Donnie who responded with a pained look. After a pause Lamar continued. "Upon seeing the bug station, just say we're coming from Reno. Vehicles with California plates just get waved through."

"Right; we're just a couple of businessmen ditching their wives for a hunting vacation at a private club."

"CC & F near the town of Huncut. We won a company fundraiser, a raffle for a three-day pheasant hunting trip; five days counting our travel time."

"Very good; you just earned yourself a cookie."

Lamar asked, "Is there a CC & F Hunting Club near Huncut?"

"Apparently."

"Apparently?"

Donnie smiled. "I'm yanking your chain. I researched the details of our cover long before we left Chicago. I told you, I do my own intel."

As the highway climbed slightly before leveling off well in front of the now visible inspection station, Lamar took the shortest line to one of the booths showing a green light. Both men felt relaxed and ready to play out the simple formality of a nod and a wave as they passed through and over the Sierra Nevada. *Nothing to see here, Inspector; just two cold-blooded killers passing through to flat line a couple of California home boys. Have a nice day.*

As Lamar pulled forward into the vehicle slot between the little guard stations, he rolled down his window and smiled at a petite and attractive woman in an imitation Smokey the Bear hat. She didn't even ask, "Where are you coming from?" like she'd recited nearly one hundred times already. Instead, she had seen the California plate and waved the truck through. But, just as Lamar hit the button to roll up his window, she yelled, "Whoa; stop!"

The two men played innocent, but adrenalin started flowing, their senses suddenly acute. Donnie and Lamar both slowly loosened the top two buttons on their light jackets.

"You guys look like hunters."

"No; not really, not yet anyway," Lamar offered. "How did you—"

"Your outfits; I'm supposed to look out for dog boxes, guns, and guys dressed like hunters. Pull over to the right please." She pointed to a small parking area just past the booths.

Lamar asked, "Is there a problem?"

Ignoring the driver, she said, "If no one comes out, just go inside that door and ask for a Department of Fish and Game warden."

Donnie leaned forward, used his woman-killer smile, and asked, "Excuse me; what's this all about?"

"DFG wants to talk to you; some hunting survey or something. I was just told to look for hunters and send them over there." She pointed and said, "It won't take long."

"Sure, no problem," Donnie replied, still smiling. As Lamar pulled past the inspection stand, he looked to his right and whispered, "What the fuck?" After a van pulled past, Lamar veered right. The two killers looked at each other. Donnie said, "I'll do the survey; stay upbeat."

A warden was just walking away from an older pickup with two dog boxes in the bed. Lamar pulled in so the passenger side faced the warden. The warden entered a few more bits of information into a handheld electronic device. He looked up, saw the pickup, and walked toward Donnie/Alex and his open passenger window. He spoke, "Morning, gentlemen; I'm Warden Perkins. Do you mind answering a few questions?"

"Of course, Officer. What's this about?"

"It's Warden, Warden Perkins."

"Sure, sorry, but—"

"Ah, some muckety-mucks in Sacramento thought a bunch of us wardens could better spend our time taking a useless unscientific survey of out-of-state hunters entering California, or California hunters returning from out-of-state. Believe me, we don't like this anymore than you do; I'll try to make this quick. Your names and home state?"

"I'm Alex Brown and this is Willy Jones. We're both from Springfield, Illinois."

"How long are you in our state and what are you hunting?"

"Three days; pheasants."

"Ever been hunting in California before?"

Just for humans, Warden. "I've been here on business before, but never to bird hunt."

"No dogs?"

"No; we understand the club will provide dogs."

"Which club?"

"CC & F, near a little town named Huncut."

"Nice club." Officer Perkins knew the high-end club well.

Out of habit he glanced in the truck bed and the backseat. He noticed two soft gun cases and two hard gun cases. The big hard case appeared way too long for a shotgun, and the smallest hard case looked way too short. *Hmmm.* Looking again with piqued interest at these thirty-something clean-cut, athletic types with new hunting clothes and a small arsenal, Gene Perkins thought, *something about these two doesn't add up. These guys are way too...plastic. Either they're just novice hunters or...?*

"What type of shotguns are you using?"

Donnie picked up the negative vibes from the warden and noticed he quit punching in information on his tablet. Donnie felt the hair on the back of his neck start to twinge. "That's kind of a funny questionnaire question."

"Oh, I'm finished; I was just curious."

"Willy and I won this hunting trip at work. We aren't what you'd call bird hunters."

Looking at the gun cases in the back again, Warden Perkins said, "Quite a few guns. They all shotguns?"

Shit; he knows they're not all shotguns. "No, two are varmint guns. After pheasant hunting, we get to shoot ground squirrels and rabbits overrunning the club, too."

Nodding, Warden Perkins asked, "Did you bring them from Springfield?"

"Yes."

"Wouldn't it have been easier to just borrow guns at the club, like the dogs, instead of bringing guns with you from Illinois?"

Lamar leaned forward and interjected, "Yeah, we sure as hell know that now. Some friends said we just had to take their Benellis. But, excuse me, Officer, we still have quite a distance to drive. How much longer?"

Gene Perkins eyed Lamar intently. Just as Lamar straightened up, Gene thought he saw something under his partially opened jacket. It looked like… a shoulder strap.

Warden Perkins straightened up and said, "Sure, no problem; and it's Warden. Thanks for your patience. Be sure to purchase your out-of-state license for all the days you hunt."

"Yes, sir, Offi…I mean Warden."

Perkins tipped his hat and said, "Good hunting." *You lying fucks.*

Donnie replied, "Thank you, Warden; have a pleasant day." *You suspicious fuck.*

Hitting his partner on the shoulder, Donnie said, "Let's go pheasant hunting."

As they drove off, Warden Perkins memorized the California plate. *These two are not what they seem.* He pulled out his pen and wrote the license number on his palm, turned and walked into the main building. Looking back one more time, he watched the Ford pickup disappear. Perkins pulled out his cell phone and speed dialed California Highway Patrol dispatch.

"Truckee dispatch; Beverly."

"Hey, Bev, this is Warden Perkins."

"Hi, Gene; you in town?"

"I'm working that damn hunting survey at the Inspection Station. Can you run a California plate for me?"

"Sure; no problem."

"1L25061."

"Checking it now."

"While I have you on the line, who do you have working down I-80, by Cisco Grove and farther west?"

"Jose Fernandez has Cisco today, and Lawrence Yun's working Gold Run. Okay, Gene; I have a 1990 Ford F-150, extended cab, gray."

"Well, that pans out," Perkins grudgingly conceded.

Warden Perkins quickly told Bev what had just transpired and his suspicions. He decided he still wanted to talk to both officers. Beverly said she'd radio Jose first since he was the closest and have him call right away. Gene recited his cell number and thanked her.

When Jose called, Perkins repeated what he had told Bev but in more detail.

"I have nothing but a bunch of hunches and bad vibes, but something isn't right with those two. You might find a reason to pull them over and check them out; rattle their cage, see what drops out. I wouldn't do it alone, though."

Jose asked, "What are you thinking?"

"I don't know; I just didn't buy their story. They're up to something, and I don't think it's pheasant hunting."

"Like drug runners?"

"Don't know; maybe, I'm not sure. I'd error on the side of caution though. I thought I saw a piece of a shoulder holster; they could be carrying concealed weapons."

"Okay, I'll call it in and get Yun to haul ass my way; I won't stop them until he backs me up. Good enough?"

"Thanks, Jose; I'll head that way, too. Have dispatch tell me where you stop them. I'm leaving right now but hang back until I'm near to light them up. I'll take the lead."

"No problemo, mi amigo. You're just adding a little spice to my otherwise dreary day."

In the Ford heading past the town of Truckee on the way to Donner Summit, Lamar asked, "Think we're cool?"

"My gut says no. That guy acted like a bloodhound that picked up a faint scent. He was snooping; those wildlife cops are savvy…always poking, probing, digging. I watched him through the side mirror; I'm sure he wrote down our license." After a while Donnie said, "Whether he acts on us or not, we better prepare in case he does. I'll hold the wheel; slip out of your holster, and I'll put everything in our travel bags. We may be able to bullshit our way past the rifles, but not concealed weapons."

Lamar asked, "Aren't you going a bit too far?"

"No, fuck no. We absolutely cannot get caught and cannot screw up this contract. If we fail, we are dead men…dead men. During this entire operation, we cannot be paranoid enough."

After Donnie stowed the guns, he said, "And what's with that bullshit about our friends said we just had to take their Benellis? Jesus Christ; I said I'd do the talking."

"You said you'd take the survey."

"You know what I meant. The more I think about that warden, the more I know he didn't buy your line one bit. I told him we don't bird hunt, then you pipe in that two of our buddies just couldn't let us go without taking their Benellis. One…what are the odds that two big-city, non-bird hunters know buddies with expensive shot guns and, two…who would give novice bird hunters their high-end shotguns? No one, that's who; your line had bullshit written all over it."

"Look, I'm sorry; I just got a little tired of his questions. I was trying to help."

Donnie had to let it go. His partner was good; just young and impatient to prove himself. They rode on in silence.

After a bit Donnie said, "We have to get off this freeway. Take the King-vale off-ramp coming up. We'll take old Highway 40; the map shows it parallels I-80 for quite a while."

Chapter Forty-eight
Valiant Effort For Nothing, Ace

Riding beside the company pilot and chief of security, Ron Townsend, Lance stared out of the unmarked jet ranger. The helicopter maintained wide circles around a monstrously large excavation similar to an open pit mine.

The Lost Hill Diggins exhibited the familiar characteristics common to all hydraulic mines. The wide scoured depression surrounded by steep barren headwalls starkly displayed the immense erosive power of water under pressure. Astute Gold Rush era geologists knew repeated massive pyroclastic mud and ash flows rushed down and buried even older gold-rich ancient river channels. Millions of years of aging and decomposition turned much of the volcanic material into rich soil, providing a fertile substrate for the development of lush forests. Tunneling under the overburden to reach the bottom of the river channels proved too dangerous as the unstable gravel walls and ceiling constantly collapsed. Manually removing the millions of tons of overburden and surface gravels would exceed the value of the rich ore hiding underneath. But, channeling vast amounts of water to these sites, then concentrating that water under tremendous pressure into the hillsides worked. Using water instead of laborers to tear away the layers upon layer of soil and ore-poor surface gravels proved economically viable. Wealthy San Francisco investors paid thousands of Irish, Chinese, and other destitute miners a pittance for backbreaking labor. They constructed rock and timber storage dams high in the Sierra, concurrent with long open ditches and boxed wooded flume systems, to import the stored water to the gold bearing sites. Diverting the water down riveted pipes generated forty-four pounds per square inch of pressure for every one hundred feet of vertical fall. Funneling and constricting the water into giant swiveling cannons called hydraulic monitors, miners now had the means to blast away the "over-burden" and reach the ore-rich river bottoms.

Lance had no clue that man created the ninety-acre amphitheater he continued to circle, or that it occurred one hundred thirty years ago. His mind instead tussled with how forcefully to greet the two Chicago thugs, men he very much disliked. The last time the three met, Donnie and Lamar were told by their boss that Lance was top dog. Through the whole disastrous encounter, neither assassin truly acknowledged nor respected his position. That needed to change.

The copter banked in a counterclockwise fashion, giving the pilot a clear view of the diggings and surrounding forest. The arc tightened as the machine dropped in altitude. A stolen, dusty, black SUV with heavily tinted windows rested in the partial shade of some scraggily ponderosa and sugar pines.

The two men situated the SUV exactly where they were told, parking on the southern edge of a wide gravelly flat. Both front doors were swung wide open, with the two men partially visible in the front seats.

Lance said, "You are clear, when I return with these two, what you're to do?"

Turning into the wind and moving into position about thirty yards to the north of the SUV, the pilot pulled the nose of the sleek helicopter up slightly then said, "Yes, sir. Right when you exit the vehicle and move away from—"

"I didn't ask for a recital," Lance cut in. "I said, are you clear?"

"Clear; yes, sir." *Jesus Christ; for an adopted son, he sure acts like his stepfather. The turd doesn't roll far away from the pile.* While musing himself with his little joke, the pilot's attention lapsed just enough to result in a rare but sloppy landing with one rung hitting sharply before the other.

Lance snapped, "Great first impression, Townsend."

"Sorry, sir." Ron partially lied. "The knee's acting up again."

Twenty-seven miles away in Cedar Creek, Whit's dad's phone rang. The clock said 6 A.M. Whit answered, and Katelyn's perky voice said, "Hey, Whit, I'm free today."

"Hot damn, but geez, Kate; when did you start charging?"

"Auh," Katelyn flatly replied. "Way too early in the morning, Whitting-ham.... Let me try again; are you available?"

"Sorry, sweetheart, as a matter of fact, after a late breakfast, Grey and I plan to head to my cabin. We're comparing notes about all this bizarre crap occurring to us." Not wanting to say it but feeling he must, Whit added, "Please join us. We could use your journalistic perspective and of course, a referee."

Sternly, Katelyn asked, "And what you know or learn, you will take to your father, right?"

"Of course," Whit lied. "But you better get driving; Tightwad Milner's buying and with you along, we can really soak him."

Upbeat again, Katelyn said, "Great, on my way."

Whit hung up but felt bad about lying to Katelyn again. *It's just not right, but what the hell can I do? Katelyn grew up in an urban liberal setting. The system— government, police, judges, lawyers and prison—dealt with bad people, not the individuals harmed.* The big difference in Whit's world, whoever these bad people are, they didn't fear "The System." They attacked without concern for society's controls. The system would actually save their asses. If the police appeared, they'd just lawyer up. *That's not going to happen.*

A little over an hour later, Katelyn arrived. They met Grey and proceeded to eat and drink way too much. After wallowing out of the restaurant, they all piled into Old Blue. Whit's truck wouldn't win a beauty contest, but she functioned well for his needs. The navy blue Ford F-250, V-10, 4x4 included an extended cab. The backseat looked like Ford's engineers couldn't decide whether to make it for passengers or luggage. It ended up being too big for luggage and uncomfortably small for riders. Whit and Katelyn rode fairly comfortably in the front. Unfortunately, due to Whit's long legs, the bench seat needed to be slid all the way back. That left Grey sitting behind Katelyn with his knees turned sideways. Grey called it Old Turd due to its low-geared rear end, rough riding heavy suspension, and manual transmission.

After a little over twenty-five minutes of leisurely driving, Whit pulled up to his rather stout 8"-diameter pipe gate with the swing arm on the right and the locking post on the left. He popped his truck out of gear, stepped on the parking brake and jumped out.

Whit turned his head back toward Grey and said, "I'll get the gate, since you can't. You drive through."

"Fine," Grey replied as he slid out of the backseat. Grey walked around the back of the truck and hopped into the driver's seat.

Katelyn asked, "Why can't you open the gate?"

"Oh, well, that's a long story," Grey replied. Before Katelyn could ask again, he said, "Get ready, I need to scoot this bench seat forward."

After moving the seat, Grey noticed Whit staring at the lock, so he tried to change the subject. Grey raised his voice and asked, "Forget the combination?" When Whit didn't respond, he added, "Need glasses?"

"No!" Whit barked, obviously lost in thought and not wanting to be disturbed.

Milner lowered his voice so only Katelyn could hear. "See that? There he goes again, off in his own little world. The simplest task can send his brain down a painfully slow, way too deliberate, and overanalyzing path. He can't just open the damn gate because of what? Some bird crapped on it and he can't figure out what it ate?" Grey mouthed out in silence, *Oh my God!* Then he added, "Maybe he saw deer tracks on top of bobcat prints. Holy crap; there's a carnivorous deer stocking a bobcat. Let's get out of here!"

Laughing, Katelyn whispered, "Milner, you're such an ass."

"I'm just saying. When he gets like this, who the hell knows? We might as well start eating our lunch here."

Katelyn said, "I think it shows intelligence, and look, something definitely seems to be bothering him."

Above and to the west of the cabin, Donnie whispered into his mic, "You said they'd be here by now."

"Take it easy," Lance whispered back. "This isn't like Downtown Chicago. You have to be patient; like hunting animals, not humans."

Donnie thought, *How the hell would you know?* "Yeah, well, we've been waiting longer than you said. These insects are eating me alive. I'm sweating like hell and it's only 10 o'clock. You should have told me about the mosquitoes and these fucking little flies that keep getting in my eyes. I'd have been more prepared."

"Soon, very soon, it will be all over." *Regardless of the outcome, I'll make sure it's over for you two assholes, too.*

Donnie whispered, "You should have let me set up on the east side of the cabin, with the sun behind me and the targets between me and their only way out."

Lance said, "You're right, except Whittingham isn't normal and this is his world. He knows stuff about nature. He'll feel, smell or sense a trap, if we're not careful. That comes from someone who knows Whittingham well, orders from above."

Donnie thought, *Yeah, but where I wanted to set up, once he drove past me, it wouldn't matter if he sensed anything. Even if I thought this Whittingham guy...or anyone was that good, I still wouldn't set up here.*

Whit swung the gate open. Grey released the parking brake and eased out the clutch without giving the engine enough gas. Old Blue jerked forward then stalled. Looking first at Katelyn then at his disapproving buddy, Grey gave a sheepish grin and shrugged his shoulders. He started the engine again but overcompensated with too much gas. As he dumped the clutch, the truck lurched forward.

"Nice work," Whit said, as he spoke into the passenger window as the truck rolled by the open gate. When the truck stopped, Whit jumped in the backseat behind Katelyn.

"You going to let me keep driving?" Grey asked with a puzzled look. Looking out the side mirror, Grey added, "Hey, you left the gate open. Isn't that one of your huge taboos?"

"That would be a yes and a yes," Whit replied. "Looks like you need some practice with a clutch; Christ, you've always driven like crap. And leaving my gate open does violate one of my rules. But I can take exception anytime it's appropriate."

Whit turned his body sideways and reached under the half-seat. Grey turned his head sideways and started to speak but stopped when he saw Whit pull out two rifle cases from under the back seat. Grey asked, "What did you mean by when it's appropriate?"

Whit slid the soft case with his Browning, A-5, 20-gauge shotgun back under the seat and started to unzip the larger case. When Whit didn't answer, Grey stopped the truck and looked around to Whit again, "Hey, Nature Boy, what did you see back there? And is that what I think it is?"

Stalling for a little time Whit said, "Keeeerist Milner, do you ever just ask one question at a time?"

"Yeah, usually that is…with normal people. You just take too long to answer."

"I saw, ah, multiple coyote tracks heading in toward the cabin. Got a doe hiding in the willows near the pond with twins. I don't like coyotes getting such an easy meal. To answer your second question, yes, this is a M1918A2, Browning automatic rifle or BAR for short. It's the one my dad somehow snuck back from Korea. He packed this twenty-pound behemoth into combat."

Milner leaned over to Katelyn and whistled the science fiction tune.

Looking seriously lost, Katelyn said, "I'm getting confused here; one issue at a time. First, the gun; you are going to shoot at a coyote with that, that thing?"

Locking a full 20-round mag, Whit said, "The shotgun won't work unless I can call the coyote in close. That isn't going to happen today with you two here. Besides, I didn't bring my varmint rifle—the Remington—so ergo, this behemoth. This puppy fires at a rate of five hundred rounds a minute."

Katelyn turned sideways to see both men, threw her right hand up and said, "Okay, fine; I didn't follow all that. But Whit, I thought you were like super hands-off about nature? Isn't shooting a coyote human interference?"

Milner piped up. "Oh, that's a big yes and no. Nature's order is God to Whit, but our Whit here has his own set of rules. He steps in with human intervention whenever he deems it appropriate."

Grey changed his inflection into a boring drawl. "Not that he doesn't understand the reality and brutality of the natural process—the food chain, life, death, wildlife population dynamics, and all that happy horseshit." Peeking in the rearview mirror, Grey studied Whit's red face then said, "How am I doing so far?"

"I thought you tuned me out whenever I try to enlighten your pitiful knowledge of nature?"

Grey replied, "I did and do; but I've heard it so many times and for so long, it just seeped in." Grey continued. "Whit doesn't even watch those African wildlife documentaries where some big-eyed kangaroo gets drug down by a bunch of lions."

"There're no kangaroo in Africa, you dork; and it's a pride of lions."

"Pride, pack, bunch, gang…whatever."

Then Grey remembered the open gate, but before he could ask Whit why seeing coyote tracks made him keep the gate open, Katelyn looked first at Whit then at Grey, and asked, "Why can't Grey open your gate?"

Whit replied, "That's easy to answer, Grey lost the right to know the combination."

No one spoke, and Kate started getting anxious for an answer, so Grey fessed up. "I was sneaking earth muffins and nature babes up here. They loved it. But apparently, I violated one of Whit's strict rules of access."

"Apparently my ass, Milner; I told you my cabin remained off limits to your debauchery."

Katelyn backhanded Grey on the arm and replied, "I see clearly now why you lost your privileges."

After dropping both back windows all the way down and putting the BAR on his lap, Whit added, "If I didn't promise his mother, on her deathbed, I'd watch out for him, I'd have disowned the rabid skunk a long time ago."

Grey's fragile ego had had enough, "Okay, you both have had your fun. Look, we're almost here; shouldn't we start focusing on why we came?"

Letting his buddy off the hook, Whit said, "Good point; pull up and park this beast."

Lance said over the mic, "Here they come. Wait until they both exit the vehicle...then take them out."

Donnie whispered, "Goddamn you Lance; there are three individuals in the truck. You said two!"

Shit; okay, act like it's no big deal. "I don't give a shit how many there are; shoot them all...no witnesses."

"This is a bolt action, asshole. One or two is easy; but three could be difficult, complicated, and messy."

Lance jabbed, "We're here because you and Lamar switched places last time and couldn't adjust to evolving situations."

"Your intel was the problem then and your intel is the problem now. I'm already on the wrong side of the cabin and dealing with glare because of you. Now there's a third target."

"I told you before; you don't know who you're dealing with here. Whit feels things, senses danger; he's not normal. Look how slow they're driving. He's already acting like he smells a rat."

The gunman said to himself, *That makes two of us, pal.*

The truck approached slowly, cautiously, corroborating Lance's concern. Even in the slight glare, Donnie could tell through his scope that the person in the passenger seat had long hair, probably a female. Shooting a woman was not a concern for Donnie, not at this point. He had to finish the contract, and that meant no witnesses. *Sorry, honey.*

Little did the assassins know that the truck's slow pace occurred more as a result of three people engaged in conversation while Grey just poked along. The occupants had no knowledge of their impending doom, although Whit felt concerned and suspicious enough to pull out the BAR. He had already registered two oddities. Whit had that funny feeling as he scanned his surroundings, enough so that he pointed the barrel of the BAR out of the driver's side back window.

"Fuck, they know something's up; see that barrel sticking out of the window?" Lance's voice started to creep up, betraying his growing jitters.

Donnie replied calmly, "Then why are they still coming?"

"I don't know, but I want you to take them out now."

"I don't have a sure shot on any of them yet. I'm waiting."

"Take out the driver, it should be Whittingham; the others will not recover fast enough to save their lives. I just want them dead. We'll deal with the mess later."

Donnie explained, "If I shoot up the truck, the cops are going to know it's a hit much sooner than if they find charred remains in a burned down cabin."

Lance paused, not knowing what to say.

Donnie continued, "And I'm sure Whittingham's not driving; that's Milner."

Lance finally reacted. "Shit, I don't care at this point; I need them all dead."

Donnie wanted to wait and said, "I'm set up to take them halfway from the truck to the porch. If I try to take them out in the parking area, I'll have to move to a better field of fire."

"So, move; just get it done."

While the truck meandered slowly toward him, the killer slid out of his hide. He moved slowly downhill, invisible behind leafy dogwood and thickets of Christmas tree sized incense cedar and white fir.

The truck pulled up close to the flat rock path leading to the cabin and stopped. The truck sat ninety feet from the cabin and two hundred forty feet from the shooter.

Donnie had set up, as best he could, for two unsuspecting souls walking up toward the cabin porch. Situated approximately one hundred fifty feet behind the cabin, at that range he could damn near do it left-handed. But now he moved parallel to his victims, down the hill to an area he had not pre-checked. Not good; plus, more sun glare. Once again, Lance had messed up a clean operation. But as Donnie moved a little further down the hill, he believed he'd be in position to shoot them in the truck or if they exited.

Grey killed the engine, but when he looked in the rearview mirror, he saw Whit spinning his finger in a circle telling him to turn around and back in. "I am not going to try and turn this tank around."

"You need the practice."

Grey tried again. "Normal people drive up forward."

"I always face out: just do it."

Looking at Katelyn, Grey asked, "Can we agree on obsessive compulsive?"

Crouched within a dense thicket of white fir, Donnie rose slowly. As he cleared his rifle past some branches to open a clear field of fire, the end of the barrel slowly approached a nesting Steller Jay. Stealthy but wary, she finally felt too threatened, screeched loudly, and bolted. The startled killer ducked and leaped wide-eyed sideways. Donnie quickly realized what had occurred and returned his focus back to his targets, still in the vehicle. The jay continued to fire off her threat call eliciting other jays to join in.

Whit understood the warning; something or someone startled Steller jays just past the cabin. Whit yelled, "Get us the hell out of here. Now, Grey!"

Grey picked up the concern in Whit's voice; he'd heard that tone enough to know not to question, just react. He didn't hesitate, started the truck, jammed it in reverse and dumped the clutch, spinning the back tires as he cranked the steering wheel.

Lance yelled, "Take the shot, take the shot!" so loud into the mic that he emitted only static.

Even so, Donnie knew instinctively what Lance screamed. Trying to assess the situation and his chances, he hesitated a second; then just said under his breath, *Ah, fuck it! I can't fail again. I know I can get the driver and stop the truck.* Donnie followed the spinning truck in the scope. He'd wait until the truck quit spinning around in reverse and stopped briefly before pulling forward. He took a breath and slowly exhaled; the truck stopped. The killer settled the sights on the base of the driver's head and squeezed the trigger. The bullet pierced the back window, exploded flesh and shattered the truck's windshield. *Lights out, bumpkin; one down.*

The gunman slid the smooth bolt action of the Mouser up and back, ejecting the spent casing. Something small drifted down in front of Donnie, but he ignored it. Sliding the bolt forward and down, he secured another round in the chamber. Seeing blood splatter, he knew he'd hit his target. *Shit, this is going to get messy.* Donnie watched, waiting for the truck and its dead driver to slowly roll to a stop. He'd go for the guy in the back, then the woman. *Just stop and show me something, anything vital.*

Whit, in the middle of the back seat, took off his dusty sunglasses to see better beyond the cabin. As he looked through the back window, the bullet punctured a hole in the glass, blasting bits of window into his face.

He closed his eyes far too late; tiny safety glass chards and glass dust slammed into his face and eyes. The boom of the rifle cracked in his ears as he grunted, "Augh!" The right side of his face slowly started oozing blood from a dozen lacerations.

Whit, with both eyes shut and blood starting to run down his face, shifted his knees onto the seat and pulled the BAR up and back out of the window. His upper body followed the gun out and he let loose with the entire twenty-round magazine in what he hoped was the direction of their assailant. Ka-thump, ka-thump, ka-thump, the large bore rifle coughed out its characteristic report. Whit's bullets went everywhere. Never being shot at before, Lance slid backwards down a slight incline and buried his face in the leaf litter and soft dark brown loam. Donnie knelt down on one knee but otherwise ignored Whit's barrage. He heard a few high-pitched zips as rounds passed by somewhere between he and Lance. *Valiant effort for nothing, Ace.*

Donnie stood back up and held the Mouser tight to his shoulder but peered beside the scope. He thought, *Shit, the driver's foot must still be on the gas pedal.* Then he realized the damn truck kept going, purposely; erratically, but purposely. Donnie couldn't believe his eyes. How could that be? He had center-punched the driver in the base of the skull. Even through the slight glare and the clutter of shattered glass he clearly saw the body jerk and blood explode. Then he remembered the something that fell in front of him, right in his field of fire. Donnie quickly looked down and saw it. *Shit!* Lying on the ground rested a branch about the diameter of a pencil with a small cluster of green leaves clinging to one end. His shot had severed the branch and slightly altered the trajectory of the bullet. The tiny piece of a black oak branch, in the path of the bullet, saved Greyson Milner's life. The black oak wouldn't even miss that tiny twig; but to the three lucky souls racing down the dirt road, it was the most important branch that hardwood had ever grown.

Donnie's bullet deflected just low and to the right, missing the base of Grey's head by four inches but passing through his right shoulder close to his neck. The searing pain caused Grey to cry out and involuntarily swerve hard to the left.

When Grey swerved back to the right to stay on the road, the inertia threw Whit further out the window and he had to let go of the twenty-pound rifle or be launched from the vehicle. "What the hell, Milner; I lost the BAR!"

"I'm shot, you asshole. You're lucky I'm still on the road."

With obvious concern in his voice, Whit asked, "Milner, how bad?"

"I have no fucking idea, but it hurts like hell. Katelyn, can you take a look?"

Donnie thought about taking quick shots at the fleeing vehicle or chasing it down with the SUV. Shooting wildly would cost him precious time. He decided on the latter and bolted toward where his partner had parked. Into his mic he said, "Lamar, get the SUV up here fast. Lance, get your ass to the SUV or—I swear—I'll leave you."

Lance got up and started to run. He thought, *Calm down; get control of your voice, clear your head, and take charge.*

Lamar had parked the SUV down a skinny little road leading to Whit's pond. Unfortunately, he'd made another lazy rookie mistake. Believing their victims didn't have a chance and not wanting to sit waiting with the sun in his face, Lamar hadn't bothered to turn the vehicle around to face out. Lamar had to drive a little farther down the road to a tiny little wide spot.

When Donnie reached where the SUV should have met him, he barked, "Where the hell are you, Lamar?"

Shit. "Twenty seconds," Lamar said.

Lance arrived wild-eyed and breathing hard.

Donnie told Lance, "I'll get in the back seat with the bushmaster."

Lamar pulled up and purposely avoided Donnie's glare. They hopped in as the SUV roared off before the doors were closed. Reaching into the back for the bushmaster, Donnie said, "The driver's hit, I'm sure of it. And that truck's a turd; we'll catch them before they can open the gate."

Lance tried to control his voice, "I told you Whit was cagey." Then, realizing that in the front seat he would be in the line of fire, Lance asked, "Are you sure this is a good idea? They have some kind of big machine gun."

"It's a BAR, but he dropped it. I saw it fall out of the truck, didn't you?"

In Old Blue, Whit stated, "They're coming after us, I'm sure of it. They think I locked the gate and that they'll catch us there. Can you drive?"

"For the time being; I think I'm losing lots of blood." Milner glanced across the cab and saw Katelyn scrunched on the passenger floorboard. She had her head down and her knees to her chest. Grey thought she was in shock. "Katelyn? Katelyn!"

She popped her head up and yelled angrily, "Don't yell at me; I'm right here. Jesus holy shit, who's shooting at us?"

Whit said, "Bad people. Doing okay, Grey?"

"Yeah, sort of. Katelyn, can you come up here and check my shoulder?"

Katelyn's wide-eyed stare looked more like a frightened cornered animal than a human. She raised her arms up and stared at Grey's blood speckled all over them. Not hearing any movement from the passenger side, Whit said calmly, "Katelyn, can you help Grey, please?"

Katelyn finally looked up and her vision returned. In the matter of a second, she was all business. Katelyn pulled herself up and settled her gaze on Grey's face, then his shoulder. "Holy shit, Grey; you've been shot!"

"Yeah, I'm pretty sure I was the first one to know. Can you take a look?"

She wiggled up closer and sat on her knees looking at Grey's blood-soaked shirt. She glanced into the back seat and shrieked, "Whit! Your face!"

"What?" Grey said, then looked in the rearview mirror. "Jesus, Whit; you okay? Did you get shot, too?"

Whit thought, *How the hell do I answer those two stupid questions?* He finally just said, "I think it's just glass, but some pieces are stuck in my right eyeball. I can't see." He sensed Katelyn still staring at him. Whit took out his handkerchief and handed it to her. "Katelyn, help Grey; he has to keep driving."

Katelyn pulled back the ripped fabric and assessed the wound. She said, "It looks like it passed straight through."

Wincing, Grey said, "The blown-out windshield was my first clue."

Katelyn glared at Grey but held her tongue. Looking back at his shoulder she continued. "What's the muscle on top of the shoulder attached to the neck?"

Simultaneously, Whit and Grey said, "Trapezius."

"There's a big jagged flap still attached to his neck. Torn muscle, but I don't see any bone or any spurting blood. I think I can stop the bleeding if I press it back down," which she did with the handkerchief.

Grey winced and gave out a sharp yip.

Katelyn said, "Shush; is there a first-aid kit?"

Whit said, "Yeah, but it's in the tool box in the truck bed. There are rags in both door's cubbyholes. The handkerchief and the rags will have to do. If you don't need them all, pass one back to me so I can cover my face. The less I move my eyes the better."

Whit thought, *she's back from the shock of damn near being killed and now she's as cool as a cucumber. Ms. City Girl has grit.*

Katelyn grabbed the rags and pressed one on top of Whit's handkerchief on Grey's shoulder.

Grey piped up. "Hey, let's lock the gate. They'll be stuck on the other side...problem solved."

"Thought of that already; too risky. I should have taken the lock and pin with us, but I locked them on the swing arm. Katelyn's the only one who could do it, and she'd take too long."

Katelyn said, "Let me try."

"No! If they show up we're deader than dead and they are following. Our best chance is to stay together and keep our lead."

Whit knew their chances of escape had nosedived when he lost the BAR. *With only a shotgun, we can't keep the assailants at bay. We need time and distance... but how? I'm blind, Grey's shot and drives a clutch like crap, and whatever the killers are driving sure as hell moves a lot faster than Old Blue.*

Two thousand feet behind Old Blue and coming on fast, Lance asked, "Why did you only shoot once? They were still in range."

Not caring to explain but deciding to anyway, Donnie said, "I was waiting for the truck to stop. I thought I killed the driver, but a branch deflected the shot. I hit a twig. Plus, it's difficult enough trying to make a kill shot into an erratically driven truck without some asshole trading my shots at 20 to 1. I decided I needed to get to the SUV and the bushmaster to overwhelm them with firepower. And now that he's dropped the BAR, we can easily finish this when we catch them. It's going to be messy, but if this Whittingham dude is as anal as you say, he locked the gate. We'll know in about ten seconds."

Already on his knees, Donnie leaned out of the passenger-side back window with his rifle on full automatic. They made the last turn and, as Lance started to sluff down below the dash, they saw the gate wide open...no truck. *Son of a bitch! More bad intel, or did Whittingham have a hunch, a premonition?* Donnie moved back inside the vehicle. No one said a word as they shot past the gate.

Finally, Lance said, "You see, Whittingham left the gate open. He knew something wasn't right. Stay sharp; Whittingham might try an ambush or take a side road."

Hitting the pavement and grinding through the gears, Milner yelled to no one in particular, but definitely aimed at Whit, "This low-geared, off-road, piece of shit is already overheating. No way are we going to make it."

Whit yelled over the air whistling through the shattered windshield, "Well, that helps our situation; you feel better?"

Sitting against the back seat of his poor abused truck, Whit had to ignore Grey, Kate, the SUV...everything, and think. They needed time.

Grey cut into Whit's thoughts and said, "It's a black SUV; I picked up a glimpse of it briefly at the back of that last straightaway."

Concentrating on holding the bloody rag over his face, Whit tried very hard not to involuntarily move his eyes. The bits of back window in his right eye felt like razor blades. As air rushing in through the shattered windshield brushed past Whit's face, suddenly an idea popped into his head. *Shit, it may work.* Whit yelled to the front seat, "Hey, can you tell if we have a prevailing wind; you know, Grey, an up-canyon drift?"

With Katelyn pressing down hard on the sizable flap of skin violently dislodged from Grey's shoulder, he uttered, "Jesus, Whittingham, what the hell are you talking about?"

Ignoring Milner, Whit explained. "We usually do starting late morning; just look out the window and tell me."

Scanning the upper branches of the trees quickly passing by, Milner noticed no movement on the branches of the pine and fir. Glancing back to the road then back to his left, he focused on the crown of a black oak struggling to compete for sunlight in between the taller conifers. The wide jagged leaves tossed back and forth.

Milner said, "Yeah, some wind, I guess. Hell, I don't know, Whit."

"Yes or no, Grey?"

"Yes, a little."

"Coming from the southwest?"

"Kind of left to right if that's what you mean."

"It is. We haven't passed the Dixon Mine turnoff?"

"No, it's still a couple of turns or so ahead of us. Why?"

"Good. Can you see the SUV?"

"Hell yes; I can see the SUV on the straight stretches, and its closing."

Very deliberately Whit said, "Okay, hotshot, listen up. If they cannot see us in the turn just before the Dixon Mine intersection, drive off the pavement with the right tires. But, pull back on to the pavement right at the intersection."

"Are you nuts? We'll lose what pitiful lead we currently hold."

"They're going to overrun us anyway; do it."

Shaking his head, Grey finally said, "Okay, old buddy; I'll trust you. I just hope you're not signing our death warrant."

Milner checked the rearview mirror just before making the wide left-hand turn in front of the unpaved Dixon Mine road...no SUV in sight. He slowed slightly while holding the steering wheel firmly and dipped the right-side tires off the pavement and onto the graveled shoulder.

The rear of the truck did try to break loose. Milner almost unperceptively turned the steering wheel slightly into the skid then back as the vehicle straightened out. They shot back on down the pavement.

"Good driving," Whit said. "Hope this works."

Milner forced what speed he could out of the poor truck. "You hope what works?"

Whit leaned forward and said, "With our momentum and the wind drift, our dust should waft down the Dixon Mine road. Those buttholes might think we turned off or, at least they may slow down to check. Either way it could give us time to get to Four Corners. If we get there unseen, we have three paved roads to choose; that puts the odds in our favor."

Nobody spoke for a few seconds, then a wincing Milner conceded, "Damn, Nature Boy; you're good."

Lance said, "Get ready; after this turn coming up, we should be on them in the next straightaway."

Donnie, on the passenger side in the backseat, leaned forward and up. Putting his right knee on the seat, he resumed his firing position, leaning out of the right backdoor window. He planned to empty a full clip regardless of the distance between them and the truck.

The SUV started into the left turn above the Dixon Mine intersection. Lamar concentrated on maximizing their speed around the turn when his brain processed the dust drifting down the dirt road on the right. He locked up all four wheels, putting the vehicle into a sideways skid. The violent move forced everyone forward and to the right. The inertia launched Donnie's upper body out of the back window. To stop himself, Donnie shot his left arm inside the vehicle and locked a death grip around the front passenger seat headrest. Unfortunately for Lance, Donnie's desperate grasp included Lance's neck. Donnie's upper body continued to pitch and twist forward and away from the car. Before he could stop his momentum, the barrel of his bushmaster banged off of the pavement.

Lamar had to let up on the brakes to prevent leaving the pavement sideways. Once Lamar straightened out the SUV, he reapplied the brakes, slowing to make the right turn.

Due to Donnie's chokehold around his throat, Lance couldn't breathe, let alone speak, until the SUV slowed down and straightened out enough to allow Donnie to reenter the vehicle. Throwing off Donnie's arm, Lance took a deep breath then turned and yelled at Lamar, "No; stay on the pavement, you idiot!"

"But they turned off just like you thought," stammered Lamar.

"No, it's a trick. Drive, now!"

Then Donnie cut in. "I don't dare put a round through this rifle; I hit the end of the barrel pretty hard on the pavement back there."

"Until this is over, I'll tell you what you will and will not do," snapped Lance.

Donnie leaned forward and hissed in Lance's ear, "Okay, bigshot; but you know if this rifle blows up, it will be right outside your fucking window. You might get a free ear-piercing, all the way through to your other ear."

The point finally seeped into Lance's furious brain. After a few seconds, he spoke in a surprisingly calm manner. "Slow down. You blew it; we're done here. Get me back to the copter."

Lamar slowed down, whipped a U-turn and shot back east up the road. Luckily, during the whole chase they never ran into one other vehicle.

In the backseat, a warning tingle shot through Donnie. The gunman sat back and looked in the rearview mirror and caught Lamar looking back. Lamar pitched his head slightly toward Lance. Donnie returned the nod.

Old Blue hit the long straight stretch; no one spoke. About halfway down, Grey said, "I don't see the SUV; I think they took the bait."

Raising his voice Grey added, "Shit, Whit; you crazy, backwoods SOB, I think you saved our butts."

Katelyn asked, "Which way when we get to four corners?"

Whit, sitting as still as possible, replied, "If we don't see the SUV by the end of the straightaway, take the shortest route to the hospital."

Grey said, "Ridge Road?"

"Duh, Milner; how long have you lived here?"

"Blow it out your ass, Whittingham," Grey said, then winced and yipped because he tried to flip Whit off.

Katelyn cut them off. "Jesus, you two; knock it off."

Grey said, "He started it."

Whit shot back, "No, you did."

Raising her voice, Katelyn yelled, "Just stop it, you bickering assholes."

That brought on a long period of silence. Finally, Katelyn said, "I don't want to hang around either one of you if you keep getting shot at. By the way, which one of you were they shooting at?"

Whit said, "Jeez, Kate, you just ended two sentences with prepositions."

Grey added, "Bad form for a journalist, I'd say."

Fuming and shaking her head, Katelyn snapped, "I'm learning damn quick how infuriating you two can be and why you both get shot...at!"

Chapter Forty-nine
Barring a Miracle

The stolen SUV returned to the Lost Hill Diggins and the helicopter. With Lamar driving, he parked almost exactly where he had when the copter arrived. Donnie wasn't too concerned when he saw the jet ranger but no sign of the pilot. He'd already liberated Lance's 9-millimeter and had his own automatic, gripped in his left hand, pointing inches from Lance's left ear.

Lance said, "This is completely unnecessary; we're on the same side."

Ignoring Lance, Donnie said, "Call out to your pilot; tell him to show himself."

Lance snapped, "Your boss is going to hear about—"

Lance stopped when he felt the end of Donnie's .45 poke him hard behind his ear. "You heard me."

Trying to cover for Ron and his intentions, Lance lowered the window and yelled, "Ron, it's okay; no one is following us. You can come out."

Ron Townsend pulled the rifle down and knelt behind a neatly piled stack of rocks and boulders. Ron didn't know that his perfect hide had been placed there over one hundred twenty-five years earlier by fifty-cents-a-day miners. What he did know was he needed to think and think fast. *How do I play this?*

Something obviously went terribly wrong. Their plan covered everything, or so they thought. Lance would exit the vehicle and separate himself from the killers, allowing Ron to get the drop on them. After liberating the killers of their guns, they'd cuff them.

If the hit went well and the assassins successfully killed Whit and Grey cleanly, their bodies would be flung into the cabin. The cabin would be torched and if burned hot enough, no evidence of murder or, at least they hoped, no conclusive proof would remain. The killers and Lance would then drive to the copter. At that point, the only individuals outside of the Inner Circle with knowledge of Sliger's involvement were Donnie, Lamar, and of course, Johnny Big Nose. Johnny couldn't talk, but the two assassins might…someday. Dead men can't blackmail, give depositions, or turn state's evidence. Ron and Lance would shove them in the SUV, shoot Donnie with Lamar's automatic and shoot Lamar with Donnie's automatic. Then the only gruesome part remaining…bust out their teeth; Lance would leave that messy detail to Townsend. Bag the ivory, pull the cuffs, toss the automatics in each killer's lap, torch the vehicle and fly away. The only mildly risky part left required Lance to drive the killer's rental pickup to a chop shop to disappear. No one around to recall events years later with ties to Sliger; just two unidentifiable toothless stiffs in a burned out stolen SUV…dead end.

But, if the hit required a messy shoot out and, say, bullet holes in Whit's pickup, they couldn't clean up all the evidence. A massive investigation could be dangerously problematic for Sliger and Johnny. Both killers would know they were liabilities and could turn fatalistic. Desperate killers, with no hope of survival, may just turn themselves in and start talking. In reality, regardless of the outcome of the hit, the end result required the elimination of Donnie and Lamar.

Unfortunately, all that intense planning turned to shit because neither Ron nor Lance anticipated Whit and Grey getting away or that the dumb-shit hitmen would foresee their precarious position.

Before Ron could make a decision on what the hell to do, he heard Lance say, "The hit failed miserably; they're still alive. We have to torch this vehicle and get the hell out of here, now."

Ron decided, *Well, that settles it, I'll just act like I was providing cover and play the rest by ear. They still need me to fly them out. If they get shitty, I'll just crash the damn copter. Hell, I'll be dead either way…but I'll take them with me. Jesus, I hate sticking my neck out for that little prick and Sliger. I made a bad choice taking Sliger's head of security job. And I'm sick and tired of dragging this rotten knee around and popping pain pills like Lifesavers. If I live through today, I'm finding a way out before I become a liability and Sliger makes me disappear.*

Screw this. Ron yelled, "I'm here; coming out." He slowly stood up, holding the rifle by the stock, pointing straight down.

Donnie exited with Lance and, pointing toward the pilot, said, "Lamar, take his rifle and check him for any other weapons."

Walking toward Lamar, staring at a .45 pointed at his belly, Ron complained, "Yeah, what's this?"

Lamar said, "Just making sure we all get out of here." He found Ron's pistol and a nice little knife in one of Ron Townsend's boots.

Ron asked, "What went wrong? I thought this was a sure thing."

Donnie said, "You can ask your boss, later. Go get some branches so we can sweep our tracks."

"Can I have my knife?"

Donnie shook his head. "No, just break the branches off. You can have your knife back after you take us to our pickup. Lamar, go with him. I don't want him accidently finding another rifle stashed out there."

Fifteen minutes later, with the completely empty SUV on fire and all weapons—except for Donnie and Lamar's automatics stored in the helicopter's back compartment—they took off. Donnie and Lamar sat behind Ron and Lance. No one spoke. It only took fifteen minutes to land the helicopter back at the rental pickup.

Donnie said, "Shut it down."

They waited impatiently and, eventually, Ron applied the overhead lever break and the blades stopped.

Donnie opened the back door and exited. He opened Lance's door and said, "We're taking the shotguns and our pistols. You'll find the Bushmaster and the Mouser in the back; get rid of them. Your pistols and the pilot's knife are back there, too."

Lance started to speak so Donnie punched him in the eye. Lance buckled forward grabbing his face.

Donnie continued, "You don't get to speak."

Ron said, "Hey, there's no—"

"I should cap you both right now," Donnie shot back. "What changes for Lamar and me if I kill you right here, right now?"

That shut them up as the seconds ticked off.

Finally, Donnie said, "Hey, asshole." When Lance slowly dropped his hands and looked up, Donnie punched him hard again then said, "Get this piece of shit out of here before I change my mind."

Ron Townsend didn't have to be told twice. He knew the sound of a man at wits' end with absolutely nothing to lose. In record time, he fired up the engine and lifted off.

Leaning against the side of the pickup with Donnie as the copter shrunk smaller and smaller, Lamar said, "Man, I thought you were going to kill them."

Donnie stood there shaking his head slowly. Finally, he said, "I should have. And it would have been more than fair because, barring a miracle, what transpired today sure as hell killed us."

Chapter Fifty
Square One

Walking down the main hallway to find Whit at the tiny fourteen-bed Cornish Hospital, Katelyn moved with purpose. The freshly patched up Greyson Milner worked hard to keep up, his stitched shoulder twinging with each step. They were heading for room fourteen.

Katelyn felt drained, exhausted from the adrenaline rush and tired of getting cryptic answers and refereeing Whit and Milner's incessant sniping. Neither provided her with straight answers. Whit spoke little and revealed less, keeping everything tight to the vest. Grey blurted out all kinds of crap...right, wrong or indifferent and also cleverly deflected pointed questions.

She liked Grey, though he reminded her of those horny, self-absorbed Washington beltway dick-wads. But he seemed different in some way, like a good guy trying really hard to be a bad guy. Once, she asked Whit about Grey's relentless sexual prowess. His response was typical Whit. "He wasn't always that way, but that's Grey now. Just like the seasons, his romances followed a logical progression for the women; hope springs eternal, then winter bites them in the ass."

For the first time, Katelyn experienced second thoughts about pulling up stakes and flinging her life into Whit's world, a totally crazy and chaotic existence. After a nurse whisked Whit away, the adrenaline wore off and shock set in. Katelyn sat on a toilet seat and started shaking and couldn't stop. Twice she spun around to throw up but didn't. Finally, she stopped shaking and calmed down.

Katelyn washed her face again and looked in the mirror at a disheveled image. "What the hell have you done?" *Bored was I? Sick of the beltway; tired of the plastic, phony, selfish lifestyle…lacking fulfillment, passion, love.* But, turning her life completely upside down to chase a dream? Because of what, an intense one-night stand?

Thinking back, she had to admit it wasn't a one-night stand; it was *the* one-night stand. She had never fallen so hard, so fast. And even after that night, she really didn't know that much about him. Well, if opposites attract, they were the personification; and Whit certainly erased boredom and the lack of excitement from her need-to-do list.

But before she pursued Whit any further, she'd need some straight talk. *I'm sick and tired of being left out of important information and decisions until after the fact.* Her anger welled up. Since Whit wasn't there, she looked over her shoulder at Grey hustling behind her and vented, "Fuck you, too!"

Puzzled, Grey immediately apologized. "Oh, ah, sorry." *What the hell just happened; did I miss something?* He tried to think back to what he had just done to anger Katelyn.

They sat in the ER under the care of an older attractive nurse who seemed to be particularly rough with Grey's shoulder. He winced and gritted his teeth often as she aggressively cleaned and washed the wound, but mostly, Grey tried to stay quiet. She finished, turned to Katelyn and said, "He's ready for stitches. I'll find Doctor Parker and send him back in."

Katelyn sensed some serious bad blood between the two and said, after the nurse left, "What's that all about?"

With his head tilted toward the wound, obviously in pain, he hissed, "Oh, ah, that's Mrs. Wagner; we call her Nurse Ratchet. She has a reputation for being a tad rough; I think she hates men."

"I think she hates you. How does she know you? And no bullshit, Milner."

"Oh, ah, well, you see, a few years back a guy that looked a lot like me dated her daughter and I think it didn't last…or end well. She keeps getting the two of us mixed—"

"I said no BS, Milner."

The door opened, and the doctor stepped in, ending Katelyn's grilling. Doctor Parker smiled at Katelyn and nodded to Grey. He put on gloves and sat down next to Grey to observe the wound. The doctor deliberately pulled open the flap on Milner's shoulder. Grey's head snapped back as his damaged nerves exploded. Looking into the severed flesh, the doctor said "Jan, ah, Nurse Wagner, did a fine job cleaning the wound." Smiling he added, "I think she's been looking forward to this day for a long time."

Katelyn and Milner looked at each other. Grey gave up all pretenses and said to the doctor, "Yeah, yeah. I guess I had that coming; but we're good, right, Doc?"

"Oh, sure, sure, Grey," Doc Parker said in a matter-of-fact manner. Then he added, "I'll even give you plenty of local before I start stitching; good stuff too, on one condition. Stay the hell away from all females in my family and at this hospital."

Looking at the tray full of curved needles, Grey looked straight into Doc Parker's eyes and seriously proclaimed, "I promise, Doc."

True to his word, Doc Parker took good care of Grey. Only toward the end did the local start to wear off, a little. When the doctor finished, he stood up and said, "I want to see you in two days…immediately if you see redness, feel increasing pain anywhere, or become nauseous."

"Okay, Doc; thanks."

Walking to the door, Doc Parker said, "Wait here. Nurse Wagner will be in shortly with some pain killers, antibiotics, and a prescription for more. Oh, the sheriff called and said to stay in the hospital until he arrives. He's tied up with the Maglioca's again. I'm sure I'll be patching up those two drunken love-birds shortly."

When Nurse Wagner returned, she actually sneered at Grey while handing Katelyn the pills, prescription, and some printouts. She turned to walk out but before she reached the door. Katelyn said, "Aren't you supposed to tell Grey how to take his medication?"

Looking straight at Grey, Nurse Wagner quipped, "I suggest he takes all of them at once." As she opened the door, Nurse Wagner turned her head back to Katelyn and said, "The dosages are on the packets, and you'll find the dos and don'ts on the printouts. Good luck, sweetie; you'll need it," Just before the door closed, Katelyn faintly heard, "with that little prick."

Katelyn crossed her arms and said, "Well, that was pleasant; care to ex-plain?"

Quickly as he could, Grey hopped down but immediately bent over and winced. Finally, he opened his eyes and said, hoping to end any further prying into his brief relationship with one of Nurse Wagner's daughters. "Hey, we better go see Whit. It could be serious, and I'm worried about the damage to his eyes."

Standing with her arms still crossed and seeing nothing further forth coming from Grey, Katelyn said, "Nurse Wagner's right."

"About what?"

Heading for the door, Katelyn said, "You are a little prick."

Still following Katelyn to Whit's room, Grey figured with the events that took place today, Katelyn had a right to be a little...testy. Grey's silhouette revealed a noticeable lump under the scrubs he was given since the nurses had cut his shirt off and threw it away. A thick layer of gauze and tape covered his newly stitched upper shoulder. A black sling kept his tucked arm against his chest.

Finding the right room, Grey caught up with Katelyn. Using his left hand, he opened the door, letting Katelyn go first. As she passed, Grey checked Katelyn's profile; she seemed to have returned to a more pleasant demeanor. Grey thought, *she must be part Portuguese or Italian...quick to flare and just as quick to calm down.*

The lights were off, and Whit sat up in bed with most of his head wrapped in white. "Hello, Benjamin," Katelyn said in a cheery voice. She walked over to the side of the bed and held his right hand.

Sensing two people had entered the room, Whit said, "Hey, guys; all in one piece?"

"Yeah, all put back together; starting to really throb though. Just like we talked about in the truck, that bullet—or at least a chunk of it—peeled up a nice slab of my trapezius muscle right by my neck. Doc Parker said any lower and a huge artery would have exploded...I'd have bled out. At least I—"

Whit cut in, "I'm fine, by the way, narcissist, thanks for asking."

Grey sounded shocked. "Why, Whit, why do you think we're here?"

Katelyn gave Grey a nasty glare, and silently mouthed, *What the hell, Milner?* Moving her hand up to Whit's forearm she asked, "What did the doctor say?"

"Well, thank you for asking, Katelyn." Turning toward where Grey stood, Whit added, "It's obvious who really cares about me." Turning toward Katelyn, Whit said, "When that bullet punched a hole through the back window, it imbedded tiny bits of glass in my right eye; plus, abrasive, almost glass dust, in both eyes. They plucked out the pieces that actually stuck in my eyeball and flushed the hell out of my eyes with—I think—a fire hose. The doc said eyes are tougher than you'd think, and he seemed pretty encouraged. I could end up with no permanent damage. My left eye appears fine. I just can't see for a while. If I move my left eye, it involuntarily moves my right eye; that's why both are wrapped. They want minimal movement for at least two or three days...probably more."

"I think we were pretty damn lucky," Grey said.

Katelyn and Whit thought about what Grey had said and nodded.

Grey continued. "Whit, had we climbed out of your truck, we would have been dead ducks. How did you know? What made you yell to get the hell out of there?"

"Unlike you, Milner, I pay attention to my environment. I should have figured it out at the gate. I tell everyone—everyone that is, who knows the combination—to leave a specific order of 3s, 6s or 9s on the tumbler. That way I know if someone has been messing with the lock. It wasn't left correctly, which is odd. As you know, only a select few individuals know the combination."

Turning to Katelyn, Grey whined, "Can this guy hold a grudge or what? Jesus, Whittingham; don't you believe in clemency, forgiveness...a second chance?"

"I also don't believe in Santa Claus, the Tooth Fairy, or the Easter Bunny. And for you to change, that would take a miracle; and I don't believe in those either."

Grey responded. "But, Whit—"

"Enough you two, geez!" Katelyn put her hands on her hips and said, "Can we get back to almost getting killed...can we? How did you know, Whit?"

"The evidence was right there; I didn't properly take heed."

Grey and Katelyn remained silent, so Whit continued. "Okay, clue one was the combination on the lock. Clue two...someone drove in recently with wide tires. I tried to think, who do I know that drives a vehicle with fat tires? I just let that slide, too."

Katelyn said, "Not entirely. You pulled out the rifle and left your gate open."

Grey added, "Yeah, and you gave us that bullshit story about coyote tracks."

Whit nodded slightly and said, "Okay, I didn't want to alarm you two with flimsy information and just...a bad feeling. My fault; I wasn't paranoid enough because I was acting too much like you, Milner."

Grey started to protest but stopped when Katelyn turned and put the palm of her hand in his face.

Whit continued. "So, clue three hit me when the Steller jays went nuts. Something startled them; that sealed the deal…that's when I yelled."

Grey couldn't take it. "Wait a frikkin' minute; little birdies came to our rescue? Are you serious?"

Whit gave a shrug. "Holy crap, you are serious." Looking at Katelyn, Grey put his good hand up like a mime. "I feel it too, Katelyn; it's the Force." Pointing to Whit he added, "And this is our very own Obi Frikkin' Whit Kenobi."

Katelyn closed her eyes, pinched her nose and sighed. "Oh, Christ, Milner, shut the hell up. I swear to God I'm going to karate chop you right in the neck." She opened her eyes and said, "Whit, please go on."

Whit stuck his tongue out toward Grey and said, "Thank you, Kate. It's not the Force, Milner…you boob-ass. It's just nature and how everything fits together. Jays, chipmunks, squirrels, Stinker, geese…pretty much all animals make great early warning systems. But you have to pay attention. Going back to jays, they're in the genus Corvus, along with ravens and crows. These birds live and act a lot like you, Milner; very intelligent, but tend to use their powers for evil, not good."

Katlyn cut in. "Can you stop bickering and jabbing each other like a couple of little kids? Someone just tried to kill us today. This is not funny. Now, damn it you two, focus."

Grey blurted out, "He started it."

"Did not."

"Did so."

Katelyn threw her hands up. "I'm out of here."

Whit reached for her, but missed. "Stop, Katelyn, please. I'm done; I promise."

Grey piped in, "Me too; sorry."

Katelyn stopped, and no one spoke. Frazzled and upset enough to cry, she felt at wit's end.

Whit said, "Sorry, Kate; sorry. It's just kind of how Grey and I…for lack of a better word…communicate. I think it's how we deal with pressure, defuse stress, decompress; hell, I don't really know. We do know this is serious stuff; we were getting there, in our own way. Stay, we'll try again and, I promise, no more digs."

Katelyn stood facing the door but didn't leave, so Whit continued. "Okay. So, at the cabin when Grey turned off the truck, that's when I heard the Steller jay's fire off. I knew something past the cabin startled them. I didn't know what but didn't want to take a chance. If it was nothing, we could always just come back."

Katelyn finally turned around and spoke. "The bottom line, your awareness, Grey's driving, and your idea about sending dust down that road saved our lives."

Grey added, "Don't forget your assistance. Without you putting pressure on my gunshot wound, I would have eventually passed out from loss of blood."

Whit added, "Bottom line, we all kept our heads and performed. That's impressive, and that's why we're still alive. We all played a part in saving each other." Whit also thought but did not say, *And our assailants made some serious fundamental screw-ups.*

Realizing how incredibly close they had come to a gruesome end, no one spoke for quite some time. Finally, Katlyn asked, "What I need to know now… where do we go from here?"

Thinking along the same line, Whit said, "Well, today was a game changer. It's all out in the open now; no doubts, no pretenses, no ambiguities. They were trying to cover up the shotgun attack on Milner as possibly jealous rage, and Ned's incident as suicide. But today boils down to only one interpretation…murder by assassination. That means they don't care anymore."

Grey asked, "Yeah, but who are they?"

Katlyn said, "I see the connection between you two, but why try to kill me?"

Going back to finish his last thought Whit said, "Whoever they are, they're not professionals; or at least they make stupid mistakes. Otherwise… we'd be dead. But if they could have taken us out, at my cabin, they probably would have gotten away clean. Since we're not dead, whoever ordered the hit and those who participated are sweating bullets right now."

No one spoke as they absorbed that news. Then Katlyn went back to her point. "Okay, but I still don't see my connection to this."

Whit said, "I don't think you are connected. Either they still wanted to kill Grey, and you and I were just collateral damage; or they wanted to kill Grey and me, and you were going to be collateral damage. Remember, you were a last-minute addition to Grey's and my plans. I think somehow they knew Grey and I were heading to my cabin, but not you."

Katlyn sighed. "Well, I guess I feel better that I'm not a direct target. But still, where does that leave us?"

Whit and Grey answered at the same time, "Square one."

Chapter Fifty-one
Blowing Smoke

Johnny "Big Nose" Ramelli and Steven Sliger needed to talk, one on one. The system Johnny devised wasn't the most secure, but it was Johnny's, and no one dared tell Johnny different. He didn't trust computers, jamming devices, scramblers, or any other type of high tech gizmo shit. Johnny figured the Feds couldn't bug every damn phone in Chicago, at least not yet.

Johnny knew he wasn't getting the whole story. He also realized Steven Sliger wasn't getting straight answers either. Johnny gets it from Donnie. Sliger gets it from Lance. But, regardless of who's at fault, Donnie was there to back up Johnny's word. He failed. Nobody makes Johnny Ramelli out to be a liar. He maintained his empire top down through respect. Johnny's form of respect happened to include immediate, violent and guaran-fucking-teed painful retribution. He levied that retribution against all parties who crossed him. Favored employees were no exception. Donnie and his ex-military buddy, Lamar, would soon become horribly mutilated examples for the rest of Johnny's employees and associates.

Leaning forward in a cushy black leather chair, Johnny stared blankly across the slightly dusty red oak desk. Staring at nothing in particular on the far wall, he listened to Steven Sliger on speaker phone, even though he knew he shouldn't. *You listening, you fucking Feds?* Johnny came to the old office building owned by a friend of a friend; in fact, someone Johnny didn't even know. He needed privacy to deal with this latest crisis. The particular office, he picked at random. Sliger's computer geek ensured a routed and scrambled secure communication at Sliger's end. All they needed was a date and time. The Feds could follow Johnny and watch him enter a building, but that was it. With whom did he meet, talk to, or phone? They had no clue. They could take pictures of everyone who left the building and follow them endlessly and, ultimately, find no connection. They could bug the phones till hell freezes over, but Johnny would never return. It became great amusement to Johnny, that any wasted time and expense he could levy on the Feds made decent payback for hounding him.

Today he was on Chicago's eastside, listening to Steven Sliger's mild tirade. No one that knew Johnny ever actually yelled at him, at least not twice. Steve Sliger artfully measured the shallow ice he walked, and he kept his tone, volume, and inflection within the underworld boss's razor-thin tolerance level.

Johnny interrupted Sliger long enough to make a point. "We go way back, you and me. It's not like we've had a problem in the past. I take care of you, you take care of me. That's how it's always worked. I ain't going to leave this unfinished." After a brief pause, he added for effect, "Not with my longest living associate."

Sliger knew immediately that "longest living associate" meant longest surviving associate. Getting the message loud and clear, Sliger toned his voice down a bit more. "This one was special; personal to me and—"

"So maybe that's the problem," Johnny cut in again. "You get emotionally involved, you get impatient. You get impatient, you get sloppy; you don't think smart, take shortcuts and unnecessary risks. And that ain't good for business. I ain't spent a day in prison yet and I ain't gunna. You understand what I'm saying?"

Sliger had hoped their conversation would go in a different direction, but it hadn't. Sliger knew exactly what Johnny meant. Sliger himself would be swept up in the housecleaning to keep Johnny's involvement hidden. *Okay; new tactic.* Sliger offered, "Hasn't everything I've done for you been to protect your empire? When I came to you with my idea, it was specifically designed to keep you out of prison while you conducted all your, ah…business ventures. I think we've done very well."

Sliger heard nothing but breathing on the phone and realized his change of direction must have hit a chord. Now it was Johnny's turn to reflect. He sat back and looked up at the ceiling.

What, twelve years ago, Sliger walks right into one of my restaurants and asks to speak with Johnny Ramelli. The defiant little shit wouldn't take no for an answer. Some of my guys had to get a little rough with him and throw him out. So, what does the little shit do? He hacks my restaurant's computers and says, "Now you'll meet with me." I'm thinking, you bet your ass I'll meet with you, you little shit. So, he says where he's staying and some of my boys go pick him up; again, not so nice like. The freak is completely unfazed.

I says to him, "You got a death wish?"

He comes right back with, "No, I want to be rich. You got a prison wish?"

Nobody talks to Johnny Ramelli like that; so even before I look at my boys, they grab this little shit and start messing him up. He blurts out, "Give me five minutes and I'll show you a computer program to launder your finances." I lift my hand and my boys stop. The little shit stands up and says, "The Feds will never touch you."

I'm intrigued by this smart-assed little shit. He sits back down and glares left and right at my two boys like he could take them out…fat chance. I changed his name from little shit to little Napoleon right then. He turns to me and says, "You'll have to pay taxes on all of it, including the dirty money, because it's passing through your legit businesses. Your produce, trucking, restaurants and disposal businesses will cover each other's increased revenue stream. How are the Feds going to mess with a tax-paying businessman with clean books?" He even said it would ebb and flow with the market, and he'd programmed periodic minor input errors to make it all look human-like and realistic.

Johnny took his eyes off the ceiling and realized Sliger had gotten him off his game. *Okay, so he's got a point; Sliger's computer geek's program worked like a charm, flowing with the seasons, the markets and demand, like clockwork.* Johnny leaned forward and said, "I'll handle the fallout; I'll be sending someone to find my guys, if they're still there. He'll set this straight."

Sliger relaxed a little, realizing he had what he wanted. But then Johnny added, "Any chance these…old high school pals of yours know what's going on…like, any connection to you?"

"No, no; we're layers removed." After a brief pause which told Sliger, Johnny wasn't convinced, he lied, "Besides, they aren't the sharpest tools in the shed. I'm twenty years in their past; absolutely no connection." Still no response, so Sliger shifted gears again. "Who are you sending?"

"Tony Bassetti, we call him—"

"Two Tap," Sliger cut in, excited after hearing Johnny's top enforcer would help. Sliger immediately regretted opening his mouth. *Shit!* Again, another long pause ensued. Sliger thought, *Shit; Johnny's thinking how the hell do I know his top man's nickname? Shit, shit, shit; I hope he's as dumb about computers as he acts. Think of something to say…change the subject.*

Before Sliger could come up with a diversion, he heard Johnny inquire, "Yeah, Tony Two Tap; so, you heard of him?"

Shit. Taking a deep breath, knowing he was putting himself somewhat out on a limb because he didn't really know if the two missing hitmen knew Tony, Sliger responded, "I heard the name from your two absent guys."

Somewhat sternly Johnny said, "You specifically said you would use your go-between and not meet the hitmen, am I right?" Not waiting for an answer Johnny added, "And why would my two professionals bring up Tony's name?"

Shit, shit, shit. Sliger knew the longer and more strung out the lie, the harder to maintain the bullshit. Quickly, and as nonchalantly as possible, Sliger said, "Oh, I didn't meet with them. Lance told me when he met your guys the second time. They couldn't figure out why they were asked to come back. They thought you'd rather send your top guy, Tony Two Tap Bassetti."

You don't build and fight your way to the top of an organization like Johnny's without having a little sixth sense, like knowing when to duck, when to punch, or when someone's feeding you a line of crap. Johnny knew Donnie and Lamar were shocked that they were asked back to California for another hit attempt; specifically, because they knew Sliger and his little poodle, Lance, had blown a gasket. They could have mentioned Bassetti's name as the go-to-guy, but that would be very uncharacteristic for the tightlipped Donnie. Maybe it was the new kid, Lamar? Shit, this Sliger is one clever son of a bitch. Either he's lying through his teeth, which means I can't trust him any longer, or people in my organization are just getting sloppy, losing their edge, talking too damn much. The sooner I make an example out of Donnie and Lamar, the better.

Sliger waited nervously, hoping his story held. The longer he waited the worse he felt. *What a stupid rookie mistake; shit. Other people blurt out shit, not ne.* If Johnny ever found out how much Sliger really knew about the mobster's Chicago Empire, Johnny would turn Tony Two Tap loose on Sliger and his Inner Circle.

Mercifully, Johnny came back to his casual tone. "Tony Two Tap knows everything you and I know; at least about the hits, that is. He knows what to do."

"Okay," was all the relieved Sliger could muster.

"Tell me, why did you really ask for my two guys to come back a second time to whack them bums you grew up with?"

Sliger thought, *Okay, focus and sell this.* "I knew you would only send me good men, and I didn't want you to get the impression I was unappreciative or that I questioned your choice. It was out of respect."

More silence. Sliger thought, *come on, Johnny; you've established who's the boss. You're used to bootlickers; eat it.*

After a few more strained seconds, Johnny said, "This time it's different. Tony don't take no orders from no one but me. Your man Lance is out, other than to assist Tony; that clear?"

"Okay, I just want to get this whole—"

"I ain't done yet," Johnny snapped. He let a long string of dead air add credence to his control of the situation. "You know about Tony; you know how Tony gets his nickname?"

Lying, Sliger replied, "No."

"Tony kills a specific way unless I tell him different. He likes kneecapping or gut-shooting whoever I tell him needs eliminating. While they're squirming and squealing, he tells them, for me, why they got it. Then Tony asks them if they are right-handed or left-handed; and whichever one they say, he shoots them in that eye. Always one in the knee or guts and one in the eye...tap, tap."

Feeling the weight of the threat, Sliger's response came back as a very quiet. "Oh."

Johnny jumped back in. "Something smells funny about this whole operation of yours. You and me have been good for each other for a long time; that counts for something. I'd be very...annoyed, if I learn different than what I'm hearing. This personal vendetta you got with these bums could start to become a problem. I don't like problems. I did you a favor by sending out my guys. They ain't screwed up for me before, not once; but, somehow, they screw up for you twice. That's a problem. I don't know what happened, 'cause I get my side of it and you get yours. I don't even give a shit what happened; I'm going to fix it…my way. Tony finds my two guys what disappeared and he really makes them disappear…poof, like smoke…no traces. Tony, he looks at this situation of yours and sees what he can do. If he can take them old buddies of yours out in what looks like an accident, robbery or like natural causes, he whacks them. He thinks it's too dicey, he walks away. That means you walk away; it's over…no more vendetta."

Johnny slowed his speaking for emphasis. "If, at that point, you go back to what you do best, then that's not a problem between us. If, instead, you don't walk away from this vendetta, that is a problem." Johnny took his phone and tapped it twice on the desk. He let silence fill the phone again, then said, "Tony's got a problem to clean up for me here but should be in California soon. He'll contact your foxy HR lady."

The line went dead and Steven Sliger realized he was holding his breath. He made a couple of gulping sounds as he sat back and tried to catch his breath. *Jesus H. Christ, that was close, but didn't I survive? No, didn't I come out the best?*

A huge revelation hit him. Sliger discovered he relished the adrenaline rush of being on the edge with Ramelli. As a control freak, this new sensation…he liked. Under pressure, hadn't he talked his way out of his flub about knowing Tony Bassetti's nickname? Wasn't Johnny Ramelli sending him his best man? Sliger yelled into the empty room, "Who's the man?"

I have the intellect, finances and cojones to do what it takes to win. No one, not even Johnny Ramelli, controls Steven Sliger. One way or another, Tony Bassetti will finish off Whittingham and Milner; he must. For my mental health, I need them gone; so, it will be done.

Chapter Fifty-two
They're Gone, Dead...Or

Walking into Ben Whittingham's hospital room, Warden Perkins greeted Whit. "Hey, poacher."

"Well, if it isn't Warden Perkins; I heard you arrested your mother last week for swatting flies out of season."

"Funny, smartass."

"Hey, you started it...and picking on a cripple, no less."

Whit stuck out his right hand. Gene took it and said, "You look like shit."

"You smell like shit."

Gene rarely could get the best of Whit. Shaking his head, he asked, "What's the prognosis, asshole?"

Chuckling, Whit replied, "Better than I look. I had pieces of glass stuck in my right eye and a few scratches on the cornea. But I'll mend, so says the docs. In fact, I see the doc this afternoon and could be released today."

"You're lucky."

"We were all lucky, Gene. We drove right into an ambush. Hey, speaking of which, what's the latest?"

"Zippo; either they were aliens and returned to the mothership or they're in a shallow grave somewhere, because they just vanished. Nothing new at the scene or at the burned-out SUV, though they did ID the vehicle's owner."

"And?"

"Stolen; it belonged to the Roseville school district. Apparently, it was boosted from a Special Ed teacher's house."

Whit asked incredulously, "We give SUVs to teachers now?"

"No; but the superintendent of the school budgeted one for himself. Since he's married, but not to the Special Ed teacher, he didn't report it missing. He hoped it would turn up…quietly. The dumbass told his wife it was in the shop. When the CHP traced it to him, they went to his house but ended up speaking to the wife. Major doo-doo hit the fan."

Whit responded, "It's always the cover-up; well, screw him."

"As it turns out, no one's screwing him at the moment. But it sounds like when his wife and the school district are done with him, he'll be royally screwed."

"Good; I like happy endings. But where does that leave the investigation?"

"Nowhere, except—"

"Except what?" Whit cut in, sitting up straighter.

"No one seems to think it's relevant or related except me, but—"

"Jesus, Gene, what? Spit it out."

"Hold your horses, cripple; geez. I'll tell you if you let me; now shut up. I was conducting one of those bullshit out-of-state hunter surveys at the bug station up on the summit last week. I ran into two youngish, ex-military types and they lied to me."

"Hell, everyone lies to cops. When was it, a Tuesday, Wednesday or Thursday?"

"Tuesday, why?" Realizing that was a dig, Gene took offense and sniped, "Hey, what are you implying?"

Whit said with a smirk, "I deal with plenty of agencies; I don't think I've ever met any of them in the field on a Monday or Friday."

"You are such an ass, Whittingham. Do you want to hear this or not?"

"Sorry; couldn't resist. Please continue."

Whit couldn't see the warden shaking his head, but finally Gene tried again. "Okay, turd. These guys were late twenties; maybe the white guy was early thirties."

"White guy?"

"Yeah, the other guy was black."

"In lily-white Logan County, he'd stick out like a sore thumb."

"Oh, gee, Whittingham, brilliant; no one thought of that. Now are you going to shut up and let me finish?"

Whit pinched his lips with his fingers.

"So these two guys say they're from Springfield, Illinois, and won a pheasant hunting trip through a company raffle. I looked in the back seat of their truck and saw four rifle cases. Two looked right for shotguns, but one was too long, and one was too short, like maybe—"

Whit spoke through his pinched lips. "A sniper rifle and a semi-automatic?"

Exasperated, Gene stressed, "Peace officers are trained to let people babble on, but not in your case. Jesus, you're annoying."

Out of the corner of his mouth, Whit muttered, "Sorry."

"So, they don't pass the smell test; but I had nothing concrete on them, so off they go."

Whit started to open his mouth, but Gene said, "Aah!"

"I had CHP dispatch connect me to their Gold Run unit and told him about my suspicions. I said I was heading that way and I asked him if he'd sort of do a routine stop on these guys. They don't show. We finally figured too late that they knew I was suspicious and pulled off of I-80 and used old Highway 40. Why would a couple of innocent guys from Illinois do that?"

"Was that a question?" Whit asked.

"No...rhetorical, so zip it." Gene continued. "I checked with the gun club they named, and the manager knew nothing of these two or any raffle."

After a long silence, Gene watched Whit rubbing his chin. Whit wanted to say something but wouldn't. Gene let Whit stew a little longer then finally said, "Okay, Whittingham; speak up before you pop."

"I think you met the assassins; why doesn't anyone else think so?"

"Beats me. Go ask them yourself; but you'll have to wait until Tuesday, Wednesday, or Thursday, of course."

"Why? Oh...clever, Gene. Okay, I deserved that. But it still begs the question, where the hell are they now?"

"Everyone investigating the case...that will talk...seems to think they ditched the truck and made it out of California in a private jet; or maybe pulled their vehicle into the trailer of an 18-wheeler and were driven out of the state, something like that. When I ran the plates to their pickup truck, it showed up as a rental out of Reno. It hasn't been returned. That fits either theory. The feds and the state investigators are losing interest because of no leads, clues, or perps. They're leaning heavily toward a domestic issue, due to your buddy Milner's involvement. That means a local issue. The big boys want to dump this back on the county and split."

Whit sat back quietly with his head resting on his pillows. Finally, he said, "They're gone, dead, or...still here."

"Or still here? Okay, what makes you say that?"

"I don't know."

They both stayed quiet. Eventually, Gene said, "Go back to your last point; they're gone, dead, or still here. If they're gone, they're gone. If they're dead, they're dead. Either way, they're no longer a problem or threat to Grey and you. But, what if they are still here?"

Another long period of pondering ensued as they both mulled over Gene's point. Whit finally snapped his fingers and said, "Maybe they can't go back. What if they were the two that messed up the first hit attempt on Grey? Now they've screwed up twice; that can't be good for their employer or whoever hired them. Both are probably furious."

Gene added, "That could mean the hit's still on; you, Grey, even Katelyn could still be in danger."

Whit replied, "I have to chew on this for a while." After maybe twenty seconds Whit continued. "I'm probably fairly safe while I'm in here. I just can't see how Katelyn's a target; she just happened to show up right before Grey and I left for the cabin. If I had to guess, Greyson and I are the targets. Can you keep tabs on Grey for a while, at least while I'm in here? He's not the most...situationally aware guy."

"Sure; I'll tell your dad what we discussed, too. The sheriff's office has more resources than DFG."

"I'll be out of here today, I hope...a few days at the latest; let's stay in touch."

"Sounds good. Rest up; if I hear anything new, I'll let you know."

As Gene headed for the door, Whit said, "Thanks, Gene. You're swiftly becoming my favorite government slug...after my dad, of course."

At the door, Gene turned back to Whit and said, "Jesus, Whittingham, do you ever give your smartass brain cells a rest?" He let the door close before Whit could answer.

Whit rested back against the raised bed and let his mind wander. *If the assassins are gone or dead, that means we're safe...at least for now. But what if they're still here? What does that mean? Well...either they're in hiding, want to finish the job, or both. I'm thinking they're in big trouble, so they can't go home. The only way to save their skin and maintain some semblance of a reputation means finishing the contract. Okay; but where the hell do two out-of-towners go...one being black...and not be seen? Hmm; limited choices...has to be some place they know or feel comfortable, with no human contact. They can't live out of their car for very long without being noticed. They have to eat, and I have a hunch they're not the live-off-the-land types.*

Chapter Fifty-three
Good Guess, Bad Outcome

Donnie only had to raise his head slightly as he already sat in a prone position. The barrel of his camo-patterned 20-gauge Benelli rested in the forked branch of a skinny, but stout, western redbud. Donnie finally felt comfortable in a sniper hide of his choosing...sun at his back, wind drifting toward him, and camouflaged to the tens. Donnie lay prone sixty feet from the gate; twenty yards, the perfect distance for the buckshot to spread a nice pattern to send Whittingham to where he deserved to go. Unfortunately, and ultimately, the hit may not make any difference. Donnie and Lamar were, in fact, in a world of shit. By the time Donnie called Johnny Big Nose and tried to explain what had transpired, Stephen Sliger had already spoken to the underworld boss. Whatever distorted version Lance told his father went straight to Johnny. As Donnie suspected, the truth didn't matter...probably never did. The fact— or at least their strong suspicion—that Lamar and he were supposed to end up as frittered scapegoats inside the burned-out SUV meant nothing. Johnny guaranteed the success of the hit. You don't turn Johnny Big Nose's words into a meaningless, empty lie...and live. Both hitmen were late for a dirt nap. Johnny ordered them back to Chicago and added, if they tried to run, they'd be very sorry.

Before Donnie called Johnny, he and Lamar drove far away from where the copter had returned them to their rental truck. In reality, it probably wouldn't have made any difference anyway; but they should have called Johnny immediately.

Sitting in their rental pickup, the two marked men tried to make a game plan. Could they talk their way out of a shattered knee and, eventually, a bullet through the eye back in Chicago? They figured their chances of survival hovered just below zero. That meant a new...stay alive...strategy. Maybe they could get out of the country and start new lives. But doing what? Sooner or later Johnny Big Nose would sniff them out. Before long they'd be found, beat to hell, and shoved in the hold of a plane or trunk of a car for a one-way trip back to Chicago.

Lamar said, "Hey, they may not find us if we go legit; you know, get real jobs."

After a brief pause, they both busted out laughing. They laughed hard enough to put tears in their eyes.

"Legit! Jesus, Lamar; that was a good one."

Then Lamar snapped his fingers and suggested, "Let's finish the contract on our own...whack those two country hicks. If we kill those two lucky sons-of-bitches—like we know how to do—maybe then we can go back home, face the music, and maybe...just maybe, live."

Donnie wrinkled his brow and said solemnly, "Yeah, lots of maybes; and what if Johnny knew or authorized our getting burned to a crisp in that SUV? Maybe he signed off on it because we screwed up the first hit. It kind of fits the Johnny I know."

Donnie and Lamar weighed the pros and cons of every conjured-up scenario. They finally settled on the best in a batch of bad choices. Their decision left them off the grid and hiding in plain sight, so to speak. They bought forty dollars' worth of junk food and water late at night from vending machines, then returned to the scene of their crime. They knew sooner or later Benjamin Whittingham would return to his cabin, maybe even with the Milner guy. Leaving their truck well hidden, the two men hiked back to the cabin and watched for five days from about a half-mile away. Finally, the cops, detectives and crime scene investigators stopped coming. Even though their meager supplies were gone, they waited another day. Starving, they moved down to the well-stocked cabin. To their surprise, they found a small root cellar out back packed with quarts and quarts of canned fruit and vegetables. The kitchen shelves contained dry goods and can food, plus beer and whiskey. They couldn't risk a fire; but cold canned soup, pork and beans, and tons of fruit and vegetables sure as hell beat nothing. Plus, cold showers and washed clothes made them feel nearly human again.

From early morning to late evening they hid near the infamous gate. Lamar took up the scout position...listening, watching, waiting. Donnie stayed in his well-concealed hide, doing the same. After three days, they decided their plan sucked. Waiting all day, then taking turns on guard duty at the cabin at night wore them down. With no heat they became sullen and depressed. Soon they needed to try something different. Just like any predator in nature, starvation, desperation, or both eventually forced all hunters to take risks…risks that could turn the hunter into the hunted. They decided to give it two more days. Then what; they had no clue. But the next morning Lady Luck, in the form of Whit's old pickup, changed everything.

In an excited voice, Lamar whispered into his mic, "Donnie; he's here!"

"I hear the pickup. Is he alone?"

"Yep; driving really slowly like he's…suspicious."

"Copy; keep me posted."

Whit's pickup eventually appeared around the bend in the road just east of the gate. Rolling up to within twenty-five feet of the barrier, Whit kicked the tranny into neutral, stepped on the parking brake, and waited.

Lamar whispered into the mic, "Why is he just sitting there in his truck?"

Donnie did not respond. He wished his less-experienced partner would keep his mouth shut and just stick to relevant information.

Whit's pickup—with a new windshield and back window—idled loudly. Sporting dark sunglasses for his still sensitive right eye, Whit felt edgy as hell. Absentmindedly, he rubbed one of the lingering itchy scabs on his cheek. Whit looked in every direction; he felt like eyes were following his every move. You get that feeling often when working alone in the woods; it's good to trust your instincts. Many times, while backtracking at the end of the day following the same game trail to return to his pickup, Whit discovered mountain lion or bobcat tracks right on top of his own. Curious by nature and almost always on the hunt, cats test the wariness of all who enter their realm. How many times, when Whit felt this exact same edginess, had big cats been watching him? Meat eaters balance risk versus reward all the time. Warden Perkins once told Whit, cats can command two-thirds of their muscle mass at one time, about twice that of a fit athlete. A one-hundred-fifty-pound mountain lion can attack with the power of a three-hundred-pound Olympian. Throw in a surprise attack with long, curved razor-sharp claws and incisors with massive crushing power and you enter into a very one-sided encounter. But Whit's concerns, at the moment, were two-legged killers.

Whit thought to himself, *hired murderers ultimately possessed the same basic instincts and traits as any predator. They stalk their prey with the same cunning, zeal, and cold indifference. Most hapless prey never know they're on the menu until it is too late. The only clear distinction is that to the predator, it's food and survival. To the assassin, it's money, maybe prestige or just sick demonic pleasure. Either way, you're dead. Is that why I feel stuck out in the open like bait?*

Whit shook his head slightly. *Focus, damn it.* Whit looked around more cautious than ever. In the two days since leaving the hospital he had not returned to his cabin. Whit wished he had his dad's BAR, but a small spring holding the safety in place broke when it fell out of his truck. Finding the spring for the WWII vintage rifle turned out to be a bigger problem; Whit still didn't have the gun. Whit did have his 1911 Colt .45 automatic, Remington Model 700 rifle and his Browning Auto-5, 20-gauge shotgun. His thoughts turned back to the investigation. Though investigators found the burned-out SUV in the Lost Hill Diggings and believed it belonged to the hitmen, they gleaned no evidence from the heavily charred metal carcass. Obviously, the perps used an accelerant as an added precaution to ensure that zero traces of hair, fingerprints, or any other evidence survived. Investigators did locate two parallel depressions in the gravel revealing that whoever used the SUV exited via a helicopter. All of the follow-up investigation on the helicopter, or any trace of a helicopter in the area that day, traveled down the same dead-end road. With not a speck of information, clues, or leads, the investigation waned.

Even the two "persons of interest" who piqued the bloodhound in Warden Gene Perkins at the California border turned out to be a dry hole. Whit remained convinced they were the assassins; but he, like Gene, lacked proof. If they were the assassins, are they dead, did they split, or are they still around somewhere lying low, waiting for another try? *I say they're here.*

Whit shook his head again, trying to stop the pointless rambling going on between his ears. *Stop daydreaming. The killers are still out here somewhere close; I don't know it…I feel it. Stay alert and stick with your instincts.*

Whit exited the pickup with his .45.

Lamar said, "He's packing, and I think he's wearing Kevlar; his jacket looks too puffy."

Almost inaudibly, Donnie replied, "Copy."

Standing next to his fender, Whit yelled, "I know you're out here, Dickheads."

"He's on to us, Donnie. He's close enough; take the shot."

Donnie watched his prey's mannerisms. Whit seemed too relaxed to know killers were present, watching, poised to strike. Whit looked more questioning than confident.

Donnie decided to wait. "He's just fishing; I'm on hold."

Whit tried again. "I figure you're here because you're dead meat if you go back to your employer. Am I right, Dickheads?" Another long period of silence, broken only by the rhythmic thump, thump, thump of a Pileated woodpecker hammering his beak into a hard, dead tree.

"I just might be your only lifeline, Dickheads; your choice." More silence. "You want to live...talk to me."

"What's that cracker saying, Donnie?"

Donnie watched Whit so intently he didn't respond. Finally, Whit walked over to the open door and tossed the .45 on the front seat. He turned and made three steps toward the gate then stopped. He moved back to the open door, reached into the idling pickup, grabbed the .45 then turned toward the gate.

Donnie said to himself, *Clever, asshole; you're a smart son of a bitch, I'll give you that.* Donnie imperceptibly followed Whit with the barrel of the shotgun. Whit took his time getting to his gate. About eight feet from the locking post, he stopped and looked around one last time. He yelled, "If you kill me, you might as well kill yourselves."

Hearing and seeing nothing, Whit finally moved up to the gate. Putting the automatic on top of the gate post, he bent over and spun the tumblers on the combination lock. Pulling off the lock, Whit stood up, retrieved his pistol and lifted out the gate pin. Whit cocked his head slightly then slowly turned around. Walking to the middle of the road, Whit scanned the surrounding forest slowly. When Whit's gaze turned Donnie's way and stopped, he felt instant panic. From around seventy feet away, Donnie pulled the trigger. Whit actually saw the flash and felt the impact an instant before the loud bang. The round, fired at a slightly uphill angle, caught Whit in the upper right side of his chest. The impact completely spun him around and flung him backwards. Whit felt incredible pain, then the side of his head slammed against the gate cross arm with a loud bong. All consciousness ceased. He crumpled in a heap, like a sack of potatoes.

"Damn," Lamar said. "That was cool."

Standing up and walking toward the prostrate body, Donnie said into the mic, "Lamar, get your ass down here. He's turning the place into a major crime scene; we have to do something about all this blood."

"What do you expect when you shoot a guy that close with double 00 buck?"

Ignoring Lamar's remark, Donnie said, "I'll open the gate. You bring up his pickup. We'll throw him in the back and take him down to the cabin. See if he has a shovel in the bed."

"On my way."

Donnie picked up the lock, confirmed the combination remained the same, then pushed open the gate. He flipped Whit over on his stomach just far enough, so Lamar could drive through. Lamar pulled the pickup forward and parked just past the gate. Reaching into the bed of the truck, he grabbed the shovel. While walking past the back of the truck, he dropped the tailgate. Tossing the shovel to the ground with a loud clang, Lamar bent down to grab Whit's shoulders to drag him to the bed of the truck. He suddenly dropped Whit and jumped back. "Shit! What the…he's still alive!"

In one smooth motion, Lamar reached across his chest and yanked out his .45. He pulled the hammer back and pointed the gun at Whit's body. Stepping forward Lamar inched up to Whit's shoulders and pointed the barrel at the top of Whit's head.

"Freeze, Lamar!" Donnie yelled in a stern voice.

Still bent forward, Lamar looked up at Donnie and saw the shotgun pointed at his head. Staring at the angry end of the scatter gun, Lamar froze. Then, with faltering bravado, Lamar asked, "What the hell, Donnie?"

"Change of plans. The next round is double 00 buck. I suggest you toss the gun."

Lamar dropped the automatic beside Whit's head then asked, "I'm listening, partner; you figure something different than what we discussed, like maybe self-preservation?"

They stared at each other for a good five seconds. Finally, Donnie dropped the barrel and said, "Jesus, Lamar; you gave me no choice. You were a split second away from killing him."

"Damn it, Donnie, I thought that was the plan."

"It was, but now I'm thinking…"

"Thinking what?"

"Look, this poor sap and the two of us are in the same boat. We're all working in the dark here. He's been set up and we've been set up…used. When he said he could be our only lifeline, well, it hit me. This guy didn't just come here; he showed up looking for us. Just like you and me, he wants answers and maybe a way out. When he leaned in and tossed his .45 back in his pickup then walked back to retrieve it, I had time to switch out the buckshot for a slug. I was betting on the Kevlar vest.

"Yeah, why the slug?"

"A slug can't penetrate Kevlar; just kick him like a mule. I probably broke a rib or two. But the spread of the buckshot would have hit his neck, arms and shoulders. I wanted to stop him, not see through him. I'm hoping I didn't puncture a lung."

"I still don't get it."

"We got nothing to lose, Lamar; we can still cap his ass, right? But, think about it; with this guy still alive, we could have more than one option. I just wasn't planning on his head banging into the gate. Look at all that blood. We don't stop that bleeding…all this won't make any difference."

"Donnie, I'm not comfortable with—"

"Lamar, aren't you tired of being played, and curious to hear what he has to say?" When Lamar just shrugged, Donnie said, "Well, I am."

Pointing the shotgun at Lamar's pistol, Donnie said, "Pick up your gun and drive this guy back to the cabin. See what you can do for him and make sure I didn't collapse a lung. I'll clean up the blood and walk."

"How do I check his lungs?"

"Watch his jugulars; if they start distending, one of his lungs has collapsed."

"How do you know all this shit, Donnie?"

"Because it was my job. Often Johnny didn't want his work force whacked, just ruffed up a bit. Lots of these shitheads just needed to be taught a lesson, put in their place, reminded to keep their mouths shut. I used to be called in to work over lots of guys. I've seen plenty of busted ribs and punctured lungs."

Reaching down and picking up his gun, Lamar said, "For a second there I thought you figured a way out of this that didn't include me…at least me not breathing."

"Lamar, right now and for our foreseeable future, you and I, we got no one else but each other; it's poisonous to think otherwise. Got it?"

Lamar put his gun in his shoulder sling and said, "Yeah, I got it. Hey, grab his legs and help me put this dude in the pickup; he must weigh over two hundred pounds."

Before Donnie returned to the cabin, Lamar had the now conscious Whit tied, sitting up, on the twin bed in the back bedroom. Whit's hands and legs were tied independently to the metal frame holding the box springs. Lamar had cut away chunks of matted bloody hair from the side of Whit's head. The impact of the shotgun blast hit Whit in a glancing blow, but still punched him hard. The surprise and shock of being shot left Whit's mind blank, blocking any memory of what occurred. Though now he knew he'd been shot. Now fully awake, Whit processed his predicament through one righteous headache. Every time he sucked in air deeper than a shallow breath, he had to close his eyes. The black guy never said a word while fixing Whit's split temple. Whit was now sporting what looked like a turban. Twice he asked the black guy, "Hey, Dickhead, did you hit me?"

The guy just ignored Whit and asked, "You want some water?"

Whit shook his head as if to say no, and immediately regretted it. Wincing, Whit said, "On second thought, please…Dickhead."

Bringing back a glass of water and lifting it to Whit's lips, Lamar said, "You got balls, asshole, I'll give you that."

"Why did you hit me?"

Looking perplexed, Lamar said, "I didn't; you hit the gate with your head, after Donnie shot you." Lamar immediately looked at Whit who was smiling.

Whit said, "Well, I at least have one Dickhead's name."

Shit. Trying to recover from yet another rookie mistake, Lamar said, "Like it will do you any good."

Lamar heard three loud pounds at the door, then, "Coming in."

Donnie entered the cabin, but before closing the door he habitually scanned out front and to the sides of the cabin. He immediately walked to the back-bedroom door and stood in the frame.

Before he could ask Lamar how their captive faired, Whit said, with as good a smirk as he could muster, "Hey, Dickhead; or should I say Donnie?"

Donnie remained facing Whit, but his eyes turned and glared at Lamar. Lamar returned a sheepish look and a nearly imperceptible shrug. Still staring at Lamar, Donnie finally said, "Like it will do you any good."

"Hell, you guys sound like parrots or two Dickheads in a pod; Warden Perkins was right." Whit was rewarded by both killers quickly glancing at each other. *Whoa, that hit a nerve.*

They both looked back at Whit until Donnie cleared his throat. Lamar saw Donnie use two fingers to gesture for Lamar to follow him out of the bedroom.

As the door closed, Whit added, "Have a nice chat. I'll see you two Dickheads later." Whit turned his head sideways to a slightly more comfortable position and closed his eyes. *Okay, Whittingham, time to think and stop agitating these assholes. That Warden Perkins shot was a lucky guess and it hit home; they know, or at least think, I know something. Use it.* As he tried to concentrate, Katelyn entered his thoughts. *Kate, what if I never see you again? What if they go after you?* Whit stopped himself. *Kate, Katelyn, you have to get out of my head; go away for a while, please. I need to think, concentrate. I'll never come back to you if I don't outfox these scumbags.* Shaking his head, as he always did to clear his mind, he winced and again regretted the movement. In between the painful breathing and searing throbs brought on with every heartbeat, Whit finally cleared his mind and listened.

In the other room, speaking in a low tone, Donnie said, "Lamar?"

"I know, I know; I did it again. That asshole got me talking, and your name slipped out. I'm sorry, Donnie. Maybe you should have shot me when you had the chance."

"Tempting, Lamar; very tempting," Donnie said straight-faced. Seeing Lamar's concerned face, Donnie slapped him on the shoulder to show he was kidding. "Did you bring up Warden Perkins?"

"No, not a word; I don't know how he knows about the fish cop."

While looking down at nothing in particular, Donnie held his index finger on his nose and his thumb under his chin. After some thought, Donnie continued. "Look, Lamar, it probably doesn't matter anyway; we're dead men. But, Jesus, try to watch what you say."

Lamar just nodded, so Donnie added, "This guy is smart, dangerously smart. We need to find out what he knows, but for Christ's sake, let me do the talking. We don't give up shit until we get information we can use, agreed?"

"Sure, Donnie, but what if he don't know nothing?"

From the other room, they heard, "Doesn't know anything. Jesus, Lamar...you moron."

Looking at each other, they both mouthed, *Shit!* Finally, Donnie rolled his eyes and waved Lamar to follow, and they reentered the bedroom.

Before Donnie could speak, Whit said, "Wood walls, wood floors, great acoustics for listening to dumbshit city tough guys trying to figure out how to stay alive. I was right out at the gate." Looking at each one and addressing them by name, Whit continued. "Donnie, Lamar, you guys are walking dead, am I right?"

"Look, smart guy—"

"No, you two geniuses look and listen. Someone's been dealing you guys and me aces and eights. So, here's how it plays. I cooperate with you...I'm dead. I don't cooperate with you...I'm dead. I have no leverage, unless...unless I can keep you two alive. You two Einsteins are in the same boat. You don't cooperate with me...you're dead; you do cooperate with me, you're dead... unless, maybe, just maybe, you keep me alive. No other options for either of us; we work together to keep breathing. That's the deal. Take it or leave it."

Neither killer spoke.

"Time to make an unholy alliance with one of the guys you tried to kill. You two Dickheads don't actually look that stupid. If you want a future, untie me so I can lie down and get some rest. I can't think straight with this splitting headache and dent in my chest." Glaring at Donnie, Whit continued. "I think you cracked at least one of my ribs, Dickhead. Give me some aspirins and about four hours. Come get me if I'm still asleep. We'll sit at the table like long lost pals and try to figure out how we can all get out of this mess. Deal?"

After a long pause, Donnie looked at Lamar, shrugged and said, "You heard our new...partner; get him some aspirin."

Lamar exhaled loudly, shook his head, and walked off toward the bathroom.

Donnie walked over to Whit, bent down and looked at Whit with a flat expression and cold eyes. Whit had seen predators stare at little hapless victims that way right before...Whack! In a flash, Donnie backhanded Whit in the chest. Whit saw white and gave out an agonizing groan as his chest screamed. He was forced to close his eyes hard while attempting not to move. He took short rapid breaths, doing his best not to expand his chest.

He heard Donnie say in an even tone, "I broke my nose once, and two days later got punched right on the snout. Goddamn that hurt but I'm guessing your chest hurts worse." While untying Whit, he added, "Some good advice, partner...stop calling us dickheads."

After being cut loose, Whit tried to gingerly scoot down the bed. With his eyes still closed, through gritted teeth, Whit managed to utter, "Deal...partner."

After delivering the aspirins, Lamar walked back into the main cabin area. Lamar whispered to Donnie, "He looks like shit. What happened when I left? I heard him yelp."

Donnie bugged out his eyes and shrugged. "I just asked him to stop calling us dickheads."

Lamar smiled. "I see; very persuasive." Returning to a serious tone, he continued. "I don't trust that guy. Who in hell in their right mind would dare talk to us like that? I think he's crazy. And how in the hell did he know we were here? And how did he hear us from the other room?"

Whispering back, Donnie said, "I can't figure him out either." With a hint of admiration, he added, "But, the guy's got coconut-sized balls. He risked his life on a hunch that we were here and wouldn't kill him. He's convinced we're all dead if we don't join forces." Looking at Lamar's despair, Donnie added, "This is unchartered territory for me too, buddy. Look, as long as we have a new partner, one of us always stays awake."

"Damn straight."

Chapter Fifty-four
Beer, Sex, Talk

Sweating profusely, Grey felt Veronica's tremors wane and her heavy breathing subside. He peeled her damp blonde hair away from his face, then gently rolled her to his left. He needed distance between their overheated, dripping bodies. She complied; but as soon as he pulled out of her, she grabbed his arm and stuffed his forearm between her legs and squeezed it up tight against her crotch. Grey thought, *Holy crap, there's no stop button on this...this...human masturbating unit.* Realizing what he'd just thought, he added, *Jesus, V's right; I am a whiner. What guy complains about too much sex, especially V sex?*

His mind quickly shifted to what Veronica revealed soon after she arrived. She'd barged in through his kitchen door, with her .45 held straight down on her right side. Seeing Grey drinking a beer at the kitchen table she said, "Hey, barkeep, this thirsty hardworking girl could sure use one of those."

Getting up and heading for the refrigerator Grey said, "Hey, V, good timing; just got in." Pointing toward her automatic he added, "Expecting trouble?"

"No, but I wasn't expecting trouble the last time I met you here, either." She turned and locked the kitchen door, then flipped her head toward the hall and added, "Beer, sex, then I have something very important to tell you." Veronica's mannerisms exhibited an uncharacteristically upbeat mood. She slid her gun in her waistband behind her back and sauntered over to Grey.

Giving her a long hug and kiss, he handed her a local pilsner and remarked, "Beer, sex, talk...awesome foreplay, V."

Veronica drained half of the beer then looked up and around the room as if catching a faint voice. "Did I just hear an estrogen-laced male snivel?"

"What I meant to say was, why not sex first?"

With a slight nod and smile, Veronica replied, "That's bullshit, Milner, but nice recovery."

Grey continued. "But I have to warn you, I've been working in the garden all day and haven't taken a shower or brushed my teeth."

"I just drove that hog two hours after working out this afternoon; no shower, so I'm in the same boat. But, I can stand a…randy roll in the hay, if you can."

Grey smelled his arm pit and made a face. Then he tipped his head toward the hall and replied, "Lead the way, musty."

Veronica drained her beer then pulled her pants out away from her waist. She sniffed the air then wrinkled her nose. Walking past Grey she smacked him in the arm and said, "Your funeral."

Thirty minutes later, lying in…odiferous, saturated sheets, Grey thought, *Well, that definitely classifies as randy sex; technically, randy sex twice.* Grey also had to admit it was also erotic as hell, in a wild sort of way. Everyone's body emitted different scents, similar but different. Veronica's, Grey had to admit, didn't assault or offend his senses at all…quite the opposite. *What is it about this woman? Hell, poor saps like me have been pondering that question ever since Eve and the apple popped into the picture. Well, beer done, sex done…now maybe she'll tell me the good news.*

Looking over at the curled up little ball that was Veronica Sanchez, Grey whispered, "V?" After no response he tried again a little louder. "Veronica?"

Not moving a muscle, Veronica moaned, "Hmm?"

"You said after beer and sex you'd tell me something very important."

Straightening out a little from her fetal position but still not opening her eyes, she muttered through a yawn. "What I meant to say was beer, sex, sleep… then I'll tell you something very important."

"That was not the deal; besides, you chose sex twice, so you used up your sleepy time strapped in the saddle."

Smiling now Veronica said, "Yeah, yeah, I did." Jiggling her hips a little for emphasis she added, "That was a goooood choice, but I'm whipped; so, goodnight."

Knowing he had to keep her talking, Grey tried another tactic. "Why the blonde hair?"

Smiling again Veronica said, "I heard blondes have more fun." Jiggling her hips again, she added, "And you know what? They're right, goodnight."

"Veronica Sanchez, I'm going to keep talking until you tell me; so try as you want, sleep is out."

Pulling Grey's forearm out from between her legs, she flicked it back at Grey. Moaning, Veronica rolled onto her back. With her hands covering her closed eyes and pouty face she said, "The problem being, if I tell you there will be no sleeping."

"Ah, come on, V; now you have to tell me."

Veronica lay motionless for fifteen seconds with her eyes still closed. Finally, she pulled her hands away from her face and formed them into six shooters, then said, really fast, "I know who hired the hitmen that tried to kill us. There, goodnight."

Grey sprung forward, leaped, and spun toward Veronica. "Holy shit, V, holy shit; who is it? How did you find out? Is that why you dyed your hair? Do I know him? Is it a he?"

Veronica reached over, found Grey's face and pinched his lips together. "Shut up; someone's trying to sleep."

Grey pulled his lips free and started bouncing on the bed, "No, no, no... no, V, this is huge. I have to call Whit. I have to call Whit's dad, I—"

Veronica cut in. "Damn it, Milner. I told you this would happen." Her eyes open now, Veronica scolded, "Before you run off all half-cocked, think."

Grey looked at her confused, raised his hands and said, "What? I mean, pardon me?"

"Exactly. Now, what will be the first question Whit or the sheriff asks you?"

Tilting his head to one side, a little lightbulb popped on. Dejected, Grey answered, "How did I get this new information, right?"

"Bingo; and since I don't exist, what's your answer?"

Grey said, "I didn't think of that." He turned away just in case his face betrayed that fact that, unknown to Veronica, Whit and Sheriff Whittingham already knew about her and her involvement during the first hit attempt.

Veronica cut into his guilt. "I'm working on empty here. I've hit the wall. I need to shut down for a while, so get the hell out of here and let me sleep. If I'm not up in twenty, twenty-five minutes, wake me and we'll talk." Grey started to speak but Veronica barked, "Put a cork in it, Milner, and leave; goodnight."

Grey leaned over and kissed her right breast. As he pulled away he gently bit her nipple. She pulled his head up to hers and kissed him, then rolled over on her side. Grey whispered, "Sleep tight, beautiful."

Grey stared briefly at her lovely profile; she was smiling. He slid out of bed and smelled the air. *PU, I need a shower, and another beer...maybe not in that order.*

After almost exactly twenty-five minutes, Grey heard the shower running. When Veronica entered the kitchen wearing one of his t-shirts, she noticed Grey cooking dinner. While still drying her blonde hair, she said, "Damn, Milner; that smells good."

"Fry pan stew; easy and tasty."

"I'm sold. How do you make it?"

"Slice bacon into little bits and toss it in a hot skillet. Throw in cubed London broil or stew meat rolled in flour. Cook it a while then add chopped onions; fry everything hot and hard. Poor in water and stew it for a while with some salt and pepper. Add flour to thicken the liquid. Next, just pour it over hot mashed potatoes with a big pad of butter right in the middle. Simple, quick, and super bad for you, but also really good. I'll flash steam some asparagus, too."

Walking right up to Grey, Veronica squared up to him and stated, "You blew it back there in the bedroom, Poker Face. Whit and his dad know about me, don't they?"

Shit; no getting out of this now. "Damn it, V; Sheriff Whittingham smelled you in this very kitchen, the night of the hit; he knew I was with a woman. I never gave him your real name." *Shit...I don't even know if I know her real name.* "He's keeping you out of it and will as long as he can. Whit knows I have a, ah...mystery woman. It's hard to hide that kind of stuff from guys who have known you your whole life. But he doesn't pry or ask questions...not his style."

Pausing a little to soak in what Grey admitted, Veronica asked, "When were you going to tell me?"

"Never, because I didn't think the issue of who tried to kill us would ever pop up. Now that it has, now that you have a name, we need to talk to them... coordinate. This is huge. By the way, you haven't given me the name yet."

Veronica looked at Grey and held up her index finger as if to say, *Wait, and don't speak.* She moved over to the refrigerator, tossed the wet towel on the counter, and grabbed a beer. She then moved over to the edge of the sink and stared out of the window into the darkness. After a long drink, she put the beer down and put her hands on the counter. Veronica closed her eyes, lost in thought...calculating, measuring her exposure, adding up her options, working out scenarios and, of course, lining out an escape plan.

Grey interfered with Veronica's well-orchestrated life. She should cut all contact and split, but couldn't...or at least, she didn't want to. She put her hands to her temples. She made a little wince then slammed her hands down hard on the counter making her beer and Grey jump. The battle raged on in her head. *"Damn it, Chiquita,"* she could hear her handler, DJ, scold, *"you're breaking all the rules of survival; end it and leave...now!"* Veronica listened to her own response; *It's not just about Grey. I'm going to whack those hitmen. Those fucks tried to kill me and deserve to die. Sorry, DJ; on this one, it's my call...so bug out.*

Finally, Veronica's expression turned neutral again. She raised her head, grabbed her tipped-over beer and drank the dregs. Turning toward Grey, she said, "Steven Sliger; ring a bell?"

"Sliger, Steven Sliger; no, nothing."

"He's the CEO of Serpentine Solutions, basically a big environmental cleanup company based in Sacramento, plus some other earlier computer ventures. That's the guy who hired the hitmen. I'm sure he's the one who put the prison screws to Whit and tried to string up your Ned."

After a long pause Grey asked, "How did you find out?"

"Can't tell you."

"Did you hurt anyone?"

Veronica almost said, *Duh,* but caught herself. "No, of course not." Grey's expression made her add, "Well, physically, a little."

The seconds ticked off. Finally, Veronica angrily replied, "Okay, probably some psychological damage there, too. But the asshole was taking advantage of fragile, unstable, gullible women. He deserved much more, so don't get all white hat on me, Milner. I found the name of the guy pulling the strings, didn't I? Now get your head out of your ass and start focusing on what's important."

That seemed to snap Grey back to reality. Finally, he asked more to himself, "What did Whit, Ned and I ever do to him?"

"That, Mr. Milner, is the key question. You guys did something."

Grey just put his hands up shaking his head. "V, it's time to coordinate with Whit and his dad."

"Whit, yes; but no cops...or I'm out."

"V, Whit's dad could really—"

Veronica snapped, "No cops or I'm out, and you're on your own."

Grey didn't want Veronica to just walk out of his kitchen door and his life for good. He wasn't sure if it was his feelings for Veronica or being wary of dealing with this Sliger dude without her that made him say, "Okay, V, okay; just Whit, no cops."

"Fine, call your buddy; I want to get this started so I...I mean, we, can finish this."

Grey said, "Tell you what, let's eat first. It's ready and we're starving. I'll call Whit after."

Softening a little, Veronica said, "You're right. I'm still tired, dehydrated and hungry." *Not a good way to be, mentally, when planning to kill and not get caught or get killed in the process.*

Chapter Fifty-five
The Enemy of My Enemy

Four hours later, even with a splitting headache and painful chest that hurt like hell, Whit managed to get out of bed. He hadn't really slept and felt worse than ever. Whit said to the assassin sitting in his bedroom watching, "I need coffee."

Lamar replied, "So?"

"So, you or Donnie start the fire; I'll take mine with at least another four aspirin. After I take a leak, I'll head into the kitchen, so we can chat."

Lamar stood up and replied, "Fine. We turned this place upside down for every gun or potential weapon. Unless you can kill us with a butter knife, don't waste your time."

Whit mimicked Lamar, "Fine."

Eventually shuffling his way to the kitchen table, Whit sat across from his two new allies of convenience. *The enemy of my enemy is my friend.*

Whit drank coffee while slowly rubbing his forehead. He pointed at Donnie. "Thanks for the love tap, made sleeping so much easier. My dad was right; the really dangerous ones don't rattle before they strike."

Gazing at Whit from across the thick sugar pine plank table, Donnie just smirked. Whit asked, "A little history, for starters, it was you two who tried to kill Greyson and the woman at his house, right?"

Looking quickly at each other, finally Donnie said, "Does it matter?"

"Look, Donnie; that was a test and you failed. If we don't trust each other from now forward, we're dead. What we tell each other, at this point, really does matter. Answering a question with a question won't cut it."

"Why don't you start? What did you do to get guys like us hired to take you out?"

"That I can't answer. I don't know." Whit saw the two killers obviously didn't believe him. "Look, if you two were initially hired to kill Grey, that's a connection...a clue. So, did you two go after Grey?"

Lamar sat back tightlipped and with his arms crossed, deferred to Donnie. Donnie finally said, "Yeah that was us."

"And here at the cabin, was that primarily for Grey or both of us?"

"Two hits; we didn't know about the woman."

"But you would have killed her, too?"

Donnie just shrugged, but could tell Whit didn't take that well, so he added, "Fortunately, as it turned out, it didn't get that far."

Not for lack of trying, dickhead. Sitting at his kitchen table drinking coffee and casually chatting with two professional killers was beyond bizarre. Whit had to draw on all his strength to focus on the big picture when he just wanted to get the drop on these two. He knew they were thinking similar thoughts. The delicate trick each side had to play was to remain too valuable to each other to be eliminated.

Feeling the need to explain further, Donnie said, "Look, Whittingham, we don't go after innocent people. Everyone we whack did something bad. We just figured you guys ripped off or screwed with the wrong people."

Whit needed to change the subject to avoid thinking about Katelyn and how indifferent they felt about putting a bullet in her head. He asked, "Why set up behind the cabin; another case of bad intel?"

"No, more like stupidity...because of our handler. He thought you would...sense us somehow if we set up on the other side of the parking lot instead of behind your cabin. Both hits were set up by this moron, not our choice, and definitely out of our control."

Lance or this Mr. Smith thinks he knows me pretty well, but how? Dropping that thought for the moment, Whit asked, "Is that common, to have an overseer?"

"No, never."

"Why this time?"

After a long pause, Lamar finally nodded his head slightly at Donnie as if to say, *What the hell, go ahead and tell him.*

Donnie continued. "We were subbed out. The guy that hired us wanted his man running the hit...the hits. Why, we don't know; we were just told by our boss to do it."

"So, who asked your boss for your services?"

"We don't know that either, but apparently he's rich." Both Donnie and Lamar did not let on that the guy became rich by suppling some fancy comuter program to Johnny Big Nose. Donnie already felt he'd given up more han Whit revealed.

Whit thought, *Some rich guy? Who the hell do we know who's rich?* "Who's he rich guy's henchman trying to run the hits?"

"Some half-assed creep named Lance, but we don't think that's his real ame."

Same name Allyson gave me; at least that checks out. Whit continued. "Okay, we're getting nowhere fast." He lifted his cup signaling for more coffee. Lamar eaned back, reached to the stove and grabbed the pot. Whit asked flatly, "So, who's your boss?"

That did it; all easiness suddenly ended. Donnie said sternly, "Ain't hapening, sport. At this point, it's better for all of us that you don't know."

"What you're telling me is when your boss cleans up a mess, he throws a wide loop...that it?"

"Yeah. If you catch my drift...this thing gets any bigger, it's going to get very, very messy. To cover his tracks, anyone even remotely close to you could be a potential target.

Nodding slowly, Whit felt stymied; he needed names. He had hoped these two were the conduit to Mr. Smith, but it wasn't so. Their boss probably purposely left them in the dark about who hired them. "You ever come up empty on a hit before?"

Caught a little off guard, Donnie said, "No, never; why do you ask?"

"Curious; just wondering how much luck Milner and I have already used up."

"A shit load, Whittingham. If you hadn't shot your mouth off at the gate, I wouldn't have switched the buckshot for the slug and just would have shot you in the face and we wouldn't be talking now. By the way, how did you know we were out here?"

Gingerly touching his damaged chest with his fingertips, Whit said, "I didn't. I just had a hunch; I live by them. Either you really did do a Houdini, were dead, or were lying low. I figured you couldn't go home and decided to go silent. But, where to hide; you only knew one secluded place—my cabin. So, when I could see to drive—no thanks to you—and after fixing my truck— no thanks to you—I came out here." Whit let that all sink in, then said, "I also figured you decided if you finished what you started, maybe you could get home…and live."

"Hunch or not, I could have just dropped you."

"Life is full of…calculated risks. I needed answers."

"Hey, Whittingham, back to my point…we don't get the call to go after angels; you must have done something to somebody."

Whit just turned up his hands and gingerly shrugged.

Donnie shook his head. "Man, this whole operation never added up. We've always been told what our targets did to get fingered. With you guys…nothing."

Nobody spoke. Finally, Donnie said, "Now I want the guy who set us all up, but—"

"Me too, Donnie." After looking at both of them, Whit added, "Look you two, I won't sugarcoat it; if I don't find and take out Lance's boss, I'm toast. I just know he's locked on and, for whatever reason, won't stop. But that's just me; you two have it even worse. You have no quarter; Lance, his boss, your boss, and the cops are all targeting you. I can move around; you can't. You know what that means?" Opening both his hands Whit smirked. "Better take good care of me; you're looking at the only guy who has a chance to save your sorry asses."

Donnie responded in a similar fashion, "That's why I just dented your chest." In a sincerer tone, Donnie added, "Since we're stuck taking good care of each other, one more problem, Whittingham, and you're not going to like it. You have to start taking deep breaths; if you don't, you could get pneumonia."

Trying one and gasping, Whit wheezed, "You're all heart…partner."

Chapter Fifty-six
Don't Answer That

At Whit's cabin, the phone rang. Donnie and Lamar stood up and said at the same time, "Don't answer that."

Whit said, "People know I'm here."

Donnie replied, "I'm warning you, do not answer."

"What the hell do you think I'll say? 'Hi, hey, guess what? I'm having coffee with the killers, come meet them, they're swell fellas.'"

"You must have told someone your theory that Lamar and I may be here. Maybe they're checking in. You could use a code word or phrase to rat us out."

Looking guilty, Whit replied, "Darn, you got me; 'the illerkays are erehay' was right on the tip of my tongue." When Donnie and Lamar didn't find Whit's humor very funny, he added, "Jesus, think about it, Donnie. If I rat you out, you'll shoot me; game over for everyone. That's not our agreement...partner."

Whit rose slowly and started walking toward the phone. Lamar slid his hand into his windbreaker, but Donnie held up his hand.

Lamar said, "I don't know Donnie. Do we trust him?"

Exhaling loudly, Donnie said, "I'm thinking, we've got no choice."

Whit picked up the receiver. "Whit here."

After a long pause, Whit heard, "Hi, Whit."

Whit knew not to reveal Allyson's identity or even her gender, so he replied, "Hey, good to hear your voice; you okay?"

"Actually, yes, though I'm still pretty tired. The surgery went well, or as best as could be expected. My prostate and much of my urethra are gone, plus a healthy amount of muscle and nerves. I have just enough urethra left to avoid a urostomy…so I won't be peeing into a bag."

"I'm a novice in this area; what's the bottom line?"

"Okay; I'm stuck with a catheter up my weezer for a little longer. The sutures need to heal without scar tissue decreasing the diameter of my urethra. Once that's done, I'm out of here. Radiation starts in a few weeks to target the remaining cancer they couldn't surgically treat. I'm set up to do that near Sacramento. No chemo at this point. Are you following me so far, neophyte?"

Pleased that some of Allyson's humor had returned, but still curious, Whit said, "I followed the gist of it; why no chemo?"

"I'll probably be too sick to function, and we have lots to do. We've delayed long enough. I can always go that route later."

"Well, that sounds positive…right?"

Allyson said soberly, "The doctors and staff are great, but pull no punches. They've given me some time; that's all they promise. What's going on at your end?"

Gingerly touching his chest, while looking at Donnie, Whit replied, "Oh, you've missed some, ah, significant escalation."

"Like what?"

Well, a couple of killer's damn near blew my head off and shot Grey through the shoulder. Later they shot me in the chest with a slug, and I fell backwards and split my head wide open. Now, as we speak, I'm sitting at my cabin drinking coffee with those super cool guys. Ignoring his mental review and Allyson's question, Whit asked, "Were you informed of any other operations going on simultaneously with your contract?"

"No; I only received my marching orders and dossiers on Ned and Grey. I figured out on my own, later, your incarceration being connected. Why?"

"Oh, as you know, with answers come more questions. When will you be able to meet?"

"Hopefully, I'm out in a couple of days. Because of my donation to the foundation, they're treating me like royalty. They are pulling my catheter today. When they're sure I can pee and don't have any infection or complications, I'm free. I may be somewhat incontinent and need pads but screw it. How about we meet in Cedar Creek, oh, say, in two days? I'll call if I need to reschedule."

"Okay, sounds good. We have much to do. Rest and heal; I'll meet you where we met last, how about noon or one."

"Okay, how about two?"

"Deal."

Whit put the phone down and Donnie asked, "Who the hell was that?"

Whit lied, "A client who has cancer."

Donnie didn't look convinced and said, "You aren't holding out on us, are you, partner?"

Before Whit could respond, the phone rang again.

Chapter Fifty-seven
Loose Ends

Tired of disappointments, Steven Sliger glared at his Inner Circle. No one spoke, but Jeff Bowman looked like he'd wet his pants. Andrea, the furthest away, could smell Jeff's body odor more than normal, and decided to start the meeting.

Looking up from her notes, she thought how difficult these last few weeks had been on her boss. He derived his power by out-thinking, out-smarting and staying one step ahead of his competition, the government, his enemies, the press…everyone. Of course, not playing fair gave him a huge advantage; but regardless, she greatly admired his string of successes. But now with this personal vendetta against his old friends, his calculating analytical mind became clouded with dangerously irrational and emotional interference. Their future, which once appeared as sturdy and as impenetrable as a castle, more and more felt like a house of cards. She had her escape plan with Sean Peterson, but for the moment she'd remain part of the team and would give her boss her best, until…?

In her standard manner, Andrea started, "It appears Dr. Zulov left his practice and bolted. Jeff accumulated many interesting tidbits to bring us to that conclusion."

Appearing fatigued, Sliger slowly turned to Jeff and asked, "What do you have?"

Jeff straightened up, pushed his glasses back up his nose, and read his notes very slow and deliberately. "Um, it appears Dr. Zulov visited the Bakersfield E.R. for a broken rib. Apparently, he fell down the stairs at his cabin. He cancelled all sessions for the following Monday."

Impatient to get to the point, Sliger said, "Yes, yes, Jeff; all good information, but get to the point." Sliger knew better than to prompt his computer genius too much.

Frazzled now, Jeff tried to read faster, and actually repeated his last sentence. "He cancelled all sessions for the following Monday. But, on Monday, he withdrew large amounts of cash from multiple accounts. Tuesday, he missed all of his scheduled appointments." Looking up at Sliger he pleaded, "That's all I have; can I go?"

Sliger flicked his hand signifying that Jeff was excused. Not waiting for Jeff to leave, Sliger asked, "Who's next?"

Lance spoke up. Even though it was Andrea's idea, he said, "We sent Moose down late Tuesday to Zulov's office. Moose scares the crap out of Zulov's secretary, so I knew she'd sing like a bird. She told Moose she had no clue of the doctor's whereabouts. She tried to call his house, but no one answered. Then she told Moose that on the Friday before, a new client—a woman—came into Zulov's office for the last session of the day. Something terrible happened and Zulov screamed for her to call the police."

Sitting up, Sliger said, "It's related; has to be. What do we know about this woman?"

Lance continued. "The name she gave was Ms. Teresa Morales. Dark hair and complexion, fortyish and very well built; kind of a biker type, too." In a mocking voice Lance added, "Andrea thinks she's Greyson Milner's girlfriend; I'm not so sure."

Ignoring Lance, Sliger turned to Andrea and asked, "How in the hell did she learn about Zulov? Who is this bitch of Milner's?"

"We have no clue, sir. She's a dead end. But for sure, she has no affiliation with Johnny Ramelli or anything to do with Chicago. My guess…she's a cop, bounty hunter, or private investigator."

Slumping back in his chair, Sliger glared at Lance. *We should have known more about her before we went after Milner. We pushed it too quickly. Those hitmen were right.*

Standing up, Sliger said, "We are shutting this operation down. Lock it up tight. Remove ourselves from everything operational; we're sitting on too many loose ends."

Lance asked, "How many loose ends can there be?"

Exasperated, Sliger stabbed a finger at Lance. "Listen, you, because they're mostly your fault. Take these down." Pointing toward the computer room door, Sliger added, "Because you're going in there and give the list to Jeff."

As expected, his stepson turned sour faced as Sliger held up his index finger. "One, find Allyson Chandler; two, find Zulov; three, find out everything you can about this Ms. Morales, and her employer; four, keep digging for any news on those two hitmen; and finally, step up our monitoring of Ned Penrose's recovery. Any relevant information comes straight to me; we'll need to act fast."

Waiting for Sliger to finish, Andrea offered, "There is one more issue, Steven."

Sliger turned her way and sniped, "Shit; what?"

"Jeff, in his haste to leave, forgot to tell you one more bit of news. Johnny Ramelli's, um, assistant—Tony Bassetti—contacted me and said he'd be arriving in California soon."

Annoyed, Sliger said, "Yes, Ramelli said Tony Bassetti would call when he arrived."

'Well, Jeff found out Bassetti's already here. He arrived a few days ago."

Sliger thought, *So, why didn't he call?* But to Andrea, he replied, "So, he came early."

Andrea tried to warn her boss, "He's been in Cedar Creek. It appears he didn't want us to know he's been snooping around; why, I don't know. But, maybe he's collecting information, without our…filter. Regardless, I think we should be very careful until we know his intentions."

Sliger said confidently, "That's bullshit; my partnership with Johnny remains as solid as ever. That's why he's sending Basetti, to help. We'll back out and let him take over. He's making sure Ramelli's two hitmen never surface and will analyze our Milner/Whittingham problem. If anyone can eliminate them cleanly, he can."

"I'd just like to caution you that—"

Sliger held up his hand and scolded, "Bassetti's the first good news you've passed on to me in quite some time. Don't spoil it."

On that harsh note, the meeting ended. Andrea stood up and replied, "Yes, sir." As she walked to the door to leave, she thought, *Dead men tell no tales… neither do dead women.*

Chapter Fifty-eight
Just Potential Victims

As the phone continued to ring again in Whit's cabin, Donnie asked, "Now what?"

In mock surprise, Whit said, "It's the FBI; I can tell by the ring." Both Donnie and Lamar didn't think much of Whit's joke, so Whit added, "How the hell should I know? Jesus, you two...lighten up."

After dialing the number to Whit's cabin and hearing it ring and ring, Grey kept saying, "Come on; pick up, pick up, pick up."

Veronica said, "Watch what you say; your phones could be tapped. I should have checked them again."

"Oh, ah, sure," Grey answered without thinking. Then, after registering what she'd said, turned to her and asked, "Do you really think so? I thought you checked the phones."

Veronica replied, "Jesus, Milner; you are one lucky son of a bitch to be alive. Someone tried to blast you into unrecognizable chunks of gigolo Jell-O, then sent a high-powered rifle round through the top of your shoulder. Now, here you stand, still not paranoid enough to take proper precautions."

"Well, when you put it that way."

Veronica almost said, *there is no other way to put it, dumb ass, not if you want to stay alive.* She decided to let it drop and replied, "And I did check your phones; they could tap the line, too. But it doesn't appear to matter; Whit's not there."

"You can never tell with Whit; he doesn't have an answering machine." *Come on, Whit; pick up, pick up.*

Donnie threw up his hands and in a resigned voice said to Whit, "Go ahead, partner, answer your phone."

Whit grabbed the receiver.

Grey heard the phone click and totally forgot Veronica's warning. He started talking before Whit could even say hello. "Whit, I have some incredible news! I know for a fact—"

"Not over the phone," Whit cut in. Whit could tell Grey had his phone on speaker.

Waving to catch Whit's attention, Donnie whispered, "Who is it?"

Whit pointed at Donnie, then slowly raised his left arm up and put his fingers together on his right shoulder. He flung them apart like an explosion. Donnie's slight nod and dour expression showed that he knew who held the phone at the other end.

Frustrated, Grey paused for a second. He also noted that Whit spoke much softer than his normal baritone voice. He continued. "Okay. But Whit, this information—"

"The last time we tried to meet at this cabin," Whit interrupted, "someone tipped off the killers that you and I were coming here and when. Eavesdropping, phone tapping, mind reading...who knows? Whoever hired the killers could have someone listening in on this conversation right now. If they are listening, I don't want them to know what we know about them."

"Oh, ah, right, right."

Whit asked, "You with your girlfriend?"

Surprised, Grey said, "Yes, as a matter of fact—"

"Good; stow it until you get here."

Grey asked, "I'm coming out there again?"

"Yep. And since, no doubt, your girlfriend dug up the information, bring her too...if she'll come."

After Veronica nodded, Grey replied, "She will. She agreed to meet with you, but not your dad or any other cops."

Looking at Donnie and Lamar to relieve their concern, Whit replied, "Deal; no cops."

Grey asked, "If someone's tapping my phone, won't those killers find out and come after us again?"

Whit replied, while looking again at his two new partners, "I know for a fact that you'll be able to walk right up to my front door without running into those assassins...guaranteed. Now, when can you show up, because we...all can't discuss anything further until you get here."

Grey said, "How about tomorrow, late morning? Oh, by the way; I'll need the combo to your gate."

"That timing works fine and, nice try, Milner. The gate will be open."

Grey thought, *damn it*, and then said, "You're an unforgiving heartless bastard, Whit."

Whit laughed, which caused him to wince and groan into the phone. He weakly replied, "I do try."

Grey asked, "Hey, you okay?"

Whit controlled his voice better and said, "Yeah, sure." Changing the subject, Whit said, "I'm running low on supplies. Can you bring about two weeks' worth of food? About half perishable and half canned. You pick; I'll pay you back."

Grey asked, "Sure; why so much?"

Lamar raised his hands up in a plate-sized circle and whispered, "Steaks."

Donnie quietly added, "Whiskey."

Whit told Grey, "I let my stores run down more than usual. Hey, buy half a dozen big ribeye steaks, and a couple of bottles of," Whit looked at Donnie, who mouthed, Bushmills. Whit said, "Bushmills."

"Will do; see you tomorrow."

"Deal."

As soon as Whit put the receiver down, Donnie said, "You're letting this get out of hand. The more that know we're here, the faster we get busted."

Whit needed to sit down. He picked up his cup and asked Lamar, "Can you grab me four more aspirin and more coffee, even if it's the dregs?"

Donnie said, "Coffee's a diuretic; probably not a good idea with that headache."

"Yeah, you're right; but I just feel like coffee. As for your concerns about who knows, so far it's only people directly involved." Looking at Donnie, he jabbed, "Just potential victims."

Lamar handed Whit four white pills and filled Whit's white porcelain cup to the brim, then said, "I don't see how this...meeting...helps Donnie and me; besides, potential victims tend to hold a grudge."

Whit took a sip of coffee, then dropped the aspirin into the black liquid. After Donnie and Lamar sat back down at the table, Whit said, "I'm here, aren't I, and you shot me. Look, you two; we need to pool our information. We need to draw Lance out and grab him around his scrawny little throat. He's the conduit to his boss."

Donnie and Lamar looked at each other but didn't speak. Whit waited then finally said, "What?"

Donnie said, "You still don't get it; you've already forgotten what I said. Anybody goes after Lance's boss; our employer will call for a massacre. The way we see it, our only option is for Lamar and I to try to disappear somehow with your help. Slim to zero chance of staying hid but there it is. You and your buddies go back to being country bumpkins; then, maybe it's over. Or maybe, even if we get to Lance and break his neck, it still may be over. But," Donnie held up his index finger for emphasis, "but, if we out Lance's boss in any fashion, there will be a bloodbath."

Trying to hide his anger, Whit said, "And what about my buddy Ned—he'll never be right! What about him?"

Donnie shrugged. "Casualty of war; life ain't fair." Donnie noted that did not sit well with Whit, so he added, "Look; like I said, the best you can hope for, the furthest we can go, would be taking out Lance. No further." Nodding at Lamar, who nodded back, Donnie finished with, "Lamar and I will help you that far."

Whit closed his eyes as his growing anger and rising blood pressure caused his head to throb timed to his heartbeats. Whit placed his elbows on the table, leaned forward, and rested his temple in his fingertips. He opened one eye and said, "If you two are so sure you can't somehow disappear and not get caught, I have another option."

The long pause that ensued divulged the other, long-shot, option weighing on Donnie and Lamar's minds.

Whit could guess, so he ended the awkward silence. "Yes…partners; you two could kill Grey, his girlfriend and me…then grovel back to your boss, hoping for redemption. Maybe, just maybe, he'd allow you to live." Whit pointed his index finger straight up, wiggled it and said, "Except…."

Lamar asked, "Except what?"

Whit said, "Except, I'm involved with another partner…partners."

Donnie and Lamar shared glances, then Donnie said, "The first phone call."

"Perhaps; and this individual already knows where to find Lance's employer." Whit watched Donnie and Lamar look at each other again, more surprised. "My other partner, for personal reasons, will not quit, whether I'm alive or not. So, Lance's boss will be exposed with or without your help." To put the final nail on the coffin, Whit added, "And if something happens to me, everything my other partner and I know, or surmise, goes to my dad, the sheriff. He'll take it to the Feds."

Looking defeated and resigned to absolutely no chance of survival now, Donnie couldn't hide his irritation and demanded, "Who's your other partner?"

Whit ignored Donnie and said, "Hell, we're all probably heading for a shallow grave or prison. Do we slither away and wait for others to choose our fate, or take our one chance? If we fail, at least we die trying...like men."

Neither Donnie nor Lamar spoke.

Whit continued. "Back to my survival option for you two. We take out Lance's boss; no cops...just us. With the information we gain, you two confront your boss straight on; make yourselves too valuable to kill."

Donnie threw his hands up and said, "How the hell do we do that?"

"Blackmail."

Donnie hit his chest and said incredulously, "I'm the guy who takes out blackmailers, snitches and cheats. I don't know of no one who ever blackmailed Johnny Big Nose and lived."

Whit thought, *Well, there's a breakthrough; at least I know who pays their checks.* "So, you're an expert on bad blackmailers. That means you know what doesn't work." When neither Donnie nor Lamar spoke, Whit said, "You want some good—"

"No!" Donnie shot back.

Lamar just shook his head and said to Donnie, "We're neck deep in it already, Donnie. Our other option no longer exists. Let's hear him out."

Whit took his cue. "Use the dirt we obtain on your boss to insure your continued ability to breathe. Each of you must find multiple attorneys and/or untraceable, trusted individuals to hold the incriminating evidence. How can your boss touch you? If something happens to either one of you, all your confidants send the information to the Feds. The way I see it, that's your only chance." Slowly standing up, Whit said, "You two want to talk this over in private?"

Lamar held up his hand to stop Whit. "Donnie...let's do it. At least it feels like a chance to me. You know we're dead men otherwise." Donnie just stared at the table. Lamar prodded, "Go ahead and tell him what Maria told you."

Donnie snapped his head toward Lamar, but Lamar's expression remained cogent, forceful, confident. Donnie looked at Whit and said, "You're right. If you'll excuse us, we do have some decisions to make...in private."

"I'm going to take a leak then head back to bed." As Whit shuffled slightly bent over toward the hallway, he tapped the knotty pine wall. "Remember… your voices carry."

Chapter Fifty-nine
It's Cool

"You are a wimp."

"I am not."

"Then why are we riding in this piece of shit? I should have taken my bike."

Grey and Veronica both knew why Grey chose to drive his company's old suburban to Whit's cabin. He didn't want to get the date machine—his sporty little Mustang—dirty.

Veronica, wearing tight black pants, a black tank top and cowboy boots, wanted to keep yanking Grey's chain. She needed him off guard and not thinking about their phone conversation the day before with Whit. She also wanted to mask her own emotions. Grey apparently missed the underlying information Whit passed to them. It registered loud and clear to Veronica. Whit told them he knew for a fact that she and Grey could walk right up to his front door without running into those assassins. Then, he had added, "We 'all' can't discuss anything further until you get here."

While Grey brooded, Veronica re-analyzed what she believed Whit divulged to them. Veronica knew Whit could never be forced to set them up for an ambush; he'd die first. And Whit sounded hurt, she assumed Whit had a run-in with the killers and that somehow, they'd agreed to some kind of truce. That's what she would have leveraged if cornered and in Whit's shoes. But, since she already knew the name of the guy who ordered the hits, she didn't need one damn snippet of intel from the two killers. In Veronica's mind, that gave her the advantage, an edge, a leg up...to exploit.

With her mind made up she turned less confrontationally toward Grey, much to his relief. "Let's take a walk sometime today and find a nice secluded spot."

Heading through Whit's open gate, Grey grinned. "That's a big 10-4, but first we need to tell Whit everything that you discovered and hear what he knows."

Grey turned serious and asked, "V, Whit made a pretty strange reference over the phone about those killers; he guaranteed we'd be safe. How the hell does he know? Do you think Whit knows they're dead or gone?"

Well, my little squeeze, you're close and not as slow as I thought. Veronica fibbed, "Maybe, Milner. Possibly, they slithered through the dragnet back to their boss with their tails between their legs. I'm betting they've been whacked."

Pulling up to the large parking area, Grey seemed relieved. "Well, that makes me feel better." But then he said, "But, why go back to your boss if you thought he'd kill you?"

Veronica stepped out of the suburban when it stopped and said, "Because some professionals are about as sharp as a plum. Forget it, Milner."

As they walked up to the porch, Whit opened the door and, while looking at Veronica, said, "We're all partners here, so everybody be cool."

Grey said, "What?"

Veronica asked, "Are they both here?"

Grey said, "What?" again.

Whit replied, "Yes, and we're on the same team now. We all need to share information against a common enemy; okay, Veronica?"

Grey finally saw the two men standing behind Whit's huge table, their chairs pushed back behind them. "Holy shit! I thought you said? Is that them?"

Veronica smiled as she walked past Whit. "It's cool."

Whit led them into the cabin where they stood across the table from Donnie and Lamar.

No one spoke until Whit lifted his hand toward the two killers and said, "Lamar, Donnie, this is Veronica and Grey." Still no one spoke, so Whit walked around to Grey and Veronica's chairs and pulled them out. "Everyone sit; we have lots to discuss."

Veronica looked across the table and asked politely, "Which one of you assholes can't handle a little bear spray?"

"Fuck off," Lamar shot back.

Veronica spread her arms and smiled back. "Just saying." *Now I know.*

Whit cut in. "Cut it out, Veronica. Knock off the taunting. Our common enemy isn't here. We're all the pawns in this chess game and need to work together."

Veronica just said, "Fine," as she moved in front of her chair. *She could tell both Donnie and Lamar were packing, and with her tight-fitting clothes, they assumed she was not.*

Knowing the most critical time to watch out for any revenge type justice occurred after the information exchange, Donnie and Lamar felt confident enough to lean forward and sit. Both kept their eyes on Veronica but lowered their gaze briefly as they scooted their chairs forward.

Grey and Veronica did the same. Just as the two killers took their eyes off of Veronica, she reached down to scoot her chair forward and lifted her right leg. She reached into her cowboy boot and grabbed a sweet little Beretta 9mm. Just as Donnie and Lamar straightened up in their chairs, she lifted the pistol, pointed it at Lamar, and squeezed the trigger twice. Bam! Bam!

Lamar leaped backwards falling like a rag doll. Veronica immediately turned the gun on Donnie. A millisecond before Veronica fired, Whit, still behind her, yanked her chair backwards. When she fired—Bam! Bam!—Donnie grabbed his neck and fell sideways.

Veronica's arms flew out sideways as she tried to regain her balance, but Whit tipped her and her chair over backwards. Whit grabbed her right wrist in his left hand and toppled on top of her on the floor. The quick movement and impact of hitting the floor caused Whit excruciating pain, but he kept a vice grip hold on Veronica's wrist.

Grey stood, stunned and immobile.

Veronica, now screaming like a banshee, thrashed around wildly. She made it nearly impossible for Whit to stay on top of her. She cussed, bit and head-butted at Whit while trying to squirm free. She yelled, "Get off me! Finish them!"

Through gritted teeth, Whit turned his head to Grey and ordered, "Get some duct tape…the closet, and start wrapping this psycho up; hurry, Grey!"

Grey backed away, then eventually turned and ran down the hall. He found and grabbed the duct tape on the top shelf and returned. Grey glanced over at the two men sprawled out on the opposite side of the table and froze. Lamar lay on his back, not moving…blood everywhere. Somehow Donnie managed to crawl over to his friend; his own neck oozing blood.

Whit yelled, "Grey, snap out of it!"

Grey slowly turned to Whit then charged to him. He started wrapping Veronica's legs together as she kicked wildly. Grey kept saying, "Sorry, V."

Whit told Grey to carefully pull the gun back over Veronica's thumb and twist to the left. He did, it worked, and they were finally able to wrap her wrists together. She fought them the entire time, but with the last of their strength they wrapped her taped wrists to her knees. The immobile ball of kinetic energy wouldn't stop screaming, so Whit made Grey tape her mouth.

Her eyes glared at Grey who kept repeating, "Sorry, V."

Whit, at last, rolled away from Veronica, obviously in severe pain. He curled into a ball on his side. Looking at Grey, Whit tipped his head in the direction of the table and said, "Help them; do what you can."

Whit knew Lamar took two bullets right through the neck. Just after he turned on the hellcat, he sensed or heard at least one round hit Donnie in the neck or face. Grey walked around the table and knelt into the blood pooled around Lamar. Lamar didn't move, but his eyes darted around wildly.

Donnie managed to lean over his buddy while holding his own neck. Blood kept pulsing out between Donnie's fingers. He kept saying, "Look at me, Lamar; look at me."

Lamar's large, white-bordered eyes finally focused on Donnie. Grey could barely watch as tears started rolling down Lamar's cheeks. Donnie started crying, too. "It's okay. Buddy, it's okay. We'll get out of this, I swear. I'll take care—"

Lamar's head started to twitch little involuntary tics. His sad, wet eyes turned glassy. Next, he stared at...nothing. Donnie dropped his head on his buddy's bloody chest.

Grey had just witnessed a cold-blooded killer display the most tender expression of compassion and grief he'd ever observed.

Whit watched the ordeal on his side while looking under the table. He finally said calmly, "Grey, take some dish towels and try to stop the bleeding... or Donnie's dead, too."

Veronica, also witnessing Lamar's last seconds, said through duct tape, "Good."

Whit painfully rolled toward Veronica and kicked her hard in the ass. She went ballistic; but, in her current condition of restraint, couldn't attack.

Grey got up and retrieved two dish towels, folded them, and after rolling Donnie on his back pressed them on to the still pulsing neck wound. The bullet ripped open Donnie's neck from just past his Adam's apple to just under his jaw bone.

Whit struggled to his feet and, using chairs for support, made his way around the table. He grabbed three place mats and gingerly lay down beside

Donnie. Donnie continued to lose too much blood and didn't look good. Whit told Grey to lift Donnie's head up gently and stuff the rolled-up placemats under Donnie's neck.

Whit took over. He folded one dish towel and fit it into the slit in Donnie's throat, then placed the second towel over the first and pressed down hard. Satisfied that pushing down along the entire length of the wound seemed to stem the flow, Whit told Grey to turn a chair sideways, slide it up to Donnie's butt and lift his legs onto it. Grey put his hands up, the gesture asking, why?

Whit stated, "We need to pool his remaining blood around his vitals."

When Grey finished, Whit said, "Good; now I need you to call my dad and tell him to get Dr. Conte out here fast."

Veronica screamed through the tape, "No, nooooooo!"

Whit yelled, "Shut up, you basket case."

Grey turned back to Whit and asked, "Doc Conte…the old veterinarian?"

"Conte served in Korea as a medic. That's where he and Dad met. Conte went back to school after the service and became a veterinarian. Just tell my dad to bring Doc Conte here right away. He'll know what it means."

Turning toward the phone, Grey asked, "But what can that old geezer do?"

Whit said, "Do what he does best; save Donnie's life if he can, and keep his mouth shut. Now move!"

Chapter Sixty
The Call

Tony Bassetti arrived in California but didn't inform Sliger for the first three days. He spent those in Cedar Creek. Dressed casually and trying hard to avoid looking too big city and too Italian thug, he actually avoided talking to most people. Tony knew his limitations. Never approachable, even as a kid, Tony just looked...scary. Tall and way too skinny, with stretched skin over sunken cheeks, large suspicious dark eyes and wire-straight black hair, Tony made people nervous...even before he spoke. That's why he brought along cheery, roly-poly Sal. Sal happened to be one of Johnny "Big Nose" Ramelli's cousins and restaurant managers. Sal's pleasant, jovial face and easy-to-talk-to, harmless demeanor just made people open up. Sal used the same story with everyone. His wife took sick—food poisoning—on their mini-vacation. While she stayed in the motel room sleeping and healing, he just wandered around town, waiting while she recovered. Sal's car received a self-induced flat, so he talked to the tire guy. He bought an old lamp and talked to the antique store owner. He ate out and struck up a conversation with whoever he sat near. Some of his best intel came one evening at a bar called Pete's Place. Sal spoke to an off-duty sheriff's officer about all the crazy stuff he'd heard happened fairly recently in this quaint little town. Over a beer, the officer told Sal that his boss, Sheriff Whittingham, knew a hell of a lot more than the press or the Feds knew. Sal acted confused, so the officer explained that someone had attacked the sheriff's son and his son's friends. The sheriff and his son sometimes deal with...problems, on their own...if you catch my drift. Sal knew cops and believed the officer. Apparently, the county sheriff and his son harbor vigilante tendencies.

Sal reported back to Tony each afternoon and evening. A picture started to emerge, and Tony didn't like it. The information certainly didn't match the feedback Johnny received from his California associate. In fact, the more Sal reported, the more Tony learned Donnie's report of events fit more accurately. Definitely these country bumpkins were not the dumb-shits Mr. Sliger conveyed to Johnny.

Outside of whatever the sheriff knew, the rumor mill around town ran the gambit of who-done-it theories. Bottom line, nobody seemed to know squat. Though the sheriff could be a problem, Tony decided he could whack Milner and Whittingham without blowback to Johnny. A botched robbery in the back parking lot at Pete's Place would work. As for Donnie and Lamar, not a peep, not a sighting, not a rumor; no one even mentioned hired killers.

Bottom line, when Sal left to return to Chicago, Tony told him to tell Johnny there was no trace of Donnie and Lamar. With no evidence that they'd left, the two were probably rotting away in some shallow graves. Maybe the sheriff and his son took them out...quietly. As for Milner and Whittingham, if Johnny wanted them dead, of course, he could snuff them. The job would create moderate exposure, as the Feds would probably jump in with both feet. Even the dumbass Feds couldn't ignore a third shooting incident. But bottom line, whatever Johnny wanted, he'd pull it off.

With Sal gone, Tony decided to head for Sacramento, nail a prostitute or two, and wait for orders. He planned to poke around Sliger's building and check out the security system and the caliber of Sliger's guards. The next afternoon, in Tony's hotel room, his cell phone rang. Tony heard Johnny "Big Nose" Ramelli's voice.

"Important shit, so listen up." Thirty seconds later, Johnny said, "You got that?"

Tony "Two Tap" Bassetti told Johnny, "Crystal clear, they're as good as dead. I'll give your associate your decision and message as soon as we can meet."

After disconnecting, Tony pulled his cell apart and threw it in his briefcase for later disposal. He grabbed another one and dialed the Serpentine Solution's number.

"Serpentine Solutions, Human Resources, Andrea."

"Hi, doll, I'm an associate of an associate of Mr. Sliger. I need an appointment ASAP.

Oh, shit! Smoothly, Andrea replied, "Yes, of course. Let me see. *Shit, he even sounds like a killer.* I'm sorry, Mr. Sliger won't be back until tomorrow afternoon. But I'll cancel his late afternoon meeting and get you right in, say four o'clock?"

"That works fine."

Andrea said, "Just call me when you arrive downstairs, and I'll come get you."

"So, you free for dinner tonight, sweetheart?"

What the…not a chance. Andrea lied, "Oh, I'm going to dinner with my boyfriend."

"Break it; I'll show you a better time; promise."

"Oh, not tonight, I think tonight he's going to finally pop the question."

"Jesus, you're a pathetic liar. How in the hell did you climb all the way up to the head of human resources?"

Too stunned to respond, Andrea heard Tony Bassetti add, "See you tomorrow, sugar."

Quickly hanging up, she fumbled for her cell phone and dialed. Sean picked up and said, "Yes, Andrea?"

As calm as she could, she asked, "What are you doing; you in town?"

She's upset, something's not right. Sean replied, "Close; I'm in Walnut Creek on a jealous husband case. Apparently, he can fool around, but went nuclear when he suspected his wife of boinking someone else."

"Do you love me?"

Whoa! Sean thought looking at his phone, *where did that come from?* Sean asked, "Everything alright, Andrea?"

"Yes; well, no. The reason I asked, well…I think we'll be seeing a lot of each other, really soon."

Okay, okay, I get it now, we're leaving. Well, shit, Sean, you did get involved. "Okay, Andrea, what are we talking here?"

"Like tomorrow afternoon."

Holy crap! Okay, no big deal; this is how it works. Just grab what you can and disappear. Trying to calm Andrea's nerves, Sean said, "I have our new identities, passports…everything, except enough cash."

Andrea sighed in relief. "Perfect, darling. I'll draw as much cash as I can at this end. Be ready no later than 3 o'clock. It will take me five minutes to meet you out front after I give you the call."

"I'll be there; you sure, Andrea?"

"Oh, yeah; totally sure, Sean."

"Me too." *I think?*

Chapter Sixty-one
The Old Vet

With the smell of drying blood and bodily fluids thick in the air, Grey opened most of the windows in Whit's cabin.

The sullen Veronica finally calmed down and motioned Grey over. She told him to take the duct tape off. Grey tried to delicately peel the tape, but Veronica just pulled and jerked her head to free her mouth. He couldn't get the tape out of her hair, so he left it dangling from the side of her head.

Grey spoke first. "I'm sorry, V; you just went berserk, whacko…crazy."

She immediately thought, *Not as sorry as you're going to be, wise guy.* Instead she said, "I need to pee."

"No!" Whit yelled. "Do nothing with her until my dad gets here. Let her pee her pants. We're not letting that banshee free until she can be handcuffed."

Veronica said, "Just stand me up and pull down my pants; I'll sit on the edge of a chair and pee right here."

Whit ignored her and said, "Why did you do it? They were going to talk, in exchange for us helping them."

Veronica hissed, "They tried to kill me, goddamnit; you, too. They deserved to die. Besides, I know who hired them. You might as well know too… some asshole named Steven Sliger. And they're employed by—"

"Johnny Ramelli," Whit cut in.

That caught Veronica off guard a little; but she just shrugged and recovered enough to say, "So, why let them live?"

Whit thought briefly then said, "Do you know the connection between the two? How this Sliger guy and Ramelli work together?" Whit could tell she didn't. He said, "These guys did, but they can't talk now."

Veronica replied, "Good, like I give a shit." But what Whit said started to sink in. *Shit; I may have screwed up. The feds have been trying to nail Ramelli for years, and I just might have killed the golden goose…geese. Goddamnit!*

Whit tipped his head up. "I hear a car, coming fast." *That was quick; nice going, Dad.*

Sheriff Whittingham parked his county cruiser, hopped out, and scurried briskly up the rock steps to the porch. Doc Conte grabbed his bag and followed.

Sheriff Whittingham smelled the blood and death when he hit the porch and pulled his service revolver. When he entered, he scanned the horrific scene and said, "What the—"

"Dad, get Doc Conte over here quick; we have a dying man hanging on by a thread."

Bill put his gun away, backed out to the porch, and helped Doc Conte up the steps. Old Doc Conte had to be pushing seventy-five. Far from his first rodeo, or bizarre scene, he moved with Bill to Whit and the ashen-colored man on the floor.

All business, Doc Conte knelt down close, put on different glasses and said, "Let's have a look." As Whit shuffled out of the way, the old vet said, "Open my bag, will you, Whit? That old clasp is a bitch."

Doc Conte pulled the blood-soaked towels away, spread the wound, and viewed inside. He reached in with his finger and pressed down. He said, "His jugular has been nicked. I have to sew it quickly, if I can. It's like a slit; I can't clamp it or he'll probably stroke. You'll have to help me, Whit."

Whit traded places with Doc Conte and placed his thumb along the leaking vein while the veterinarian prepared a curved needle and thread. As Doc Conte worked, he said, "I'm going to partially block the vein with the stitches, but enough blood should be able to pass by. It will need to be fixed later. Tucking the place mats under his neck gave you something to press against, probably kept him from just bleeding out."

Doc Conte looked over at the black man and all the blood. "Shot though a carotid and probably the spinal cord; nothing anyone could have done."

Bill paced impatiently. "If he's stable, I'll call this in. That guy needs plasma or blood and fast."

Whit said, "Whoa, Dad, no can do. These two guys are the assassins." Tipping his head toward Veronica, he added, "And loony as a pet coon over there is Grey's mystery woman…and the shooter."

Holding his forehead and wincing, Bill said, "I'll be go to hell. Son... you're killing your old man. I can't just—"

Doc Conte interrupted, "This guy needs a transfusion immediately. Any of you O-negative?"

Bill shook his head then pointed at his son. "Both AB positive."

Grey threw up his hands. "I don't know."

From behind them they heard, "I'm O-negative."

They all turned to Veronica. No one spoke, so she said, "Okay, I shot them. I got a little carried away. I'm impulsive like that, especially when I run into someone who tried to kill me." Still no one spoke, so she continued. "Okay, I screwed up; he possesses information my, ah, employer needs to nail his boss. So...hook me up."

When again no one spoke or moved, she exclaimed, "I'll be good."

Chapter Sixty-two
Promise Me

Whit thought, *who in the hell is Steven Sliger? Why put hits on my friends and me? And, why does that name ring a bell?* Whit stayed awake much of the night frustratingly racking his brain for answers.

Actually, both Whit and his dad traded off staying up while everyone else—Doc Conte, Grey, the heavily sedated Donnie, and the volatile and unpredictable Veronica—slept, or at least nodded off. Neither Whit nor his dad trusted the snoring, serene-looking hellcat. Just because Veronica hid her fangs and retracted her claws didn't mean she'd suddenly turned docile. She'd tricked Whit once; he refused to give her another opportunity.

Veronica's transfusion pulled Donnie back to semi-consciousness. The sew job turned out sloppy but effective enough to stop virtually all the bleeding while still allowing the vein to partially function. The vet eventually superglued the wound and finally stopped further seepage. In the early morning, Doc Conte agreed to take Donnie to his old veterinary clinic attached to his residence…as long as Sheriff Whittingham kept two officers posted at Donnie's side.

Veronica said that as soon as Donnie could be moved, she could arrange some Feds to transport him to a safe location…a holding pen, kind of like in witness protection, but more bars and a whole lot less freedom.

Murderous Lamar had to disappear. Veronica's snap shots had in fact torn open his carotid and nicked his spinal cord. The immobile bastard virtually bled out. Grey and Veronica wrapped him in a large tarp. Grey watched Veronica spit on Lamar before they covered his head. *Jesus, V.*

Even though Whit walked slowly through the woods leading the way, the two pallbearers struggled with the deceased. They had to stop six times during the procession's half-mile march. Whit stopped at one of the many well over-grown mine shafts he'd discovered as a kid. From tossing rocks down this one, Whit knew it dropped straight down for a long, long way. They un-wrapped Lamar and slid him to the edge of the shaft. Veronica gave him a little shove and said to herself, *I won, you lost, asshole.* The body slid down away from them and into…oblivion.

Veronica quipped to Whit as they backed away, "His body the only one down there?"

Though Grey appeared oblivious, she noticed Whit took a little too long to say, "Yep." He coldly stared at her just a little too long also.

She noted to herself, *Whoa, Whit. Welcome to hell. You're not who you appear to be either.*

Back at the cabin, Whit told Grey and Veronica that the blood-soaked tarp and all of Whit's tacky, saturated floor planks needed to be burned. They spent most of an hour prying planks and hauling them down to Whit's big cleared burn area. Whit found just enough plywood to temporarily cover his cabin floor. They bleached blood spatter and wiped down everything. Veronica collected anything burnable that remained of the killer's possessions. Fortunately, when Whit's dad left with Doc Conte and Donnie, he took all of Donnie and Lamar's guns and ammo.

Donnie and Lamar's rental pickup remained as the only evidence and loose end. Donnie weakly whispered to Whit where he and Lamar had hidden the vehicle. Whit figured he could find it. He'd drive it to Blue Hole, drain the fluids, then use his truck to push it into the deep pond. As a kid, he'd done it before for his dad; that vehicle had completely disappeared from view before it passed halfway to the bottom. *Like father, like son.* But at the moment Whit didn't have time and didn't say anything about the killer's pickup to Grey and Veronica. He left them to tend to the fire, as he needed to clean up and go meet Allyson.

After a hot shower and gingerly slipping on clean clothes, Whit realized he could breathe in a little deeper without much pain. Maybe the glancing blow of the shotgun slug only spread and severely bruised his ribs. Fighting with Veronica certainly stretched his chest muscles but didn't seem to increase the damage.

When he came out of his cabin, Veronica and Grey walked up from the fire and met him at his truck. Veronica offered, "I'm sorry I went batshit loony on you. I have a problem with…my—"

"Temper, maybe?" Whit finished for her, then added, "Shit Howdy, Veronica, you're sly like a fox, woman. But what's done is done; forget it. We need to focus on bigger fish to fry."

As he gingerly slid into his truck, Whit said, "Make sure everything burns to ash, then go home. I'll be in touch. Oh, Grey, the gate...3963."

Grey rubbed his hands together and said, "Great!"

Veronica said, "Think about it, genius; he'll just change the combo after today." When Grey looked dejected, she pointed to the fire and said, "Hey, Smokey; after we're done burning, you still owe me a stroll in the woods and a roll in the hay."

Exasperated, Grey said, "After all this. After everything that's happened, you can think about sex?"

Walking back down the hill to the burn pile, Veronica said over her shoulder, "Yep, one more fire you need to put out."

Following her, Grey said, under his breath, *Unbelievable.*

Whit's dad had locked the gate when he left. They didn't need anyone, like Warden Perkins, accidently dropping by. As Whit opened his gate, he stopped and snapped his fingers. "I'll be damned...Sliger Mine Road."

About four years ago, Whit had worked on a salvage logging operation, following a large wildfire, in the neighboring county. He had to open and lock a gate to access the sale area. About two miles before the gate, Whit remembered a funky old wooden sign hanging by one nail at the intersection of a skinny overgrown road. He could barely read the engraved words, Sliger Mine Road, carved on the old gray plank. Sliger cannot be a coincidence...not a name like that.

He drove into town without giving the name, Sliger, another thought. After filling his truck with gas, Whit thought about buying coffee, but dropped the idea. Driving to his old high school, he pulled around the parking lot until he saw Allyson sitting in the same older, white Chevy Impala. Whit parked, walked over to the passenger side and maneuvered in. He noticed she looked well and told her so.

"Thank you. I feel pretty good; weak, but surprisingly good." She added, "Hey, where's my coffee?"

Whit put his hands up and said, "Sorry. I see you're in the same old ride."

"Yeah, it's registered to another one of my aliases. I picked it up because it had a bench seat. When I started having problems, I found bucket seats too uncomfortable. I pay a shop to keep it and run it periodically when I'm not around."

Whit decided to jump in with both feet. "Steven Sliger."

That caught Allyson way off guard, but she recovered quickly. "How did you find out?"

"It's a long story, but I just learned his name."

"Do you know him or know about him?" Allyson asked.

"I looked him up enough to know what he does and where to find him, but Sliger means nothing, other than I've heard the name before. About forty-five miles south and east of Cedar Creek, an old wood sign reads 'Sliger Mine Road.' It has to be linked. I just don't know how to quickly find out the connection."

They both thought for a while until Allyson touched Whit's side. "Hey, why don't you ask Katelyn to dig through some of the local archives? She is a reporter, you know."

Whit snapped his fingers and said, "That's a great idea. Sharp as a tack, Allyson. Can I borrow your phone?"

After giving Katelyn the name, she said she'd check. But just before Katelyn hung up, she said, "Whit, I'll do it; but only on one condition. Any information I find, you take to the police. Promise me, Whit."

Whit said, "Of course."

Coldly Katelyn pushed, "Whit, promise me."

Hating being cornered, Whit lied, "I promise. Kate, you're the best."

Cheery again, Katelyn replied, "Don't I know it, you lucky dog."

When he handed the phone back to Allyson, she said, "You lied through your teeth. You're not taking anything to the police."

Not wanting to answer, Whit asked, "What's your idea about snatching Lance?"

She turned slightly toward him and said, "Easy; I just walk up and stand in front of Sliger's building and call. My presence will get to Lance or Sliger damn quick. Sliger will send Lance out, I'm sure of it."

"Snatch him in the open, in public? Sounds a tad risky."

"I don't think the coward will come out otherwise. But, as soon as I see him, I'll walk toward their underground garage. You be at the bottom of the ramp. We snatch him, dump him in the trunk and zoom."

Whit thought, *Simple, but in their backyard.* He asked, "They have security?"

"Some; but I'll tell Lance to come out alone, and that if I see anyone else, I'll leave and head straight to the police. If we start out front, I think Lance will feel safe enough. Plus, Sliger will be dying to know what it will take…financially, to guarantee my silence."

Whit tried to think of the downsides to her simple plan. Allyson cut into his thoughts. "I want to do it tomorrow."

"Whoa, too early. I need to think about this, case the place, especially the parking garage."

"Whit, if you think about it too much, we won't do it." When Whit didn't respond, she added, "How about in the late afternoon, like three o'clock, maybe three-thirty? Grab him, and scram before the evening commute. We'll have plenty of time today to check the layout."

When Whit still didn't answer, Allyson said, "I start radiation next week. If it wipes me out, snatching Lance gets much tougher."

Whit turned to Allyson. "For the moment, let's say we're on. If I think of something or get a bad feeling about this, we hold off."

Allyson said, "Fair enough. You up for a drive to case Sliger's fortress?

Putting on his seatbelt, Whit said, "Deal…as long as we stop on the way, so I can buy you a coffee."

Chapter Sixty-three
This Guy Doesn't Exist

True to Veronica's word, thirty-six hours after one of her 9mm rounds ripped through the side of Donnie's throat and after Doc Conte's heroic emergency services, two Federal officers arrived in a shiny, black Lincoln Navigator. Parking near a sheriff's sedan, the two entered the old veterinarian's small clinic. They spoke with Doc Conte privately for a few minutes, handed him a thick envelope, then proceeded into the small operating room to claim their prize.

Weak, drugged, but more coherent than he let on, Donnie listened with his eyes closed to the two sheriff deputies and the two agents.

Hands shook, but no badges or names were exchanged. The lead agent said, "Have you heard from your sheriff?"

"Yes sir; he said to expect you. The sooner mystery man here gets gone, the better." Flicking his hand back and forth between himself and his partner, the sheriff's officer added, "We don't like being kept in the dark; but sometimes that's how the sheriff works."

The agent walked up to Donnie and said, "With this one, the less you know the better." He smacked Donnie gently a few times in the cheek with the back of his hand, leaned closer to the bed and said, "You listening, sport?"

Donnie blinked and opened his eyes but didn't speak.

Doc Conte entered and said to both agents, "No rough stuff; as I said, I've only quickly stitched the vein and superglued along the whole area. He still needs surgery. Either of you have medical training?"

"The basics, but we have a real doctor waiting at the plane. Your patient will be fine."

Doc Conte ignored the jab since he'd just received a nice stipend for his services and for, of course, his silence. After checking Donnie's vitals, the veterinarian pulled back the sheet and he said, "I need you to sit up carefully."

Donnie made eye contact with everyone in the room, then rose up slowly and slid his legs off the bed. Even though he looked woozy and unstable, the second agent stepped forward with shackles.

Doc Conte asked, "Are those really necessary?"

The first agent replied, "You have no idea, Doc; besides, standard procedure." Wrapped with a chain around his waist linked and locked to handcuffs and ankle bracelets, Donnie stood up.

The lead agent started to address the sheriffs, but one cut him off. "Save your breath. Sheriff Whittingham already gave us the lecture." Looking at Donnie he added, "This guy doesn't exist. You two don't exist. My partner and I were never here."

Nodding, the two agents put a hand under the hunched-over killer's armpits and slowly started walking. By the time they reached the Lincoln, the sheriff cruiser had already pulled away. The lead agent put Donnie in the back seat on the passenger side. He walked around the vehicle and climbed in the other side. The second agent took the driver's seat.

Donnie watched as the agent wrapped his shoulder harness and seat belt around him. The agent said, "I put you on this side so the shoulder harness wouldn't ride on your wound. Consider yourself…precious cargo."

Donnie just turned and looked out the window.

The lead agent continued. "Okay, Donnie; we have about an hour before I turn you over to some…professionals. You start talking to me voluntarily, or you talk eventually; but either way, you will talk. The difference—and I want you to pay very close attention—the difference, if you talk to me, I just may have a career move in store for you. If not, well, what's left of you will be dumped in front of one of Johnny Ramelli's restaurants."

That raised an eyebrow, but Donnie continued his silence.

Trying a different tact, the agent said, "I had a hard time convincing Veronica, once you were in our custody, not to finish what she'd started. She's difficult to control; you're lucky to be alive."

Donnie looked at the agent and said, "Screw her. I tried to kill her, she tried to kill me. We're even."

Good, he's talking. "That's not Veronica, in her world, someone wins and someone loses." Donnie sat back and closed his eyes. The agent knew the thug kept weighing the pros and cons of his bleak future.

For twenty minutes, they just rode in silence. Finally, Donnie turned to the agent and asked, "What's your name?"

"I'm called Desk Jock...DJ for short."

In a little stronger voice, Donnie asked, "So you're not the FBI; who sends you your W2?"

"Doesn't work that way, Donnie. For quite some time, you will only be answering questions. All privileges, and ultimately your future, will solely depend on how well you cooperate right now."

Donnie nodded slightly then turned to look out the window again. DJ continued. "One serious point to remember, your former employer—the man and his organization you protect with your silence—wants you dead. Kind of a lose/lose situation, don't you think? Johnny Ramelli may personally kill you himself then have you dumped into a trash compactor for disposal with the rest of his garbage."

Donnie continued to look out the window, but DJ knew he had Donnie's ear. "So, we know you're a tough guy; but we also know you're not stupid. You have a slim window of opportunity here if you start talking now before we initiate coercive techniques. If you don't, next stop—your last stop—will be Chicago."

Donnie thought, *I laughed my ass off when Lamar said, "Hey, we could go legit." Well, this definitely isn't legit but what the hell choice do I have?*

Donnie turned his head toward his new boss, of sorts, and said, "Okay, you have your convert. I'm in, but I do have one question I need answered first."

DJ thought a little while, then nodded.

"How will you keep...Ms. Psycho from killing me?"

Grinning, DJ replied, "I have absolutely no idea."

Chapter Sixty-four
They Need to Disappear

"Christ, Lance; you need to pay more attention to human behavior. Don't just listen to what she says; look at her mannerisms, tiny facial tics, posture. I'm telling you, Andrea's acting differently."

Sliger scolded Lance alone in his conference room, trying to educate his stepson on nuance. Sliger knew something left Andrea with a burr under her saddle, a bee in her bonnet, a damn bug up her ass. It was more than just being left out of the loop on the scheme to kill Ned and Allyson; there's something else...bigger. The last time Andrea serviced him, her effort lacked...enthusiasm. Hell, 90 percent of her blowjob consisted of just jerking him off. Of course, none of this did he mention to Lance.

Lance sat back in his chair pouting. *He's just mad at Andrea because she must have just jerked him off the last time they had a special session.* Of course, he didn't mention that to Sliger. Lance leaned forward in his chair and said, "She sits in here like a mannequin and answers you like a robot—'Yes sir, Mr. Sliger; No sir, Mr. Sliger'—all the time. I don't see any difference."

"You're wrong, Lance; she's stewing. Andrea doesn't hang her emotions out on her shirtsleeve, like you do. Shit, you're a walking neon sign. That's my fucking point. You are an open book, she's not; but I can read you both loud and clear. Until you can check your emotions and detect other people's subtle signals, you'll always be second tier. I need better than that."

Lance sat back staring at his stepfather, brooding once again. *I stayed because you showed me how to accrue power, control people. I learned fast back then. Maybe you used to be a better mentor; now you just badger me all the time.*

Sliger yelled, "Stop pouting like a little girl. I need you to keep an eye on

Andrea. She's up to something. Lately, she's maintained steady contact with Sean Peterson. I want you to—"

Sliger heard a slight hum and realized someone had walked past a sensor in the hall. He turned to his monitor and saw Andrea with the limping head of security, Ron Townsend, in tow. Sliger pushed the button to activate a speaker in the hall. Sliger angrily said, "What's he doing here? I'm busy."

"I asked Ron to come up with me; we have a situation and something very important to show you."

Sliger growled loudly then turned to Lance and said, "Pay attention and watch her closely." As Andrea and Ron entered and walked toward his desk, Sliger scolded, "Limping is a sign of weakness; the wrong impression for the head of my security, Townsend."

Ron's right leg no longer retained a functioning meniscus. His femur and tibia/fibula painfully ground bone on bone. Sliger informed Ron his knee replacement would occur on his schedule...not Ron's. That was eight months ago. By 10 o'clock, excruciating pain became Ron's daily companion.

Ignoring his pain and Sliger's insult, Ron walked to the side of Sliger's desk and said, "Sir, locate the security camera at the front of the building, by the ramp to the parking garage."

Sliger grudgingly obliged, looked at the screen, then leaned forward to confirm what he saw. Sliger sat back in his chair and flicked his fingers at Lance to come look. As Lance advanced, Sliger said to no one in particular, "So, she's back."

Lance recognized the dark-haired beauty dressed all in black.

Andrea said, "Allyson called me about five minutes ago and asked for Lance to step out and speak with her. She also told me she had a price in mind for her continued silence. Oh, and if anyone else comes within three hundred feet of her, she'll head straight for the police."

Lance pointed to the image on the screen. "That woman hates me; I can't go out there. Why doesn't security just rush her?"

Not wanting to reveal Johnny Ramelli or Tony Bassetti's names with Ron Townsend in the room, Andrea said, "Steven, we have an employee of an associate of yours arriving around four o'clock. It's imperative to resolve this issue with Ms. Chandler quickly and quietly. I suggest Lance meets her pronto, find out what she wants, and move on from there."

Sliger looked up at Lance, whose shoulders sank. *Look at that; he hasn't learned a goddamn thing.* "It's extremely important that my next meeting goes

moothly. Get your ass down there; find out her price and get her the hell away
.om the front of the building."

Lance pleaded, "I need backup. I want Moose."

Sliger said, "You can't have Moose." Turning his chair and pointing at Ron
.e added, "Or this cripple either; no one. She's your problem; get down there
nd resolve this…now."

Lance offered, "Maybe I can grab her and wrestle her to the ground. We
an bring her up the garage elevator and deal with her privately."

Thinking it over, Sliger stood up and said, "Fine, whatever; but I guaran-
ee you, whatever she knows or thinks she knows is stored with someone else.
f anything happens to her, it goes to the press or the cops or both. If it comes
o that, we have plenty of lawyers to deal with whatever she thinks she has on
.s. Feel her out and play it by ear. But, deal with it quickly and quietly; and no
ops. Now all of you get out."

As Ron, Andrea and Lance marched down the hall; Andrea said she
.eeded to wait for Sliger's four o'clock to call and turned into her office.

At the same time, Lance tapped Ron on the shoulder and said, "Just a
ninute." He ducked into his office and walked over to his closet. Finding his
vinter coat, Lance reached into an inside pocket and pulled out a thin black
.nife. The small four-inch switchblade gave Lance an added measure of courage.

As Ron and Lance exited the elevator, they saw Moose and motioned
.im over toward the front sliding doors. Lance said to Ron, "Tell Moose
vhat's going on." Ron nodded, then Lance added, "If I can get the drop on
.er, come running."

Ron just nodded again. Lance straightened his jacket, looked up and down
.he street out front, then walked through the fast-moving sliding door.

He glanced right, saw Allyson standing near the parking garage ramp, and
:ook off in her direction. As he approached, he noticed she looked considerably
:hinner but otherwise as gorgeous as ever in her tight-fitting, all black outfit.
More than a little apprehensive, he stopped about ten feet away.

Ron and Moose lost visual on Lance and decided to go to the monitors.

Lance said, "So, you wanted to see me?"

Allyson turned to face Lance. As he looked her over, his gaze froze. *Ah,
shit.* Fairly well concealed in her black glove next to her black purse rested—
what else—a damn black Lady Colt. She said sternly, "Down the ramp."
Knowing the woman's volatile disposition, Lance immediately complied.

Moose and Ron reached the monitors just as Lance led the way down the ramp and into the parking garage. Moose said, "Maybe he's taking her down there where we can grab her." He turned and headed for the elevators.

Instinctively, Ron said, "No, Moose, too noisy; use the stairs." Ron thought *Looks to me like she's in control. Maybe she's here to take out that little shithead.*

Whit stood behind a pillar watching Lance and Allyson approach. He planned to pull in behind Allyson when they passed, grab Lance and stuff him in the trunk. Whit, with his back to the stairs, did not notice the huge head that filled the small window in the stairwell door. That odd sensation like when a mountain lion secretly watches you, hit Whit. Just as Moose pulled his head back, Whit straightened up and snapped his head around to check the stairwell door for the tenth time. Whit said *hmm* to himself, then turned back around. He decided after Allyson and Lance moved a little closer, he'd step out.

At that moment, Moose pushed down the release bar and bolted the fifteen feet he needed to close the distance to Whit. Whit spun around and ducked just in time to avoid a huge right fist. With his chest still bruised and weak, Whit threw a pathetic right near Moose's spleen...with no effect. Quickly, he added a good left uppercut into a pair of huge balls. A beastly groan exited Moose's lips as his knees buckled and he crumpled forward...unfortunately, right on top of Whit.

Allyson and Lance looked toward the disturbance to their right and heard Whit say from under the mountain of flesh, "Keep going, get him in the car." Allyson felt stuck between a rock and a hard place. She couldn't help Whit and keep control of Lance. She decided to do what Whit said and jabbed Lance in the back with her pistol.

Moose, in obvious pain, still managed to grab Whit's upper body in a bear hug and pin him down. He moaned, "In about two minutes, I'm going to pinch you in two."

Whit struggled to get free, but his efforts appeared hopeless. On his back with a banged-up chest and 350 pounds of rhinoceros on top of him, he could barely breathe, let alone fight. Every time Whit exhaled, he couldn't force as much air back in as the last time. Whit's only hope now depended on Allyson. If she could drug Lance quickly enough and lock him in the trunk, Whit might be able to last long enough. She could rescue him by shooting this...blob in his fat ass.

When Allyson reached her car, she told Lance to stop about ten feet back. She walked way around Lance and popped the trunk. Lance put his right hand in his jacket pocket. She motioned him forward and said, "Bend over and stick your head way in there."

When Lance complied, he pulled the knife out as he put his hands ahead of his body in the trunk. Allyson crossed her body with her left hand and looked down. Taped to her purse, she grabbed the plunger of a syringe full of milky white Propofol.

Lance decided it was now or never; he pushed back and spun around sweeping with his left arm. The impact forced Allyson to step back to regain her balance. Lance backhanded her right wrist with his left hand as the switch-blade snapped open. His grip kept the gun pointing away. He completed his pivot and drove the four-inch stiletto up into the left side of Allyson's ribcage.

She didn't cry out but made a painful grimace. Lance grinned and loudly exclaimed, "Now, I'll watch you die, bitch." She lost grip of the gun, and Lance let her fall backwards with his knife still embedded in her side.

Whit heard Lance's voice and knew Allyson needed help. With the last of his strength he tried to break free, but Moose had regained much of his might and started crushing Whit. He felt like one of those poor deer mice wrapped in the coils of a constrictor. Those snakes often squeezed so hard that the little mouse's eyes popped right out. Whit realized he was passing out. A final thought gripped him: *I've failed...failed everyone.*

As Whit's eyesight faded to black, his mind registered a loud whack. Then his captor yelled and released his grip. Whit gasped but remained too exhausted to fight. He heard the monster say, "Why did you hit me?"

Ron Townsend said, "Mr. Sliger won't want him dead; not yet, Moose."

Whit looked in the direction of the voice and saw an older security guard putting his collapsible baton to his side.

Moose stood up, rubbed his thigh and complained, "But he punched me in the nuts."

Obviously the boss, the older security guy ignored Moose and said, "Get him up and follow me." He took off toward Allyson's car but turned his head back to Moose and added, "Make sure he doesn't whack the family jewels again."

Moose roughly collared Whit and violently wrenched his left arm around Whit's back and bent his wrist up. The pain made the still gasping Whit walk on his tiptoes.

Allyson blinked slowly as she watched the three approach. Lance spoke before anyone else. He pointed the pistol at Whit, then Allyson, and said, "Hold him tight; put her in the back seat."

Ron Townsend said, "I'm sure Mr. Sliger wants them upstairs."

Lance yelled, "You're addressing Mr. Sliger!" Smugly he continued. "I caught them and I'm going to deal with them. My dad will be entertaining an important guest and can't be bothered. He told me to deal with this situation. That's exactly what I intend to do. They need to disappear."

Ron decided not to argue, bent down, and carefully picked up Allyson. She suppressed, as best she could, any sounds of discomfort as he carried her to the car. He opened the back-passenger door and, as gently as he could, set her in. Before he pulled his head away, he whispered, "I'm sorry."

When Ron stood up and closed the door, he saw Lance walk to the other back door. Lance told Moose, "Put Whittingham in the trunk and one of you get in the driver's seat; we're taking a ride to Cedar Creek. I haven't decided whether they kill each other or die in a murder/suicide. I'll figure it out on the way."

Ron said, "That's not going to happen."

Incredulous, Lance roared, "What the hell did you say?"

Ron continued. "Too risky and not thought out; I'm not doing it and neither is Moose. If you want this done, do it yourself."

Lance couldn't speak, and his face turned beet red. Lance finally hissed, "Put Whittingham in the driver's seat. I will do it myself and return to deal with your insolence later. You have no idea what's in store for you."

Lance opened, entered, and slammed the back door. Ron tipped his head at Moose, who walked Whit to the driver's door and stuffed him in.

Lance yelled through the open window, "Get the fuck back upstairs and tell my dad what I'm doing. You assholes might as well start packing." He turned to Whit and said, "Start driving and remember, Whittingham, this gun will be pointed at the back of your head the whole time."

Whit started the car and said, "You can't let Allyson suffer like this; she needs—"

"What's the difference? Would you rather I just put a bullet in her head right now?" When Whit didn't answer, Lance bumped the barrel of the automatic at the base of Whit's skull and said, "Shut up and drive...the speed limit."

Chapter Sixty-five
Lead the Way, Doll

Sitting in her office waiting for the dreaded phone call from Tony Bassetti, Andrea realized she couldn't concentrate. She knew her career at Serpentine Solutions terminated today. No matter what Tony told Sliger, the trajectory of Serpentine Solutions and everyone in the Inner Circle raced in one direction—downhill.

If Tony told Sliger he planned to whack Milner and Whittingham and make their deaths appear random or accidental, she knew it just wouldn't work. Even the Feds couldn't ignore that many assaults aimed at the same individuals. If Tony told Sliger to end his vendetta against Milner and Whittingham, Sliger would go berserk. She knew Sliger wouldn't stop, putting them at odds with Johnny Ramelli and his organization. Hell, just sign your own death warrant right now and be done.

No; she was done, finished, out of it. That meant just walking away. Andrea's next roll of the dice was tying her future to Sean Peterson, a man she really didn't know that well. *But, what other choice to escape exists?*

She stood up to fill her coffee mug for the third time—a rarity for Andrea—when the phone rang. She leaned over and grabbed the phone. "Serpentine Sol—"

"Yeah, I'm downstairs waiting for my escort, Sweetness."

A little surprised, Andrea said, "Oh, ah, be right down; you're a little early."

"Yeah, well, how else are us early birds gunna catch us them worms?"

What the hell does that mean? Andrea replied, "Yes sir; I'm on my way."

She hit the button for Steven's private office. Sliger barked, "What?"

"Mr. Bassetti has arrived downstairs."

"Bassetti? He's early; did he see anything going on out front?"

"I don't think so, he didn't mention anything. But I haven't heard from Lance, Ron, or Moose."

After an annoyingly long pause, Sliger said, "Bring him up; let's get this over with so Bassetti goes to work on my...old pals." Sliger abruptly disconnected.

Andrea speed-dialed Sean and left a message. "Come get me out front, now!"

She hustled out of her office to the elevator leading to the ground floor. Andrea wanted to get a visual on Lance, Ron, or Moose and see if they had neutralized Allyson. As the door opened, she started out and nearly ran into Sliger's four o'clock.

"Oh," she said, a little startled as he walked by her. He wore a dark pinstriped suit and dark fedora just like in old forties gangster movies. Under one arm he carried a rectangular package about twice the size of a Kleenex box. She started to speak, but he held up a hand in her face.

When the doors closed, he dropped his hand. She tried again, "Good afternoon, Mr. Bassetti."

"How you doin', Sweetness?" Bassetti saw Andrea staring at the box and said, "A little gift from my boss to your boss."

Andrea just smiled. *No way in hell am I attending that meeting.*

When the elevator door opened, Tony said, "Lead the way, doll."

Hoping to follow, Andrea just smiled and moved down the hall. When they reached Sliger's huge double doors, the right one clicked and automatically swung open. They walked in. When Tony moved even with Andrea, she immediately turned for the door and said, "I forgot some paperwork for Mr. Sliger; I won't be a minute."

With the package under his right arm, Tony couldn't reach for her. He quickly said, "I want you to stay; this will only take a minute."

With her back to Tony and partially out the door, she held up her index finger and kept walking.

To stop her, Tony would have had to make a scene; he decided to let her go. *Fuck; she was supposed to be part of this. She looked scared, sounded scared, smelled scared; she knows. She's not coming back. Well, just to make sure, I'll wait, a bit.*

Sliger walked out of his inner office, smiled and said, "Tony Bassetti; I hope you have good news."

Tony smiled at Sliger as he walked up to the big desk.

Sliger asked, "Where's Ms. Moran?"

Tony pointed over his shoulder and said, "Said she forgot something and would be right back." *The bitch is probably heading down the elevator right now.* He asked Sliger, "Where's your kid?"

Sliger said coldly, "My stepson happens to be out on an important assignment."

Tony said to himself, *Shit, I was supposed to address all four of them, can't stop now.*

Placing the package on Sliger's desk, Tony said, "A little gift from Johnny. You must be special; he don't do that for many of his friends." *Like shit he don't.*

Still standing, Sliger tried to lift the taped cardboard box but it was quite heavy. He slid the box in front of his chair and said, "It's heavy; what's in here?"

Tony just shrugged and said, "Gold maybe?"

Sliger used his letter opener to slice the tape.

Tony glanced at the big double doors, now hoping his assessment of Andrea's flight remained correct. He'd have to find and deal with Andrea and Lance later.

Sliger pealed back the top and stared at thick plastic and said, "What is it?"

Tony pulled out his pistol and, just as Sliger looked up, shot him in the lower right abdomen. The gun made a little "phtt" sound. Sliger clutched his side, shocked, and fell back in his chair.

Tony walked around the desk and said, "Johnny sends his regards."

Nothing registered with Sliger except pain; this all felt like a dream. He pulled his hand away and looked at the small hole in his shirt. "What's...what's going on?"

Tony closed the box and put it under his left arm. He then transferred the pistol into his left hand then grabbed Sliger. "Come on; we gotta go see your computer guy."

Still confused as the two of them half walked and half staggered to Jeff's computer room door, Sliger moaned, "Why did you shoot me?"

Tony replied, "Johnny wanted you to know your vendetta against your old buddies is over and told me to, ah, punctuate the point. He said if I didn't make it absolutely clear, you wouldn't stop."

Sliger groaned, "Okay, okay, I get it. I'll stop; now get me some medical attention."

"Your sweet thing was supposed to do that. But since she didn't return, I'm gonna take you to your computer guy."

Suddenly, Sliger's fog cleared away. *Shit, Johnny didn't send Tony Bassetti to kill Milner and Whittingham; he sent him to kill me. Well, he can't do this. I know too much about Johnny that will come out.*

Defiantly, Sliger said, "Your plan won't work. You can't get in without the combination and I won't reveal it. That means we make a deal."

Tony let go of Sliger, who fell to the floor with a groan. The stunned Sliger watched as Tony punched the right numbers in the keypad. Tony smiled at Sliger and said, "Your Jeff's a genius, can't deny it. But, he's a social idiot; just too damn trusting."

Tony stepped in and scanned from left to right. Past a bunch of huge blinking mainframes to the far right, Tony saw the computer geek's back. Jeff had on earphones and stared at multiple monitors. Tony quickly walked up behind Jeff and slugged him with his pistol hard at the base of the skull. Jeff toppled forward knocking off his earphones as he moaned and grabbed for the back of his head. Tony pulled out an ice pick from inside his vest, grabbed Jeff's greasy hair firmly, and rammed the tip deep into Jeff's right ear. Tony reefed the handle down, then up. When he extracted the pick, nothing happened at first; then Jeff started jumping and flipping, hitting all kinds of functions at random on his keyboards. To Tony, Jeff flailed like a chicken with its head cut off.

Tony stabbed the ice pick in Jeff's back, then ran back to Sliger who had managed to crawl about ten feet from the door. Tony grabbed Sliger by the collar and dragged him through the computer door and allowed the door to close. Sliger kept screaming, "Everyone will know. Everyone will know. If I go down, so does Johnny."

Tony slid Sliger up beside his twitching computer man. Sliger ignored Jeff and said, "You kill me and all the dirt I have on Ramelli automatically goes to the Feds."

Tony brought a chair around in front of Sliger and sat down. "The best part of my job, I get to tell people where they fucked up, so pay attention. The last conversation you done with Johnny, you spoke my nickname. Johnny knows you ain't supposed to know nothing about me. He don't believe your bullshit story. Johnny thinks your computer guy's been snooping into his affairs. Johnny can't take no risk like that."

Sliger remained silent.

"So, what does Johnny do?" Tony poked the now lifeless Jeff in the back with his pistol. "Johnny calls this moron right here and asks him. This poor bastard ain't got no filter, no sense, and tells Johnny everything."

Shit, shit, shit. Sliger shot back, "Jeff doesn't know where I hide the dirt on Johnny."

"Bullshit, I know the dirt you got on Johnny is stored right in here. I also know you disabled this place's sprinkler system. If the shit hit the fan, to cover your ass, you needed all this stuff to burn up quick like and complete."

Sliger said to himself, *Shit, Jeff, you dumbshit.* "I have state of the art security cameras all over this place."

"A guy in a pinstriped suit wearing a fedora that don't look up, that's all you got. I already got my airtight alibi back in Chicago. Plus, good ole Jeff here told Johnny that you're so paranoid and controlling, your entire security camera system feeds to and is stored…right in here."

"There will be evidence left…Johnny's evidence too. He's cutting his own throat; it's suicide."

Tony stood up and said, "That's why Johnny sent you this present." He pulled a playing card-sized package out of the box and said, "Ignition device; burns to ash." Then he lifted a large vacuum sealed package from the box and said, "Accelerant; actually, a common computer cleaning solvent." Jerking the ice pick out of Jeff's back, he poked a half a dozen holes through the plastic. Tony turned the package sideways and squeezed liquid all over Jeff's back. He spoke calmly. "As long as I spray this stuff around and don't concentrate it too much, no sign of an accelerant. But one damn hot, evidence-eliminating fire."

Sliger tried to shuffle away from Jeff. *Oh God, oh God,* "Wait, wait, it's not too late. We can still make a deal, you and me…anything you want."

Tony doused Sliger then set the package down. He knelt next to Sliger. "All I need from you is to know if you're right-handed or left-handed."

Sliger put out his hands and yelled, "No, no, I won't—"

Tony jammed the ice pick deep into Sliger's right eye and said, "Doesn't matter, I already know."

Tony quickly pulled out the ice pick and moved back to keep Sliger's twitching, jerking body from flicking blood on his suit. He wiped the ice pick off on Sliger's pant leg and placed it back inside his vest. Tony stood up and reviewed and rehearsed what had taken place and what he still needed to do. *The hard-plastic bullet in Sliger's side won't survive the extreme heat of the fire. With only soft tissue damage to these two, the intensity of the fire should eliminate all evidence of…assassination. I need to wedge open the door to Sliger's office and the one to this smelly turd's private quarters, then turn this computer room's huge ventilation system on high. After I finish spraying the solvent around, just crush the two chemicals together in the ignition devise. Four minutes to get out of the building and…poof.*

Two minutes later Tony "Two Tap" Bassetti crushed the packet and tossed it on Sliger's bloody lap. He grabbed the now empty box, placed it under his arm and briskly moved out of the computer room and through Sliger's conference room. Not until he reached the huge double doors did he put his pistol away. When the door opened, Tony strolled to the elevator like a man without a care in the world.

Chapter Sixty-six
Trevrep

Sitting at her work station at the Sacramento Bee, Katelyn's excitement waned as call after call to Whit's cabin went unanswered. She tried Sheriff Whittingham's home and left a message. Finally, she tried Grey's house.

"Milner Organic Produce and Supply."

"Grey, it's Katelyn. Where's Whit?"

"Hi, Kate; I don't know. He met with Allyson yesterday and said he'd be in touch, but I haven't heard a peep."

Oh, no. "Grey, we have to find him before he does something…terrible. I found out some very important information about Steven Sliger, but it makes no sense to me. I'm sure Whit will know."

Grey thought about Whit's strict order and admonishment. *"Katelyn must never learn about Donnie, the disposal of Lamar's body, the bloody mess we cleaned up at my cabin, or anything to do about going after Sliger or Lance. If anyone's going to blow it, Milner, it's you."*

Knowing Whit took off with Allyson to kidnap Lance, Milner lied, "I'm sure he's around; probably working or driving into town. We'll find him." Frustrated, Katelyn remained silent, so Grey said, "Tell me; maybe I can put meaning to your information."

"Okay, um, okay. Whit asked me to look for the name Sliger in archives. I found the name in articles from the Foothill Democrat, and obituaries in The Nugget."

Grey said, "The Nugget? That paper went out of business when we were kids. What relevance to—"

"Just listen, Grey."

"Oh, yeah, sure, sorry; I'm just trying to—"

"Grey, shut the hell up!" Katelyn dropped the phone to her side, looked straight up and said, "Jesus." She waited a few more seconds then tried again. "Wilhelm Sliger owned a hard rock mine in the county south of yours. He married in 1908 and had three sons—Wilhelm Jr., Albert, and Jonathan. Albert died as a child; Wilhelm Jr. was killed as a young man in a mining accident. Jonathan eventually inherited his dad's mine. He married in 1931 and had two daughters, Christiana and Elisabeth. You follow me so far?"

Not seeing where any of this led or what Katelyn thought she had, Grey said, "Yeah, but—"

"Okay, now listen," Katelyn cut in. "Christiana married but apparently never had children. Elisabeth married a guy named Robert Neuton in—"

"Holy shit! Holy shit!"

"What, Grey? What?"

"Holy shit!"

"Grey, stop swearing and talk to me."

"Robert Neuton is Jonathan Neuton's dad, Jonathan Fucking Neuton!"

"Who's Jonathan Neuton?"

"Neuton is Sliger, Sliger is Neuton."

"Milner, stop with the cryptic babbling and walk me through this."

"Okay; Jesus, Kate. Jonathan Neuton grew up with us, since childhood. He was part of the gang, the seven of us. He was an odd little kid but okay. Fun, he fit in and was super smart. As we grew older he became harder or colder. We nicknamed him Trevor, after Trevor Howard, a British actor that mostly played stoic, emotionless British officers. Jonathan liked his nickname. But when we reached adolescence, he grew worse."

Katelyn asked, "What do you mean worse?"

"Oh, you know; indifferent or just plain mean to kids he felt his lesser. Plus, he had no patience or tolerance of animals, like everyone's pets. He considered them filthy and disgusting. The guy turned arrogant, really arrogant. And, he became fascinated with the Nazis and the SS. He believed most people were inferior, or at least stupid, and needed to be herded, manipulated, controlled. He acquired a kind of love/hate relationship with women, too; attracted to them but repulsed by them at the same time, if that makes any sense."

"Kind of; I'm getting a mental picture. What happened?"

"We continued to distance ourselves from him and eventually changed his nickname to Trevrep."

"Why Trevrep?"

"I think Ned figured it out. It's 'Pervert,' spelled backwards. He eventually found out. That, plus some other revelations, caused a complete relationship meltdown with the rest of us. That occurred at the end of our senior year. He really hated us. He left school and basically disappeared. No one's heard from him or even really thought about him in, what, twenty years."

Katelyn said, "Obviously, Jonathan Neuton changed his name to his mother's maiden name, Sliger. Over the last twenty years Sliger must have devolved into a psychopath, a nut case, a revenge-seeking whack job. But Grey, in Sacramento, there's a very successful businessman named Steven Sliger. We have to tell Whit's dad and get the police involved. I'm afraid Whit and Allyson know and will go after Sliger. He'll confront Sliger and—"

"Okay, Kate. *Clever girl; Jesus, if she only knew.* I'll go find the sheriff and talk to him. What are you going to do?"

"As soon as I can leave work, I'm heading for Cedar Creek. We have to find Whit and stop him. I'll head for Whit's dad's house first."

Grey said, "V's in the shower. She has to leave for, ah, work...whatever that is. As soon as she's gone, I'll go to Whit's cabin. If he's not there, I'll leave a note on his gate and head back."

"Okay." Someone in the news room ran up to Katelyn's cubicle and she said, "Wait a second, Grey."

Grey could tell Katelyn put the phone against her clothes as he barely heard her say, "I'm on it. Tell Danny to grab the van and meet me out front."

When Katelyn returned, she said, "Shit, Grey, I'm screwed; big fire downtown; I gotta go."

Chapter Sixty-seven
My Old Pal

Whit looked quickly in the rearview mirror at Lance's smug expression as he drove up the parking garage ramp under the Serpentine Solutions building. He slowed at the turnstile as a metallic female voice spoke while the stop arm lifted.

"Serpentine Solutions provides free parking for our environmentally sensitive employees and guests."

Lance told Whit to head west on a one-way street with a single letter for its name. Whit took the I-5 onramp to head north. Lance told Whit to take Business 80 east and just keep driving the speed of the traffic, all the way to Cedar Creek. Whit couldn't see Allyson crumpled against the back-passenger door and thought, *I have less than an hour to get the drop on this murderous freak. I hope Allyson can hold out. I need to induce conversation, get him talking. Obviously, this move on his part hasn't been clearly thought out. If I can rattle him or cater to his arrogant ego, maybe he'll drop his guard. If not, I'll just have to crash this car and take my chances.*

Whit asked, "How you doing, Allyson?"

Before Allyson answered, Lance cut in. "Like I said, what's the difference?"

Whit replied, "Because, you dumb ass, if you plan to make it look like we killed each other, the difference in the time of death could blow that theory."

Shit. After thinking a while, Lance responded, "Then a murder/suicide. You killed her first because of what she did to Penrose; then you became distraught, guilt-ridden, and killed yourself."

"Won't fly; everyone, including my dad, knows Allyson and I are working together. Besides, anyone who knows me, even a little, knows that's not in my character."

Shit! Getting mad, Lance said, "Then I'll just kill you both and drive away."

"Murder the sheriff's son, after all your pathetic failed attempts against my friends and me? Throw in the death of the woman specifically looking for you outside of your daddy's building? Can you say murder one investigation, subpoenas, warrants, a microscopic detailed search into Serpentine Solutions?"

"Just shut up and drive." *Shit, I didn't think this out. I should have listened to Townsend and taken them upstairs. I need to think of—* Whit lifted his arm and Lance jumped back and pointed the gun at Whit's head.

Whit held up and shook his handkerchief, tossed it in the back and said, "Better wrap that around the knife and apply pressure...if you want to keep your options open."

Lance didn't respond to Whit. After he noticed Whit looking in the rearview mirror, Lance grabbed the cloth and threw it at Allyson. "Here."

Allyson, shriveled up against the far door with her eyes closed, didn't move at first. Eventually, she slowly reached around until she found the handkerchief. She gingerly wrapped it around the base of the knife and tried to apply pressure.

They drove on in mostly silence for about twenty minutes. Twice Whit asked Allyson how she felt. Both times she weakly said, "Okay." The last time she added, "Cold."

When they started up the foothills and turned north on the state highway, Allyson started coughing. Whit looked over his shoulder at her and noticed she wasn't holding the handkerchief against her wound. He said, "Allyson? Allyson!"

Lance put Allyson's pistol against the base of Whit's neck. "Just drive."

"I'm pulling over. Shoot if you want, but I'm stopping."

Lance wasn't sure what to do; shooting Whit on a state highway would seriously complicate everything, especially his escape. He finally said, "Don't try anything or I shoot and take my chances."

Whit pulled into a wide turnout and stopped. He scooted across the front seat, looked down at Allyson and grimaced. He started to open the passenger door. Lance, tracking Whit with the gun, said, "Very slowly; move very slowly."

Whit opened the passenger door and walked slowly to the back door. He opened it just enough to hold Allyson up, then pulled the door open. She gave no resistance and sluffed into his arms. She inhaled and exhaled in rapid little breaths.

Whit looked at her ashen face and softly said, "Allyson, I'm here."

Allyson's eyes half opened, and she whispered, "The...envelope."

Lance asked, "What did she say? What did she say? Tell me."

Whit thought quickly and said, "I've...lost all hope."

Lance said, "What's that mean?"

Whit slid her in farther and laid her down. "Don't know and doesn't matter; she's dead."

Lance said, "Fine; about time." When Whit snapped his head up and glared at Lance, Lance glared back unafraid. He had the gun; he felt in charge. "Move damn slowly, get back in, and drive."

As Whit retraced his steps back to the driver's seat, he thought, *I hope when Allyson's attorney doesn't hear from her, he doesn't end up sending the envelope to Benjamin Whittingham....dead man.*

As they closed in on Cedar Creek, Lance bragged, "I know what I'm going to do with you two and it will work out perfectly. You were supposed to be charcoal in your cabin. Well, nothing's changed." Lance tapped the window with Allyson's gun and finished, "Except the location."

Whit, sounding defeated, asked, "It won't make any difference one way or the other now. Why don't you tell me who Steven Sliger was, before he changed his name?"

Lance leaned forward and goaded, "You're the great Benjamin Whittingham, mister super powers of insight. You tell me."

Whit thought, *Lance couldn't lean that far forward if he still wore his seatbelt.* To Lance, Whit said, "Obviously, it's someone who knows Ned, Grey and me; that's the common thread. But we are so different; different lifestyles, jobs, relationships. How could we all be the target of one person?"

Lance smirked, "Indeed."

"Someone would have to know us all well. Plus, the attacks are so visible, brutal, and meant to be. That means someone who really hates us, all...three... of us." *Son of a bitch!*

Realizing Whit knew, or was very close to knowing, Lance leaned forward again and tapped Whit on the side of the neck with the little automatic and excitedly asked, "Yes? Have you come up with—"

Realizing the barrel of the gun pointed parallel to his neck, instead of into his neck; Whit snapped his right hand up, grabbed the pistol and held it tight. At the same time, he jammed the car to the left, across the road, and over the bank.

Lance made funny little squealing sounds as inertia sent his body toward Allyson. He tried to pull the trigger, but the firing pin struck the side of Whit's index finger. As the car slid down sideways and then rolled over, Lance lost grip of the gun as he slammed hard to his left, then all over like a rag doll.

Whit's airbag didn't deploy, but his seatbelt and the steering wheel kept him in the driver's seat. He hit the side of his head hard against the window and the door frame. Momentarily shaken up, he tried to clear his head. He eventually realized the car rested down on the driver's side. Then he smelled gas and saw smoke.

Whit popped his seat belt and realized Lance lay partially on him, unconscious, in a heap. Whit didn't see Allyson. He pulled himself free and stomped repeatedly on Lance until he gained good footing. As Whit stood, he rolled down the still functioning passenger window. *I could grab Lance and jerk him out ahead of me.* Seeing the fire building, Whit decided, *Too bad, asshole; that's what yappy little mongrels like you get for jumping off the porch and trying to play with the big dogs.* Whit jumped three or four times until his arms cleared the window enough to hoist himself out. He backed away from the car and the highway. Whit heard then felt a whoosh of heat as the underside of the car ignited. Whit backed away further as he assumed the gas tank must have buckled or ruptured.

Whit never found Allyson and realized she was still inside the car. Lance must have broken his neck—or just never regained consciousness—as he never cried out. Hearing a car slowing down on the highway, Whit slipped away through the trees and brush heading north to Cedar Creek. Looking back one last time Whit silently said, *I'm sorry, Allyson. Whatever your attorney directs me to do, I'll do it.* Turning his attention to his new task, Whit thought, *Time to focus on my old pal, Jonathan Neuton.*

Chapter Sixty-eight
You're Hiding Something

Two hours after a frantic Good Samaritan called in the tragic vehicle fire south of Cedar Creek, Whit had already hiked to his dad's house and eaten some cheese, salami and an apple. He then showered and made numerous phone calls. He told everyone to meet in the back room of Pete's place at ten o'clock. Everyone except Katelyn; she had driven straight to Whit's dad's house after reporting on the four-alarm fire in Downtown Sacramento. She saw and ran to Whit and held him without speaking for a long time. Katelyn felt so relieved.... initially. Later she grew guarded, suspicious, a little standoffish as Whit explained briefly what had transpired. She wanted more detail about the car fire she drove past south of town. Whit said he'd walk through the whole story completely once everyone involved in this nightmare met.

Whit mocked surprise at Katelyn's revelation that Steven Sliger was in fact Whit's old ex-friend, Jonathan Neuton. She also told him she felt 99-percent sure Steven Sliger, or Jonathan Neuton, would be identified as one of the victims in a huge fire that had occurred in Sliger's Downtown Sacramento building. She asked Whit straight out if he had anything to do with the fire at Serpentine Solutions. He answered truthfully, he did not. *Not that fire anyway.* He also wondered who else had it in for Sliger. That fire, the timing, no way could it be a coincidence.

When Whit, Katelyn, Grey and Ned met in the back room of Pete's Place, they noticed Stacey acted ill-tempered and short. Ned told them, "Her sister is on a date, so Stace can't get out of work. She's fuming because she can't join the meeting."

Stacey stood at the door to the back room with her arms crossed. She said, half in jest, "I hate you all." She turned to Whit and added, "Your dad called looking for you and your motley crew. As soon as he's finished with the double fatality south of town, he's coming straight here."

Whit asked, "And his mood?"

As she turned to leave them, Stacey replied, "Very similar to mine."

Whit groaned as they all sat down. He started, "I think you all know Katelyn found out that Steven Sliger, the guy who orchestrated all the attacks on us, is—or was—in fact, Jonathan Neuton."

Grey said, "How do you grow up in Cedar Creek as a happy little kid then turn into someone so damn sick and evil?"

Whit replied, "Well, it doesn't matter anymore; apparently he's tater tots."

Katelyn said, "I'll get a call as soon as the paper hears confirmation. But unofficially, one of the dead is Sliger."

Whit spoke up again. "What I'm about to reveal to you concerns the death of Lance, Sliger's protégé." Whit turned to Ned and said, "And I'm sorry Ned, Allyson, too." Other than Ned's nostrils flaring, his only other response was just a slight nod.

Whit started in, "Allyson knew Lance's connection to Sliger and where to find him."

Grey asked, "Shouldn't we wait for your dad?

Whit shook his head. "No, who knows when my old man will finish with that wreck? Besides, I want to get this all out."

Katelyn asserted, "Like a dry run, ahead of your official statement to the authorities?"

Caught a little off guard, Whit turned to her and replied, "Nice jab, Kate." Knowing where her ire originated, he apologized. "I should have gone to the police like I promised, I'm sorry." No one spoke or even looked up from the table, so Whit continued. "Allyson and I figured we needed something more solid, so they all wouldn't lawyer up. Allyson felt Lance was a coward and would turn on Sliger to save his ass. It made sense; I went with it."

Whit could tell Katelyn didn't accept his reasoning but kept going. "Allyson and I tried to snatch Lance. Allyson actually had him, but some giant ogre of a security guard got the drop on me. Lance somehow stabbed Allyson and took her gun." Whit turned to Ned and lied, "She died instantly, Ned; she didn't suffer."

Again, Ned remained stone-faced and nodded.

"Allyson was placed in the back seat of her car. Lance sat behind me, holding Allyson's gun to my head, as I drove. He ordered me to drive to Cedar

Creek. Ironically, Lance planned to kill me up here and burn Allyson and my body in Allyson's car."

Katelyn said, "Whit, you said you had nothing to do with the fire at the Serpentine Solutions building."

"I didn't. I didn't even know the place caught fire."

Katelyn followed like a prosecutor. "That happened sometime around 4 o'clock. There's a huge time discrepancy between then and the time Allyson's car crashed and caught fire."

Whit tried but failed to hide his growing anger. "Yes, Ms. Investigative Reporter. I only told you the Reader's Digest version at my dad's house; be patient." *She's mad and knows I'm not telling the whole truth.*

Whit pushed on. "Lance fumbled with a bunch of scenarios of how to plan my murder and his escape. He wanted our bodies found far away from Sacramento. Lance bragged how he'd pull it off. But I continued to find flaws in his plans. He eventually came up with just shooting me and burning the vehicle with Allyson in it, too. Because he'd have to torch his ride, Lance figured to do it at night; less chance of being seen while he got away. Lance had me pull over near Dry Creek down a side road. We didn't pull back onto the highway toward Cedar Creek until dusk."

Everyone seemed satisfied except Katelyn. "I know you, Whit; in all that time, you didn't try to get the drop on him?"

"I would have tried something if I had a ghost of a chance. He sat behind me the whole time, Kate. He'd have pumped at least four shots into me before I turned around. But what he didn't know…before we made it to Cedar Creek, I was going to crash Allyson's car anyway."

Katelyn pressed. "Then how did you get the drop on Lance?"

"Patience, prosecutor," Whit snapped. "I'm getting there."

Ned said, "Come on, Kate, give Whit some slack; he's sitting here alive, isn't he?"

That hit home. Katelyn's expression changed, and she looked a little embarrassed. She put up her hands and said, "You're right, you're right, I'm sorry. The journalist in me took over." She leaned over to Whit, rubbed his shoulder and whispered, "I'm sorry."

Whit gave her a quick, neutral nod and continued. "Lance is the cocky type and I finally started him talking…more like bragging. He came up behind me and, for emphasis, tapped me on the neck with Allyson's gun. To lean so far forward, he couldn't be wearing his seat belt. Plus, I felt the barrel of the gun more parallel to my neck than pointing into my neck. I grabbed the gun tight in my right hand and jerked the steering wheel hard left. Over the bank we sailed and…smash. I stayed in place, but Lance flew all over the place. We rolled and eventually hit a big rock. I think Lance flew into the dashboard and knocked himself out."

Everyone seemed to absorb and weigh what Whit told them. Finally, Katelyn put her coffee down and said, "Could you have saved him and pulled Allyson's body out of the vehicle?"

Whit knew what Katelyn implied. Allyson and Lance's bodies burning to a crisp ultimately turned out to be very convenient for Whit. Especially since Whit left the scene, thereby ostensibly removing himself from the incident or any involvement.

Whit looked at Katelyn and said, "Truthfully, Lance…maybe; but not Allyson. I was a little shook up; banged my head. When my head cleared, I saw flames and smelled gas. I made the decision to bail and stuck with it."

No one spoke for a while and Whit prayed Grey wouldn't inadvertently blurt out something in front of Katelyn.

Katelyn finally sat back and said, "God, can it really be all over?" She snapped her fingers. "Just like that?"

Whit looked at Grey and said, "I'm thinking if Sliger's dead and those hit-men remain long gone and never turn up, then yes, it's over."

From out in the main bar, they heard significant commotion, then nothing. Sheriff Bill Whittingham had entered the bar looking around. Everyone at the bar turned, saw the badge, then became morgue silent.

Before Bill spoke, they heard Stacey say, "Back room."

Bill stormed into the back room and right up to their table. He looked everyone over then addressed them by name. "Ned, Peckerneck, Kate." He turned to Whit and said, "Benjamin, you're in a heap of trouble, boy."

After a few seconds of silence, everyone nervously laughed. Whit asked his dad in an innocent voice, "What makes you think I'm involved?"

Bill pointed a finger at his son and bellowed, "Christ, Benjamin; since you were born what shit storm that has ever hit this county not involved you?"

Everyone turned to Whit waiting for his response. Whit said, "Guilty; but you know more than you're telling."

Again no one spoke; Bill put a boot on an empty chair and leaned forward. He said evenly, "The security officer at the high school saw you sitting with

Ned's, ah, ex-girlfriend, in the school parking lot. He took down the license, the make and model of the car and later told me. It's the charred vehicle. I just made an educated guess about tonight and that you were involved; thanks for the confirmation." Bill sat down and said, "Let's hear it."

Fifteen minutes later, Whit had recited the day's events again for his dad. He finished with, "I doubt if the true identities of the two will turn up anywhere; not without some serious digging by the Feds, if they get involved. And Dad, I really need to stay out of this…if possible." Everyone looked at Bill, who didn't say a word.

The sheriff was just about to speak when a deputy entered the back room. He walked to the chair, now occupied by the sheriff and reported, "Sir, we've removed the two bodies…pretty severely burned and towed the vehicle."

Realizing the deputy would not have come find his sheriff just to tell him routine information, Bill said, "And?"

"Well, sir, the coroner said the victim in the front, well, one of his hands burned off."

"I saw it in Korea with white phosphorous; hell, once everything burns off the bones there's nothing left to hold them together."

Katelyn noticed Whit look down and stare at his drink.

"No, sir; the wrist was attached. The hand burned off between the wrist and the fingers, because the bones were all shattered, like—"

"Thank you, Sergeant; that will be all."

The Sergeant persisted. "But sir—"

When Bill shot out of his chair, the officer stopped and nearly stood at attention. Looking his deputy right in the eyes, Bill said, "Take off your shirt and badge, go find a table in the bar and wait for me."

"Sir?"

"Have Ms. Cummings bring over two pints, your pick. It's late, and I say we're off duty. I'll be with you in a minute."

The wide-eyed deputy stammered, "Yes sir," turned, and left.

Bill turned to the table and said, "You young people need to go home before I institute a curfew. We'll sort this out tomorrow. Deal?"

Everyone nodded and stood up as Bill left.

They all exited out the back door to the bar's tiny parking lot. Katelyn and Whit hopped into Katelyn's car, but she waited until Grey and Ned left. She turned to Whit and said, "What aren't you telling me?"

Shaking his head, Whit sternly suggested, "How about, thank God it's over and I'm so glad we're alive and safe."

"Of course, yes, of course. But I know you, Benjamin; you're hiding something."

Whit put his head down and didn't talk for a while. Finally, he said to his feet. "You know, Kate, when you're doing something wrong and while you're doing it, you know it's wrong, but you don't stop yourself? Then, later you feel bad because it's not you...not who you are?"

"Whit, what did you do?"

Whit turned to Kate and said, "I could have pulled Lance from the car; I'm pretty sure I had time. I'll never know for sure now, but I didn't even try. He was below me when I scrambled out. To get out of the passenger window, I had to jump quite a few times to gain purchase. Each time I did, I heard my boots crushing bones. I'm pretty sure now; I must have smashed the hell out of one of Lance's hands. Even if he came to, he couldn't have lifted himself out. Fortunately, I didn't hear him scream or cry out. He was either already dead or never regained consciousness. I'll have to live with that."

Katelyn leaned over and put her head on Whit's shoulder. "Oh, thank God; I thought you killed Lance and used the fire to cover it up."

Whit said, "Kate, as angry as I get, I could never turn into someone like that."

Katelyn grabbed Whit under his chin and said, "Oh, I like that, Mr. Whittingham, I like that a lot." She let him go and added, "I worry so much about you and your, your brooding dark moods. It scares me sometimes."

"I'll admit, Kate; I've had some...dark episodes in my past. But, I'm not going back there; you've changed me...forever."

Katelyn smiled. "We can't stay at your dad's house tonight and...celebrate like I plan. We're heading for your cabin."

"Works for me," Whit said grinning back.

Katelyn said, "I hope it works out for Stinker."

A little confused, Whit asked, "What works out for Stinker?"

Katelyn smiled as she pulled her car on to Main Street. "Stinker's new roommate, I hope it works out for her, too."

Whit put his head on the headrest, smiled, closed his eyes and said to himself, *Shit Howdy!*

Chapter Sixty-nine
Epilogue

Katelyn stood up in her cramped Connecticut condo's little den and said to herself, *Well, I made it through the happy-ever-after, rainbows-and-unicorns, Cinderella ending without crying.* She raised her hands and halfheartedly cheered, "Hal-Le-Friggin'-Lujah."

She stretched and looked at the clock, *Jesus; it's three in the morning.* Quieter, she said to her pseudonym, "Sam Lund, you just finished the book, and it's a good one." *I finished, I did it, I should feel...more elated? But regardless of the Hal-Le-Friggin-Lujah...not this time. I have everything down that took place, as close as anyone alive can recall. Well, except for the wishful, make-believe prologue and the rosy ending. Screw it; I'm done with what goes to print. This is what Sam Lund wrote, this is what the public will read, and this is the story that will sell.*

Too tired and too numb to cry, Katelyn just sighed and said, "But...I would have been so damn happy."

She closed her eyes and rolled her head back and around in slow circles. *Hell; go to bed and do the epilogue in the morning.*

No, no, do the epilogue now, while you're still fired up and can recall what happened to everyone...or at least what you guess happened. Readers always want to know which direction each character's lives travel.

Katelyn took a bathroom break and grabbed a Mountain Dew. She knew she'd regret the caffeine rich drink later but needed the boost. Katelyn returned and sat. *Okay, Sam Lund, start with the obvious ones and avoid....*

Epilogue

Jeff Bowman

Poor Jeff Bowman burned to a crisp, sure as hell…so said the coroner. If the brilliant, sorrowful soul could have been left alone with a steady supply of electricity and surrounded by his computers, he'd have survived fine and been content without interacting with another human. Unfortunately, as in nature, survival on the fringe rarely works out. Many who knew or came into contact with Jeff, while he was alive, speculated that after the fire, he surely must have smelled better.

Steven Sliger

Steven Sliger's empire collapsed following his mysterious, ignominious and fiery demise. With almost all of his soft tissue consumed, the autopsy revealed no indication of foul play. In the volatile confines of the computer room, even though the area near the bodies burned extremely hot, fire investigators could not positively rule in or out the use of an accelerant. The environmental movement in many articles and opinion pieces praised Steven Sliger's innovation and vision. Attorney for Earth Wild, Luna Waxman, spoke at his celebration of life, embellishing about how a beautiful green beacon no longer lit the way along their righteous path. Definitely, all of his competitors and many of his employees did not fully share that view.

Lance Sliger

As far as the police were concerned, Lance Sliger started out as a missing person. Witnesses confirmed that just before the fire at Serpentine Solutions, Lance spoke to the head of security, Ron Townsend, and his huge subordinate, Moose. The two were quoted as saying, "Lance walked out of the building to meet some lady." He never returned and was never heard from or seen again. Officials finally identified the male body, severely burned in the fiery car crash south of Cedar Creek. Through dental records, a match confirmed the remains belonged to a Larry Baker. Upon contact from the authorities, Larry Baker's mother initially said her son had died a long time ago. Upon prompting, she cleared up the confusion for the police. She told the authorities, her estranged son just started calling himself, Lance Sliger. She reluctantly took charge of the remains.

Allyson Chandler

Allyson Chandler never existed. No tax information, social security number, fingerprints, birth certificate, green card, criminal records, bank accounts or any other form of identification ever surfaced. Evidently the woman entered the country illegally and lived under many aliases. The remains of the woman killed in the burned out white Impala south of Cedar Creek could not be positively identified. The car was registered to a fictitious owner named Hannah Stanford.

Andrea Moran

Witnesses at Serpentine Solutions confirmed Andrea Moran uncharacteristically and unprofessionally rushed out of the building and jumped into private investigator Sean Peterson's car. The two never returned. Police detectives searched both Moran and Peterson's residences and found virtually all of their possessions. A check of financial accounts proved the two withdrew substantial cash on the same day they disappeared. Both appeared to be on the run for unknown reasons and remained persons of interest.

Lamar Jackson

Even though Lamar Jackson's last residence placed him in Chicago, he just ceased to exist. Bills piled up, calls were never returned, and eventually his landlord finally took possession of his apartment and belongings. Everyone just figured he'd left and started a new life somewhere else. No one cared enough to even file a missing person's report.

Donnie Sloane

Donnie Sloane's military records included an honorable discharge. Sloane's only known employment, following his discharge was a bouncer job in one of

Chicago's finer Italian bars and restaurants. However, the man abruptly disappeared from his Chicago job, never to return. Rumors that he entered the federal witness protection program and that he fingered a high-ranking Chicago mob boss could not be confirmed.

Tony Bassetti

Even though airport cameras in San Francisco International Airport caught an individual with a striking resemblance to Tony Bassetti, his rock-solid alibi in Chicago precluded any further investigation into his involvement with the intense inferno that converted Steven Sliger and Jeff Bowman into pork rinds. However, seven months later, authorities found Tony "Two Tap" Bassetti dead in a couple's apartment in Santa Barbara. Apparently, someone gave Tony a taste of his own medicine...a bullet in the kneecap and one in the right eye. A bum and snitch for the Santa Barbara police department said he had a good description of two couples leaving the apartment the night of the shooting. They walked right by him. The couple that lived in the apartment, he'd seen numerous times and regarded them as an odd match. The female was short, but a beauty with an hourglass figure; the guy looked like a gun safe...a chunk, blocky and thick. The two individuals escorting the couple away that night kind of looked like cops. The female, attractive but hard-looking, walked with purpose and seemed to be in charge. The man, tall and fit, looked like an athlete. The most striking feature he possessed was a nasty scar across half of his neck. As the bum cowered by a dumpster when the four walked by, he distinctly heard the woman in the back say to the couple in front, "I may have a use for you."

Johnny Ramelli

A huge federal racketeering indictment landed on Johnny "Big Nose" Ramelli's lap soon after someone punched Tony Bassetti's ticket. Apparently, the Feds retained a star witness rumored to be one of Johnny's ex-enforcers. Johnny's proclamation that he would never spend one day in a federal prison turned out to be...not true.

Gene Perkins

Gene took his lieutenant's position as the head of the local Fish and Game office. His previous boss, Lieutenant Dalton, moved to Sacramento. The rumor mill among the employees presumed Lieutenant Dalton's poor handling of a previous female employee problem and the Benjamin Whittingham fiasco forced him out. Out, of course, in the world of bureaucracies, meant a promotion up the ladder. Gene became a regular and good friend to a small group of Cedar Creek locals that met every Tuesday night at a bar called Pete's Place.

William "Bill" Whittingham

Bill easily won reelection for his sixth term as sheriff of Logan County, despite the growing knowledge of his mental blackouts. When confronted during the campaign, Bill admitted to reoccurring dreams, flashbacks, and nightmares of violent battles he'd fought with his platoon in Korea. He addressed his disorder with honest frankness and actually garnered support from his constituents. Many locals also noted, to their surprise, that Sheriff Whittingham quit calling Greyson Milner...Peckerneck.

Ned Penrose

Ned Penrose remained proprietor of Penrose Stationery with a new partner, Stacey Cummings. Following a strange phone call from a law firm in New Orleans, Ned received an award which included a cash payment of $250,000. Apparently, a Spanish philanthropist named Louis Escobar periodically searched out and rewarded individuals who exhibited a selfless and long-standing record of exemplary community service. The reclusive donor of the "Noble Service Award" stipulated only one requirement—the beneficiary could never contact Senor Escobar. Asked what he planned to do with the money, Ned quipped, "I'm going to keep running the store...until it's all gone."

Stacey Cummings

Stacey continued to run her bar, Pete's Place, with her sister; and she became half owner and partner of Penrose Stationery. She refused Ned Penrose's initial proposal of marriage due to his previous, disastrous track record. She opted for a five-year engagement to avoid all the paperwork and to see...how it goes.

Greyson Milner

Grey returned to seriously focusing on his organic produce and farm supply business. He also began a three-year renovation project of the family Victorian.

Grey became far less self-absorbed and made a concerted effort to treat female acquaintances with considerably more respect. He also took a lead from Ned and joined numerous local service clubs and organizations.

Veronica Sanchez

The mysterious and mercurial V, and her Harley, pulled out of Cedar Creek the day Allyson, Lance and Steven Sliger died. She never returned and, as far as anyone knew, never made any attempt to contact Greyson Milner again. Everyone believed that at some point she'd push her luck too far; you can't live on a razor's edge forever. In some lonely forgotten back woods, the demons, evils spirits, and ghosts that haunted her so would finally disappear as some dirt bag tossed her lifeless body into a shallow grave.

Benjamin Whittingham

Whit proposed to Katelyn at his cabin the night the attacks on he and his buddies ended. With Stinker, the ring-tailed cat, as witness, Whit even knelt on one knee. He returned to working in the woods and remained a vocal advocate for sound forest and wildlife practices and prudent government oversight. Whit's dimensionless love for his wife and later, two sons, eventually rounded off his rough edges and further diminished his...darker side. He worked less to devote more time to his true love, his boys, and lifelong friends.

Katelyn Summers

Katelyn Summers said yes before Whit got past "Will you-." She fell head-over-heels in love with Whit the first night they'd met. She couldn't explain it and really didn't care; he was the one. They moved into his cabin in the mountains where he built her a woman cave, so she could write. They had two sons, William Michael and Justin Abraham. The city woman grew into a mountain girl. She learned to garden, can fruits and vegetables, fly fish, hunt, and even clean game while turning into a damn fine cook. Due to growing boys, Katelyn learned how to make love to Whit anywhere and everywhere the kids weren't; and, when need be, to be as quiet as a church mouse.

Chapter Seventy
More Sorry than You'll Ever Know

The last two entries in the Epilogue upset Katelyn badly. Sitting back in her chair, the crying returned. Katelyn viciously wiped tears out of her eyes. She muttered, "Goddamnit...Goddamnit. Why couldn't you just—"

She stopped complaining...pointless. Benjamin Whittingham would never change; he'd proven she couldn't change him. True to himself, he was a goddamn throwback; old school, an eye for an eye, don't tread on me, free spirit, wild animal, kill or be killed...Christ, she could go on and on. How could someone so gentle, compassionate, loving, turn so...self-righteous, violent, pitiless?

She closed her eyes, rested her body against the back of the chair, and put her hands on her head. *Yes, Katelyn, everything's written; written for the public consumption, everything except...why I'm not with Whit and can never be. Shit; with what I know, he really should be in prison.*

She opened her eyes and said to herself, *I need to write the last chapter...the truth. Spell it out for me; spell it out...clear the air. But no one, absolutely no one, can ever read it.*

She demanded the truth from Whit and he told her...everything. *Why didn't I just let it go? Why did I force an ultimatum, and why the hell did Whit tell me? I guess Whit was right all along; we lived in two worlds, too far apart.*

Sliger and his stepson were no different than a psychopath like Charles Manson. Of course they had to be stopped. But didn't the system take care of Manson? Why couldn't Whit trust the police and the courts? That's the glue that binds society together, for Christ's sake. If we breach the law to our own ends, don't we ourselves become

Sliger...Lance...Manson? If Sliger hadn't died, Whit never would have stopped. He'd have just kept hunting, stalking, pursuing until he killed Sliger...or died trying.

What her alias, Sam Lund, could reveal in the book, Katelyn could not. But Katelyn had to finish with the truth...for herself. Leaning forward, committed now, she pursed her lips once again. Katelyn began at that cataclysmic night when the gang met at Pete's Place...where it all ended; a day of death and a night of shock, when she gazed into her lover's eyes...for the last time.

The Truth

Bill turned to the table and said, "You young people need to go home before I institute a curfew. We'll sort this out tomorrow, deal?"

Everyone nodded and stood up as Bill left.

They all exited out the back door to the bar's tiny parking lot. Katelyn and Whit hopped into Katelyn's car, but she waited until Grey and Ned left. She turned to Whit and said, "What aren't you telling me?"

Shaking his head, Whit sternly suggested, "How about, thank God it's over and I'm so glad we're all alive and safe?"

"Of course, of course I feel that way. But I know you, Benjamin Whittingham; you're hiding something."

"Kate, it's over...all of it. Let's go home and re-start our lives without... all this."

"I can't start out thinking you did something bad, terrible, horrible enough that you won't or can't tell me. That's no foundation for a lifelong relationship." When Whit looked away and didn't respond, she knew whatever he kept from her was devastating. She said softly, "Whit, be honest with me, please."

Maybe Katelyn's right; she'd always wonder. Katelyn would never stop trying to find out. But if I tell her the truth, she'll blanch and won't understand.

"Whit, please; I have to know...no secrets between us."

I knew this day would arrive. I knew it way back in Virginia, the first morning. Whit closed his eyes and sat stiffly. Neither spoke for quite some time. Finally, Whit opened his eyes and as he looked straight ahead, he said, "That cut on my head, I wasn't hit by a falling limb in the woods, like I told you. I was attacked again at my cabin, by the assassins. I wore a Kevlar vest because I guessed they were hiding there. They shot me with a solid lead round from a shotgun and I banged the side of my head on my gate."

Over the next eight minutes, Whit described his brief partnership with the killers, V shooting Lamar and Donnie, his dad's and Doc Conte's involvement, Lamar's disposal, and Donnie disappearing with some mysterious federal agents.

Whit finally looked over at Katelyn. He could tell she felt betrayed and barely held back her anger. When she finally spoke, she asked, "Why did you keep all this from me?"

Whit flipped up his hands. "Katelyn, what was the point? In reality, for your sake, the less you knew the better...legally speaking."

Katelyn saw right through Whit's logic. "That may be true, but that's not why you didn't tell me." Angrily she continued. "You didn't tell me because you were going after Lance and Sliger and you didn't want me to know." When Whit didn't respond, she yelled, "You lied to me. You said you'd go to the police when you found solid evidence."

Whit tried to explain. "Kate, if the police arrested them, those bastards would have hired a high-end law firm and walled themselves off. Hell, look what the justice system did to me. Try to understand my—"

"What really happened today?" Katelyn cut in.

Whit's fists tightened as he forced out, "Kate, don't ask. For our sake, don't ask me to explain any more than I have tonight."

Now it was Katelyn's turn to look straight ahead. She said sternly, "You tell me the whole truth right now or I will never," she turned to face Whit, "never trust a word you say, ever again."

Whit felt cornered. *How do I deal with an ultimatum like that? She's put me in a burning building, ten floors up. I can choose to burn to death or leap to my death. Our relationship dies if I tell her; our relationship dies if I don't tell her.* Whit put his palms to his temples and tried to think. *What the hell do I do?* Whit thought about his dad and mom. *No matter how bad—and there were some really bad—his dad always told his mom the truth. Somehow, they worked it out.*

"Okay, Kate, okay. I just want you to know, I love you and always will; nothing will ever change my feelings. But those bastards came after my friends and—"

Katelyn threw up her hands and he stopped. He waited but she didn't speak. *She doesn't care a wit about my motives. Okay, okay,* Whit took a deep breath. He cleared his throat, closed his eyes and began. "It was around three-thirty; I was in the parking garage under Serpentine Solutions. Allyson prodded Lance down the parking ramp with a gun in his back."

Whit stood behind a pillar watching Lance and Allyson approach. He planned to pull in behind Allyson when they passed, grab Lance and stuff him in the trunk. Whit, with his back to the stairs, did not notice the huge head that filled the small window in the stairwell door. That odd sensation, like when a mountain lion secretly watches you, hit Whit. Just as Moose pulled his head back, Whit gave in to that funny feeling. He straightened up and snapped his head around to check the stairwell door, for the tenth time. Whit said *hmm* to himself, then turned back around. He decided, after Allyson and Lance moved a few more feet closer, he'd step out.

At that moment, Moose pushed down the release bar and bolted the fifteen feet he needed to reach Whit. Whit spun around and ducked just in time to avoid a huge right fist. With his chest still bruised and weak, Whit threw a pathetic right near Moose's spleen, with no affect. Quickly, he added a good left uppercut into a pair of huge balls. A beastly groan exited Moose's lips as his knees buckled. He crumpled forward, unfortunately, right on top of Whit.

Allyson and Lance looked toward the disturbance to their right and heard Whit yell from under the mountain of flesh, "Keep going; get him in the car." Allyson felt stuck between a rock and a hard place. She couldn't help Whit and keep control of Lance. She decided to do what Whit ordered and jabbed Lance in the back with her pistol.

Moose, in obvious pain, still managed to grab Whit's upper body in a bear hug and pin him down. He moaned, "In about two minutes, I'm going to pinch you in two."

Whit struggled to get free, but his efforts appeared hopeless. On his back with a banged-up chest and 350 pounds of rhinoceros crushing him, he could barely breathe, let alone fight. Every time Whit exhaled, he couldn't force as much air back in as the last time. Whit's only hope now depended on Allyson. If she could drug Lance quickly enough and lock him in the trunk, Whit might be able to last long enough. She could rescue him by shooting this…blob in his fat ass.

When Allyson reached her car, she told Lance to stop about ten feet back. She walked way around him and popped the trunk. Lance put his right hand in his jacket pocket. She motioned him forward and said, "Bend over and stick your head way in there."

When Lance complied, he pulled the knife out as he put his hands ahead of his body in the trunk. Allyson briefly looked down as she crossed her body with her left hand. Taped to her purse, she grabbed the plunger of a syringe full of milky white Propofol.

Lance decided it was now or never. He pushed back and spun around, sweeping with his left arm while releasing the blade of the tiny stiletto. Slightly off balance, the impact forced Allyson to step back. Lance backhanded her right wrist with his left hand. His grip kept the gun pointing away. He completed his pivot and drove the thin, four-inch blade up under the left side of Allyson's ribcage. She didn't cry out but made a painful grimace. Lance could feel her losing grip of her gun and said, "Now I'm going to watch you die, bitch."

Ever the arrogant bully when he perceived total control over a victim, Lance registered too late the determination that returned to Allyson's eyes. She head-butted Lance on the bridge of his nose. Lance released her, screaming as he backed up holding his face. Allyson shoved him and he fell backwards into the trunk, banging his head on the lid.

She staggered forward and smashed him on the temple with the butt of her gun. With blood still spouting out of his nose, Lance flopped backwards. With the last of her strength, Allyson jabbed Lance in the thigh with the needle and depressed the plunger.

Still holding the gun, she staggered back then fell on her side. Pinching the knife in her left hand, Allyson watched the back of the car. She listened as Lance moaned and feebly yelled out. Once, while pinching his nose, he peeked over the trunk. He tried to climb out but dropped back when Allyson raised her gun.

Whit heard Lance scream and knew Allyson needed help. With the last of his strength he tried to break free, but Moose had regained much of his might and started crushing Whit. Whit felt like a little deer mouse wrapped in the coils of a constrictor. The snakes often squeezed so hard that the mouse's eyes popped out. Whit realized he was passing out. His last thought: *I've failed...failed everyone.*

As Whit's eyesight faded to black, his mind registered a loud whack. Whit opened his eyes but couldn't focus. Whit's brain could no longer tell if he was being squeezed or crushed or both...then he passed out.

Allyson blinked slowly as she watched the back of her car. She realized if Lance tried to get out of the trunk again, she couldn't do anything to stop him. Her mind kept saying, *Allyson, get up, go help Whit.* But her body wouldn't respond.

The head of security raised his voice and said again, "Hey, fella, you can't stay here."

Whaaa?

Whit felt a slap to his face, so he started swinging.

Someone pinned his arms down and said, "Take it easy and take some deep breaths. Snap out of it."

Whit did and finally opened his eyes, eventually focusing on an older guy. He wore the same uniform as the huge gorilla that attacked him. The guy said again, "You're running out of time; can you sit up?"

With help, Whit spread out his legs and tipped his upper body upright. Whit leaned forward with his head between his knees and took deep breaths.

The guy said, "Let's try standing."

When Whit stood up and looked down at the big goon, he noticed a nasty crease across the unconscious man's temple. Whit asked, "What happened to him?"

Whit's guardian angel pointed to his collapsible baton and said, "Don't worry about Moose; he'll be alright."

"Moose...Jesus...figures; who are you?"

"Oh, just an old fool who's seen the light. I just retired." He pointed to Moose and said, "He just retired too, but doesn't know it yet. Look, you better get going." The guy pointed Whit toward the main part of the parking garage and gave him a little shove.

Ron Townsend watched Whit stagger off, put his baton away, then bent down over his unconscious subordinate. To extract Whit, Ron had grabbed two fistfuls of fabric, pulled, and slowly rolled Moose's body over. Now, he looked down at his unconscious partner.

Ron gently slapped both huge jowly cheeks and said, "Moose, come on, Moose."

It took a whole two minutes, but finally Moose groaned, "Ohhh, ohhh, my head. Who hit me?"

Ron looked up as a white Impala shot up the exit ramp and lied, "That guy you jumped had backup. By the time I could get this bum knee down the stairs, they were gone. And you know what? We better get gone, too."

Moose made it to all fours and asked, "Where are we going?"

"I have no idea, but we're done here. This place just smacked an iceberg and is listing badly; we're not going down, too. Come on; we deserve an extended vacation...then new employment." Slapping his right leg, he added, "Besides, I'll need someone to watch over me after my surgery."

During Moose's trauma-induced sleepy time, Whit staggered, then walked, then ran to the crumpled heap behind the white Impala. He called Allyson's name softer and softer as he approached. "Allyson, Allyson, Allyson."

When he knelt down and touched her, she moaned, "Where's Lance?"

Whit looked up. "In the trunk, out like a light."

She smiled weakly and said, "Help me into the car."

Whit saw the position of the knife and said, "Allyson, I think you're hurt badly; we have to get you to a doctor."

"No." After a couple of breaths she said, "We take Lance...and go." When Whit didn't move, she squeezed his hand and said, "I'll make it."

Whit jumped up and pulled open the driver's side backdoor. He returned and, as gently as possible, picked up Allyson and gingerly carried her to the backseat. He laid her in the backseat as far as he could, then dashed behind the car to pick up her gun and purse. Whit opened the passenger side backdoor and slowly slid Allyson all the way into the back seat. He lifted her head and slipped the purse under her head. Whit yanked out his handkerchief and wrapped it around the hilt of the evil little knife. He took Allyson's right hand, separated her fingers, placed them over his cloth and whispered, "Can't risk taking it out. Press down gently and don't stop."

Whit looked around, surprised that during the whole ordeal, not one person entered the garage. He eased the passenger backdoor closed and walked to the trunk.

Whit reached in, grabbed Lance's hair, and jerked up his torso. He drew back his arm to smash Lance's face, then realized Allyson had already broken his nose. Whit turned Lance's hair loose and watched the unconscious body flop back down. He slammed the trunk lid closed.

Whit softly closed the driver's backdoor, hopped in the front seat and fired up the car. Backing out slowly, Whit said, "Nice job on asshole's nose."

Allyson responded weakly, "Thank you."

Whit put a 49ers baseball cap on and tilted his face down as he drove up to the turnstile. A metallic female voice spoke as the stop arm lifted. "Serpen-

ine Solutions provides free parking for our environmentally sensitive employees and guests."

As Whit pulled out of the parking garage, he added, "And kidnappers,
oo."

Whit headed west on a one-way street named after a single letter. He took
he I-5 onramp to head north, then asked, "How we doing? Allyson?"

"Fine...cold."

Whit said, "I'm going back to Cedar Creek up I-80. If you get any worse,
I'm stopping at the ER at Sac. Valley Faith or Mercy St. Michael."

No answer.

"Allyson, are you still bleeding? Allyson!"

"No...I think," she meekly replied.

Yeah, but what about internally? Whit said, "My fault; I'm sorry, Allyson. I
messed up. I let a guy the size of a Beluga whale get the drop on me."

Knowing if she didn't keep talking Whit would head for a hospital, she
asked, "How did you get away?"

"I didn't; another security guy whacked the goon on the noggin and rolled
the thug off of me."

"Why?"

"Sounded like rats leaving a sinking ship."

Whit continued the small talk with Allyson; she mostly returned one-word
answers. After thirty minutes, they finally started climbing up the foothills,
and Whit felt like they just might make it.

Whit asked her for the fiftieth time, "How are you, Allyson?"

"Okay...as long...as I...don't move."

Only a couple of miles farther, Allyson coughed and started taking short
rapid breaths. Whit said, "I'm stopping at the Dry Creek Rancheria Clinic."

To Whit's surprise, in a very clear voice Allyson said, "When my lawyer
doesn't hear from me...he'll send you...the envelope."

"Allyson? Allyson!" Whit looked up and saw the Dry Creek Road off-
ramp just ahead. He pulled off and drove to the first wide spot. Whit maneuvered to the outer most edge, stopped and leaped out.

He slipped in beside Allyson and held her gray cheeks. His eyes turned
red as he said, "Hey."

Allyson's eyes opened halfway; her quick shallow breathing decreased. She
slowly whispered, "Please...go to Spain...see...my mom...tell...."

She exhaled one last time, and Whit felt her life slip away. Tears rolled off his face and splashed onto her lifeless eyes. He closed her eyes and touched her face gently. *Goddamnit, Goddamnit to hell! I'm sorry, Allyson…I'm so sorry I let you down.*

Whit realized he had to get moving. He drew away from Allyson and trudged back to the driver's seat. Whit took back roads all the way to the state highway and turned north. Within twenty miles of Cedar Creek, Whit knew how to end this. *Too much death…and not enough.*

As Whit drove, he checked the fuel gauge. *A little over half…plenty.* Whit popped open the glovebox looking for matches. He found a Bic lighter. *Even better.*

Whit drove twelve more miles then turned right and over a cattle guard onto Bean Ranch Road. Bits of gravel periodically shot out of the tire tread and banged into the fender wells. Whit stopped at an old Powder River gate; half green and half rust. He opened, pulled through and closed the gate, then drove on. After about a quarter mile, he turned left down a skinny dirt road bordered by thick manzanita and buckthorn. Whit stopped at a little picnic area under a valley oak shaded flat, next to Badger Creek. Himalayan blackberry encased both sides of the creek's riparian zone with thick, thorny, mounds of live and dead canes. The Bean family periodically fought back the berries at their secluded little shady picnic site. Barring Jesse Ray or his son, Alex, surprising Whit, he had about two and a half hours to wait before evening…plenty of time.

Whit slid the stiletto out of Allyson's side with his handkerchief and grabbed Allyson's Lady Colt. He exited the vehicle, then crawled under the car's engine compartment. Whit saw what he needed, then slithered back out. He took his t-shirt off and snapped it several times, then put it back on as he walked to the trunk.

Whit pulled the automatic out of his back pocket, cocked it, then popped the trunk and stepped back, just in case. Lance and his dried-blood covered face lay motionless in the trunk. Knowing the drug had worn off long ago, Whit leaned forward and flicked Lance's nose.

Lance roared in pain, held up both hands and pleaded, "I just do what I'm told; it's not me."

"Get out."

"I didn't mean to hurt her. I just follow orders."

Pointing the pistol in Lance's face, Whit said, "Shut up and get out." After Lance climbed out, Whit grabbed the tire iron and flicked the gun toward the creek.

Lance walked on periodically looking back at the tire iron in Whit's left hand. Lance said, "I can fix this. I have access to—"

Whit slapped the tire iron against Lance's back and said, "Shut up!"

Near the creek, Whit made Lance lie on his belly and place his hands on top of a long log the Beans had slabbed for a bench seat. Whit rolled a smaller log round over and sat to the side of Lance. The awkward position forced Lance to cock his head up and back just to look at Whit.

He asked, "Who is Steven Sliger?"

Lance hesitated then said, "Look, you don't—"

Whit slammed the tire iron down on Lance's left wrist, shattering every carpal bone.

Lance screamed and rolled onto his back. "Ahh, ahh, ahhhh, ahhhh! My hand...you've ruined my hand!" He used his right hand to cradle his left wrist.

Whit let Lance go on for a good three minutes. When the screaming subsided, Whit calmly said, "We are going to start again. Put your right hand on the log or I'll step on your left."

Not looking at Whit, Lance scooted forward and meekly set his right hand on the log. Whit suggested, "Need I remind you not to hesitate, lie, or try to negotiate?"

Whit never had to touch Lance again. Twenty-five minutes later, Whit knew way more than he could believe. *Jesus. Jonathan Neuton, you sick son of a bitch.* Looking down at Lance, Whit thought, *If this wannabe killer hadn't screwed up, Ned, Grey, Katelyn and I would be dead. And poor Allyson over there... time to cull the herd and start killing my way up the scum ladder.*

Whit leaned forward and said, "Hey." When Lance slowly brought his head up, Whit backhanded Lance in the forehead with the tire iron. Lance flopped onto his back, twisting at the air like an upside-down turtle. Whit moved over his prey, bent down, and clutched the scrawny murderer's throat in his left hand. Whit squeezed hard.

Lance's wild frantic brown eyes stared into the cold blue of Whit's. He feebly flailed and grabbed at Whit with his one good hand.

Whit said calmly, "What were you doing while Ned slowly suffocated? Did you watch him like I'm watching you? In nature, predators do the same;

not an ounce of compassion for their victims. Humans aren't supposed to ac like this…yet here we are. Horrifying isn't it?"

Whit straightened his arm and added downward pressure to his grip. A Lance's struggling waned, the last words his oxygen-deprived brain registere hissed from his executioner. "See you in hell, asshole."

Whit sat back down. He tossed the knife in the edge of the creek an broke apart the gun. Rubbing down each part for prints, Whit threw eacl piece way downstream, deep within the wall of blackberries. He cleaned th knife of blood and prints and flung it even further into the berry thicket.

Whit sat in the shade by the creek for nearly two hours, mostly just starin at the water. He watched water skippers hunt, mud daubers fly in and collec nest material, a water snake pass by, and even observed a covey of valley quai emerge from the berries to feed in the late afternoon. Whit felt numb…men tally and physically exhausted. Eventually dusk arrived; Whit dragged Lanc back to the car and yanked his jacket off. Whit tossed the jacket on the sea with his handkerchief and stuffed the lifeless body on the passenger floorboard

Ten minutes later, Whit pulled out onto the state highway with both th driver's window and the passenger's window open. He'd already unscrewed th gas cap.

About two miles from town, with no cars in either direction, Whit slowl crossed the centerline. He angled off the highway's left shoulder and down th embankment. He turned the wheels to the right and the car rolled over onc completely, then partly again. The car stopped against a large rock and som lanky pine trees as it came to rest on the driver's side. Whit popped his seatbelt found his handkerchief and Lance's coat, then climbed up and out of the pas senger window.

Whit pulled out his pocketknife, flipped open the blade, then flicked or the Bic lighter. He relocated the rubber segment of gas line near the inline fil ter and sliced it in two. With the lighter in his mouth, he soaked Lance's coat and his handkerchief with what drained out of the line. He tossed them ontc the passenger door. Grabbing his handkerchief, he lit it and flung it into the back seat. He lit the jacket and let it slide down into the front seat.

Whit backed away from the car and the highway. When the front seat fab ric caught fire, he tossed the lighter in the window. Eventually the fuel drip ping out of the severed gas line and the gas escaping from the uncapped gas tank filler lit with a whoosh.

Whit said quietly, "I'm sorry, Allyson; no other choice."

Whit continued to back away into the tree line as the fire really took off. Whit heard a car approaching; it slowed down. Whit turned and started hiking north.

Katelyn sat frozen. She hadn't stopped crying, and barely heard Whit since he revealed how he had killed Lance.

After Whit finished, neither spoke. Whit put his handkerchief on Katelyn's lap, but she didn't touch it. She kept wiping her eyes with her hands. She felt devastated, humiliated…and furious. Didn't her love mean anything? How could he lower himself to a…a savage? Why hadn't her love, stopped him…changed him…softened him?

Her anger dominated all other emotions when Whit tried to speak. "Kate, they tried to kill my friends. They tried to kill me. Had they shot Grey and me at my cabin, they'd have mercilessly killed you. I had to—"

"Not your call, not your duty, and not your charge," Katelyn snapped. "Never was."

"After what they tried to do to poor harmless Ned, I had no choice."

"You always had a choice. We all do, the police, the courts, the—"

"Ah, hell, Kate; I had to find the assassins myself. Where were all the investigators? Gone."

Katelyn threw her hands up and over her ears. "Shut up, shut up, shut up!"

Whit looked at Katelyn but didn't speak. He couldn't change what he had done and, apparently, she couldn't accept or live with it.

She spoke so softly Whit could barely hear her. "I thought we meant something, I thought I meant something…to you. If I truly did you—"

"Kate, I never knew love…. what it meant, how it felt, before you. But murderers came after my friends. I had to protect my—"

"Damn it, Whit; you can't make those decisions; vigilantism turns you into one of them. How is it okay for you to torture, slaughter, murder?" Whit just looked forward, so she added, "And, if miraculously Sliger had survived the fire, you'd still pursue him…outside of the law."

Again, Whit didn't say anything which corroborated her thought. She asked, "And your dad's going to cover all this up?"

After a long pause, Whit said, "Yes, unless you say different."

"You know I won't. I can't." Quietly she whispered, "I love you too much." Shaking her head slowly at first then faster and faster, she turned and yelled at Whit, "I hate you for making me part of this!"

Whit put his hand out to her. She cringed. "Don't touch me." Before Whit could speak, she continued. "I'm so angry at you. You can't take the law in your own hands. Don't you understand? We are a nation of laws, not a lawless nation. It makes you the same as Sliger, or a corrupt politician, or a dirty judge." She avoided saying unethical cop, but, that's exactly how she felt about Whit's dad. "It's against everything I believe in."

Whit wanted to plead with her, tell her not to make any rash decisions… that they could work everything out, over time. She just needed to give him a chance. But he just sat there.

She started crying again and softly said, "Please go."

Whit's mouth opened but nothing emerged. He wanted to say something, anything, to change her mind. Whit couldn't come up with even one damn word that would help. Slowly and sadly, Whit opened the door and stepped out. She started her car. As Katlyn pulled away, he walked alongside the open door. He was about to yell, "Katelyn, stop!" But she sped up just enough that the door closed.

Standing in the dark, watching her disappear from his life, Whit grabbed his head and looked up. The Big Dipper sparkled down brightly as Whit spoke back to the heavens. "Oh, Kate, I'm sorry… more sorry than you'll ever know."

Epilogue

Katelyn Summers

Katelyn abruptly quit her job in Sacramento and moved back to the East Coast. She never returned to work in the beltway or any other reporter job. She briefly visited a few friends or old coworkers, but none knew of her present location. Rumors of a writing career could never be confirmed, as nothing written by Katelyn Summers was ever published.

Benjamin Whittingham

Benjamin Whittingham returned to his world of biology, forestry and small-town life. His nearly solitary life included his dad, his friends, and his pet ring-tailed cat. Whit and his friends continue to meet regularly at their favorite bar. Out of character and without explanation, Whit traveled to Spain. He spent most of a week there, then returned to stay two weeks in the D.C. area with Mike Ho and his wife and kids. Whit's friends in California believed he spent most of that time searching for his Kate. Upon his return, if Whit ever found her, he never said.

9 781480 999152